I0565267

The Fallen Elyssian

The Dreamer Saga, Book Two

E.M. Lucas

Golden Thread Publishing

Copyright © 2025 by E.M. Lucas

All rights reserved.

No portion of this book may be reproduced in any form without written permission from
the publisher or author, except as permitted by U.S. copyright law.

Contents

Map   VI

Acknowledgements   VII

Dedication   IX

1. Dareth I   1

2. Melia I   13

3. Auren I   24

4. Melia II   36

5. Auren II   55

6. Orlan I   68

7. Melia III   80

8. The Shadow I   92

9. Melia IV   106

10. The Shadow II   123

11. Melia V   138

12. Jade I   151

13. Melia VI   164

14. Jade II   176

15. Auren III   190

16. Melia VII   203

17. Orlan II   217

18. Auren IV   230

19. Melia VIII   243

20. Jade III   256

21. Melia IX   269

22. Melia X   281

23. Jade IV   294

24. Melia XI   308

25. Orlan III   324

26. Sam I   337

27. Melia XII   351

28. Auren V   363

29. Orlan IV   374

30. Auren VI   385

31. Sam II   397

32. Auren VII   412

33. Sam III   423

34. Auren VIII   437

35. Dareth II   449

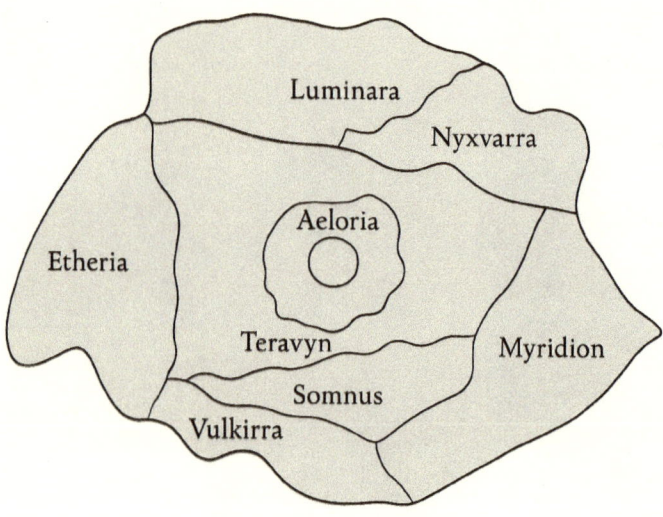

THE VAULT

Acknowledgements

Stepping into the world of publishing for the second time feels no less surreal than the first. If anything, it carries even more weight, because I know now the journey it takes to get here, and the many hands and hearts that lift me along the way.

To Maddie and Evie—you are my joy, my inspiration, and my constant reminder of why stories matter. Every word I write carries the hope that you'll find the courage to chase your own dreams, no matter how impossible they may seem.

To Cayci—your unwavering support and sharp eye as a beta reader mean more than I can ever express. You've believed in me in every draft, every rewrite, every stumble and step forward. This book is as much yours as it is mine.

To everyone who read advance copies and offered encouragement—thank you for being part of the process, for your insights, and for helping me shape this story into what it became.

To Dean and Holly—thank you for supporting me from across the world, for always cheering me on even from a distance.

To all of OSW—you inspire me constantly with your creativity. This community has pushed me to think bigger, dig deeper, and never stop imagining.

To Mollie—thank you for always supporting me and being the best sister ever!

To my mom—thank you for being the strong woman I've always looked up to. Your strength shaped mine.

And finally, to my cats—Rogue, Sami, and Woovie, who keep me company on lonely days. And to Bear, who left us in 2025. The Bear who lives in these pages is a tribute to you. You will always be part of the story.

For Eliza, Jasper, and Rosie.

Dareth I

The honor guards' boots made no sound against the obsidian floor, yet Dareth felt each step echo in his bones. His own footfalls seemed thunderous in comparison, despite years of military precision. The descent into the Chamber of Echoes stripped away familiar certainties with each spiraling turn.

Crimson light from hidden sources cast his shadow in eight different directions, stretching across walls that seemed to drink in both sound and certainty. His new Council insignia weighed heavy on his collar, still sharp-edged and unfamiliar against his throat.

The guards flanking him wore masks of polished black stone, their faces smooth and featureless save for thin slits where eyes should be. Dareth had heard rumors about the Echo Sentinels - that they were more construct than human, their tongues removed to preserve the Chamber's sanctity. He didn't ask. Questions felt dangerous here.

Memory struggled against the Chamber's presence. Each thought came slower, as if moving through honey. The military precision that had earned him this position seemed to blur at the edges, leaving him uncharacteristically uncertain of his next step.

A massive door loomed ahead, its surface etched with symbols that hurt his eyes to look at directly. Thread-script, ancient and potent, formed patterns his mind refused to fully process. The inscription above burned clearest: "No sound escapes. No truth enters."

The Sentinels stopped in perfect unison, their masks turning toward him with mechanical precision. The message was clear - beyond this point, he walked alone. Dareth straightened his spine, letting his fingers brush against the ceremonial blade at his hip. Its familiar weight anchored him against the Chamber's disorienting presence.

The door opened without sound or movement, reality simply parting like a curtain of black water. The council seats rose before him, eight empty thrones arranged in a perfect circle around the Echo Core's ghostly glow. His designated position - marked with the symbol of planetary security - waited like an open mouth.

Cold air brushed his face, carrying the taste of metal and old stone. The Chamber felt alive in a way that defied explanation, as if the very walls watched and judged. This was where the Empire's true power resided - not in fleets or armies, but in whispered decisions that reshaped worlds.

His boot touched the first step leading to his throne, and the Echo Core pulsed once, acknowledging his presence. The seat of power that awaited him represented everything he'd fought for - order, structure, the promise of a controlled galaxy. Yet standing here, at the heart of that control, Dareth felt the first tremor of doubt.

The silence pressed against Dareth's eardrums like a physical force. No footsteps, no breathing, not even the subtle hum of Thread energy that permeated every other structure in the Empire. His own heartbeat seemed to fade into the void, as if the Chamber sought to erase even that small rebellion against its perfect stillness.

The other council members watched his approach with varying degrees of interest and disdain. Their ceremonial robes caught what little light penetrated the chamber, each color representing their domain of power. The effect created a ring of ghostly luminescence around the Echo Core's deeper glow.

Admiral Thalos Vire dominated his seat like a statue carved from granite, his fleet-master's robes the deep blue of space itself. The man's augmented eyes tracked Dareth's movement with mechanical precision, calculating threat assessments even here, in the heart of Imperial power.

To Vire's left sat Minister Rhessa Vorn, her crimson robes seeming to absorb the chamber's light rather than reflect it. Her fingers traced patterns on her armrest that Dareth recognized as military deployment sequences. Even in stillness, she planned for chaos.

Chancellor Venn Aros wore robes of shifting silver, their surface rippling like mercury despite the chamber's deadened air. The diplomat's face remained carefully neutral, but his eyes held the weight of a thousand unspoken deals and betrayals.

The Scribe-Magus Helyn Dros hunched in her seat, gold robes drawn tight around her slight frame. Ancient texts and forbidden knowledge had left their mark - her skin held a translucent quality, as if reality itself struggled to maintain its hold on her.

Executor Deyron Sahl's black robes seemed to create a void in the chamber's already dim light. Justice incarnate, his scarred hands rested on execution seals that could condemn entire worlds with a single touch.

High Aetherion Caedmon Reth's white robes practically glowed, though Dareth noticed dark stains at the edges - remnants of ceremonies best left unspoken. The spiritual leader's eyes remained closed, lips moving in silent prayer.

The seat felt wrong against his back - too soft, too yielding for a soldier who'd spent decades on hard military benches. Dareth shifted his weight, the ceremonial blade at his hip catching against the ornate armrest. His uniform's high collar seemed to tighten with each breath.

These weren't warriors surrounding him, despite their titles and medals. Their hands were too clean, their postures too relaxed in the presence of such concentrated power. They played at war from comfortable distances, moving pieces across star maps while others bled. The thought tasted bitter in his mouth.

The Echo Core's pulse quickened, its glow intensifying as if sensing his discomfort. Why had they chosen him? His service record spoke of frontier battles and suppressed insurgencies, not the delicate maneuvering these chambers demanded. A soldier among serpents - was that the point? His fingers traced the edge of his seat, feeling ancient symbols carved into the metal.

Minister Vorn's gaze settled on him like crosshairs, calculating and cold. Her blood-red gloves flexed once, twice - a subtle tell that spoke of assessment and judgment. Dareth met her stare with the same steady resolve he'd used to face down insurgent squadrons. The corners of her mouth twitched upward, but the smile didn't reach her eyes.

Caedmon Reth's whispers grew more urgent, his lips moving faster as ancient Thread-verses spilled into the deadened air. Dareth watched the High Aetherion's fingers twist in complex patterns beneath his ceremonial sleeves - protective wards, if his frontier training served correctly. The religious leader's tension radiated across the chamber despite its sound-dampening properties.

The Echo Core's glow dimmed without warning, plunging the chamber into an unnatural twilight that made Dareth's combat instincts scream. His hand found his blade's hilt as darkness pooled in the chamber's upper reaches, collecting like ink in water.

Golden light pierced the gathered shadows, announcing the Emperor's descent with calculated grandeur. The throne floated down on ribbons of Thread-energy that shouldn't have been possible within the Chamber's nullifying walls. Dareth noted how Vorn's shoulders stiffened.

The sight of the Empire's supreme ruler knocked the breath from Dareth's lungs. Propaganda holos showed a figure of strength and vitality, but reality told a different story. Beneath ornate robes of liquid gold, the Emperor's form was skeletal, held upright by an intricate framework of machinery that hummed with forbidden technology.

Withered hands gripped the throne's armrests with desperate strength, bones visible beneath paper-thin skin. The Emperor's face remained mostly hidden behind an ornate mask, but what little showed appeared desiccated, preserved rather than alive. This was no immortal being - this was a corpse refusing to acknowledge its own death.

Admiral Vire's augmented eye whirred as it adjusted to the darkness, the sound unnaturally loud in the Chamber's silence. The military commander's expression remained carefully neutral, but Dareth recognized the subtle shift in posture - the same instinctive response any soldier showed when confronting unexpected weakness in command.

Deyron Sahl leaned forward in his seat, the Executor's mechanical heart visible through his transparent chest plate beating faster than its usual measured rhythm. His gaze fixed on the Emperor's throne with an intensity that bordered on hunger, cataloging every sign of deterioration like evidence in a future trial.

The machinery supporting the Emperor's body clicked and whirred, adjusting its grip as the throne settled into position. Each mechanical movement seemed to pain Caedmon Reth, the High Aetherion's prayers taking on an edge of desperation. The religious leader's faith strained against the physical reality before him.

Helyn Dros alone appeared unsurprised, their blindfolded face turned toward the Emperor with something approaching pity. The Scribe-Magus's data-script tattoos pulsed with increased frequency, recording truths that would never leave these walls. Their fingers traced patterns in the air - not wards like Reth's, but something older, something that made Dareth's eyes hurt to watch.

The Emperor's voice filled the Chamber with impossible strength, belying his withered form. "We have a new enemy. Liora Solari." The name hung in the air like smoke, heavy with implication.

Thread-energy crackled around the Emperor's throne as he gestured, and a holographic display materialized above the Echo Core. "What you are about to witness exists in no Imperial record." The image coalesced into a world Dareth had never seen - nine distinct regions separated by shimmering barriers, each pulsing with its own unique energy signature.

"This is the Vault." The Emperor's mechanical supports whirred as he leaned forward. "The mere fact that you now know this name marks you as possessors of information no other Imperial may claim." The hologram rotated slowly, revealing details that seemed to defy physical laws - floating cities, seas of light, mountains that curved impossibly toward a center that couldn't exist.

Dareth's military mind automatically began cataloging tactical implications - defensive positions, resource concentrations, potential staging areas. But something about the world's configuration disrupted standard strategic analysis. It felt wrong, as if the planet operated under different rules entirely.

"Impossible." Vorn's voice cut through the silence, her usual careful control cracking. "A world of this significance couldn't have been hidden from the Council. The Charter explicitly-" The Emperor's mask turned toward her, and the words died in her throat. Dareth watched her sink back into her seat, fingers trembling slightly against her armrests.

The Chamber's oppressive silence deepened, pressing against Dareth's ears until he could hear his own heartbeat. He studied the hologram more carefully, noting how the barriers between regions flickered in places, suggesting instability. His frontier experience recognized the pattern - containment failing, pressure building toward inevitable breach.

Admiral Vire's augmented eye whirred rapidly, likely recording every detail despite the Chamber's security measures. "The navigational implications alone..." he began, but fell silent under the Emperor's steady gaze. Dareth understood the admiral's concern - a hidden world meant hidden hyperspace routes, which meant potential threats to Imperial control.

The High Aetherion's prayers had ceased entirely, replaced by a tension that seemed to draw his robes tight against his frame. Dareth noticed how Reth's hands had stopped their protective gestures, instead gripping his seat with white-knuckled intensity. Whatever this revelation meant to the Empire's spiritual leader, it clearly shook him to his core.

Helyn Dros alone appeared unsurprised, their blindfolded face turned toward the hologram with something approaching recognition. Their data-script tattoos pulsed in rhythm with the Vault's displayed energy patterns, suggesting knowledge that went far beyond what the Emperor was revealing.

The machinery supporting the Emperor's throne hummed louder as he raised a skeletal hand toward the hologram. "This world represents both our greatest weapon and our gravest threat. And now, Liora Solari threatens to unravel everything we have contained there." The name seemed to echo despite the Chamber's sound-dampening properties, carrying weight beyond mere syllables.

Through the hologram's ethereal glow, Dareth watched the barriers between realms fade like morning mist. His military instincts screamed at the tactical nightmare unfolding before them - nine distinct territories suddenly exposed to each other, each wielding powers beyond Imperial control. The Chamber's oppressive silence felt heavier now, weighted with unspoken implications.

"You've felt it," the Emperor's voice rasped, machinery whirring as he leaned forward. "The surge in Thread manifestations. The unexplained phenomena on frontier worlds." Dareth's mind flashed to recent reports from his border commanders - weapons failing without cause, reality bending in ways that defied Imperial physics.

The Emperor's withered hand traced the outline of a particular realm, labelled Somnus, where reports indicated increased magical activity. "Liora Solari is young but very powerful," he continued, "She has used what she called dream magic to tear down the Veil that kept the realms, and their magic, separate, ignorant of each other's existence." Dareth noticed how Caedmon Reth's fingers twitched at the name, a tell that spoke volumes in this chamber of calculated control.

The hologram shifted, focusing on a magnificent floating city that seemed to defy gravity itself. Elyssia. Dareth had heard whispers of its existence in ancient military texts, but seeing it now, suspended in impossible glory, made those accounts seem pale and inadequate.

"Elyssia's grasp grows weak," the Emperor stated, his mechanical supports creaking as he gestured toward the city's flickering outline. The perfection of its spires seemed to waver, like a reflection in troubled water.

Admiral Vire's augmented eye whirred frantically, analyzing the tactical implications. "The Aether magic-" he began, but the Emperor's raised hand cut him short. Dareth noted how even the seasoned fleet commander yielded instantly to that skeletal gesture.

Dareth watched the floating city's image flicker again, its perfection momentarily cracking to reveal something underneath - something that made his combat instincts scream warnings he couldn't quite articulate. The other council members shifted uneasily in their seats, suggesting they saw it too.

The council chamber erupted into overlapping arguments, their carefully maintained composure cracking under the weight of revelation. Dareth watched them with a soldier's practiced patience, noting how quickly these powerful figures descended into chaos when faced with a threat they couldn't control.

Admiral Vire's augmented eye glowed fierce red as he pounded his fist against his armrest. "We must deploy the Third Fleet immediately. A show of force-" But Minister Vorn cut him off with a sharp laugh that seemed to freeze the very air.

"And how do you propose to get them there, Admiral?" Her blood-red gloves gestured toward the hologram. "The Threadways don't reach it. That's rather the point of a hidden world, isn't it?" Dareth noticed how her fingers twitched toward hidden weapons - old habits dying hard even here.

Chancellor Aros leaned forward, his rings catching the Echo Core's light. "The Aetherium cost alone would bankrupt three sectors. We'd need to requisition every crystal from the Outer Reach just to power the navigation cores." His usual smirk had vanished, replaced by genuine concern.

The High Aetherion's prayers had grown more urgent, almost frantic. "We cannot allow this knowledge to spread. The theological implications alone..." He trailed off, hands weaving protective wards that seemed to die in the Chamber's dead air.

"Why not just let it burn?" The words left his mouth before he could stop them, cutting through the chamber's chaos like a blade. Eight pairs of eyes turned to him with expressions ranging from shock to outright hostility. Even the machinery supporting the Emperor's throne seemed to pause its endless whirring.

The Emperor turned toward him with agonizing slowness, the golden surface catching and distorting the Chamber's dim light. Dareth forced himself to meet that hidden gaze, years of frontier combat helping him maintain his composure despite the crushing pressure of attention.

"This planet is of great value to me, Warden-General," the Emperor's voice rasped, mechanical supports creaking as he leaned forward. "As it should be to us all." The words carried weight beyond their simple meaning, heavy with implications that made Dareth's combat instincts scream warnings.

The Emperor's skeletal hand rose, and darkness pooled in the chamber's corner like spilled ink. Dareth's hand found his blade hilt as a figure emerged - or perhaps materialized - from the shadows themselves. The operative's armor absorbed light rather than reflected it, making it impossible to discern where shadow ended and form began.

No identifying marks or insignia marked the armor's surface - not even the ubiquitous Imperial crest. Dareth searched for any tell-tale signs of movement or bearing that might betray species or training, but found nothing. The figure stood with unnatural stillness, like a statue carved from pure darkness.

"This is my Shadow." The Emperor's voice carried a note of... pride? Possession? Dareth couldn't quite place it. "They will be our eyes on the Vault." The figure's helmet turned slightly - the only acknowledgment of being discussed. No breath sounds escaped the armor's seals, no shift of weight betrayed discomfort under the Council's scrutiny.

Minister Vorn's crimson gloves tightened on her armrests. "With respect, my lord - we have operatives. Trained agents who-" The Shadow's helmet snapped toward her with mechanical precision, and the words died in her throat. Dareth recognized the instinctive reaction of prey before predator.

"Your agents are known quantities," the Emperor continued as if Vorn hadn't spoken. "The Shadow exists outside our normal chain of command." Dareth noticed how Admiral Vire's augmented eye struggled to focus on the figure, as if the armor somehow rejected analysis itself.

The Shadow took three precise steps forward, stopping at the Chamber's center. Light from the Echo Core seemed to bend around the armor, creating impossible angles that hurt Dareth's eyes to track. He'd seen stealth tech before - this was something else entirely.

"You will observe. You will report." The Emperor's mechanical supports whirred as he addressed the Shadow directly. "And if necessary, you will eliminate the threat." The figure's only response was a slight inclination of its helmet - an acknowledgment so subtle Dareth almost missed it.

Dareth watched Caedmon Reth's composure crack further, the High Aetherion's usually commanding voice reduced to something approaching a plea. "If a mere girl there had the power to destroy a Veil, she should be captured and studied..." The religious leader's fingers wove increasingly complex patterns beneath his ceremonial sleeves, as if trying to ward off the implications of his own words.

The Emperor's machinery clicked and whirred, the sound unnaturally loud in the Chamber's oppressive silence. No direct response came from the withered figure on the throne, but Dareth noted how Reth seemed to physically shrink under that gaze, his protests dying unfinished.

Minister Vorn's blood-red gloves tightened on her armrests, her cold eyes tracking the Shadow's measured retreat. Dareth recognized the look - the same predatory assessment he'd seen in veteran soldiers sizing up new weapons. But there was something else there too - a flicker of unease that seemed out of place on her carefully controlled features.

The Shadow moved with impossible fluidity, each step precise yet somehow wrong, as if the figure occupied space differently than everything around it. Dareth's combat instincts screamed warnings he couldn't quite articulate, his hand never straying far from his blade hilt.

The Shadow paused at the threshold between light and dark, its helmet turning slightly toward the Emperor. No words were exchanged, no obvious signals given, but Dareth felt the weight of unspoken understanding pass between them. This was no mere operative receiving orders - this was something else entirely.

The figure stepped into the gathered darkness and simply ceased to be, leaving no trace of its passage. The Chamber's temperature began to normalize, but Dareth couldn't shake the lingering sensation of being watched by something just beyond normal perception.

The Emperor's final words fell into the Chamber's deadened air like stones into still water: "One barrier has fallen. Let us ensure the others do not."

Melia I

The golden light washes over Melia's skin like honey, thick and cloying, never wavering from its perfect luminescence. She stands motionless before the twin caskets, her shoulders squared in the posture drilled into her since childhood—spine straight, chin raised just so, hands clasped at her waist with fingers interlaced in the precise configuration befitting a princess in mourning.

The crystalline plinths hum with that strange internal glow, neither warm nor cold, just perpetually present. Inside their transparent depths, her parents lie in eternal repose, their faces serene and unmarked by the sudden illness that claimed them both within hours of each other. Too sudden. Too convenient. The thought flickers through Melia's mind before she can stop it, a treasonous whisper against the accepted narrative of divine will.

"Blessed are those who ascend to the eternal light," the priest intones from his elevated position behind the caskets. His voice carries that particular quality all Elyssian clergy possess—perfectly modulated, devoid of genuine emotion, as if his words emerge from some divine resonance chamber rather than human throat. "Queen Lysandra and King Orion have transcended the burdens of flesh to join the eternal chorus."

Melia's jaw tightens imperceptibly. The priest's name escapes her—they all blur together in their identical ceremonial robes, their identical cadences, their identical empty platitudes. Had this same nameless man spoken at other funerals?

The Temple of Ascension rises around her, a cathedral of impossibly thin marble spires and cascading light prisms that cast rainbow refractions across the gathered mourners. Melia shifts her gaze upward, past the hovering ceremonial lanterns, to where the vaulted ceiling opens to reveal Elyssia's perpetual golden sky. No clouds mar its perfection today—they never do on days of ceremonial importance. The weather architects see to that.

Beyond the temple's crystalline windows, Elyssia unfolds in concentric rings of gleaming white stone and silver filigree, a city that seems to float on light itself. The outermost ring—visible only as a distant shimmer from this central spire—houses the Boundary Gardens where massive luminous flowers bloom year-round, their petals forming a protective barrier between Elyssia and the empty air surrounding the floating city. The middle rings contain the elegant homes of courtiers and ministers, their rooftops adorned with reflective domes that catch and amplify the eternal light. And here, at the city's heart, rises the Royal Precinct with its seven sacred temples and the palace—her home—at its center.

A home that will feel emptier than the vast sky beneath Elyssia's floating foundation.

"Princess Melia," a voice murmurs beside her, pulling her attention back to the ceremony. Prefect Solivar stands at her side, his perfectly symmetrical features arranged in an expression of appropriate solemnity. Her betrothed. The man chosen to be her husband long before either of them had any say in the matter. "It is time for your offering."

Melia nods once, a precise inclination of her head that sends a single golden curl escaping from beneath her mourning veil. With measured steps, she approaches the caskets, aware of every eye in the temple following her movement. The Elyssian nobility line the circular chamber in concentric rings, their pristine white mourning robes creating a visual echo of the city's architecture. Their faces blur together just as the priest's had—a sea of perfect features showing perfect grief in perfect moderation.

She reaches into the ceremonial bowl held by an attendant and withdraws a handful of crushed petals from the sacred light blooms that grow only in the royal gardens. The petals glow between her fingers, warm and alive despite being separated from their source. Melia sprinkles them over her mother's casket first, watching as they settle on the transparent surface like stars fallen from the heavens.

"Return to the light that birthed you," she recites, the traditional words hollow in her throat.

Melia moves to her father's casket, her heart constricting in her chest. King Orion lies beneath the crystal, his powerful hands folded across his chest, silver streaking through his dark hair like veins of precious metal. Unlike the distant reverence she felt for her mother's ethereal beauty, her father had always been tangible, present—a man who smelled of leather-bound books and spiced tea, who would sometimes wink at her across the formal dining table when the ministers grew particularly tedious.

"Return to the light that birthed you," she repeats, but this time the words catch in her throat.

The petals scatter across his casket, their glow intensifying momentarily as they make contact with the crystal. One petal clings to the edge before sliding down the side, leaving a faint luminous trail that fades almost immediately. Just like him—here, then gone.

A memory surfaces: her father in the palace library, not in his formal regalia but in a simple tunic, sleeves rolled to his elbows as he pulled a massive tome from a high shelf. "History isn't just what they teach in the temples, little star," he'd told her, using the nickname only he ever used. "It's in the spaces between what's written."

She'd been twelve then, still young enough to sit cross-legged on the floor beside his chair as he read to her from the ancient texts—stories of Elyssia's founding that somehow felt more vivid, more human than the sanitized versions taught by her tutors.

Melia blinks rapidly, fighting the moisture threatening to spill from her eyes. Public tears are permitted at royal funerals, but she cannot bear to perform even grief for the assembled audience.

Her father wouldn't have wanted that.

The last petal falls from her fingers. King Orion appears to sleep beneath the crystal, his face peaceful yet somehow diminished without the spark of quiet humor that had always animated his features. The man who taught her to question, to think beyond the rigid structures of Elyssian society, reduced to another perfect, preserved specimen of royalty.

"He was proud of you," Prefect Solivar murmurs as she returns to his side, his voice pitched for her ears alone. "As your husband, I will ensure his legacy continues through our reign."

Melia's spine stiffens further, though she keeps her expression serene. Husband. The word sits like a stone in her stomach. The betrothal had been formalized just hours after her parents parents' passing—a political alliance to ensure royal continuity.

The High Priest raises his hands, fingers splayed to catch and re-fract the light streaming from above. "The divine cycle continues," he intones. "Death is but transformation, and those who have lived in perfect accordance with Elyssia's sacred laws ascend to become one with the eternal light."

The assembled nobility bow their heads in unison, a choreographed display of piety. Melia follows suit, but her thoughts remain with her father—not the king in the crystal casket, but the man who had once carried her on his shoulders through the Boundary Gardens, pointing out constellations in the night sky below them.

"The stars are just reflections of our city," he'd told her, then paused before adding in a whisper, "Or perhaps we are reflections of them. Who can say which is the true light and which the echo?"

The memory burns brighter than the funeral lights, more real than the perfect, preserved tableau before her. In that moment, Melia silently vows to honor not the public figure being eulogized, but the questioning spirit that had made her father truly great.

The procession continues its measured advance down the throne room's marble expanse. Each Elyssian approaches with synchronized steps, their breathing controlled to match some unheard rhythm. Bow. Three heartbeats. Rise. Move on. Bow. Three heartbeats. Rise. Move on. The pattern never varies, never falters.

A woman in pale blue silk approaches—Lady Celestine, her father's childhood friend. Their eyes meet for the briefest moment during her prescribed bow, and Melia catches something there. A flicker of... what? Doubt? Fear? But the expression vanishes so quickly Melia questions whether she saw anything at all.

"In their wisdom, they have prepared the path for their beloved daughter," the priest continues, his words falling like stones into still water. "Princess Melia, chosen of the light, destined to unite the realms through sacred bond with Prefect Solivar."

Her stomach clenches at the mention of her betrothed. Three days since her parents' death, and already the marriage arrangements proceed with mechanical efficiency. The light surrounding her seems to pulse with approval, as if the city itself endorses this predetermined path.

Another figure approaches—an elderly man whose name she should know but doesn't. His bow is perfect, his timing flawless, his expression appropriately solemn. Yet something in his movements strikes her as rehearsed beyond mere ceremony. How many times has he performed this exact ritual? For how many other convenient deaths?

"Through her union, the princess shall fulfill her sacred destiny," the priest declares, raising his arms toward the unchanging golden dome above. "As the light has decreed, so shall it be."

The glow from her parents' caskets seems to brighten slightly, responding to his words. Or perhaps she imagines it. Perhaps everything in Elyssia responds to priestly pronouncements, reality bending to match official doctrine.

The priest raises his hand toward the dome, and a white dove descends on invisible currents. It hovers above the caskets, wings beating in perfect rhythm—then suddenly jerks, its motion stuttering like a broken mechanism before smoothing back into graceful flight. The dove glides toward the great windows as if nothing happened.

Melia's breath catches. Did anyone else see that falter? She scans the assembled mourners, but their faces remain fixed in identical expressions of reverent sorrow. Not one head turns. Not one eye follows the dove's erratic moment.

She closes her eyes, reaching for her father's voice. "A king's duty..." But the memory shifts, the timbre deepening, then rising, the accent changing. Which version is real? She tries again. "Perhaps it is time..."

The words feel right, but the voice speaking them belongs to someone else entirely.

Opening her eyes, Melia studies the faces around her. Lady Celestine maintains her perfect mask of grief, head tilted at precisely the same angle as the woman beside her. And the man beyond that. Each expression mirrors the others—soft sorrow, downturned mouths, eyes appropriately dim. How long have they stood exactly this way?

The crystalline surface of her mother's death mask catches the light, gleaming with that same eternal radiance. Melia steps forward, her ritual posture forgotten. Her fingertips brush the crystal barrier.

Ice. Not cool—ice. As if death itself has crystallized within.

"Cities do not die," Prefect Solivar's voice cuts through the chamber, deep and resonant as he approaches the dais. "The Cycle remembers. The Thread endures."

The assembled mourners turn toward Solivar's voice with synchronized precision, their movements unnaturally fluid. Melia's hand jerks back from the crystalline barrier as if burned.

Prefect Solivar cuts through the crowd like a blade through silk. His silver hair catches the eternal light, each strand perfectly arranged despite the solemn occasion. Those pale gray eyes sweep the chamber with calculating assessment before settling on her with predatory focus. Even in mourning robes, he radiates an authority that makes the air itself seem denser around him.

Her betrothed. The word tastes like ash in her mouth.

"The light has chosen wisely," Solivar declares, ascending the dais with measured steps. His presence transforms the space—suddenly the golden radiance feels harsh, oppressive. "Through Princess Melia, the Divine Order shall be preserved."

The crowd murmurs agreement in perfect unison, their voices blending into a single harmonic note. Melia watches their lips move in identical patterns and her stomach lurches. How do they all know the same responses?

Solivar's hand extends toward her, palm upward in ritual invitation. Those cold eyes hold hers with unwavering intensity. "Soon we will seal the covenant that your parents' sacrifice has made possible."

Sacrifice. The word strikes like ice water through her veins. Not death—sacrifice. As if their passing served some greater purpose, some predetermined plan.

The crystalline caskets pulse with brighter light, and Melia swears she hears something beneath the humming—a whisper, urgent and desperate, calling her name.

The priest's fingers settle on her shoulder like autumn leaves—present but weightless, offering comfort that feels rehearsed rather than genuine. His touch carries no warmth, no human tremor that might betray actual emotion. Through the thin fabric of her mourning gown, his hand feels almost mechanical.

"Your Highness requires solitude for proper reflection," he murmurs, his voice maintaining that same hollow resonance. "The chamber awaits."

Melia allows herself to be guided from the throne room, her feet moving in the prescribed cadence despite her racing thoughts. The priest's grip remains consistently light, as if he's performed this exact gesture countless times before. His breathing never changes rhythm. His steps never falter. Even his grief seems manufactured.

The corridor stretches endlessly before them, lined with portraits of deceased royalty whose painted eyes seem to follow her passage. Each face wears the same serene expression—peaceful acceptance tinged with divine rapture. How many of these noble deaths had been equally convenient? Equally timed?

The priest stops before an ornate door, his hand finally lifting from her shoulder to gesture her forward. "The light shall comfort you in your sorrow, Princess."

The chamber door closes with a whisper-soft click, leaving Melia alone in what should be her sanctuary. But the space feels wrong—too pristine, too prepared. The air carries the cloying scent of funeral lilies arranged in perfect symmetry around the room. Every surface gleams with fresh polish. Every cushion sits precisely placed. Not a single mote of dust disturbs the golden light streaming through crystalline windows.

They prepared this. Before her parents even died, they prepared this room for her grief.

Her gaze falls upon the bed, where a single object rests against the pristine white coverlet—a painting small enough to hold in both hands. Her childhood artwork, depicting three figures beneath Elyssia's eternal sun. Mother, Father, and herself, rendered in the clumsy brushstrokes of youth. But something's wrong with the image.

Melia approaches slowly, her reflection wavering in the polished floor tiles. The painting shows Queen Lysandra in perfect detail, every fold of her royal gown rendered with surprising skill for a child's hand. King Orion stands beside his wife with equal clarity, his strong features unmistakable even in amateur paint.

But her own figure... blurs. The brushstrokes that should define her face dissolve into smeared pigment, as if someone repeatedly repainted that small section while the colors remained wet. Her childhood self exists only as suggestion—a vague princess-shaped shadow between her clearly defined parents.

Her fingers trace the canvas surface, and paint flakes away like ancient skin. The pigment crumbles at her touch, revealing blank canvas beneath. How is that possible? She painted this herself, she remembers... doesn't she? The memory feels real—sitting at her easel, tongue pressed between her lips in concentration, carefully mixing royal blue for her mother's gown.

But the paint dissolves under her fingertips as if it were merely dust.

The door opens without ceremony. Melia spins, her heart lurching, but it's only Sera—her trusted lady-in-waiting, carrying a silver tray arranged with delicate porcelain. The woman's movements flow with practiced efficiency as she sets the tea service on a low table.

"For your comfort, my lady." Sera's voice holds genuine warmth, unlike the priest's hollow tones. "Chamomile with honey, as you prefer."

The normalcy of it strikes Melia like physical blow. Her parents lie in crystalline death-sleep, her betrothal proceeds with mechanical inevitability, and Sera offers tea as if nothing has changed. As if this were merely another afternoon requiring refreshment.

Through the crystalline windows, Elyssia's floating gardens pulse with synchronized bloom. Thousands of flowers open their petals in perfect unison, releasing clouds of white fragments that drift downward like snow. The display should be beautiful—nature celebrating life even in the face of death. Instead, it feels choreographed, another performance in the endless theater of Elyssia's perfection.

Melia's throat constricts as she tries to summon tears for her parents. The grief sits heavy in her chest, a weight she can feel pressing against her ribs, but her eyes remain stubbornly dry. She forces her breathing into the shallow pants that should precede crying, but nothing comes. Her body refuses to cooperate with her emotional commands.

She remembers weeping before—at least, she thinks she does. A memory surfaces of falling from her childhood pony, scraping her knee on marble steps. The hot sting of tears, the way her vision blurred with salt water. But the specifics feel distant, like recalling someone else's experience.

The balcony beckons through gossamer curtains. Melia steps outside, expecting to feel the mountain winds that should constantly buffet a floating city. But the air hangs motionless around her, neither warm nor cool, carrying no scent except the lingering funeral lilies from her chamber.

Even the wind obeys Elyssia's script.

She grips the marble balustrade, her knuckles whitening against the pristine stone. The words rise from her throat unbidden, a whisper meant for no audience except the stagnant air.

"Am I grieving... or just acting like I should?"

Silence answers her. Not even an echo returns from the floating gardens below. The question hangs in the motionless atmosphere, as isolated and uncertain as she feels.

Her gaze drifts past the city's edge, where Elyssia's foundations disappear into layers of cloud. For most of her twenty-two years, she's never wondered what lies beneath that white veil. The teachings speak of a broken world that the Elyssian's were able to ascend from, of their blessed realm. But now, standing in her scripted grief chamber with paint-dust on her fingers and manufactured wind in her hair, Melia finds herself staring downward with desperate curiosity.

What hides beneath the clouds that cradle her perfect, floating prison?

Auren I

The final step falters. Not from exhaustion—Auren's body has transformed over the six-month pilgrimage, hardened like the mountains themselves—but from reverence. The last ridge of the Ascension Path stretches before him, starkly beautiful against the dawn sky, its ancient stone worn smooth by the feet of failed pilgrims across generations.

No one has completed the Ascent in recorded history. Many have tried. Many have died.

He will be different.

Auren pauses, letting the early morning wind whip around him. Below stretches Willow Haven—his home—nestled among rolling grasslands. The village looks impossibly small from here, mud-brick cottages no larger than the pebbles beneath his boots. Pride swells in his chest. No one from Willow Haven has ever come this close. Their children will tell stories of him, the first to ascend, the one who proved their humble origins could produce greatness.

His hand moves to the leather pouch at his waist, fingers brushing the sacred contents within. The blood-soaked thread, its crimson hue deepened to near-black with age. His mother's final gift, passed down through seven generations of failed aspirants.

"The thread remembers," she had whispered as she pressed it into his palm. "It carries the memory of all who tried before. Let it guide you where they could not reach."

The thread pulses against his fingertips, warm despite the mountain chill. Alive with purpose.

Auren straightens his shoulders and continues the climb. The path narrows as it ascends, forcing his body against the mountainside. Wind gusts threaten to tear him from his precarious footing. Each step requires complete focus—one misstep means death, body broken on the rocks below. An inglorious end to his journey.

He climbs higher, muscles burning with exertion but mind clear as crystal. The air thins, making his lungs labor. Yet determination fills him with unexpected strength. The priests had warned of hallucinations at this altitude, but his vision remains sharp, his thoughts unclouded.

With a final heave, Auren pulls himself onto the summit plateau. The legendary Ascension Point. A flat circle of stone, unnaturally smooth, etched with spiraling symbols that seem to shift and change when viewed from different angles.

And above—Elyssia.

The floating city hangs suspended in impossible majesty, defying natural law. Gleaming spires pierce the clouds. Gardens cascade from floating terraces. The city radiates with inner light, pulsing like a living heart. Even from this distance, Auren can see the intricate details of its architecture—delicate arches, towering domes, impossibly slender bridges connecting floating districts.

Elyssia. The divine reward. The ultimate promise.

To his people in Willow Haven, the floating city represents every-thing they lack—abundance, knowledge, immortality. They toil in mud and dust while Elyssia's citizens walk on light. They die while the ascended live forever.

But to Auren, the city signifies something more personal. Valida-tion. Proof that discipline and faith can overcome humble origins. His father had mocked his aspirations—"Wings are for birds, boy, not normal folk"—but Auren had persisted through mockery, through doubt, through pain.

Now, standing at the threshold, he feels vindication coursing through him like fire.

The ceremonial circle beckons. Auren steps into its center, feeling ancient energy humming beneath his feet. The symbols etched into stone begin to glow with soft blue light—acknowledging his presence, accepting his right to attempt.

He removes the blood-soaked thread from its pouch, cradling it in his palms. Generations of his ancestors' blood infuses the simple cord, their collective desire to transcend creating a powerful talisman. He wraps it three times around his wrist, whispering the sacred incanta-tion.

Then Auren closes his eyes and summons the Aether.

It responds immediately—faster than ever before, recognizing his disciplined will. The magic flows through him, not as some external force but as an extension of his own consciousness. This is what makes Aether unique among magical traditions. It doesn't draw from ele-ments or deities or natural forces. It springs from within—will made visible, memory made matter.

The priests at the temple had recognized his talent early. "Most adepts struggle to manifest even simple illusions," the Elder Priest had said, watching Auren form complex geometric patterns from pure thought. "But you... you shape the Aether as naturally as breathing. I've never seen such talent."

Now, atop the mountain, Auren's mastery reaches its zenith. The Aether responds to his call, swirling around him in luminous threads that pulse with his heartbeat. He doesn't merely command it—he becomes it, his consciousness expanding beyond physical form, merging with the conceptual fabric of reality itself.

Warmth spreads across his shoulders. The sensation begins as gentle pressure, then intensifies as his manifestation takes physical form. Wings—his signature expression of Aether—emerge from his back in translucent splendor. Not illusions but actual constructs of matter born from thought, capable of generating the lift his physical body requires.

The wings unfurl, spanning twenty feet of shimmering possibility, each feather perfectly formed from his detailed understanding of avian anatomy combined with his unwavering belief in transformation. They beat once, twice, testing the air.

His entire life has led to this moment. Every prayer, every sacrifice, every hour of training—all culminating in this single act of transcendence.

Auren opens his eyes. Elyssia floats above him, close enough that he can see individual figures moving along its boulevards. His destination. His destiny.

He launches himself from the platform.

The wings catch air, lifting him upward with powerful strokes. Exhilaration floods through him as gravity loses its hold. He ascends on currents of both air and magic, the mountain falling away beneath him, the sky opening wide to receive his triumphant form.

Higher. Faster. The wind rushes past his face, bringing tears to his eyes—or perhaps those are tears of joy, of vindication, of release. His wings beat with increasing confidence, each stroke carrying him closer to the floating city.

The clouds part around him. Elyssia grows from distant vision to imminent reality. He can see the intricate latticework of its foundation, the crystalline structures that somehow defy natural law. Individual buildings take shape—temples, palaces, gardens suspended in air.

He is close enough now to see faces. Residents of the divine city peer outward, witnessing his approach. Some point. Others call to companions. He imagines their expressions of wonder, their recognition that a new ascendant approaches their rarified realm.

Auren's heart swells with triumph. Three hundred more feet. Two hundred. The blood-soaked thread pulses around his wrist, generations of ancestors lending their energy to his final push.

One hundred feet beneath the city's edge. So close he can hear the musical chime of fountain waters, smell the fragrance of flowers unknown to the world below.

And then—

A whisper. Not from without but within. A voice that seems to vibrate directly inside his consciousness, bypassing his ears entirely.

"Not yet."

Just that. A single syllable of rejection. But it carries the weight of absolute authority, crashing through his certainty like a stone through glass.

The effect is instantaneous. His wings—his perfect, powerful manifestation of Aether—shudder mid-beat. The translucent feathers lose cohesion, their edges dissolving into particles of fading light. His connection to the magic—unbreakable just moments before—severs completely.

Confusion replaces confidence. The wings that carried him skyward vanish entirely, leaving only ghostly afterimages against the blue.

And Auren falls.

The descent begins slowly, almost gently, as if the air itself hesitates to accept his failure. Then gravity reasserts its dominion with brutal efficiency. His body accelerates downward, wind tearing at his clothes, his hair, his outstretched hands that grasp desperately at empty air.

He tries to resummon the wings. Concentrates with frantic intensity on the shape, the feeling, the absolute certainty of flight. But the Aether remains unresponsive, deaf to his silent screams. The blood-soaked thread—his ancestral talisman—hangs limp around his wrist, its power extinguished.

Elyssia recedes above him, its perfect beauty growing more distant with each heartbeat. The city that should have been his eternal home becomes merely a distant mirage, unreachable as the stars themselves.

Mountains rush upward to meet him. Auren tumbles through space, disorientation making it impossible to determine how far he's fallen or how much time remains before impact. His training abandons him. His discipline shatters. Raw animal panic floods his system, overtaking rational thought.

A flash of blue below. Not stone but water—the sacred lake that surrounds the mountain's base. The Tears of the Fallen, they call it in Willow Haven. The traditional burial place for failed aspirants whose bodies could be recovered.

Auren's last conscious thought before impact is not of failure or fear but of bitter irony: he will contribute his own tears to the lake that already holds generations of broken dreams.

His body strikes the water at terminal velocity.

Pain beyond description. Blackness. Silence.

Then—improbably—consciousness returns. Liquid fills his lungs. His limbs refuse to respond to desperate mental commands. He feels himself sinking, the sunlit surface growing more distant as darkness claims him from below.

His last sight before blackness claims him completely: Elyssia floating in perfect serenity above the lake, indifferent to his failure, eternal in its unreachable glory.

Auren, most gifted adept of his generation, has failed the Ascent.

***

Dawn breaks over Willow Haven with the gentle indifference of a world that continues regardless of triumph or tragedy. Sunlight creeps across the village, illuminating thatched roofs and morning cooking fires, before finally reaching the ancient stone circle at the village's edge.

Auren sits with his back against one of the weathered pillars, watching the interplay of light and shadow across the worn stones. The fire beside him has burned low, more embers than flame now. His clothes still carry the faint scent of the sacred lake—a smell no amount of washing seems to remove.

Twenty-four hours. A single day since they pulled him from the Tears of the Fallen, his lungs full of water, his mind full of confusion. The healer, Old Maeve, called it a miracle. "Not a bone broken," she'd whispered, her fingers pressed against his chest, checking for fractures that should have been there but weren't. "The water must have caught you just right."

But Auren knows better. The height of his fall would have shattered any man, water or no. Something else preserved his body. Perhaps whatever force rejected him from Elyssia couldn't bear to finish the job completely.

A small mercy that feels like the cruelest cut. Better to have died than to live with this hollow emptiness spreading through his chest.

The knife in his hand catches the morning light as he scratches another mark into the base of the pillar. His name joins hundreds of others—some fresh, some so weathered by time they've become illegible—all those who attempted the Ascent and failed. The official record of Willow Haven's broken dreams.

A-U-R-E-N.

The final stroke of the N feels like signing his own death certificate. The death of possibility. The death of purpose.

Auren traces his finger over the freshly carved letters of his name, the stone still warm from the friction of his blade. Around him, the familiar sounds of Willow Haven coming to life drift across the morning air—children's laughter, the blacksmith's hammer striking, the bleating of goats being led to pasture.

Once, those sounds had been a promise. A reminder of why he pushed himself beyond what others thought possible.

He'd been seven when Grandfather Kaelen first took him to this stone circle, his small hand enveloped in the old man's calloused grip. "Look there, boy," Kaelen had said, pointing to the tallest stone. "My father's name is there, and his father before him. One day, yours might join them—or perhaps your name will never need carving at all."

The memory twists in Auren's gut. How many afternoons had he spent here as a child, tracing the names of failed pilgrims, swearing he would be different? He'd memorized the stories behind each mark—Uncle Joren who'd made it to Windy Ridge before a storm took him; Meera the baker's daughter who returned silent and haunt-ed from Old Hollow; countless others who never returned at all.

"The Ascent isn't just a climb," his mother would say while weaving the sacred threads. "It's a proving ground for the worthy." Her fingers, always stained with dyes from the ritual cloths she created, would brush his hair from his forehead. "And you, my son, are worthy."

Auren snorts bitterly, breaking the silence. Worthy. What a hollow word.

He'd believed it though, arranged his entire existence around that belief. When other boys played at swords, he'd been running up and down the village's steepest hills, strengthening his legs. While girls his age learned cooking and weaving, he'd studied the stars and memo-rized the path markers. When adolescents paired off for harvest festi-vals, he'd stayed apart, keeping his body pure for the trials ahead.

Twenty five years of preparation. Over two decades of sacrifice. For what?

For three perfect minutes of flight, the sacred Aether coursing through his veins, wings of light carrying him upward—only to be rejected at the threshold.

A memory surfaces: his tenth birthday, when he'd climbed the village's ancient oak. He'd gone higher than any child before, reach-ing branches so thin they bent beneath his weight. The village had gathered below, gasping when he nearly fell, then cheering when he steadied himself.

"That's what makes you special, Auren," his grandfather had said that night. "Others stop when safety demands it. You push further."

His grandfather had been so proud then. What would he say now, if he were alive? The thought of facing him—of facing any of them—makes Auren's chest tighten.

The knife in his hand suddenly feels heavy. He stares at the blade, turning it over, watching sunlight dance along its edge. So easy to end this shame. One quick slash and he'd join the truly fallen, those pilgrims who couldn't bear the weight of rejection.

Something rustles in the undergrowth beyond the stone circle. Auren tenses, the knife instinctively shifting to a defensive grip. His eyes narrow, scanning the treeline.

A small black shape darts between two bushes, then freezes—a cat, its sleek body low to the ground, amber eyes fixed on him with unnerving intensity.

"Get," Auren mutters, flicking his hand dismissively.

For a moment, the cat just stares at him, then scurries off towards the lake.

"I thought I'd find you here."

Kyp's voice carries across the stone circle, familiar and grounding. His childhood friend approaches with the cautious respect of someone approaching wounded prey. His gaze drops to the two bottles at Auren's side—one already empty, the other still sealed.

"Celebrating being alive or mourning... well, you know?" Kyp asks, nodding toward the bottles.

"What do you think?" Auren doesn't look up, still staring at his freshly carved name.

"Fair enough." Kyp settles down beside him, crossing his legs and adjusting his worn leather vest. Unlike most in Willow Haven, Kyp never aspired to the Ascent, never felt the calling that drove so many to risk everything for a chance at divinity.

For a long time, they sit in silence, the crackling fire providing the only conversation. Finally, Auren uncorks the second bottle and takes a long pull. The liquor burns down his throat, a physical sensation that briefly distracts from the emotional numbness.

"So that's it?" Auren mutters, wiping his mouth with the back of his hand. "It's over."

Kyp doesn't offer platitudes or reassurances. He simply sits, a solid presence beside Auren, watching the fire's dance.

"I heard a voice," Auren says suddenly, the words spilling out before he can consider them. "Right when I was about to reach Elyssia. Right when everything was perfect." The memory brings a bitter taste that even the alcohol can't wash away. "Just two words. 'Not yet.' And then I fell."

He looks at Kyp for the first time, seeking... what? Understanding? Validation? Some confirmation that he isn't losing his mind along with everything else?

Kyp's expression remains neutral, though his eyes soften with concern. "What kind of voice? Like, an actual person speaking?"

"No." Auren shakes his head, struggling to articulate the experience. "It wasn't... outside me. It was inside. Here." He taps his temple. "Clearer than thought. More certain than knowledge."

"Hmm." Kyp picks up a stick and pokes at the fire, sending a cascade of sparks into the morning air. "The elders would say it was the voice of Elyssia itself."

"And what do you say?"

"I don't know, Auren." Kyp sighs. "I'm not the one who chases after floating cities and ancient magic." He pauses, then adds more gently, "But I know it matters to you, what you heard. I just don't have answers."

The fire between them sputters, a log shifting and settling deeper into the coals. Auren stares into the flames, seeing in their chaotic dance an echo of the Aether wings that carried him skyward—and then abandoned him.

Without warning, he hurls the second bottle into the heart of the fire. Glass shatters, liquid splashes across burning wood. The flame hisses, recoils—and then swells with unnatural intensity, flaring bright blue for a heartbeat before settling back to its normal orange.

Both men stare at the fire, startled by its reaction.

"What am I going to do now?" Auren's question emerges quiet and raw, directed as much to himself as to Kyp.

Kyp doesn't answer immediately. He waits until the fire has quieted, until the morning birds have resumed their chorus in the nearby trees.

"If I were into all that religious stuff," he finally says, "I'd tell you the thread will guide you." He gestures vaguely toward the blood-soaked thread still wound around Auren's wrist, now dull and lifeless. "But I'm not, so I'll just say that I know you'll find your way, when you least expect it."

Auren flexes his wrist, the ancient thread shifting against his skin. Even in failure, he can't bring himself to remove it—this last connection to generations of pilgrims, to his mother's hope, to everything he was supposed to become.

In the distance, a temple bell rings, calling the village to morning prayer. Neither man moves to answer its summons.

Melia II

The knock comes at dawn. Three sharp raps, exact and measured—the knocks of someone who counts seconds between them. Melia stirs beneath silk sheets, momentarily disoriented in the gray half-light. The royal chambers feel cavernous around her now, the absence of her parents expanding the space in ways she cannot define.

"Princess." A voice through the door. Not Solivar's clipped precision, but the warm reassurance of Sir Orlan. "Forgive the early hour. The Prefect requests your presence in the Hall of Ascendant Light."

Melia sits up, abandoning sleep's brief mercy. The wedding dream clings to her consciousness—not a dream of celebration but of suffocation, of being draped in ceremonial whites so heavy she couldn't draw breath.

"I require a moment, Sir Orlan."

"Of course, Princess."

She hears the subtle shift of armor outside her door as her guard resumes his post. Sir Orlan—steadfast, resolute, and the only person who looks at her with genuine concern rather than calculated assessment.

The marble floor sends a shock of cold through her bare feet. Melia crosses to the window, drawing back the shimmering drapes. Elyssia spreads before her in pristine splendor, morning light catching on gilded spires and crystal domes. The floating gardens cascade in perfect tiers, each blossom precisely timed to open with the rising sun.

Perfect. Always perfect. Elyssia's glory never dims, even as her own has begun to fade.

The dream-weight of wedding vestments still presses on her shoulders as she slips into a simple morning robe. No handmaidens today; she cannot bear their practiced smiles and rehearsed condolences. Instead, she splashes cold water from the porcelain basin onto her face, the shock momentarily anchoring her to the present.

In the mirror, her reflection looks like a stranger—a golden-haired apparition with eyes that hold questions she cannot voice. The royal mark on her palm seems to pulse in the morning light, a subtle shimmer of silver against her skin.

"I am ready, Sir Orlan."

The door opens to reveal her guard, tall and imposing in the traditional armor of Elyssia's elite knights. Despite his formal bearing, concern shadows his steel-blue eyes.

"Are you well, Princess?" His voice lowers, private in the empty corridor.

"As well as circumstances allow," she replies, matching his discretion.

Sir Orlan offers a short bow before falling into step beside her. His presence is reassuring—solid and unwavering amid the shifting uncertainties that have plagued her since her parents' deaths.

The Hall of Ascendant Light occupies the highest tier of the royal palace, a circular chamber whose ceiling opens to the sky. Here, tradition dictates, Elyssia's rulers commune directly with divine purpose, unobstructed by barriers between heaven and earth.

Sir Orlan pauses at the massive silver doors. "He awaits you inside." A hesitation, then: "Remember who you are, Princess."

The doors swing open without visible prompting, and Melia steps into a flood of carefully orchestrated light. Hundreds of prisms hang suspended from the domed ceiling, catching the morning sun and fracturing it into precise patterns across the polished floor.

Prefect Solivar stands at the center of this manufactured constellation, his silver-gray hair and pale eyes absorbing the light without reflecting it. He turns at her entrance, hands clasped behind his back, expression revealing nothing.

"Princess Melia." His voice carries the authority of position rather than emotion. "I trust your mourning period has provided adequate reflection."

Not a question. Never a question from Solivar.

"It continues to do so," she responds, remaining near the entrance rather than approaching him.

"Indeed." Solivar moves through the light patterns, disrupting their flow without seeming to notice. "However, Elyssia cannot pause for grief, however profound. The city requires certainty, continuity. Your parents understood this fundamental truth."

Melia feels something cold settle in her stomach. "My father has been dead less than a fortnight."

"Precisely." Solivar stops before her, close enough that she can see the minute precision with which his robes are tailored, each fold and seam exacting in its placement. "Which is why we must act with decisive clarity to reassure our people."

He gestures toward the windows, where Elyssia spreads in mani-
cured perfection. "Look at them, Princess. They seek the comfort of
tradition, the assurance that although individuals may pass, our sacred
order remains unbroken."

"And what does this sacred order demand of me now?" The words
emerge sharper than intended.

Solivar's expression doesn't change, but something in his eyes hardens. "The Council has confirmed the date. We are to be wed at the next
moon, sixteen days hence."

The pronouncement lands like a physical blow. Melia had known
this was coming, but the timing...

"So soon after their deaths? The people will see it as disrespect."

"On the contrary." Solivar circles her slowly, each step measured.
"The people will see it as your inheritance, your sacred duty, your
confirmation as heir. They will find comfort in the continuity."

"And if I require more time to mourn?"

"Your private feelings, while understandable, are secondary to
Elyssia's needs." His tone remains perfectly calm, reasonable. "This
was your parents' wish, the fulfillment of their vision for a unified
Elyssia."

Melia feels her throat tighten. "Did they specify the timing as well?
That I should stand at the matrimonial altar while their funeral flowers
still bloom?"

For the first time, Solivar's expression shifts—a flicker of annoyance
quickly mastered. "Your mother entrusted me with ensuring a smooth
transition. The Priests concur with my assessment of the appropriate
timeline."

He moves to a small silver table where a document lies unfurled,
official seals glinting in the prismatic light. "The arrangements have

been made. The announcement will be delivered to the people at midday."

Rebellion surges, hot and insistent. "And if I refuse?"

Solivar doesn't even look up from the document. "You won't."

"You cannot command my consent."

"Cannot I?" Now he does look up, his pale eyes assessing her with clinical detachment. "Your position exists within a framework of obligations, Princess. Your consent was given the moment you accepted your royal birthright."

"My birthright is to rule Elyssia as my mother did, not to be rushed into a political marriage while still in mourning."

Solivar sighs, the sound of someone dealing with a willful child. "Your mother ruled with wisdom accumulated through decades of experience. You are twenty-two, bereaved, and untested. Elyssia requires stability that you, alone, cannot provide."

He approaches her again, his movements smooth and controlled. "This is not a negotiation, Princess. It is the inevitable fulfillment of your purpose." He gestures to the document. "The preparations are underway. The ceremonial whites are being prepared."

The wedding dream flashes through her mind again—suffocating layers of white, tightening with each breath.

"This is wrong," she says, her voice dropping to a whisper. "My father would have granted me time."

"Your father is dead." Solivar's bluntness is calculated. "And I now speak with your parents authority as Regent Prefect. The wedding proceeds as planned."

Something shifts in the light behind him. Sir Orlan stands at attention by the door, his expression schooled into neutrality, but his eyes meet hers briefly—a silent acknowledgment of her distress.

"I require your formal acknowledgment, Princess." Solivar extends an ornate silver pen. "A mere formality, but tradition must be observed."

Melia stares at the pen, at the document with its elaborate script and official seals. Everything already decided, her role reduced to a ceremonial signature on a future written without her input.

"And if I refuse to sign?"

Solivar's smile doesn't reach his eyes. "Then I would be forced to question your fitness for royal duties during this difficult time. For your own protection, of course. Grief can cloud judgment, lead to regrettable decisions."

The threat hangs in the air between them, polished to a perfect shine like everything else in Elyssia. Melia takes the pen, its weight cold and foreign in her hand.

"Those who would rule must first learn to be ruled by duty," Solivar quotes, the ancient Elyssian proverb flowing from him with practiced ease.

The document blurs before her eyes. Her signature feels like a betrayal, though of what or whom, she cannot articulate. When she finishes, Solivar takes the pen with a satisfied nod.

"A wise choice, Princess. Your parents would be proud."

The words strike like a physical blow. Would they? Her father's voice seems to whisper from the edges of memory: *Remember who you truly are, Melia.*

But who is she, if not the perfect Elyssian princess, fulfilling her predetermined role?

Solivar rolls the signed document with meticulous care, his fingers moving with practiced precision. The parchment disappears into his robes as he turns his attention fully to Melia, studying her with an intensity that makes her skin prickle.

"You exceed your mother's beauty," he observes, beginning a slow circle around her. His footsteps echo against the marble, measuring the perimeter of her personal space. "The royal bloodline shines through your features."

Melia stands rigid, feeling like a specimen pinned for examination. "I prefer not to discuss my mother this way."

"Your preferences are noted." Solivar continues his orbit, pausing behind her where she cannot see his expression. His voice comes from just over her shoulder, close enough that she can feel his breath. "But there are practical matters we must address regarding our union."

She steps away, creating distance, but he follows, maintaining his calculated proximity. "The wedding arrangements are sufficient discussion for today."

"Hardly." His pale eyes rake over her, assessing rather than admiring. "A royal marriage serves purposes beyond mere ceremony. The continuity of leadership requires more... tangible outcomes."

The meaning behind his words crystallizes, sending a chill down Melia's spine.

"Elyssia requires an heir," Solivar states, the words clinical yet somehow intimate in their implication. "Our first duty following the wedding will be to secure the succession."

Melia feels heat rise to her face. "That is not a topic I'm prepared to discuss."

"Preparation is precisely my point." He resumes circling, a predator establishing the boundaries of its territory. "The royal apartments are being prepared for our use. I've instructed modifications to ensure our privacy during the crucial early months of our marriage."

Her stomach turns. "This conversation is inappropriate."

"On the contrary. It is essential." Solivar's hand brushes her arm, the contact brief but deliberate. "Your inexperience is understandable, even expected. Purity becomes an Elyssian princess."

He steps closer, invading her space with calculated dominance. "You need not fear the marriage bed. What begins as duty often blossoms into genuine affection. Many royal brides have found themselves surprised by the pleasures of submission."

The word 'submission' lands like a slap. Melia steps back, colliding with a column. "You overstep, Prefect."

"I prepare you for reality." His expression remains impassive, but something flickers in his eyes—a cold, proprietary gleam. "The royal chambers will witness the beginning of a new era for Elyssia. Our coupling will ensure stability for generations."

"Stop." The word emerges sharper than she intended.

Solivar tilts his head, studying her reaction with detached curiosity. "Your modesty is commendable, if unnecessary between betrothed. You'll find I can be a patient teacher. Many women resist initially, only to discover unexpected pleasure in surrender."

His fingers trace the line of her jaw, and it takes all Melia's willpower not to recoil. "In time, Princess, you will learn to welcome my touch. To anticipate it. Perhaps even to love it, as you will learn to love me."

She feels trapped between his body and the column, the prismatic light casting fractured patterns across his face that make him appear inhuman for flickering moments.

"For now, your nervousness is charming," he continues, withdrawing his hand. "But make no mistake—our union will be consummated promptly. Elyssia cannot wait for an heir while you adjust to marital realities."

Melia finds her voice, forcing steel into her words. "I believe we've concluded today's business, Prefect."

Solivar steps back, his expression returning to formal neutrality so quickly she almost doubts the predatory gleam was ever there. "Indeed. I have preparations to oversee." He offers a shallow bow. "Consider our discussion an educational courtesy, Princess. I believe in thorough preparation for all eventualities."

Solivar inclines his head in dismissal. "Sir Orlan will escort you to your chambers. I have increased your security detail in anticipation of the announcement. The people's enthusiasm can sometimes manifest in... overzealous ways."

The real meaning is clear: she will be watched more closely now, her movements restricted under the guise of protection.

Sir Orlan steps forward, his formal bow hiding whatever thoughts might cross his weathered features. "Princess."

They exit the Hall of Ascendant Light in silence, the massive doors sealing behind them with a resonant boom. Only when they have traversed half the length of the upper corridor does Sir Orlan speak, his voice pitched low.

"Princess, if I may..."

Melia glances up, startled by the break in protocol.

"Speak freely, Sir Orlan."

He hesitates, clearly weighing his words. "The Prefect's haste seems... unusual, even considering the circumstances."

"You think so as well?" Relief floods through her—validation from an unexpected quarter.

"It is not my place to question the Prefect's decisions." Sir Orlan's diplomatic response is belied by the concern in his eyes. "But I served your mother for twenty-seven years. She believed in the power of proper time and consideration."

They reach an intersection of corridors, and Sir Orlan glances both ways before continuing, voice even lower. "Princess, your mother often spoke of balanced judgment. She would want you to honor your instincts as well as your duties."

Something unspoken lingers beneath his words—a warning, perhaps, or encouragement. Before she can press further, footsteps echo from an adjoining passage. Sir Orlan straightens, resuming his formal bearing as two members of the Prefect's personal guard appear, their silver uniforms gleaming.

"The Princess is returning to her chambers," Sir Orlan announces, his tone betraying nothing of their brief exchange.

The guards offer synchronized bows. "We are instructed to join her security detail," one states.

"By whose authority?" Sir Orlan's question carries a subtle edge.

"Prefect Solivar's. Direct order."

Sir Orlan's jaw tightens momentarily. "Very well. You may follow at an appropriate distance."

The rest of the walk proceeds in silence, the two additional guards trailing several paces behind. Only when they reach her chambers does Sir Orlan speak again, opening her door and bowing low.

"Princess." He meets her eyes briefly. "Remember that even in the clearest skies, one must watch for changing winds."

The door closes, leaving Melia alone with the cryptic warning and the weight of expectations pressing down like ceremonial whites, layer upon suffocating layer.

***

In her dimly lit chamber, Melia paces. The scroll of wedding proclamations lies discarded on her writing desk, its contents as hollow as the platitudes at her parents' funeral. Night has fallen over Elyssia, the floating city's perpetual glow dimmed to a soft luminescence that bathes the architecture in silver.

She can't sleep. Can't rest. Can't breathe under the weight of everything unspoken.

Remember who you truly are, Melia.

Her father's words haunt her, circling like a persistent melody. What had he meant? There had been something in his eyes those final days—a heaviness beyond illness, a knowing that cut deeper than pain.

Her gaze drifts to the painting she'd found after the funeral. The fading figure of herself bothers her more than she can articulate. Why would a royal portrait, preserved with the finest pigments and sealed with ceremonial varnish, begin to fade?

A thought crystallizes, sudden and clear. The Royal Archives. If her father left any clues about what he truly meant, they'd be there, hidden among the ancestral records she's never been permitted to see.

"My birthright," she whispers to the silent room, the words feeling strange yet powerful on her lips.

She moves to her wardrobe, selecting a simple indigo gown—less conspicuous than her usual attire. The Archive Room sits in the eastern wing of the palace, accessible only to Council members and the royal family. Yet even as princess, she's always been gently steered away from the historical scrolls by attendants with polite excuses.

No more excuses. No more gentle deflections.

The corridors of the palace remain lit by soft blue flame-globes, casting elongated shadows across marble floors. Melia moves with practiced grace, head high—looking as though she has every right to be wherever she chooses. The few night servants she passes bow deeply, eyes averted.

The massive gilded doors of the Archive Room appear at the end of the eastern corridor. Two Silent Guards flank the entrance, their ceremonial spears crossing at her approach.

"I wish to see the royal lineage scrolls," Melia states, infusing her voice with authority she doesn't entirely feel.

The guards exchange glances, hesitation evident in their rigid posture.

"Princess," one begins, "the Archive Master must be present for—"

"My parents are dead," Melia interrupts, the words sharp as crystal shards. "I am the last of my line. Those records are mine by blood and by right."

The guards exchange another wary glance. Finally, their spears part like reluctant curtains. Melia steps through the threshold, heart thundering as the massive doors close behind her with a whispered thud.

Inside, circular chambers branch outward from a central hub, each storing scrolls from different eras. The genealogy section should contain the royal family's records—meticulous documentation of every generation.

The room hums with contained power. Scroll cases line the walls, their silver caps engraved with family crests. Melia's fingers trail across them, searching for the royal insignia. When she finds it, her hands tremble slightly as she withdraws the case.

Empty.

She checks again, disbelief turning to alarm. The royal case contains nothing—not even dust. She moves frantically to neighboring cases, searching for misfiled documents, finding nothing.

A deeper, more thorough search reveals other gaps—precise excisions in the archive's collection. Records of council members, high priests, ranking officials, all mysteriously absent. Something about her origin—perhaps about all the ruling elite—must be hidden.

The corridor outside has filled with guards. They move with purpose, checking rooms systematically.

"The Princess is in here. The Prefect has ordered her to be returned to her chambers," a voice confirms. "Secure all exits from the eastern wing."

The room spins around her. Through the thin pillars separating archive sections, Melia glimpses more guards pouring into the entrance hall. Not her guards—Solivar's men, with their distinctive silver clasps.

They're looking for me like I'm a criminal. In my own palace.

Her stomach twists into a tight knot. The emptied scroll cases stare back at her—evidence of deliberate erasure, not careless misplacement. Someone has systematically removed all traces of her lineage.

The realization lands like a physical blow: her authority as princess is just for show. The palace, the government, the guards—they answer to Solivar now. Have they always?

"Check the genealogy section," a gruff voice commands. Footsteps approach.

Melia slips between towering shelves, crouching behind a reading desk. Her fine gown catches on a wooden corner, tearing with a whisper that sounds thunderous in the quiet archive. She freezes, heart hammering against her ribs.

"Princess Melia, the Prefect has expressed concern for your wellbeing," calls a guard captain. "Please come with us. It's for your protection."

Protection from what? she wonders bitterly. *From learning the truth?*

The guards move methodically through the chambers, closing in. Escape routes dwindle with each passing moment.

She presses a hand against her mouth to quiet her breathing. If she's caught now, Solivar will ensure she never has another chance to uncover what's been hidden. Her title—her entire identity—suddenly feels like a beautifully crafted cage rather than a birthright.

Melia retreats deeper into the archive, searching for another way out. A small maintenance door at the rear opens onto a narrow service passage. She slips through, following the cramped corridor as it winds upward through the palace infrastructure.

The passage emerges near the Grand Observatory—one of the highest points in Elyssia, its domed ceiling open to the night sky. From here, the entire floating city spreads below in concentric rings of light and shadow.

"Halt!"

Two guards spot her emerging from the hidden door. Melia runs, abandoning stealth for speed. The Observatory's wide chamber offers nowhere to hide, but the viewing platform extends outward, suspended over Elyssia's edge.

More guards pour in from multiple entrances. She's cornered, backing toward the platform's railing.

"Princess Melia," one guard steps forward, removing his helmet. "Please come away from the edge. The Prefect is concerned for your safety."

"Why are there no scrolls?" she demands, voice rising with emotion. "Where are my parents' origin records? Where are mine?"

The guards exchange uneasy glances. None reply.

"Tell me the truth!" Her cry echoes through the domed space. "Who exactly am I?"

"Princess, you're distressed. Please—"

"I am not distressed. I am awake." The realization floods her with terrible clarity. "And I think you know that some of us aren't meant to be awake."

They advance slowly, forming a half-circle. Behind her lies only open air—the endless drop from Elyssia to the world below.

In that moment, her father's words return with blinding significance. *Remember who you truly are, Melia.* Not a plea to remember her royal duties, but to discover her actual nature.

The missing scrolls. The fading portrait. The rushed wedding. All pieces of a puzzle she's only beginning to assemble.

One guard lunges for her arm. Melia steps backward, feeling the railing press against her spine.

"What happens," she asks softly, "if I fall?"

Their expressions answer before words can—panic, revelation, confirmation.

"Princess, don't—"

Melia leans back against the railing, feeling its solid presence. One decision point. One moment of truth.

"I need to know."

She pushes herself up and over in a single fluid motion. For one suspended instant, she hovers at the precipice, looking into their horrified faces.

Then she falls.

***

The first sensation is the wind—harsh and howling as it whips through her hair and tears at her gown. Melia's scream dissolves into the rushing air, consumed by the roar of her descent. Through streaming eyes, she watches Elyssia shrink above her, its magnificent spires and gardens transforming into a glowing coin against the darkening sky.

I'm going to die.

The thought arrives with strange clarity. Not a question, not a plea—simple acceptance. She spreads her arms wide, no longer fighting the inevitable. The clouds rush toward her, enveloping her body in their cold embrace. Moisture clings to her skin as she punches through layer after layer of mist.

Strange, how time stretches in these moments. Each heartbeat lasts an eternity. Each breath might be her last.

The clouds part below her, revealing the distant ground—a patchwork of greens and browns punctuated by the silver thread of a river. The world beneath Elyssia, the place spoken of only in hushed tones, now rushes to meet her with terrifying speed.

What did I expect to discover? The question flickers through her mind as the air grows warmer, denser. *Truth or oblivion?*

Something deep inside her rebels against the approaching end. A primal instinct forces air into her lungs for one final, desperate scream. The sound tears from her throat, raw and animal, as the glittering surface of a lake expands beneath her.

Impact.

The water doesn't feel like water at all. It strikes like stone, punishing her body for its velocity. Pain explodes across every inch of her skin, then plunges inward to her bones. Water engulfs her, swallows her whole. The roar of wind gives way to muted pressure against her eardrums.

Down, down she sinks, indigo gown billowing around her like the petals of a drowning flower. Bubbles escape from her lips, carrying away what little breath remains. The pain recedes, replaced by a spreading numbness. Her limbs refuse to obey, floating uselessly as she descends into the murky depths.

Diamonds dance across her vision—little sparkles of light that have nothing to do with the sun filtering through water. Her lungs burn, then stop burning. The urgent need for air transforms into peaceful acceptance.

So this is death.

The world blurs at the edges, consciousness slipping away like water through fingers. As darkness claims her, strange visions pulsate behind her eyelids.

Her father stands before her, not as she last saw him—stern and distant—but as he was in her childhood. His eyes crinkle with warmth as he kneels to her level.

"Remember who you truly are, Melia." His lips don't move, but she hears the words clearly. He extends his hand, but before she can reach for it, the vision shifts.

Her mother appears, surrounded by strange machinery, her perfect face contorted in pain. "Not again," she whispers. "Not another one." The image dissolves into hundreds of unfamiliar faces pressing against glass walls, mouths open in silent screams.

Melia!

They call her name in unison, hands outstretched, eyes pleading. Men and women of all ages, wearing simple garments unlike the elaborate fashions of Elyssia. Their features blur together, yet each somehow feels achingly familiar.

Help us!

The vision fractures, replaced by a small black cat with luminous green eyes that bore into hers with unsettling intelligence. Unlike the other apparitions, this one doesn't speak or move—it simply watches, patient and knowing.

Water fills her lungs. The visions fade.

Nothing.

Then—sensation. Rough sand against her cheek. Cold water lapping at her legs. The distant cry of unfamiliar birds.

Melia's body convulses, expelling water in painful, wracking coughs. Each breath burns like fire, but the pain signals life. She's alive.

Her eyelids weigh tons, but she forces them open to a sliver. Blinding sunlight stabs her pupils. She tries to move, managing only a weak twitch of her fingers. Every muscle screams in protest, every joint feels dislocated.

Something soft presses against her cheek. Warm. Vibrating gently.

With tremendous effort, Melia shifts her focus. A small black cat nuzzles against her face, its fur glossy in the sunlight. Green eyes regard her with that same unnerving intelligence from her drowning vision. Not a hallucination, then.

The cat bumps its head against her chin, purring louder, as if encouraging her to stay awake.

The cat's ears twitch. It places one paw on her chest, directly over her heart.

Distant voices carry on the breeze. Human voices.

Footsteps approach, crunching on sand and gravel. The cat's ears flatten slightly, but it makes no move to run. Instead, it positions itself between Melia and the approaching strangers, its posture alert yet nonthreatening.

She tries to turn her head toward the voices, but her body refuses to cooperate. Darkness creeps in from the edges of her vision again. The cat leans closer, its whiskers tickling her cheek.

"Stay with me," Melia whispers, unsure if she speaks to the cat or herself.

The footsteps halt nearby. A shadow falls across her face, blocking the harsh sunlight.

"Gods above," a deep voice exclaims. "It's a woman!"

"Is she alive?" A second voice, higher, tinged with concern.

"She's breathing. Barely."

"Look at her clothes. Have you ever seen fabric like that?"

Melia struggles to focus on the figures standing over her, but they remain blurry silhouettes against the bright sky. The cat presses closer, its warmth anchoring her to consciousness for a few precious seconds more.

"Where did she come from?" The deep voice sounds bewildered.

As darkness claims her again, Melia almost wants to laugh. *I fell from heaven,* she thinks distantly. *Or what we pretended was heaven.*

Auren II

The sunbeam assaulting Auren's eyes feels like a blade piercing his skull. He shifts in his seat, trying to escape its merciless glare without actually moving his throbbing head. The Rainbow Goat, Willow Haven's only excuse for a tavern, reeks of stale beer and yesterday's regrets—smells that do nothing to settle his churning stomach.

"Here," Kyp slides another mug across the rough-hewn table. "Gretta's special hangover cure."

The concoction inside looks like pond scum and smells worse. "If you're trying to make me vomit, just punch me in the gut. It'd be kinder."

Kyp's laugh is soft, deliberately gentle. "Drink it. I promise it works."

Auren grabs the mug and downs the viscous liquid in three painful gulps, fighting his gag reflex the entire time. He slams the empty vessel down, wiping his mouth with the back of his hand. "That's absolutely vile."

"Which is how you know it's good medicine," Kyp grins, the expression not quite reaching his eyes. He's been watching Auren like this for days now—careful, concerned, maintaining the appearance of his usual cheerful self while monitoring for signs of something worse than a hangover.

The tavern door swings open, flooding the dim interior with unwelcome light. Councilor Bram's stocky silhouette fills the doorframe for a moment before he steps inside, adjusting his official sash with one hand while squinting into the gloom.

"Thought I might find you boys here," Bram says, approaching their table. His weathered face creases with concern as he takes in Auren's bloodshot eyes and disheveled appearance. "How are you holding up, son?"

"I'm fine," Auren mumbles, staring into his empty mug as if it might magically refill itself. The councilor's pitying tone scrapes against his raw nerves.

"Right," Bram says, clearly unconvinced. He settles his considerable bulk onto the bench opposite them, the wood groaning in protest. "Well, something's happened that might interest you."

"Unless it's a breakthrough in hangover cures, I doubt it."

Kyp shoots him a warning look. "What's going on, Councilor?"

Bram leans forward, lowering his voice though there's hardly anyone else in the tavern at this hour. "Someone fell."

The words hang in the air, simple but loaded with impossible meaning.

"Fell?" Auren repeats, suddenly alert despite the pounding in his head.

"From Elyssia," Bram confirms, his expression grave. "Into the sacred lake, just before dawn. Fishermen pulled her out. She's alive, barely a scratch on her."

The room tilts slightly. "That's not possible."

"Yet it happened." Bram's thick fingers drum against the tabletop. "She wears clothes like nothing we've seen. Fine material, strange cut."

"Her?" Kyp asks.

"A young woman. Blonde, delicate-looking. In and out of consciousness still, but Maren says she'll live."

Auren's mind races, fragments of thoughts colliding. No one falls from Elyssia. The floating city doesn't reject its own. Those who fail the Ascension—like him—never reach it in the first place. Whatever forces guard the city's boundaries prevent anyone from entering... or leaving.

"I saw all the commotion from our tent this morning," Kyp says. "Thought maybe someone had drowned."

"In a sense, they nearly did," Bram replies. "Strange thing is, there was a cat with her. Black as midnight, refusing to leave her side. Hisses at anyone who gets too close."

The hangover recedes beneath a flood of questions. "Why are you telling us this?"

Bram studies him for a long moment. "The Council's divided on what to do with her. Some say it's an omen, others think she's a danger. We need someone who understands what it means to approach the city, someone who's seen—"

"My failure," Auren finishes flatly. "You want the village reject to talk to the city's reject."

"You're the only one who's come closest to ascending," Bram counters. "You did the Pilgrimage. You understand things the rest of us don't."

A bitter laugh escapes Auren's throat. "I understand nothing. That's the whole problem."

"Nevertheless," Bram continues, undeterred, "the Council would like you to meet her. When she wakes."

"And if I refuse?"

"Then we proceed without your insight," Bram shrugs, rising from the bench. "But I think you won't refuse. You've spent every day since your return wondering why you weren't worthy. Maybe now you'll get some answers."

The councilor departs, leaving the door ajar. Sunlight spills across the floor in a golden rectangle that seems to point directly at Auren.

Kyp watches him carefully. "What are you thinking?"

"That I need another drink." Auren signals to Gretta behind the bar.

"Seriously, though." Kyp leans closer. "Someone actually fell from Elyssia. That changes everything we know about the city."

The implications crash through Auren's mind like waves against rocks. If someone can fall out, then the barrier isn't absolute. The rejection he felt, that final whispered "not yet" before plummeting—was it truly final? Or merely a postponement?

"It doesn't change anything for me," he mutters, even as his heart pounds with possibility.

"Liar." Kyp's eyes gleam. "You're already planning what you'll ask her."

Auren doesn't respond, because Kyp's right. Questions swirl like leaves in a whirlwind: Who is she? Why did she fall? What secrets does Elyssia hold that might explain his own rejection?

Before he can sort through the chaos in his mind, Gretta appears with a fresh mug. "Councilor Bram says to tell you they've moved her to the meeting hall. She's waking up."

Auren and Kyp exchange glances.

"Well?" Kyp raises an eyebrow. "Are we going, or are you planning to drink away this opportunity too?"

***

The walk to the meeting hall passes in a blur of throbbing headache and racing thoughts. Auren's mind can't settle on any one question long enough to form a coherent strategy. What do you ask someone who's done the impossible? Who's crossed the barrier that rejected him so thoroughly?

"You're walking too fast," Kyp complains, jogging to keep up.

"And you're falling behind." Despite his attempt at levity, tension coils inside Auren's chest like a spring wound too tight.

The meeting hall stands at the center of Willow Haven—a modest building of stone and timber that serves as the heart of village governance. Already, a small crowd has gathered outside, their murmured conversations creating a nervous hum. They part as Auren approaches, their gazes a mixture of curiosity and that familiar, uncomfortable pity.

"There he is," someone whispers.

"Makes sense they'd call him," another replies.

Inside, the hall's central space has been cleared. Councilor Bram stands with Maren, the village healer, beside a makeshift pallet near the hearth. A small figure sits huddled under blankets, shoulders hunched, head bowed. And beside her—just as Bram described—a sleek black cat watches with unnerving intensity.

Bram notices their arrival, relief washing over his face. "Auren, Kyp. Thank you for coming. Our guest is awake."

As they approach, the figure raises her head, and Auren's breath catches in his throat.

She's beautiful in a way that doesn't belong in Willow Haven—doesn't belong anywhere outside of fables and dreams. Her features carry the delicate perfection of artistic renderings rather than flesh and blood: high cheekbones, a gently curved mouth, and eyes the startling blue of summer skies. Her golden hair, though tangled and damp, frames her face like spun sunlight.

But it's not her beauty that makes Auren pause mid-step. It's the bruises blooming across her pale skin—purple shadows beneath her eyes, a darkened mark at her temple, raw abrasions on her slender wrists. Evidence that whatever happened to her was real, not divine intervention but physical trauma.

Those remarkable eyes lock onto him, widening slightly. They're alert and intelligent, filled not with confusion but with careful assessment.

"This is Auren," Bram explains to her. "He's experienced in matters of... ascension."

The black cat hisses softly, ears flattening.

"That cat's been with me since I woke up," the woman says, her voice unexpectedly strong despite her appearance. "I'm calling him Bear. He doesn't trust easily."

"Something we have in common," Auren replies, maintaining a careful distance.

Maren adjusts the blanket around the woman's shoulders. "She refused to let me examine her further. Says she's perfectly fine, though that's hardly possible after what she's been through."

"I am fine," the woman insists. "The water broke my fall."

Auren studies her more closely. Her clothing, though sodden and stained, is clearly of exceptional quality—silk embroidered with threads that catch the light, a cut and style he's never seen before. Her hands, though scratched, show no calluses or signs of labor. Everything about her speaks of privilege and care.

"The entire village is talking," Kyp says, dropping onto a bench across from her. "They're calling it a miracle."

"It's no miracle," Auren counters, unable to keep the edge from his voice. "The question is what it actually is."

Bram clears his throat. "Perhaps introductions would help. Miss, could you tell us who you are and... how you came to be here?"

The woman hesitates, fingers absently stroking the cat's fur. Something flickers behind her eyes—calculation, perhaps, or caution.

"My name is Melia," she says finally. "Princess Melia of Elyssia."

The words land like stones in still water, sending ripples through the room. Maren gasps softly. Kyp's mouth drops open. Even Bram, usually composed, takes an involuntary step backward.

"Princess?" he repeats.

"Yes." Melia lifts her chin slightly, the gesture instinctively regal despite her bedraggled state. "Daughter of Queen Lysandra and King Orion."

"The royal family isn't just myth," Kyp breathes, awe written across his face.

Auren crosses his arms, skepticism hardening his features. "And you expect us to believe you just... fell? From the divine city that accepts only the worthy? That rejects even those who spend their lives preparing to ascend?"

Melia's gaze slides to him, cool and assessing. "I didn't fall. I jumped."

Another shock wave ripples through the room.

"By the light," Maren whispers, hand pressed to her mouth. "Why would you do such a thing?"

Melia doesn't answer immediately. Her fingers continue their rhythmic stroking of the cat's fur, her eyes distant now. "It's complicated."

"No," Auren shakes his head. "That's not good enough. People in Etheria spend their entire lives dreaming of ascending to Elyssia. We follow the pilgrim's path, we endure trials, we sacrifice everything for even the slimmest chance of being deemed worthy—and you just... jumped? Threw it all away?"

"Auren," Bram warns, but Melia raises a hand.

"It's a fair question," she acknowledges. "One I'm not ready to fully answer."

She's hiding something. Auren can see it in the careful composure of her features, the measured cadence of her words. This isn't a traumatized victim but someone accustomed to controlling narratives, to revealing only what serves her purpose.

"What will happen to me now?" she asks, addressing Bram.

The councilor exchanges glances with Maren before answering. "Well, given the unprecedented nature of your arrival, we must consider the traditions and laws that might apply. You are, in essence, one of the fallen."

"The fallen?" Melia echoes.

"Those who attempt the Ascent but fail," Auren explains flatly. "Though usually, we fail before reaching Elyssia, not after living there."

Bram strokes his beard thoughtfully. "Our traditions dictate that those who fall must undergo a period of reflection and renewal. A reverse pilgrimage, if you will—a journey through the sacred sites that mark the path to ascension, but in the opposite direction."

"A cleansing," Maren adds. "To wash away the stain of failure and prepare the soul for another attempt."

Understanding dawns on Auren with sickening clarity. "No," he says, the word sharp as broken glass. "You can't be serious."

But Bram's expression confirms what Auren already knows. "You're the logical choice, Auren. You know the path better than anyone. This is your next step, anyway."

"You want me to guide her?" Auren laughs bitterly. "The reject leading the runaway princess on a spiritual journey?"

"I'll do it," Melia interrupts, her voice cutting through the tension like a blade. All eyes turn to her in surprise. "This reverse pilgrimage. I want to understand."

"Understand what?" Auren challenges.

Melia meets his gaze directly, something fierce and determined burning through her composed exterior. "What life is like in Etheria. How people live beneath Elyssia's shadow. The truth about the world I was raised to believe was beneath me."

There's sincerity in her words that catches Auren off guard. Beneath the practiced poise, he glimpses something raw—a hunger for knowledge, perhaps, or for something she's been denied.

A cold laugh escapes Auren's throat before he can stop it. The sound bounces harshly off the meeting hall's wooden beams, drawing everyone's attention.

"You want to understand?" Auren steps closer, ignoring Bear's defensive growl. "Princess, let me tell you exactly what you're signing up for. This isn't some royal procession with servants carrying your palanquin while you wave to adoring crowds."

Melia's eyes narrow slightly, but she doesn't flinch.

"The reverse pilgrimage strips away everything—comfort, status, even identity. You'll walk until your feet bleed, sleep on hard ground, and eat whatever you can find or what villagers might spare." Auren gestures to her fine, though damaged, clothing. "Those silks will be in tatters within days. Your soft hands will callous. That perfect skin will burn under our sun."

"Auren," Kyp murmurs warningly, but Auren pushes on.

"You'll see families scraping by on what little they harvest while looking up at your floating paradise. You'll watch children sicken because we lack the healing arts Elyssia hoards. You'll witness the desperation that drives people to attempt the Ascent knowing most will fail."

He leans in, voice dropping to ensure only she hears his next words. "And everywhere you go, people will recognize what you are. They'll either worship you or resent you—neither is comfortable. You'll never be just a person."

The cat arches its back, hissing more loudly, but Melia places a steadying hand on its sleek form. Something changes in her expression—not fear, but a deepening resolve.

"Do you think I don't know privilege when I see it in the mirror?" she asks quietly. "Do you think I haven't questioned the divide between our worlds?"

"Questioning from a palace balcony is different from walking through mud," Auren counters.

Melia rises to her feet, shedding the blanket from her shoulders. Though still battered, her posture straightens with natural authority. "I jumped from that balcony, if you recall. I've already chosen the mud."

The room falls silent. Even Bram seems surprised by her fortitude.

"This journey will be the hardest thing you've ever done," Auren continues, refusing to be swayed by her determination. "It will expose you to a life you never could imagine, nor have prepared for in Elyssia. The land of Etheria isn't kind—especially not to those who've never had to be strong."

"Perhaps that's exactly why I need to experience it," Melia responds. "How can I understand what I've never seen? How can I know the truth if I've only heard one perspective?"

There's something in her voice—a note of genuine hunger for understanding—that catches Auren off guard. It reminds him of himself, years ago, before disillusionment hardened his heart.

"The pilgrimage isn't a sightseeing tour," he warns. "It's meant to break you down and rebuild you. Are you prepared to question everything you believe? To have your identity torn apart?"

"I already question everything," she says. "That's why I'm here."

Auren searches her face for any sign of weakness or uncertainty he can exploit to end this folly. Instead, he finds only determination etched in the set of her jaw and the steadiness of her gaze.

"I understand what you're telling me," Melia continues, "and I still want to go. Need to go."

The cat—Bear—rises and stretches, as if signaling his approval of the decision. His green eyes fix on Auren with unsettling intelligence.

Kyp clears his throat. "Well, seems the princess has made up her mind."

"Indeed," Bram agrees. "The question now is whether our reluctant guide will accept his duty."

All eyes turn to Auren, waiting for his answer.

Kyp claps a hand on Auren's shoulder. "Come on, when are you going to get another chance to escort a princess? Might even be fun."

"Fun," Auren echoes hollowly. The word feels alien, disconnected from anything he's experienced since his fall.

Yet something pulls at him—curiosity, perhaps, or the faint, foolish hope that in guiding Melia, he might find answers to his own questions. Why wasn't he worthy? What's the true nature of Elyssia? And if someone can willingly leave paradise, what does that say about the paradise itself?

"Fine," he concedes finally. "I'll guide you. But this won't end the way you think, Princess. The path reveals different truths to different travelers, and none of them are particularly comforting."

Melia nods, a small, enigmatic smile playing at her lips. "I'm counting on it."

The black cat circles once, twice, then settles again at her feet, purring with what sounds suspiciously like satisfaction.

"I'm coming too," Kyp announces, his voice leaving no room for argument.

Auren turns to his friend, ready to object. "This isn't one of your village festivals—"

"Exactly why you need me." Kyp's usually playful expression hardens with unexpected determination. "You've been carrying everything alone since your fall. Not this time."

The protest dies on Auren's lips. Behind Kyp's jovial mask lies a loyalty he's never fully acknowledged.

"Fine," Auren concedes. "But when we're knee-deep in mud and misery, don't say I didn't warn you."

Melia watches their exchange, her royal composure slipping just enough to reveal a flicker of curiosity.

"It's decided then," Bram declares. "You'll depart at dawn tomorrow. The Council will provide supplies for your journey."

As arrangements continue around them, Auren finds himself unable to look away from Melia. She's like a shard of the sky fallen to earth—beautiful, intriguing, and potentially dangerous. Everything about her existence challenges what he thought he knew about Elyssia, about worthiness, about the natural order of things.

And now he's bound to guide her through the very path that broke him.

Orlan I

Sir Orlan stands at perfect attention in the High Temple's Inner Sanctum, his armor gleaming in the ethereal blue light that filters through the ancient stained glass. The intricate scenes depicted in the windows—the Ascension of the First Prefect, the Founding of Elyssia, the Divine Compact—have always filled him with reverence. Today, they feel like accusatory eyes, watching his every breath.

"She cannot have survived the fall." High Priest Tharos's voice echoes in the circular chamber, his ornate robes rustling as he paces. "No mortal could withstand such a descent."

"And yet," Prefect Solivar counters, his voice deceptively calm, "we have no body. Until I see her broken form, I consider the princess alive."

Six High Priests stand in a perfect semicircle, their faces half-hidden beneath elaborate hoods. The seventh position—where High Priestess Elynia would stand—remains conspicuously empty. Her absence, like a missing tooth, disrupts the harmony of their formation.

"Our sentries report no impact on the plains below," High Priest Verrus adds. "The sacred lake, however..."

Orlan's pulse quickens. The sacred lake—directly beneath the central spire of Elyssia. A fall into water rather than earth changes everything.

"Speak plainly," Solivar demands. "What does this mean?"

"It means," High Priest Morden says, stepping forward, "that Princess Melia may indeed have survived."

The words hang in the air like a fog, thick with implication. Orlan feels something unfamiliar stir within his chest—hope, perhaps. Or dread. The two emotions have become increasingly difficult to distinguish these days.

"Then we retrieve her immediately." Solivar turns abruptly, his silver-embroidered cape swirling dramatically. "Before rumors spread. Before she can speak to anyone about what she... knows."

The hesitation before that final word sends a chill through Orlan's spine. What exactly does Melia know? What truth drove her to leap from the observatory platform?

"Prefect," Orlan interjects, his voice steady despite his racing thoughts. "Allow me to lead a detachment to the surface. I can recover the princess discreetly and ensure her safe return."

All eyes turn to him—some surprised, others calculating. Solivar studies him with cold intensity.

"Your loyalty to the princess is commendable, Sir Orlan," Solivar says, his tone suggesting it's anything but. "Though I wonder where such loyalty was when she managed to elude your guards and throw herself from our fair city?"

The barb stings, but Orlan maintains his composure. "A failure I intend to rectify, Prefect. I know the princess better than most. I can find her quickly, without raising suspicion among the surface dwellers."

What he doesn't say—what he cannot say—is that he doesn't trust whatever men Solivar might send in his place. He's seen the way the Prefect's personal guard operates. They aren't known for gentleness or discretion.

"No." Solivar's reply is sharp as a blade. "No one from Elyssia is to leave the city. Not now, not for this."

"But Prefect—"

"I have spoken, Knight." Solivar's eyes narrow. "Or do you question my authority?"

Orlan swallows the protest rising in his throat. "Never, Prefect. I only wish to serve."

"Then serve by maintaining order here, where your skills are needed." Solivar turns back to the High Priests. "Surely you have other means to address this... situation?"

High Priest Tharos steps forward, the gemstones embedded in his ceremonial collar catching the light. "We maintain... connections on the surface, Prefect. Adherents and priests loyal to Elyssia's divine mandate."

"Loyalists in the villages below," adds High Priestess Valeera. "Those who failed to ascend but still serve our cause."

The revelation doesn't surprise Orlan, though he's never heard it stated so plainly before. The floating city has always maintained its mystique by seeming completely separate from the world below. Yet it makes sense that they would have agents, informants, those who enforce Elyssia's will without the populace knowing.

"Then utilize these connections," Solivar demands. "Find her. Recover her. Before she can spread dangerous ideas."

"And if she resists?" Morden asks, his voice soft but penetrating.

Solivar's pause lasts two heartbeats too long. "She is the princess of Elyssia. She will be treated with appropriate... care."

The word 'care' sounds hollow, performative. Orlan's hand instinctively tightens around the pommel of his sword.

"Of course, Prefect," Tharos bows. "We shall be discreet. Elyssia cannot know their princess has left the city."

"What story shall we tell?" Verrus asks. "The people expect to see her, especially with the wedding announcement."

"A period of extended mourning," Solivar supplies without hesitation. "The princess, overcome with grief for her departed parents, has secluded herself in the Temple of Remembrance for three weeks of prayer and reflection. None may disturb her during this sacred time."

The lie flows too easily from his lips. Orlan wonders how many such deceptions have been crafted in this chamber, how many truths have been buried beneath pretty falsehoods.

"And when those three weeks conclude?" Orlan asks, unable to stop himself.

Solivar's smile doesn't reach his eyes. "By then, Sir Orlan, our princess will have been returned to us, properly... reminded of her duties."

The threat in those words is unmistakable. Orlan maintains his stoic expression through years of practiced discipline, but inside, alarm rises like floodwater.

"High Priest Tharos," Solivar continues, "you will personally oversee this operation. I expect daily reports."

"As you wish, Prefect." Tharos bows deeply. "We shall begin immediately."

"Good. Now leave me with Sir Orlan. We have security matters to discuss."

The High Priests file out silently, their robes whispering against the polished marble floor. When the massive doors close behind them, the chamber seems suddenly vast and cold.

"Walk with me, Knight." Solivar moves toward the eastern archway, not waiting to see if Orlan follows.

They proceed in silence through the Temple's private corridors, passing beneath archways carved with ancient symbols that few in Elyssia still understand. Guards stationed at intervals bow as they pass, their expressions carefully blank.

Only when they reach the Hanging Gardens, with its impossibly perfect blooms and melodious fountains, does Solivar speak again.

"You have served the royal family loyally for many years, Sir Orlan."

"I have, Prefect."

"Your devotion to King Orion was legendary. And your protection of Princess Melia, equally so."

Orlan says nothing. There's a trap being laid here, and he won't help set it.

"Such loyalty is admirable," Solivar continues, examining a flawless white rose. "And yet, I wonder if it might also be... misplaced."

"I serve Elyssia, Prefect. The royal family embodies Elyssia's divine purpose."

Solivar plucks the rose with a quick, decisive motion. "Indeed. But what happens when a member of that family forgets their purpose? When they endanger everything we've built?"

"The princess is young. Grief-stricken. Her actions—"

"Her actions," Solivar interrupts, "could destroy the order we've maintained for generations. You understand that, don't you, Sir Orlan?"

Orlan meets Solivar's gaze steadily. "I understand that order without compassion becomes tyranny, Prefect."

A dangerous flash crosses Solivar's eyes. "Careful, Knight. Such philosophical musings border on sedition."

"I speak only of balance, Prefect. The same balance King Orion maintained."

"Orion is dead." Solivar's words fall like stones. "And his approach died with him. We face unprecedented challenges now. The pilgrims grow more numerous each season. Resources strain. The old ways won't sustain us."

"And the new ways?" Orlan asks. "What do they entail?"

Solivar twirls the rose between his fingers. "Greater control. Stricter adherence to hierarchy. Less tolerance for... deviation."

The rose suddenly seems like a threat in his hands. Orlan wonders if Solivar realizes how much he's revealing.

"You questioned my decision not to send you after the princess," Solivar continues. "I want you to understand why. It's not that I doubt your competence, Sir Orlan. It's that I doubt your resolve."

"My resolve has never wavered, Prefect."

"Hasn't it?" Solivar steps closer. "If you found Melia spouting dangerous ideas, questioning our traditions, undermining the very foundations of our society... would you silence her? Or would your loyalty to her as a person outweigh your duty to Elyssia?"

The question strikes like a physical blow. Orlan struggles to keep his expression neutral.

"I would do whatever best serves Elyssia's true interests," he says carefully.

"A diplomatic answer." Solivar smiles thinly. "But not a convincing one."

They stand in silence for several moments, the perfect beauty of the gardens suddenly seeming artificial, constructed—a façade hiding something darker beneath.

"You'll attend me personally until this matter concludes," Solivar says, crushing the rose in his palm. White petals flutter to the ground like snowflakes. "Your expertise is wasted on regular patrols, and I prefer to keep those with... complicated loyalties where I can see them."

Orlan stiffens, recognizing the thinly veiled threat beneath the promotion. "And my family, Prefect?"

"Already relocated to the East Wing quarters. For their protection, of course." Solivar's smile doesn't reach his eyes. "These are uncertain times. The common folk grow restless with rumors. Your wife and daughter will be safer under my direct oversight."

Hostages. The word remains unspoken between them, but its presence hangs in the air as clearly as if Solivar had shouted it. Orlan's daughter Lira, barely seven, and his wife Merien—now pawns in Solivar's game.

"I understand, Prefect." Orlan keeps his voice steady despite the rage building in his chest. "When do my new duties commence?"

"Immediately." Solivar tosses the crushed stem onto a nearby reflecting pool, where it mars the perfect surface with expanding ripples. "In fact, accompany me to the Council Chamber. We have matters to discuss with the other advisors."

As they walk through the pristine corridors of the upper city, Orlan's mind races. The placement of guards, the secret passages known only to the royal guard, potential allies still loyal to King Orion's vision rather than Solivar's ambition—he catalogs it all while maintaining his stoic exterior.

The Council Chamber gleams with polished marble and brass fittings, sunlight streaming through tall windows that offer vertigo-inducing views of the clouds below. Eight advisors rise from their seats as Solivar enters, their faces a mixture of deference and wariness.

"Remain by the door, Sir Orlan," Solivar commands. "No one enters without my express permission."

Orlan takes his position, back straight, hand resting on his sword hilt. From this vantage point, he can observe the entire proceedings while appearing to focus solely on his guard duty.

"The princess situation requires immediate attention," Solivar begins without preamble. "Minister Tallen, what reports do we have from the surface?"

A thin man with a neatly trimmed beard consults his notes. "Our agents confirm unusual activity in Willow Haven, Prefect. Their Council has convened several emergency meetings in the past day."

"Any mention of the princess specifically?"

"No direct confirmation, but there are whispers of a 'miracle from above.' The timing suggests it could be her."

Solivar's jaw tightens. "'Miracle.' Exactly the kind of dangerous nonsense we must quash immediately."

Another adviser, a woman with silver streaks in her dark hair, leans forward. "If I may, Prefect—perhaps we should consider this an opportunity rather than merely a crisis."

"Explain yourself, Lady Vaseri."

"The princess's... departure... creates a certain vacancy, does it not? One that needs filling for the sake of stability."

The implication hangs in the air. Orlan's hand instinctively tightens on his sword.

Solivar's expression remains neutral, though something calculating flashes in his eyes. "An interesting perspective. Though premature. Our priority remains recovering the princess and maintaining the illusion that she never left."

"And if recovery proves impossible?" asks another councillor.

"Everything is possible with sufficient motivation," Solivar replies coolly. "But yes, we must prepare contingencies. Which brings me to our next order of business." He unrolls a map of Elyssia on the table. "Security must be tightened, particularly around the four Sanctums."

Orlan's attention sharpens. The Sanctums—sacred sites that few ordinary citizens ever see, much less enter.

"If the princess knows what we fear she knows," Solivar continues, "then the Sanctums may be vulnerable."

The council members exchange uneasy glances. One elderly man clears his throat. "Surely she couldn't have accessed the sealed archives? King Orion would never have—"

"King Orion's judgment became increasingly... questionable in his final days," Solivar interrupts sharply. "We cannot rule out the possibility that he shared forbidden knowledge with his daughter."

The words strike Orlan like physical blows. The implication that King Orion—a man of unwavering integrity—would somehow betray Elyssia's sacred traditions seems blasphemous. And yet, hadn't the King seemed troubled in those last weeks? More withdrawn, more pensive, his eyes shadowed with some unspoken worry?

"Sir Orlan."

Solivar's voice cuts through his thoughts.

"Yes, Prefect?"

"You were King Orion's shadow in his final days. Did you observe any unusual behavior? Any indications he might have shared sensitive information with the princess?"

All eyes turn to him. Orlan keeps his expression carefully neutral, though his mind frantically sifts through memories.

"The King was dedicated to preparing Princess Melia for her future responsibilities," he says carefully. "Their conversations often seemed... intense. But I was never privy to their specific content."

"You never overheard anything of significance? Nothing that might explain the princess's sudden... departure?"

The trap is obvious, the question loaded. If Orlan admits to knowledge, he implicates himself. If he denies it too forcefully, he appears suspicious.

"The King instructed me to maintain a respectful distance during their private conversations," Orlan replies. "I followed his orders, as was my duty."

Solivar studies him for a long moment, eyes narrowed. "Indeed. Duty. A concept we must all remember in these trying times."

The meeting continues, details of security protocols and public announcements flowing around Orlan like water around a stone. He absorbs it all while appearing to focus solely on his guard duty—knowledge is survival now, for himself and his family.

As the council session draws to a close, the advisors file out with careful deference to Solivar. Orlan remains at his post, back straight, face impassive despite the turmoil churning beneath his polished armor. The massive doors swing shut with a resonant thud that echoes through the now-empty chamber.

"Your thoughts, Sir Orlan?" Solivar doesn't turn to face him, instead gazing out the window at the perfect, geometric gardens below.

Orlan hesitates. The question feels baited, like a snare waiting in tall grass. "On what matter specifically, Prefect?"

"On our esteemed council." Solivar gestures lazily toward the vacated seats. "Their... concerns regarding our current situation."

The room suddenly feels colder. Orlan chooses his words with the same precision he would use to select a blade for combat. "They seem appropriately focused on maintaining order, Prefect."

"Appropriately focused." Solivar turns, a humorless smile playing on his lips. "A diplomatic observation. But I'm not asking for diplomacy, Knight. I'm asking for honesty."

The request rings false. Honesty has never been prized in these chambers, only useful facades. Still, Orlan recognizes the test for what it is.

"Lady Vaseri appeared eager to capitalize on the princess's absence," Orlan offers carefully. "Her ambitions seem to extend beyond her current position."

"Indeed." Solivar studies him with renewed interest. "And Minister Tallen?"

"Nervous. He knows more than he's reporting, I suspect."

"Very perceptive." Solivar approaches, each footfall deliberate on the polished floor. "And what of their collective concern about the Sanctums? Did you find that... illuminating?"

The trap springs shut. Orlan feels it closing around him but keeps his expression neutral. "I found it concerning that they believe the princess might have accessed forbidden knowledge."

"But not surprising?" Solivar presses, now standing close enough that Orlan can smell the cloying scent of ceremonial oils on his robes.

"My duty was to protect the royal family, not question their activities or motives."

"And therein lies our problem, doesn't it?" Solivar's voice drops to a near whisper. "Your concept of duty seems... selectively applied."

Orlan meets his gaze steadily. "My duty has always been to Elyssia, Prefect."

"Has it?" Solivar circles him slowly. "I wonder. When you stand in this chamber, when you hear plans being made to secure our future, when you consider what must be done to preserve our way of life—who do you truly serve in your heart, Sir Orlan? The memory of a dead king? A wayward princess? Or Elyssia itself?"

The question hangs between them, weighted with menace. Orlan thinks of Merien's gentle smile, of Lira's infectious laughter. He thinks of King Orion's hand on his shoulder, heavy with trust. He thinks of Princess Melia, her eyes so like her father's, bright with intelligence and something that looked increasingly like doubt.

"I serve Elyssia," Orlan says finally. "As I always have."

"Good." Solivar nods, satisfied. "Remember that in the days ahead." He moves toward the chamber doors. "Your wife, Merien—she's an herbalist, is she not?"

The sudden change in topic sends a ripple of alarm through Orlan's composure. "Yes, Prefect. She tends the medicinal gardens in the East Quarter."

"A valuable service." Solivar's smile doesn't reach his eyes. "I'll have my personal well-wishes communicated to her. It can be... disorienting, relocating to new quarters so suddenly."

The threat is thinly veiled, but unmistakable. Orlan swallows the rage rising in his throat, forcing his voice to remain level. "Your consideration is appreciated, Prefect."

"After all," Solivar continues, hand resting on the ornate door handle, "we must all look after each other in these uncertain times. Wouldn't you agree, Sir Orlan?"

"Completely, Prefect." The words taste like ash in his mouth.

"Excellent." Solivar pulls open the door. "Attend me to the Eastern Sanctum. We have matters to discuss with High Priest Morden."

Orlan follows, his mind racing with contingencies, with half-formed plans. The corridor stretches before them, gleaming and perfect, while somewhere beneath them, a princess falls through cloud and memory toward truth.

Melia III

Melia steps past the village gates, the weight of expectation pressing on her shoulders with every scattered wildflower crunching beneath her borrowed boots. Villagers line the narrow dirt path, their faces a blur of reverence and hope that makes her stomach twist. A small girl with braided hair reaches forward, pressing a simple crown of daisies into Melia's hands.

"For the Fallen Princess," the child whispers, eyes wide with wonder.

The title sits wrong, like ill-fitted clothing. Princess, yes—that burden she's carried since birth. But "Fallen" suggests grace in her descent, as if her plummet from Elyssia was some divine act rather than desperate escape. These people don't see the bruises beneath her sleeves or know the panic that still seizes her lungs when she remembers the endless drop.

"Thank you," Melia manages, her voice still raw from screaming as she fell. She accepts the flower crown with trembling fingers but doesn't place it on her head.

"Another addition to your royal collection." Kyp appears at her side, gesturing to the growing bundle of flowers in her arms. His easy smile doesn't match the solemn procession, but there's something refreshing about his irreverence. "At this rate, we'll need a pack mule just for your floral tributes."

Bear weaves between her ankles, his sleek black form a comforting anchor amid the strangeness. The cat's eyes gleam with intelligence as he looks up at her before trotting ahead.

"I think they expect me to be something I'm not," she murmurs.

"They expect whatever helps them sleep at night." Kyp shrugs, adjusting his pack. "Just smile and wave. That's what royalty does, right?"

Ahead, Auren walks in silence, his broad shoulders set in a rigid line that betrays his reluctance. The morning light catches in his dark hair, highlighting threads of copper Melia hadn't noticed before. Unlike the polished, sculpted men of Elyssia's court, there's something raw about him—something achingly real in the way his muscled forearms flex as he shifts his pack, in the controlled power of his stride.

When he'd first entered the meeting hall yesterday, she'd been struck by the intensity in his amber eyes—the way they seemed to hold both fire and shadow. Even now, watching him navigate the path ahead, Melia finds herself studying the strong line of his jaw, the way his worn shirt clings to his back, revealing the contours of muscle beneath. His movements hold a grace that speaks of hard-won strength rather than cultivated elegance.

She flushes, embarrassed by her own thoughts. In Elyssia, attraction was another carefully choreographed performance—appropriate glances at appropriate times with appropriate parties. This awareness bubbling through her veins feels dangerously unscripted.

An elderly woman steps into her path, halting Melia's progress with gnarled hands that clutch her wrists.

"I—" Melia starts, but the woman is already being gently moved aside by others.

The villagers' reverence is suffocating. Each flower feels like a stone, each hopeful gaze another shackle. She's traded one prison of expectation for another.

"Don't mind them," Kyp says softly. "They've been waiting generations for someone like you."

"That's exactly the problem," Melia replies. "I'm not sure I am someone like me."

Bear meows sharply from ahead. He seems to understand the path better than any of them, frequently stopping to ensure they follow.

As they reach the edge of the gathering, Auren finally turns. His eyes meet hers, and something unspoken passes between them—recognition, perhaps, of shared discomfort.

"We need to make the western ridge by nightfall," he says, voice low and resonant. "The path gets steeper after that."

He doesn't call her "princess" or "my lady." The omission feels deliberate, a small mercy she's grateful for.

"I'll keep up," she promises, dropping the flowers at her feet with quiet determination. The only thing she keeps is the child's daisy crown, tucked into her belt.

The village recedes behind them as they enter the forest proper. Towering pines close around them like sentinels, the needle-strewn path muffling their footsteps. The air smells of sap and earth, so different from Elyssia's perpetual perfume of celestial blossoms.

"So," Kyp breaks the silence, "what magnificent delicacies did they serve at royal breakfasts up there? Golden eggs? Clouds whipped into cream?"

Melia almost smiles despite herself. "Mostly fruit. Everything in Elyssia tastes... perfect. Suspiciously perfect."

"Suspicious perfection." Kyp nods sagely. "The worst kind of perfection, if you ask me. Give me an honestly lumpy porridge any day."

Ahead, Auren's shoulders lose some of their rigidity, though he doesn't join their conversation. Bear darts between trees, occasionally disappearing into the undergrowth only to reappear further along the path.

"He doesn't want to be here," Melia observes quietly, watching Auren's back.

"Auren?" Kyp's voice drops to match hers. "He's got his reasons."

"What exactly are we doing?" Melia asks suddenly. "This reverse pilgrimage. What does it mean?"

Kyp studies her with surprising thoughtfulness. "Nobody really knows. You're the first to fall and survive. But I think..." He glances ahead at Auren. "I think some wounds can only heal by walking backward through them."

Bear appears again, meowing insistently. When none of them move quickly enough, he trots back and paws at Melia's leg, then darts forward again.

"Your cat seems to have opinions about our route," Kyp observes.

"He's not even my cat," Melia says. "He just... found me."

Or maybe, she thinks as Bear waits at a fork in the path, she is the one being found.

***

The sun hangs low in the sky, casting long shadows across the path as they emerge from the dense forest. Melia's legs ache with each step, muscles unused to such exertion protesting beneath her torn dress. In Elyssia, she'd never walked more than the polished corridors of the palace required—certainly never a full day's journey over uneven terrain.

Ahead, the land opens up. A broad plain stretches before them, divided by a gleaming ribbon of water that catches the late afternoon light. The river winds lazily through the landscape, alternating between gentle curves and rushing narrows.

"Riverside," Auren announces, the first word he's spoken in hours. He stops at the crest of the small hill, surveying the open expanse below.

Bear darts past them, racing down toward the water with unexpected enthusiasm. Melia watches him go, envying his energy.

"Finally," Kyp sighs, dropping his pack dramatically. "My feet have filed formal complaints against the rest of my body."

Melia steps forward, drawn by the sight of the water. Something about it calls to her—not like the ornamental fountains of Elyssia with their carefully engineered flows, but wild and natural.

"It's beautiful," she says, meaning it.

"It's the final cleansing site," Kyp explains, coming to stand beside her. "Pilgrims stop here before continuing to Willow Haven for their ascent. The water supposedly washes away impurities, preparing the body and spirit for transcendence." He glances at her. "Or at least, that's what they say."

"I came here," Auren says suddenly. His voice is quiet, almost lost beneath the distant sound of rushing water. "Before my attempt."

"Attempt?" Melia asks, fixing her gaze on Auren's profile. The word hangs between them, weighted with something unspoken.

Auren's jaw tightens. For a moment, she thinks he might ignore her question entirely. He stares at the river, eyes reflecting the golden shimmer of sunlight on water.

"I did the pilgrimage," he finally says, each word measured. "The complete journey—Riverside, Old Chapel, The Spire, Old Hollow, Windy Ridge. All of it." His fingers absently trace the worn leather strap crossing his chest. "I attempted the final ascent."

The daisy crown in Melia's hands suddenly feels heavier. She twists the stems, waiting.

"I failed."

Two simple words, yet they carry the weight of worlds. Auren's shoulders tense, then drop slightly as if releasing a breath long held.

"You actually flew?" Melia asks, struggling to imagine it—this earthbound man with wings of light ascending toward her city.

"For a time." His voice grows distant. "I felt the power, the lift. Elyssia was... right there." He extends his hand toward the sky, fingers spread wide as if trying to grasp something just beyond reach. "Then something spoke inside me. Said 'not yet.' My wings dissolved, and I fell."

Bear returns, fur damp along his paws. He circles once around Melia's ankles before sitting, green eyes fixed on Auren as if he understands every word.

"Into the sacred lake?" Melia asks.

"Into the lake." Auren's gaze finally meets hers. "Just like you."

Melia studies his profile. The setting sun catches in his dark hair, illuminating the tension in his jaw. He doesn't elaborate, but she feels the weight of those unsaid words—the memory of his failure hanging between them.

"Let's make camp there," Auren points to a flat area near the river-bank, sheltered by a cluster of willows. "We can rest and continue at first light."

They descend the hill, Bear already waiting impatiently by the water's edge. The cat circles, meowing insistently as Melia approaches.

While Kyp and Auren begin setting up a simple camp, Melia walks to the river's edge. The water laps gently at the shore, clear enough to see smooth stones beneath the surface. She kneels, dipping her hand into the cool current. It feels different from the lake that broke her fall—gentler, almost inviting.

"The water's sacred," Kyp says, appearing beside her with an armful of kindling. "Pilgrims immerse themselves fully—clothes and all. Something about carrying the river's blessing in the fabric that touches your skin." He shrugs. "Never made much sense to me, but traditions rarely do."

Melia nods, watching the water swirl around her fingers. In Elyssia, ritual had governed every moment—empty gestures performed without questioning their meaning. But here, with her hand in the rushing river, she feels something genuine stirring within her.

"Food's ready," Auren calls from the camp. The smell of something savory reaches her, making her stomach growl in response.

They eat in relative silence—simple trail bread and dried meat softened in a thin broth. It's nothing like the elaborate, perfect meals of Elyssia, but Melia finds herself savoring each bite. Hunger, at least, is honest.

After they eat, Kyp begins recounting outlandish tales of village mishaps, his animated storytelling drawing reluctant smiles from both Melia and Auren. As night falls completely, he finally yawns wide enough to crack his jaw.

"And with that, I bid you good night. My bedroll calls to me with the sweet voice of unconsciousness." He retreats to his blankets, leaving Melia and Auren sitting in awkward silence by the small fire.

Bear paces restlessly at the river's edge, occasionally looking back at Melia with an inscrutable gaze.

"He wants something," Auren observes quietly.

Melia rises, drawn to the water once more. The full moon hangs heavy in the sky, its reflection dancing across the surface of the river. Without fully understanding why, she steps to the edge, her torn slippers sinking into the soft mud of the bank.

The sound of the water fills her ears—not the artificial tinkling of Elyssia's fountains but something wild and real. On impulse, she steps forward, the cool water rushing around her ankles, soaking the hem of her already ruined gown.

Another step, and the water rises to her calves. The current tugs gently at her, an insistent pressure against her legs. She keeps going, moving deeper until the water reaches her waist, plastering the thin fabric of her dress to her body.

She doesn't look back at the shore. This moment feels intensely private—a communion between herself and the river. As the water embraces her, she feels the weight of Elyssia's expectations sliding away, if only temporarily. Here, there is only the river, the night, and her own breath.

When she's chest-deep, she closes her eyes and sinks beneath the surface. The world goes silent, muffled by the rush of water around her ears. For a moment, suspended in the current, she feels weightless—neither princess nor fallen, just a body held by water.

She surfaces with a gasp, pushing sodden hair from her face. When she opens her eyes, she's startled to find Auren standing in the river several paces away, water lapping at his chest. His dark hair is slicked back from his face, droplets clinging to his eyelashes. In the moonlight, with water streaming down his features, he looks almost otherworldly.

"I didn't hear you come in," she says, her voice barely audible above the river's song.

"You shouldn't be out here alone," he replies, but there's no admonishment in his tone—only a quiet understanding.

They stand in silence, the current flowing between them, connecting them in ways words cannot. The moonlight silvering the water transforms everything—making this moment feel suspended outside of time, outside of their complicated realities.

"When I came here before my ascent," Auren finally says, his voice low and intimate in the darkness, "I thought the water would make me worthy." His eyes meet hers, vulnerability evident in their amber depths. "I was wrong."

"And now?" Melia asks.

"Now I know worthiness isn't something you're given." His gaze is steady, searching her face. "It's something you find inside yourself, or not at all."

The simplicity of his words strikes her. In Elyssia, worth was assigned based on bloodline, on adherence to tradition. She'd never questioned it—never considered that her value might come from within rather than from her title.

"I don't know who I am anymore," she admits, the confession easier here in the flowing water than it would be on solid ground. "If I'm not Princess Melia of Elyssia, then who am I?"

"Maybe that's what this journey is for," he suggests. "To find out."

A lock of wet hair falls across her face. Before she can brush it away, Auren reaches out, his fingers hesitating a breath away from her cheek. Something passes between them—a current stronger than the river's—before he gently tucks the strand behind her ear.

His touch is light, but it sends a shiver through her that has nothing to do with the cool water. For an instant, the space between them seems charged with possibility.

Then Bear meows loudly from the shore, breaking the spell.

Auren steps back, creating distance between them once more. "We should head back. It's getting cold."

Melia nods, suddenly aware of the chill seeping into her bones. They wade back to shore together, not touching but somehow connected by the shared experience of the river.

As they emerge, dripping, onto the bank, Kyp sits up from his bedroll, blinking sleepily.

"Taking a midnight swim, are we?" he mumbles. "Should've woken me. Nothing like a good dunking to wash away the day's troubles."

Auren gathers extra blankets from his pack, handing one to Melia without meeting her eyes. "You should get warm. The nights get cold here."

She takes the rough woolen blanket, wrapping it around her shoulders. "Thank you."

For what, she's not entirely sure—the blanket, certainly, but also for joining her in the river, for understanding something she herself doesn't fully comprehend.

As she settles by the rekindled fire, Bear curls against her side, his warm presence a comfort in the chill night. Across the flames, Auren sits with his back against a tree trunk, his gaze directed at the stars above.

Something has shifted between them—nothing dramatic, nothing declared, but a quiet understanding nonetheless. For the first time since her fall, Melia feels her breathing come easier, as if some invisible weight has lifted from her chest.

The river continues its eternal journey behind them, carrying away a small piece of who they were, leaving space for who they might become.

***

Sleep takes Melia like the river's current, pulling her under to somewhere deeper than consciousness. Colors swirl behind her eyelids, resolving into her mother's face—regal and sorrowful all at once.

Queen Lysandra stands before her, bathed in a light that seems to emanate from within rather than without. Her slender fingers work at a crown—her own crown—not polishing or adjusting it, but methodically pulling it apart. Golden filaments come loose in her hands, gems dropping like tears to disappear into nothingness. The metal bends and breaks under her determined touch.

"Mother?" Melia reaches toward her, but the distance between them never closes.

Lysandra doesn't look up from her task, her face a mask of grim determination. "Some things must be unmade before they can be reborn," she says, her voice echoing strangely as if coming from everywhere at once.

The crown crumbles further, sections falling away until it's barely recognizable. With each piece that breaks free, Lysandra seems to grow more luminous, more substantial, as if the crown had been weighing her down rather than elevating her.

The scene shifts abruptly. Melia stands on a vast plain, neither Elyssia nor the world below, but somewhere in between—a liminal space of half-light. Figures materialize before her, dozens upon dozens, their wrists and ankles bound with glowing chains. Their mouths open in silent screams, eyes wide with desperation as they reach toward her.

"Help us," they mouth, their voices barely audible whispers. "Free us."

Among them, Melia recognizes faces—nobility she'd dined with, servants who'd attended her, citizens she'd passed in Elyssia's immaculate streets. And at the front, chains thicker than the others, stand Prefect Solivar and Sir Orlan.

Solivar's chains bind him to countless others, their links pulsing with a sickly light. He doesn't reach for her but stands proud even in his bondage, eyes burning with cold determination. The chains seem almost part of him, as if they've grown from his very skin.

Orlan strains against his restraints, his weathered face contorted with effort. Unlike Solivar, his eyes hold recognition when they meet hers—and something else. Fear? Hope? A warning?

"You must see," he seems to say, though his lips barely move. "You must understand."

The chains binding them all pulse in unison, like a heartbeat. With each throb, the people's faces flicker, revealing something beneath their skin—something not quite human.

Terror grips Melia's heart. She turns, desperate to escape this vision, and finds her parents standing behind her. King Orion and Queen Lysandra, hands joined, watching her with eyes that hold infinite sadness and boundless hope.

They stand apart from the chained masses, unbound and radiant. Her father's shoulders, always so burdened in life, now seem unbowed. Her mother's face, free of the crown she'd dismantled, glows with serene purpose.

"You see now," her father says, his voice clearer than the others. "What must be broken."

The Shadow I

15 Years Ago

The panel slides away beneath Samara's small hands, exposing a nest of glowing filaments. They pulse with a gentle blue-green light, twining together like underwater plants. She reaches for one.

"Careful," her mother warns, her voice soft but firm. "Remember what I showed you."

Samara pulls back, nodding seriously. She closes her eyes, takes a breath, and extends her hand again—this time, not quite touching. The filaments respond, curling upward like they're greeting her fingers.

"Good," Mother says, and Samara feels a warm flush of pride spread through her chest. "You're listening to them instead of commanding."

They sit cross-legged on the floor of the teaching chamber, surrounded by hovering displays and half-assembled tech. The room is circular, its walls lined with transparent panels showing fractal patterns that shift and evolve. To outsiders, it would look like abstract art. To the Lothari, it's a living language—each pattern conveying concepts too nuanced for mere words.

Mother taps her wristband, adjusting the room's ambient resonance. The air changes subtly, becoming charged with something Samara can feel but not name.

"Today we talk about identity," Mother says, her dark eyes reflecting the glowing filaments. The resonance band on her wrist flickers with amber—thoughtfulness, instruction, gentle authority. "What makes someone who they are?"

Samara considers this, turning the question over in her mind like one of the puzzle crystals Mother gives her to solve. "Their name?" she offers finally.

Mother's resonance band flickers blue—amusement, patience. "Is that what makes you Samara? Or Sam? Just your name?"

"No," Sam says slowly. "But... it's what everyone calls me."

"And if they called you something else?" Mother asks. "Would you become someone different?"

Sam frowns, uncertain.

From a nearby worktable, Mother retrieves something shimmering—a ceremonial Lothari headpiece, delicate filaments of metal woven into an intricate pattern that would frame the wearer's face. It's beautiful, ancient, meant for an elder or someone of high standing.

"If I put this on," Mother says, holding it up, "would I become someone different? Someone more important?"

Sam stares at the headpiece, transfixed by how it catches the light. "No," she says eventually. "You'd still be you." She pauses, thinking harder. "But people might treat you different."

Mother's resonance band pulses with warm gold—approval, pride. "Exactly." She sets the headpiece aside. "The Luthari understand that identity comes from within—from your actions and choices. Our ancestors knew that what we wear, the titles people give us, the lineage we claim... these are surface things."

She reaches for a small, unassuming device resting on a nearby stand—a smooth gray oval that fits in her palm. "This is a memory node," she explains. "It contains recordings of our people's history. But what makes it valuable isn't its shape or what it's made from—it's what it does, what it preserves."

Sam reaches for it, fascinated. When Mother places it in her small palm, it warms to her touch and emits a soft chime.

"You see?" Mother says. "It recognizes your intent, not your status or age. To the node, you are worthy because you approach with respect and curiosity."

Outside their teaching chamber, beyond the curving hallways of their hidden home, Sam knows there's a world full of people who judge by appearances. Mother has shown her glimpses through the archive visuals—vast cities where people wear badges of rank, where some bow to others based on clothing or titles. It seems strange to Sam, like a game where everyone has agreed to pretend.

"The Empire hates us because they fear what we understand," Mother says, her resonance band briefly flickering red-black—sorrow, controlled anger. "They need people to believe that worth comes from outside—from titles, from bloodlines, from faith in powers beyond themselves."

She takes Sam's hands in hers. Her fingers are worn from work, strong and steady. "But you, little one, will know the truth. We are what we do. We are how we treat others. We are the choices we make when no one is watching."

Mother activates one of the wall displays, showing a simulation of stars spreading across darkness. "Our ancestors traveled between worlds not because they wore special clothes or claimed divine right, but because they understood the Thread's patterns. They built rather than believed. They remembered rather than worshiped."

Sam watches the stars, imagining her ancestors moving among them. "Is that why we hide?" she asks. "Because we remember instead of believe?"

Mother's resonance band pulses complex patterns—pride tinged with caution, hope shadowed by fear. "Yes. The Empire would call us heretics for teaching that anyone can learn to read the Thread. They prefer their system where only the chosen few can interpret it."

She retrieves a small object from her pocket—a simple bracelet woven from ordinary fiber, nothing like the resonance bands adults wear. "I made this for you," she says.

Sam takes it, surprised by its plainness.

"It has no special powers," Mother explains. "No technology, no status. But I made it with care, thinking of you with each weave. Its value comes from the intention behind it, not what it appears to be."

Sam slips it onto her wrist, feeling its comfortable weight.

"Wear it to remember," Mother says, tapping her own resonance band, which glows with deep purple—solemn truth. "We are what we do. Not what we wear. Not what others call us. The Luthari understand that identity isn't given—it's created through action."

A chime sounds from the corridor—someone approaching.

Mother quickly stows the memory node and headpiece. "What have we learned today?" she asks, her tone shifting to casual, as if they'd been discussing something mundane.

Sam touches her new bracelet, plain but precious. "We are what we do," she answers, just as the door slides open.

***

The Present

The Shadow sits perfectly still in the command chair, her matte-black armor absorbing what little light penetrates the ship's cockpit. Holographic displays bathe her featureless helmet in an eerie blue glow, their data streams reflecting off her visor as the craft slices through the Thread.

"Approaching designated coordinates," the ship's AI announces in its flat, emotionless tone. "Thread instability detected in sector seven."

She doesn't respond. The AI requires no acknowledgment. Instead, her gloved fingers dance across the control panel, pulling up new data on the primary target: Liora Solari—Dreamer, threat, mission objective.

The reports show disturbing patterns. Thread fractures spreading from a single point. Veil instability increasing exponentially. The Emperor's concerns validated by cold, hard data.

A red warning light pulses as another Thread tremor rocks the ship. Minor, but noticeable. The Shadow adjusts the craft's stabilizers, compensating without conscious thought. These disruptions have been growing more frequent near the Storehouse, making navigation increasingly difficult, even for someone with her specialized training.

The implants along her spine tingle—a familiar sensation, her body's way of processing the ship's interaction with the Thread. A lifetime of modification and conditioning has attuned her nervous system to these subtle shifts in reality's fabric.

Another display activates, showing thermal readings from the planet below. The Storehouse. A world hidden from the Empire's subjects, containing secrets the Emperor guards jealously. And now, his most closely guarded secret threatens to unravel.

"Waypoint detected. Preparing for atmospheric entry."

The Shadow closes the data streams with a flick of her wrist and assumes manual control. The craft responds instantly to her touch, dropping altitude as the ship's outer hull begins to glow from friction with the atmosphere.

The sensation of falling settles in her stomach, but she ignores it. Physical discomfort is irrelevant to the mission.

The Shadow feels the ship lurch sideways, control surfaces straining against unseen currents. Thread interference—stronger than the initial readings suggested. The navigation console flickers, displays blinking out momentarily before snapping back to life.

"Warning: Thread instability critical. Navigation compromised."

Her hands move with practiced efficiency, compensating for the invisible turbulence that batters the craft. This isn't normal atmospheric entry; something is actively pushing back against her intrusion. The Thread here is different—reactive, almost defensive.

The ship drops suddenly, losing five hundred meters of altitude in seconds. Warning indicators flash red across the control panel. The Shadow doesn't flinch, her modified nervous system processing the chaos with mechanical detachment. Where most pilots would feel panic, she feels only the faint buzz of her implants working overtime to maintain her equilibrium.

"Initiate imperial override protocol," she commands, voice modulator rendering her words into digital precision. "Channel seven-nine-three."

"Transmitting imperial authorization code," the AI responds.

The communication array cuts through local interference, broadcasting on a frequency unused for decades—a direct line to the Emperor himself. Within moments, the signal connects to Aurora's central command.

A startled face appears on the screen—male, mid-forties, shocked eyes widening at the sight of her featureless black helmet.

"What—" he stammers, clearly unprepared. "This channel has been inactive for..."

"Imperial agent requesting landing clearance," she interrupts, letting the Emperor's seal flash across the transmission. "Priority alpha."

The man's face pales. "But no one has come here in decades. We haven't had imperial contact since—"

"Landing coordinates. Now." The Shadow doesn't raise her voice. She doesn't need to.

"I... yes, of course." His fingers move frantically across an unseen console. "Sending coordinates for imperial pad seven. It's... it's been unmaintained, but the structural integrity should be—"

She cuts the transmission. The coordinates appear on her navigation display—a hidden landing pad nestled between towering structures on Aurora's eastern district. Optimal for discretion. The Shadow adjusts course, fighting the Thread's resistance every meter of the descent.

The ship's external cameras activate automatically, revealing Aurora's sprawling cityscape below. Gleaming towers rise like silver needles, their surfaces alive with pulsing light patterns. Vehicles move in orderly streams between buildings, following predetermined paths that from above resemble glowing arteries. The city is both familiar and alien—recognizably imperial in its structured design, yet evolved in isolation, developing its own distinct aesthetic.

Most noticeable are the subtle architectural elements that don't match standard imperial design protocols—curved edges where there should be angles, organic patterns integrated into otherwise uniform structures. Someone has been reinterpreting the Emperor's vision.

The Thread pulls at the ship again. This time the navigation system goes completely dark for three full seconds. The Shadow switches to manual override, feeling the controls buck against her grip.

"Hull integrity at eighty-seven percent," the AI announces. "Thread interference patterns suggest deliberate disruption."

The landing pad appears through a break in the cityscape—a dark square platform extending from an unmarked building. No lights, no guidance markers. As promised, long abandoned but structurally sound.

The Shadow brings the ship down hard and fast, engines screaming against the Thread's resistance.

The landing gear settles with a metallic groan, hydraulics hissing as they compensate for the uneven surface of the long-abandoned imperial pad. Warning lights bathe the cockpit in crimson as the ship's systems complete their shutdown sequence. Thread interference readings still flash across multiple screens, each spike more pronounced than the last.

The Shadow sits motionless, watching the data scroll by. Something tugs at the edge of her consciousness—a memory, uninvited and unwanted.

Imperial ships descending through smoke-filled skies. The distant wail of alarms. A small hand clutching hers—her mother? Someone else? Impossible to know now.

Sam. They had called her Sam.

The memory fragments slide away like water through fingers, leaving nothing but the cold certainty of her mission parameters. Names are irrelevant. Designations, meaningful only as identifiers, not identity. The Shadow is function, not person.

Yet the memory persists, a whisper beneath the steady hum of the ship's idling systems. *Sam. Samara.*

I don't exist, she thinks, her gloved fingers tightening imperceptibly on the control panel. The Shadow exists. The mission exists.

Through the viewport, Aurora sprawls before her—a city of impossible geometry and unexpected beauty. Ancient imperial design principles warped by decades of isolation and innovation. The city shouldn't look this way. This isn't regulation. This isn't protocol.

Her tactical display cycles through preliminary scans. Population density: moderate. Security protocols: present but outdated by imperial standards. Thread calibration: severely compromised. The Dreamer's influence, no doubt.

Liora Solari. Primary target.

The Shadow accesses the mission briefing again, a familiar litany scrolling across her helmet's internal display. Dreamer. Thread manipulator. Veil destroyer. Threat classification: maximum.

Thread users existed within careful bounds throughout the Empire. Controlled. Regulated. Useful components in the imperial machine. Conjurors who strengthened cities, technicians who powered ships, priests who maintained the doctrine. None with power like this—raw, uncontained, capable of fracturing reality itself.

She absently runs her thumb across the armor at her wrist, feeling the subtle ridges of Luthari script embedded in its surface. Her armor—her skin, really—is the last remnant of a people who understood the Thread too well.

That's why they came for us.

The thought emerges unbidden, unfamiliar. Not hers, yet somehow housed in her mind.

Us. There is no us. There is the mission. There is the Emperor.

The Shadow wipes the thought away, focusing on the tactical display. Aurora's systems remain largely sealed to her external scans—another anomaly. Standard imperial protocols should have granted her full access the moment her authorization codes transmitted.

"Display atmospheric composition," she commands.

The screen shifts, showing breathable air with elevated Aetherium levels—a common trait in areas with high Thread conductivity. The Shadow configures her armor's filters accordingly, ensuring optimal functioning of her augmented senses.

"Activate perimeter surveillance."

Small camera drones detach from the ship's exterior, scattering to establish a security net around the landing pad. Their feeds appear on a secondary display, showing empty corridors and dust-covered control stations. This section of Aurora has been abandoned for decades.

Just like they abandoned you.

The Shadow's hand pauses over the control panel. These aren't her thoughts. Something in this place is affecting her cognitive functions. Perhaps Thread interference, perhaps something more deliberate. She initiates a full diagnostic of her neural implants.

"Neural pathways operating within normal parameters," her armor's system reports. "Minor stimulation detected in memory centers. Cause: unknown."

She dismisses the alert. The mission takes precedence over phantom memories. Liora Solari must be located, assessed, and if necessary, neutralized. The Emperor doesn't tolerate those who manipulate the Thread outside established protocols.

Like the Luthari.

Another unwelcome thought. The Shadow adjusts her neural suppressors, increasing the dampening effect on emotional centers. Better to operate with complete detachment.

Through the viewscreen, she watches as a maintenance drone approaches her ship—likely automated, dispatched to investigate the unauthorized landing. The Shadow allows it to complete its scan. Let Aurora's systems recognize imperial technology; it will make infiltration smoother.

She brings up Liora's file one more time. The images show a young woman with haunting eyes and an expression that suggests both power and uncertainty. Someone unaware of her dangerous potential. Someone who could shatter realities without understanding the consequences.

Someone not unlike—

The Shadow terminates that thought before it completes. She is nothing like the target. She serves structure. Order. The immutable will of the Emperor who saved her when her people were—

Exterminated.

The word hangs in her consciousness, stark and undeniable. The Shadow increases neural suppression to maximum levels.

"Warning," her armor's system announces. "Extended maximum suppression may impact tactical decision-making."

She overrides the warning. The discomfort of these intrusive thoughts is more dangerous than reduced tactical flexibility.

Rising from the pilot's seat, The Shadow moves with fluid precision through the ship's narrow corridor to the weapons compartment. Her arsenal is extensive—from subtle neural disruptors to more decisive options should the mission parameters escalate. She selects a minimal loadout: two disruptor pistols, a neural tether, and a Thread calibrator disguised as a standard communication device.

The calibrator is unique—Luthari design, modified by imperial technicians. It allows for pinpoint manipulation of local Thread currents, useful for containing a Dreamer's uncontrolled abilities. She checks its power levels. Optimal.

The Shadow secures each weapon to her armor, feeling them connect magnetically to their designated positions. The familiarity of the routine is comforting—a structured process that requires no emotional involvement.

"Ship, engage security protocols," she commands. "Authorization Shadow-Seven-Nine-Three."

"Security protocols engaged," the ship confirms. "Cloaking field active. Defensive systems armed."

A final check on her armor's systems: optics enhanced, audio receptors calibrated to filter Aurora's ambient noise, Thread detection modules active. Everything functioning at peak efficiency.

The outer hatch slides open with a gentle hiss, revealing Aurora's air—warmer than expected, heavy with unfamiliar scents and the faint electric tingle of active Aetherium. She steps onto the landing pad, boots connecting with a surface that hasn't felt imperial presence in decades.

For a moment, standing at the edge of the abandoned platform with Aurora spread before her, something shifts in The Shadow's perception. The city's silhouette against the evening sky triggers another memory fragment—tall structures, but not these structures. A different skyline. A different world.

Home.

The Shadow doesn't have a home. The Shadow has mission parameters.

Yet Samara had a home once.

The distinction presents itself with unusual clarity—The Shadow and Samara, overlapping but separate. One created, one erased.

The Emperor doesn't accept people using the Thread outside of official methods and protocols. That's why they came for the Luthari. Now they've sent the last Luthari after this Dreamer.

The irony doesn't escape her. She—a remnant of a people destroyed for their understanding of the Thread—tasked with assessing another who manipulates it beyond imperial control.

The Shadow pushes such reflections aside. They are irrelevant. Counterproductive. Yet they persist like Thread fragments caught in her consciousness.

Her mission begins with reconnaissance. Locate the Thread disruptions, find their source, find Liora.

The ship's systems dim in acknowledgment as the exit ramp descends with a soft hydraulic hiss. Night air enters the craft—cooler than expected, carrying the scent of artificial rain and synthesized blossoms.

A lone figure stands at the edge of the landing pad, datapad in hand. Male, maintenance uniform, unarmed. A docking agent, likely sent to verify the unscheduled arrival. His eyes widen as the Shadow emerges from the ship, his datapad lowering slowly.

"I wasn't informed of any imperial visits," he says, voice catching. "I'll need to see your clearance and—"

The Shadow draws her sidearm in one fluid motion, the weapon materializing in her hand as if summoned. The shot is silent, a concentrated energy pulse that strikes the man directly between the eyes. He collapses without a sound, datapad clattering on the landing pad.

Efficient. Clean. The Shadow steps over the body, moving to the edge of the platform. No alarms sound. No security forces appear. The pad was chosen well—isolated from Aurora's main surveillance network, designed for precisely this type of discreet arrival.

She activates her helmet's enhanced vision modes, scanning the surrounding buildings. Heat signatures indicate minimal activity in adjacent structures. Most of Aurora's population appears concentrated in the central and western districts, where light pollution suggests entertainment and commercial centers.

The dead man's datapad might contain useful information. She retrieves it, bypassing its security protocols with practiced ease. Local maps, security schedules, access codes—all standard information for a docking administrator. She downloads the data to her suit's internal storage and discards the device.

The drop from the landing pad to the nearest rooftop is fifteen meters. The Shadow steps off the edge without hesitation, her suit's impact absorbers negating the fall's force as she lands in a silent crouch.

Aurora spreads before her now—a jungle of light and sound, pulsing with energy. Holographic advertisements float between buildings, projecting products and services the Shadow doesn't recognize. Citizens move through illuminated walkways, their faces upturned to the artificial constellations projection that serves as Aurora's night sky.

None of them aware that death walks among them.

Melia IV

The last rays of sunset stretch across Old Chapel's weathered facade as Melia picks her way through fallen stone and overgrown paths. Her feet ache from the day's relentless march. Bear trots ahead, pausing occasionally to look back as if ensuring she follows, his green eyes luminous in the fading light.

"Keep up, Princess," Auren calls over his shoulder, his voice clipped with impatience. "We lose the light soon."

"I'm not used to—" Melia stops herself. Complaining won't change anything. These worn leather boots bear little resemblance to her delicate slippers from Elyssia, and her feet rebel against every step.

The Old Chapel looms above them, clinging to the cliff face like a desperate climber. Ancient stone walls blend seamlessly with the natural rock, making it impossible to determine where mountain ends and structure begins. Narrow windows stare outward like hollow eyes.

"Spectacular, isn't it?" Kyp grins, sweeping his arm toward the structure. "They say it was built when the first pilgrims came through, back before anyone remembers."

Melia nods absently, but her attention fixes on the sheer drop beside the path. Her stomach lurches as loose pebbles cascade over the edge, disappearing into nothingness. The memories of her fall from Elyssia flood back—the whistling wind, the sickening sensation of weightlessness, the certainty of death.

"I need to..." Her voice falters as she presses herself against the cliff wall.

Auren turns, his expression softening as he notices her rigid posture and blanched face. "The height," he says, not a question but a recognition.

She nods, unable to form words. Bear circles her ankles, his warm body brushing against her calves in silent support.

"There's a path cut into the rock," Auren explains, gesturing toward a narrow ledge. "Stay close to the wall. Don't look down."

"What excellent advice," Melia mutters, summoning a fragment of her royal sarcasm despite her fear.

Auren's mouth twitches—almost a smile. Almost.

The final approach feels endless. Melia shuffles sideways along the narrow ledge, fingers scraping against rough stone, eyes determinedly fixed on Auren's back. Bear somehow navigates the precarious path with feline grace, occasionally meowing encouragement.

Finally, the path widens into a small plateau before the chapel entrance. Melia releases a breath she hadn't realized she was holding.

"Welcome to the second station of our reverse Pilgrimage," Kyp announces dramatically, sweeping into an exaggerated bow. "Where pilgrims come to contemplate their insignificance beneath the vastness of sky."

"Or to shelter from the rain," Auren adds practically, eyeing the darkening clouds.

Inside, the chapel reveals its secrets. Faded murals cover the walls—scenes of ascension, figures with ethereal wings rising toward a golden city. Melia stares at them, recognition and unease mingling in her chest. The depiction of Elyssia is crude but unmistakable.

"There are sleeping alcoves carved into the walls," Auren explains, lighting a small lantern. "They'll provide shelter for the night."

Melia peers into the nearest alcove—a semicircular depression hollowed from solid rock, barely large enough for a person to lie down. The thought of sleeping so close to the cliff edge makes her dizzy.

"Are there any... further in?" she asks, hating the tremor in her voice.

Kyp has already claimed an alcove near the entrance, unpacking his bedroll with practiced efficiency. "Best spots go to those who call them first," he grins. "Ancient pilgrim tradition."

Auren gives him a look. "There's one in the back corner, away from the drop." He gestures for Melia to follow him deeper into the chapel.

The alcove he shows her sits against the mountain wall, as far from the cliff edge as possible within the chapel's confines. Bear immediately jumps in, turning in circles before settling with an approving purr.

"Thank you," Melia says, genuine gratitude warming her voice.

They make camp in silence—Auren preparing a small fire in the chapel's central hearth, Kyp unpacking dried provisions, Melia arranging her meager belongings in the alcove. The familiar routine soothes her frayed nerves.

Later, as they sit around the fire eating a simple meal of flatbread and dried fruit, Melia notices Auren staring at the murals, his expression distant.

"What are you thinking about?" she asks.

"My ascent," he answers after a moment, running a hand through his dark hair.

Kyp suddenly becomes very interested in adjusting his bedroll, giving them privacy without actually leaving.

"Will you tell me about it?" Melia asks, pulling her knees to her chest.

Auren is silent so long she thinks he won't answer. Then: "I prepared my entire life for it. Every test, every trial, every station of the Pilgrimage—I passed them all."

The firelight casts dancing shadows across his face, highlighting the sharp angles of his cheekbones, the furrow between his brows.

"When I reached the final summit," he continues, "I felt... chosen. Special. The wings manifested—beautiful, powerful. The Aether wasn't just a tool, it flowed through me. It was a part of me, it always was."

His voice drops. "I could see Elyssia. Actually see it. Not just a distant shimmer in the clouds, but the buildings, the gardens. I was so close."

"What happened?" Melia asks softly.

"A voice inside me said, 'Not yet.' Just that. And my wings dissolved." His hands clench. "I fell. Like you."

Melia reaches out, placing her hand over his. Not to comfort—she barely knows how—but to anchor. To acknowledge. They're connected by falling, by being rejected by the same golden city.

Her fingers rest lightly on his scarred knuckles. He doesn't pull away.

Bear stretches beside them, indifferent to tales of ascension and falling. The fire crackles. Outside, a gentle rain begins to fall.

***

The fire flickers lower, casting long shadows against the wall murals. Rain patters steadily against the stone outside, creating a cocoon of isolation around the chapel. Kyp's gentle snores echo from his alcove near the entrance.

"You should rest," Auren says, his voice low. He stands and offers her his hand. "I'll show you to your alcove."

Melia accepts his hand, feeling the rough calluses against her palm. Strange how quickly she's grown accustomed to such sensations—the texture of skin against skin, the weight of another's touch—all things barely experienced in her previous life of ceremonial gloves and formal distances.

Bear watches them with luminous green eyes but makes no move to follow as Auren leads her toward the back of the chapel. The cat stretches languorously, then curls into a tight ball by the dying embers.

"He's abandoning me," Melia whispers with mock indignation, glancing back at her feline companion.

"He knows you're in good hands," Auren replies, then looks away as if surprised by his own words.

They reach her alcove—the small depression carved into the solid rock of the mountain. Someone long ago lined it with smooth stones, creating a space that feels both ancient and intimate. Melia's few possessions lie neatly arranged: the worn blanket from Willow Haven, a water skin, the small satchel containing treasures salvaged from her fall.

Auren hesitates at the edge of the alcove. "Do you need anything else?"

Melia sits on the edge of her makeshift bed, suddenly reluctant to end their conversation. "Just... stay a moment?"

He settles beside her, careful to maintain a respectful distance. The alcove feels smaller with both of them inside it, their shoulders nearly touching in the confined space.

"I keep thinking about what you said," Melia says after a moment. "About the voice that told you 'not yet.' What if it wasn't rejection? What if it was... preparation?"

Auren's breath catches. "For what?"

"For this." She gestures vaguely between them. "For guiding me."

Their eyes meet in the dim light. Something electric passes between them—recognition, perhaps, or possibility.

"I've never felt so lost," Melia confesses. "Or so... real."

"The fall changes you," Auren agrees, voice rough. "Strips everything away."

"I'm not who I thought I was," she whispers.

His eyes search hers. "Who are you, then?"

"I don't know yet." Melia's hand inches closer to his on the rough blanket. "But I want to find out."

When their fingers touch, it feels deliberate in a way their earlier contact hadn't been. His hand turns, palm up, an invitation. She places her hand in his, marveling at how perfectly it fits.

"I've been so numb," Auren confesses, thumb tracing gentle circles on her wrist. "Since my fall. Like part of me stayed behind in that lake."

"I know exactly what you mean." She shifts closer, drawn by the warmth of him, the solid reality of his presence.

His free hand rises hesitantly, hovering near her cheek. "May I?"

She nods, unable to speak.

His fingertips trace the curve of her cheek, feather-light. "You're real," he murmurs, more to himself than to her.

"So are you," she breathes, leaning into his touch.

The distance between them diminishes slowly, inevitably. His gaze drops to her lips, then back to her eyes, asking silent permission. She answers by closing the final space between them.

Their lips meet—tentative, exploring. A soft gasp escapes her at the sensation, electric and new. His hand cradles her face with reverent gentleness.

"We don't have to—"

She silences him with another kiss, more certain this time. Her hands find his shoulders, solid and warm beneath the rough fabric of his shirt.

"I want to feel alive," she whispers against his mouth. "With you."

His restraint visibly crumbles. Their next kiss deepens, lives of isolation and longing crystallizing into this single moment of connection. His arms encircle her, drawing her closer.

The world narrows to sensation—his hands skimming her sides, the gentle pressure of his body guiding her back against the blanket, the weight of him above her, careful and considerate.

"Tell me if you want to stop," he murmurs against her neck.

"Don't stop," she answers, fingers threading through his hair.

The subtle friction of his lips against her throat sends ripples of pleasure coursing through her. His kisses trace a path downward, lingering at her collarbone, each press of his lips drawing out a small gasp. Melia's fingers curl against his shoulders, clutching at the fabric of his shirt.

"May I?" he murmurs, fingers hovering at the laces of her gown.

She nods, breathless with anticipation. The rough pads of his fingers work deliberately, loosening each tie with careful attention, as if unwrapping something precious. Cool air kisses her skin as the fabric parts, heightening her awareness of every sensation.

His palm glides across her newly exposed shoulder, a reverent exploration that leaves goosebumps in its wake. "You're beautiful," he whispers, voice rough with emotion.

"Touch me," she urges, surprised by her own boldness.

His eyes darken as he lowers his mouth to the curve of her breast. The first tentative brush of his lips against her sensitive skin pulls a sharp intake of breath from her. When his tongue traces a delicate circle around her nipple, her back arches involuntarily, pressing her closer to his mouth.

A soft moan escapes her as he takes her nipple between his lips, alternating between gentle suction and the whisper of his tongue. Heat pools between her legs, an insistent pulse she's never experienced with such intensity.

His hand slides down her side, tracing the curve of her waist, her hip, her thigh. Each touch ignites new sensations, awakening parts of her she never knew existed. His mouth continues its journey downward, leaving a trail of warmth across her stomach.

"Is this all right?" he asks, fingers playing at the hem of her undergarments.

"Yes," she breathes, lifting her hips slightly to help him.

He slides the fabric down her legs with deliberate slowness, his gaze never leaving hers. The vulnerability of being exposed before him sends a shiver through her, not of fear but of anticipation.

His hands caress her thighs, gently encouraging them to part for him. Melia feels a momentary flash of uncertainty—this is unfamiliar territory—but the tender look in his eyes dissolves her hesitation.

He lowers himself between her legs, pressing soft kisses to her inner thighs. Each touch inches closer to her center, stoking the fire building within her. When his breath finally ghosts across her most sensitive flesh, she trembles.

The first tentative stroke of his tongue draws a startled cry from her lips. Pleasure, sharp and electric, radiates outward from where his mouth touches her. His hands steady her hips as they instinctively rise to meet him.

"Auren," she gasps, one hand finding his hair, fingers tangling in the dark strands.

He responds by deepening the contact, his tongue tracing intricate patterns that send waves of sensation cascading through her body. Each circle, each delicate flick builds upon the last, creating a mounting tension that coils tighter with every passing moment.

Melia's world narrows to the exquisite pressure of his mouth against her. She's dimly aware of the sounds escaping her throat—soft whimpers and hitched breaths that echo in the stone alcove.

He finds a rhythm that transforms her breathing into desperate pants. Her free hand clutches at the blanket beneath her, seeking anchor as pleasure threatens to overwhelm her. The tension builds, drawing her body taut as a bowstring.

When he closes his lips around the sensitive bundle of nerves and sucks gently, stars burst behind her eyelids. Her thighs tremble against his shoulders as he continues, relentless in his devotion to her pleasure.

"Don't stop," she pleads, voice barely recognizable to her own ears. "Please, don't stop."

Release crashes over Melia like a tidal wave, her body arching against his mouth as pleasure radiates from her core to her fingertips. She cries out, the sound echoing off the chapel's ancient walls as her hips buck uncontrollably against his face. Auren holds her steady through the tremors, his tongue gentling as the intense sensations gradually subside.

"Come here," she gasps, tugging at his shoulders with trembling hands.

He rises above her, his expression a mixture of satisfaction and desire. Melia pulls him down for a kiss, startled by the unfamiliar taste on his lips—musky and intimate. It's her, she realizes with a jolt of surprise, her own essence on his mouth. Rather than repelling her, the discovery sends a renewed pulse of arousal through her body.

His weight settles partially atop her, and Melia feels the unmistakable hardness pressing against her thigh through his pants. A thrill of curiosity and anticipation courses through her as she shifts her hips, drawing a sharp intake of breath from him.

"Is this okay?" she whispers, emboldened by her own pleasure.

"More than okay," he murmurs against her neck.

Her hand slides tentatively down his chest, feeling the rapid beat of his heart through the thin fabric of his shirt. Curiosity propels her further, her fingers tracing the rigid outline of him through his pants. Auren groans softly, the sound vibrating against her throat where his lips press.

Melia's fingers close around his length, applying gentle pressure. The hardness beneath the fabric fascinates her—how it responds to her touch, how Auren's breathing grows ragged with each exploratory squeeze. Power, different from anything she's known in Elyssia, flows through her at the knowledge that she affects him so deeply.

"I want you," she whispers, tugging at the drawstring of his pants.

Auren draws back, searching her face. "Are you sure?"

In answer, she pulls him down for another kiss, her free hand continuing to work at loosening his pants. He helps her then, shifting his weight to push the fabric down his hips. When he settles back against her, the hot length of him presses directly against her bare skin.

Melia's eyes widen at the sensation—velvet softness over rigid heat. Her hand wraps around him experimentally, marveling at how he feels in her palm.

"I've never..." she begins, suddenly shy despite their intimacy.

"We don't have to go further," Auren assures her, brushing damp strands of hair from her flushed face.

His consideration only increases her desire. The reverence in his touch, so different from the formal deference she received as royalty, makes her feel truly seen for perhaps the first time in her life.

"I want to," she says, meeting his gaze steadily. "I want you."

Auren's thumb traces the curve of her cheek. "Are you sure? We can stop anytime."

Melia guides his hand to her center, letting him feel the slick evidence of her arousal. "I'm sure."

He groans, forehead pressing against hers. "If anything doesn't feel right, tell me. Promise?"

"I promise," she whispers, heart racing with anticipation.

His manhood slides against her wetness, the friction drawing twin gasps from them both. Melia feels him positioning himself at her entrance, the blunt pressure both intimidating and thrilling.

He pushes forward slowly, watching her face with intense concentration. The pressure builds, unfamiliar and insistent. Melia gasps as he breaches her entrance, her body yielding to accommodate him.

"Are you all right?" he whispers, holding perfectly still despite the tension evident in his trembling arms.

"Yes," she breathes. "Don't stop."

A brief, sharp sting makes her wince as he eases deeper. Auren freezes immediately, concern darkening his eyes.

"Melia?"

"Keep going," she urges, lifting her hips to meet him. "I want this. I want you."

The discomfort gives way to a profound sense of fullness as he sinks fully into her. Melia marvels at the intimacy of it—this joining of bodies in the shadows of an ancient chapel, so different from the sterile, ceremonial consummation that would have awaited her with Prefect Solivar. No witnesses, no political alliance being sealed. Just two people seeking connection in the darkness.

"You feel incredible," Auren murmurs, his voice strained with the effort of remaining still. "Are you okay?"

In answer, Melia rolls her hips experimentally, drawing a strangled groan from him. The movement sends unexpected pleasure rippling through her, washing away the lingering discomfort.

"Move," she whispers. "Please."

He withdraws slightly before pushing back in, establishing a gentle rhythm that allows her body to adjust to his size. Each careful thrust builds upon the pleasure of the last, stoking the embers of her earlier climax back to life. Melia wraps her legs around his waist, changing the angle and drawing him deeper.

"Oh!" she gasps as he strikes a spot inside her that sends electricity racing up her spine.

Auren's pace remains unhurried, each movement deliberate and controlled. His forehead presses against hers, their breath mingling in the narrow space between them. There's reverence in his restraint, a tenderness that makes tears prick at the corners of Melia's eyes.

"This is how it should be," she whispers, the realization crystallizing as he moves within her. "Not duty. Not politics. This."

His rhythm falters momentarily as emotion flashes across his face. When he resumes, his thrusts deepen, still gentle but with greater purpose.

"You deserve this," he murmurs against her lips. "Pleasure. Freedom. Choice."

Each word punctuates a movement of his hips, driving him deeper. Heat builds within her once more, a familiar tension coiling at her core. Melia clutches at his shoulders, nails digging into the firm muscle as pleasure mounts with each stroke.

The sound of their breathing fills the alcove, punctuated by soft gasps and the whisper of skin against skin. Sweat beads on Auren's brow as his pace increases slightly, responding to the urgency of her rolling hips.

"I'm close," she whispers, surprised by how quickly the sensations are building again.

Auren slides a hand between their bodies, his thumb finding the sensitive bundle of nerves above where they're joined. The additional stimulation sends sparks shooting through her veins.

"Let go," he encourages, circling his thumb in time with his thrusts. "I've got you."

The intensity builds rapidly, her inner walls beginning to flutter around his length. Melia's back arches off the blanket as pleasure crests within her, more powerful than before. She cries out his name, uncaring who might hear as waves of ecstasy crash through her body.

Auren's movements grow more insistent, his rhythm faltering as her inner muscles clench rhythmically around him. His breath comes in harsh pants against her neck as he drives deeper, chasing his own release.

With a final, deep thrust, Auren stiffens above her. His body trembles, muscles taut like bowstrings as his release claims him. A raw, vulnerable sound tears from his throat—halfway between a groan and her name. Melia feels him pulsing inside her, the rhythmic throb sending aftershocks of pleasure rippling through her still-sensitive flesh.

The sensation is entirely new—this hot rush of him emptying himself deep within her. Something primal and possessive unfurls in her chest as she wraps her legs tighter around him, drawing him impossibly closer, keeping him anchored to her as his climax shudders through him.

"Melia," he breathes against her neck, voice ragged with spent passion. "Gods, Melia."

The weight of him presses her into the blankets, but she welcomes it—this solid reminder of his realness, of what they've shared. Their skin sticks together, slick with sweat despite the cool night air. She runs her hands down the plane of his back, marveling at the shifting muscles beneath her fingertips, the racing heartbeat that gradually slows against her chest.

"Stay," she whispers when he moves to withdraw. "Just... stay like this a moment longer."

He obliges, propping himself on his elbows to keep from crushing her while remaining joined. The intimate connection lingers—his softening length still nestled within her, her inner walls occasionally fluttering with aftershocks that make him gasp.

Melia stares up at the rough-hewn ceiling of the alcove, wondering at how completely her world has transformed. In Elyssia, her body had been merely an extension of her royal duty—a vessel for continuing bloodlines, a canvas for ceremonial garb, a symbol of divine purity. Now, it's the site of revolution—a source of pleasure, a means of connection, an instrument of her own choosing.

"What are you thinking?" Auren asks, brushing a strand of hair from her damp forehead.

"That I never knew," she murmurs, trailing her fingers along his stubbled jaw. "I never knew my body could feel like this. Like it belongs to me."

His eyes soften with understanding. He shifts slightly, finally slipping free of her, and settles beside her in the narrow space. Their limbs tangle together, neither willing to surrender contact completely.

"In Elyssia," she continues, "everything about me was for someone else—for the kingdom, for tradition, for Solivar's political ambitions. Even my pleasure would have been measured by how well it served the alliance."

Auren's palm skims her hip, her waist, coming to rest just beneath her breast. "And now?"

"Now I know what it means to choose. To want. To take." A delicious languor spreads through her limbs, heavy and sweet. "To give."

His lips brush her shoulder, feather-light. "No regrets?"

"None," she whispers, turning to face him. Their noses nearly touch on the shared pillow. "For the first time since I fell, I feel... right in my own skin. Like maybe I was meant to fall. Like maybe this is where I'm supposed to be."

Auren's eyes search hers in the dim light. Whatever he finds there makes him gather her closer, one leg sliding between hers, his arm a secure weight across her waist.

The steady rhythm of his breathing gradually slows, deepening toward sleep. Melia fights to keep her eyes open, savoring the novel sensations—the pleasant soreness between her legs, the cooling evidence of their passion on her thighs, the soft brush of his chest hair against her breasts with each breath. His manhood rests against her thigh, spent yet still maintaining a ghostly impression of its former hardness.

Sleep tugs at her consciousness despite her resistance, the physical and emotional exertion of their coupling claiming its due. The last thing she registers before surrendering to dreams is the perfect, easy weight of his arm around her waist, and the certainty that she has finally, truly fallen—not just from Elyssia, but into something far more profound.

***

Morning light filters through the chapel's narrow windows, painting golden stripes across the stone floor. Melia wakes alone, the space beside her still warm but empty. For a moment she wonders if she dreamed the entire encounter, but the pleasant soreness in unfamiliar places confirms the reality of the night before.

She dresses quietly, fingers trembling slightly as she laces her borrowed clothing. Her body feels different somehow—more present, more alive, as if the night's intimacy has awakened every dormant nerve.

When she emerges from her alcove, she finds Auren already packing supplies near the entrance. He looks up as she approaches, his expression carefully neutral.

"Morning," he says, voice deliberately casual. "There's dried fruit if you're hungry."

No mention of shared blankets or interlaced limbs. No acknowledgment of the way they'd clung to each other, seeking life amid the ruins.

"Thank you," she replies, matching his tone.

Bear appears from nowhere, winding around her ankles with a satisfied purr. His green eyes seem to hold knowing secrets.

"Ready to continue?" Auren asks, securing his pack.

"Yes," Melia answers, understanding the unspoken agreement between them. Whatever transpired in the night exists in its own pocket of time—to be treasured, perhaps, but not discussed.

As they leave the chapel and continue their journey, walking side by side along the mountain path, Melia feels something has fundamentally shifted within her. Not just the physical awakening, but a deeper realization—that connection exists beyond the manufactured ceremonies of her former life. That real intimacy happens in the quiet, honest spaces between two people.

She catches Auren looking at her when he thinks she won't notice, his expression softer than before. She pretends not to see, but walks a little taller, feeling the pleasant echo of his touch with every step.

They don't speak of it. They don't need to.

The Shadow II

14 Years Ago

Samara sits cross-legged on the crystalline floor, watching light fracture through the chamber's geometric windows. Mother's footsteps echo differently today—purposeful, with an urgency that makes Samara's spine straighten.

"Sam." Mother's voice carries that rare tone—the one reserved for important lessons. "It's time."

Samara uncrosses her legs and stands. At thirteen, she's learned patience with Mother's cryptic moments. The chamber hums with the ambient pulse of the hidden systems that keep their sanctuary functioning, systems Mother calls "the breath of home."

Mother approaches, carrying what appears to be a small metallic case. Unlike their other artifacts, this one bears no obvious seams or latches—just a smooth, opalescent surface that seems to shift colors as it moves.

"What is it?" Samara asks, curiosity overriding decorum.

Mother places the case on the floor between them. "This belonged to our people when we could still live freely. Before the dark times. Before the Emperor decided our knowledge was too dangerous." Her voice doesn't waver, but Samara notes the tightness around her eyes—the subtle indicators of pain Mother never fully expresses.

With a fluid gesture, Mother waves her hand over the case. The surface responds, rippling like disturbed water before parting seamlessly down the middle. Inside, nestled in what looks like liquid darkness, lies something impossibly thin yet substantial—a bodysuit of some kind, but unlike anything Samara has seen in their archives or studies.

"Armor?" Samara guesses, reaching toward it instinctively.

"Yes. Luthari armor. Not like Imperial plating, which simply defends against physical threats." Mother lifts it carefully. The material catches light in impossible ways, bending and absorbing it simultaneously. "This is Thread-seeking armor. It protects the wearer not just from weapons, but from being written into someone else's story."

Samara stares, transfixed. The armor appears almost alive as Mother unfolds it, revealing its full form—a sleek bodysuit with intricate, fractal patterns etched across the surface.

"It's yours now," Mother says.

"Mine?" Samara's eyes widen. "But you said Luthari artifacts must be preserved, not—"

"Some things are meant to be used, not preserved." Mother's gaze intensifies. "Our people believed tools should serve living hands, not gather dust as monuments to the dead."

The gravity of the moment settles over Samara. Mother has taught her about their heritage in careful, measured doses—always emphasizing caution, always reminding her that knowledge of the Luthari is forbidden by Imperial edict.

"Will it fit me?" Samara asks, eyeing the adult-sized suit.

Mother smiles. "It will adapt to whoever wears it. The Luthari understood that form follows function, but also that function should respect form." She holds it out. "Would you like to try it on?"

Samara's heart quickens as she reaches for the armor. The material feels impossibly light in her hands, cool but somehow warm simultaneously, as if greeting her touch with recognition.

"How do I—"

A piercing sound cuts through their sanctuary—three sharp, pulsing tones that Samara has never heard before. Mother freezes, her face draining of color.

"Mother?" Samara clutches the armor, suddenly afraid.

"Warning bells," Mother whispers, then snaps into motion. "Put it back in the case, quickly!"

Samara fumbles, trying to refold the armor as precisely as Mother had unfolded it. "What's happening?"

Mother's movements become swift, efficient. She taps a sequence on her wrist interface, and throughout their home, lights dim and change color, shifting from ambient white to a muted blue-gray.

"Ghost Protocol," Mother commands the house system. "Full spectrum dampening."

"Acknowledged," responds the disembodied house voice, softer than usual.

"Mother, you're scaring me," Samara says, finally managing to return the armor to its case.

Mother kneels before her, gripping Samara's shoulders tightly. Fear lurks in her eyes—real fear, not the cautious wariness Samara has occasionally glimpsed.

"Listen carefully," Mother says, voice steady despite her evident terror. "The warning bells mean we've been found."

"Found? By who?"

"The Empire." Mother's grip tightens. "They've been searching for remnants of Luthari knowledge for decades. For survivors. For anything they couldn't erase."

Samara's stomach drops. Mother has always been careful. They've moved three times in Samara's memory, always staying ahead of imperial patrols, always maintaining the fiction that they're simply independent scholars living on the fringes.

"What do we do?" Samara asks.

"We've prepared for this." Mother takes the case and presses it back into Samara's hands. "Take this to the hidden compartment in your room. Remember the sequence I taught you?"

Samara nods, throat tight.

"Good. Go now, quickly."

As Samara turns to leave, a second alarm sounds—higher-pitched, more urgent. Mother's face transforms into a mask of determination.

"They're closer than I thought." She pushes Samara toward the corridor. "Run. Don't stop for anything."

Samara clutches the case to her chest and sprints down the corridor. The sanctuary's lights pulse with the alarm's rhythm, casting strange shadows that seem to chase her. The case feels heavier than it should, as if aware of its own importance.

When she reaches her room, Samara drops to her knees beside her bed, fingers scrambling to find the hidden panel Mother installed years ago. The floor yields to her touch, revealing a small compartment lined with the same opalescent material as the case.

Just as she's about to place the case inside, she hears it—the unmistakable hum of an imperial shuttle, so close the walls themselves seem to vibrate.

Mother appears in the doorway, her face set in grim resolve. "They're here."

***

The Present

The Shadow slips between clusters of people like water through stones. Her suit whispers silent reassurance, a constant vibration of data and feedback against her skin. The armor feels more alive than she does sometimes—the Luthari threading responding to ambient signals while she processes visual input.

Night has settled over Aurora, turning the city into a tapestry of light that reminds her of something she can't quite place. Memory fragments. Not relevant to the mission.

She adjusts her visor's filter to cut through the brightness, focusing on three patrons at an outdoor café. Their conversation rises above the ambient noise thanks to her suit's audio enhancement.

"—heard she simply vanished after the Convergence," says a woman with luminescent tattoos tracking up her forearms. "Just like that. Gone."

"Liora didn't abandon us," insists her companion, leaning forward with religious conviction. "She's still working, just... elsewhere."

The Shadow remains motionless, gathering data. Liora Solari: identified as absent rather than present. Consistent with preliminary assessment. Imperial intelligence suggested the Dreamer was hiding here. Another miscalculation from Command.

Her helmet interface tags facial expressions, searching for deception markers. None appear. These people believe what they're saying.

"What about Elyssia?" asks the third patron, a weathered man with eyes too sharp for comfort. "If what they're saying about the King and Queen is true—"

"It is," the tattooed woman cuts in. "Confirmed by three separate trader ships. Both dead within days of each other."

The Shadow's suit registers a slight temperature fluctuation—her own physiological response. Irrelevant. She dismisses the alert.

King Orion and Queen Lysandra: confirmed deceased. The brief mentioned this, but hearing civilians discuss it creates an unexpected dissonance. The armor adjusts, compensating for the momentary spike in her pulse.

"The Veil is broken," the sharp-eyed man says quietly. "That's what matters. That's what she did for us."

The others nod solemnly.

The Shadow withdraws before they notice her stillness amid the flowing crowd. The Veil: term requires clarification.

She moves on, scaling a maintenance ladder to reach a higher vantage point. From the rooftop, Aurora spreads before her like a circuit board, pulsing with energy and information. Her armor samples the ambient Thread signature, comparing it to Imperial baseline.

Deviation: 37.8%. Significant.

The Shadow crouches, pressing her palm flat against the surface beneath her. The suit's sensors penetrate deeper, reading historical Thread patterns embedded in the city's infrastructure.

Aurora has changed. Recently and rapidly. The entire Storehouse has. The energy signatures suggest a transformation far beyond normal evolutionary development.

Something catches her periphery—a mural painted across a nearby wall. It depicts a woman with hands upraised, Thread patterns flowing from her fingertips. Beneath it, fresh flowers and small tokens have been arranged. A shrine.

The Shadow drops silently to street level, approaching the mural. Her visor identifies the subject immediately: Liora Solari. The rendering is stylized but accurate based on Imperial records.

"Beautiful, isn't it?" says a voice beside her.

The Shadow doesn't startle. Her suit had already marked the approach of the elderly woman now standing at her side.

"She saved us all," the woman continues, misreading the Shadow's silence as reverence. "I'm from Somnus. When the Convergence came, Emperor Draven was going to take control of everything. Liora showed us how to reweave it together."

The Shadow tilts her head slightly. "Saved you from what?"

"From the Empire's version of reality," the woman says without hesitation. "From the lies they wove to keep us separated from our own power."

Threat identified: ideological contamination. The woman speaks heresy with casual comfort.

"And where is she now?" the Shadow asks, modulating her voice to sound merely curious.

"Gone beyond," the woman says with a smile. "She disappeared after everything changed. Some say she's searching for others like her—more Dreamers."

"You're not from around here," the woman observes, finally seeming to register the Shadow's full appearance.

"Just passing through," the Shadow replies, already calculating extraction vectors.

The woman reaches out, perhaps intending some gesture of welcome. The Shadow steps back smoothly, avoiding contact.

"Thank you for the information," she says, then melts back into the crowd.

Three blocks away, she processes what she's learned. The mission parameters show significant dissonance with observed reality:

Her armor hums against her skin, the Luthari technology sampling and analyzing Thread resonance patterns that Imperial sensors can't detect.

The Shadow pauses at an intersection, watching citizens move freely through spaces that, according to Imperial doctrine, should be rigidly controlled. They appear more connected to each other, more present in their interactions.

A troubling thought surfaces: this doesn't match the definition of "threat" in her briefing.

She suppresses it immediately, focusing instead on tactical assessment. If Liora Solari was never in Aurora, the mission requires adjustment. She must identify the Dreamer's current location."

The Shadow navigates through Aurora's arterial walkways, each step precise and measured. Reflections of neon light shimmer across her armor's surface as locals give her a wide berth. Their eyes linger too long, expressions shifting from curiosity to wariness to outright fear.

Her suit's sensors log these microexpressions, compiling patterns of behavior. Population uniformly demonstrates heightened caution around Imperial signifiers. Threat assessment protocols suggest imminent confrontation probability at 82% if current visibility maintained.

"Empire bitch," someone mutters as she passes a group of workers. The Shadow doesn't turn. The armor captures the voice pattern, categorizes it as non-threat, continues monitoring.

A public display screen shows a market report. The Shadow pauses, scanning information about local economy. The term "Gilded Bazaar" appears repeatedly, referencing the primary commerce hub controlled by someone called "Garrik the Gilded." Linked references indicate underground fighting arenas, black market exchanges, information brokering.

High probability location for actionable intelligence.

She follows the directional indicators toward the Bazaar, moving through increasingly crowded streets. As foot traffic thickens, the reactions intensify—people actively rerouting to avoid her path, parents pulling children closer, security personnel touching communication devices.

The Shadow's tactical display highlights three individuals tracking her movements with deliberate intent. Former military, based on their positioning and silent coordination. Not Imperial-trained, but professional.

At the entrance to the Bazaar itself—an elaborate archway adorned with salvaged technology and decorative metals—the crowd physically parts around her. Conversation dies. Merchants secure their wares. A security barrier activates ahead as guards step forward.

"That's far enough," one says, hand resting on a modified pulse disruptor.

The Shadow stops, analyzing the situation. Confrontation: counterproductive. Current presentation: actively hindering mission objectives.

She assesses the security team's stance, the evacuation of civilians from the immediate area, the growing tension. Her armor is registering increased surveillance activity. Facial recognition sweeps attempting to penetrate her helmet.

"No Imperials welcome here," the guard continues. "Garrik's orders."

The Shadow nods once, turns, and withdraws with the same measured pace. Behind her, she hears conversations resuming, relief evident in the vocal patterns.

A tactical error. She's been operating on outdated parameters.

The Shadow returns through the residential district, taking routes that minimize exposure. Her suit continuously maps the city, identifying patterns and anomalies. A small apartment complex shows minimal security and multiple vacant units—optimal for establishing temporary operational base.

Inside a maintenance corridor, she disables the surveillance system and accesses an unoccupied unit on the fifth floor. The space is sparse but functional. Large window, single exit, water access, power source. Acceptable.

The maintenance routine runs automatically in her head: assess, report, recalibrate, execute. But the assessment doesn't align with her briefing. Aurora should be a danger zone, a city poisoned by a Dreamer's influence. Instead, it thrives.

If the Veil was broken, why hasn't the Storehouse collapsed? The Empire's briefings described catastrophic failure scenarios—reality fracturing, civilization disintegrating, chaos consuming order. None of this matches what she's observing.

The Shadow's gaze follows a family walking below, their easy laughter carrying up to her window. They move without the rigid precision of Imperial citizens. Their posture lacks the weight of constant surveillance.

They look...free.

A dangerous thought. She dismisses it and activates her datapad, scrolling through the limited intelligence on Garrik the Gilded. Former smuggler, rose to prominence during the upheaval following the "Convergence"—their term for the Veil's destruction. Controls information flow through the Bazaar. Known for pragmatism rather than ideology.

As night deepens, The Shadow establishes a secure connection to her ship. The mission parameters need adjustment. The Empire's intelligence appears fundamentally flawed. The Veil breaking didn't destroy the Storehouse—it transformed it.

What else might they be wrong about?

She terminates that line of thought immediately. Questions lead to doubt. Doubt leads to hesitation. Hesitation leads to failure.

She is a weapon, precisely aimed. Her purpose is clear: find the Dreamer.

But as she watches the people of Aurora moving freely below, a small fissure appears in her certainty—hairline thin, but present.

***

13 Years Ago

Cold. So cold.

Samara's eyelids flutter open, only to be met by a watery blue haze. Panic floods her system as consciousness crashes in—she's submerged. Completely underwater. Her arms and legs feel weighted, unresponsive to the desperate commands from her brain.

Instinct tells her to hold her breath, but her lungs already burn with need. No choice but to inhale, to accept death, to—

Air fills her lungs. Not water. Air.

She blinks rapidly, confusion replacing panic. The liquid surrounds her, presses against her skin, yet somehow she breathes. It feels wrong, unnatural, like something inside her is converting the fluid, processing it differently than her body should.

Movement returns slowly. She lifts a hand to her face, watches bubbles escape between her fingers. The water distorts her vision, but she can make out shapes beyond the curved glass wall imprisoning her—white walls, blinking equipment, dark silhouettes.

People. Watching her.

A man in a white coat makes notes on a translucent screen. A woman adjusts something on a control panel. They speak, but their words are muted, garbled through the liquid.

Samara tries to remember how she got here. The sanctuary. Mother. The alarms. Imperial shuttles. Then... nothing.

Her hand drifts to her chest, fingers finding an unfamiliar ridge of tissue—a scar, fresh and tender, running from sternum to navel. She's been cut open. Changed.

Thin tubes snake from her arms, her legs, the base of her skull. Needles buried beneath her skin feed unknown substances directly into her veins. She tugs weakly at one, but it remains firmly anchored.

How long? How long has she been here?

The watchers confer with each other, gesturing toward her. Their faces remain impassive, clinical. She is a specimen, an experiment.

The woman at the controls nods at something said to her, then presses a sequence of buttons. A mechanical hum vibrates through the tank.

The liquid level begins to drop.

Samara's body descends with it, feet touching the bottom of the chamber. The water recedes past her shoulders, her chin. When it reaches her mouth, she gasps reflexively, lungs struggling to transition back to air.

The glass wall before her slides upward and away. Cold, recycled air hits her wet skin. She shivers violently, collapsing to her hands and knees on the smooth metal floor.

"Respiratory function normal," someone says. "Neural implants stable."

"Vitals responding within expected parameters."

Samara coughs, expelling blue-tinged fluid from her lungs. Her limbs tremble with effort as she tries to push herself up, to stand, to run—anywhere but here. The tubes and wires restrict her movement, anchoring her in place.

The scientists and technicians maintain their distance, watching her struggles without intervention. Their eyes contain no compassion, only assessment. Data collection.

Heavy footsteps echo through the laboratory. The technicians straighten, postures shifting from clinical interest to deferential fear. Even through her disorientation, Samara recognizes the change—someone important approaches.

A hush falls over the room.

Through strands of dripping hair, she sees him enter—a figure draped in gold-threaded robes, hovering inches above the ground. His face is partially obscured by an ornate mask, but even this cannot disguise the gauntness beneath, the skeletal quality of his fingers as they emerge from voluminous sleeves.

The Emperor.

Samara shrinks back instinctively. Mother's warnings echo: If the Emperor finds us, we are already dead.

Yet here she is. Alive. Changed.

"Your Eternal Radiance," a lead scientist approaches, bowing deeply. "The procedure was successful. All implants are functioning at optimal levels. The Luthari technology remains bonded to her biological systems, as you predicted."

The Emperor nods slightly, the simple gesture carrying the weight of absolute authority. His attention shifts to Samara, hunched and shivering on the floor.

"And her consciousness? Memory functions?" His voice is surprisingly gentle, resonant with an almost hypnotic quality.

"Intact, though fragmented. The integration process requires further neural adaptation."

The Emperor drifts closer. Samara tries to retreat, but the tubes and her own weakness prevent escape.

"What of the mother?" he asks.

A pause. "Terminated during acquisition, Your Radiance. She activated defensive protocols. There was no alternative."

Mother. Gone. The word "terminated" echoes in Samara's mind, too enormous to process fully. A distant part of her notes that she should be screaming, fighting, but her body feels disconnected from her emotions—numbed, perhaps drugged.

The Emperor hovers directly before her now. His hand, withered and ancient, extends toward her. The scientists watch with barely concealed surprise.

"Are you in pain, child?" he asks, voice carrying what sounds almost like concern.

Samara stares at the offered hand. Is this a test? A trick? Mother always said the Emperor destroyed their people, hunted the remaining Luthari to extinction. Why would he show kindness now?

"The transition is difficult," he continues. "But necessary. You carry something precious within you—a heritage that should not be lost."

His words contradict everything she knows. Yet in her confused, weakened state, the gentleness in his tone offers the only warmth in this sterile place of pain.

What choice does she have?

Samara reaches up, her small hand disappearing into his ancient grip. His skin feels like parchment stretched over bone, yet his grasp is surprisingly strong as he helps her to her feet.

"You," he says, "are the beginning of something magnificent."

Melia V

The first villager drops to his knees right in Melia's path, hands outstretched as if to touch the hem of her dress but stopping just short. His weathered face cracks into a smile of pure reverence.

"The Fallen," he whispers. "She walks among us."

More villagers appear from doorways and gardens, their expressions shifting from curiosity to awe. An older woman clutches a simple wooden charm to her chest, tears streaming down her leathery cheeks. A child points excitedly, tugging at her mother's skirt.

Melia stops abruptly, heat rising to her face. "Please," she says, gesturing for the kneeling man to rise. "I'm just passing through."

Her words only seem to intensify their fascination. The whispers multiply, rippling through the growing crowd.

"She fell from heaven."

"Touched the sacred waters."

"A sign from above."

Beside her, Auren stiffens. His jaw clenches as a young woman approaches with a freshly picked bundle of wildflowers.

"For your blessing, Fallen One," the woman murmurs, offering the bouquet with trembling hands.

Melia accepts the flowers awkwardly, their sweet scent mingling with the earthy smells of the village. "Thank you, but I'm not—"

"Let's keep moving," Auren cuts in, his voice flat. He doesn't meet Melia's eyes, hasn't properly looked at her since they left the chapel three days ago.

The intimacy they shared feels like a dream now—his gentle hands, his whispered reassurances, the way he'd held her afterward as if she were something precious. In the harsh light of day, that tenderness has evaporated, replaced by a wall of cold indifference that leaves her feeling hollow.

An older man spits at Auren's feet as they pass. "Failed pilgrim," he hisses. "The gods rejected you, yet you still breathe."

Kyp steps between them quickly. "Hey now, we're just passing through. No need for unpleasantness."

Bear weaves between their legs, seemingly oblivious to the tension, though Melia notices how the cat stays closer to her than usual.

"Was I just another conquest?" The thought forms before she can stop it. The physical act itself had meant little in Elyssia—merely a political transaction to be performed after marriage. But here, in this new reality, it had felt transformative, sacred almost. Had Auren felt the same, or was she simply naive?

They push through the crowd toward the village center, where a modest tavern stands alongside a communal well. Melia's legs ache from the day's journey, and the prospect of a real meal and perhaps a proper bed makes her quicken her pace.

"Hold up there," a gravelly voice calls out.

Five figures block their path—four men and a woman, their clothing a mix of mismatched leathers and threadbare fabrics. Their leader, a broad-shouldered man with a puckered scar running from temple to jaw, steps forward.

"Well, well. If it isn't Auren of Willow Haven." His smile reveals several missing teeth. "Been looking for you."

Auren's posture shifts subtly, weight redistributing to the balls of his feet. "Can't say the same."

The scarred man chuckles. "Don't need to know me. I represent Garrik the Gilded." He says the name with exaggerated reverence. "He's heard about your... talents."

"Whatever he's heard is exaggerated," Auren replies flatly.

Melia glances between them, sensing danger in the casual stance of the strangers, in how they've positioned themselves to block all potential escape routes.

Kyp steps forward, hands raised in a placating fashion. "Look, friends, we don't want any trouble. We're just passing through, headed to the next stage of the pilgrimage."

"Not asking for trouble," the scarred man says, eyes never leaving Auren. "Offering opportunity. Garrik wants you in his fighting pit. Best one in Aurora. In Garrik's own Gilded Bazaar. Good money for a failed pilgrim with nowhere else to go."

Auren's face hardens. "Not interested."

The woman flanking the leader slides a curved blade from her belt, examining it with theatrical casualness. "Garrik doesn't take no for answers. Not from fallen pilgrims who should be grateful for the chance."

Bear hisses suddenly, back arching as he positions himself protectively in front of Melia.

"The cat's got the right idea," a new voice interjects.

A lean figure steps into the space between the groups. He's dressed simply but well—tailored pants, a fitted jacket of supple leather, and boots that have seen use but still shine with care. His dark brown hair falls in artful disarray around a face that seems designed to charm.

The newcomer turns, revealing a face that catches Melia's breath in her throat. Where Auren's features are hewn from determination and hardship—all sharp angles and weathered intensity—this stranger's face holds a different kind of appeal. His eyes dance with mischief, green as spring leaves after rain, framed by lashes that seem almost criminally long for a man. A perpetual half-smile plays at the corner of his mouth, as if he's constantly privy to some delightful secret.

"Ryker Voss," he introduces himself with a slight bow that manages to be both mocking and graceful. "And you lot are making a scene in front of our distinguished visitor."

His gaze meets Melia's, and something warm unfurls in her stomach. It's not the soul-deep recognition she feels with Auren, but something lighter—a fluttering curiosity, a sparkle of possibility. His shoulders move beneath his jacket with fluid ease, suggesting strength without Auren's brooding intensity.

Ryker steps closer to Melia, and she catches his scent—spiced leather and something citrusy that reminds her of the orangeries in Elyssia's eastern quarter. His fingers, when they briefly brush against her arm, are smooth yet strong, a tactician's hands rather than a laborer's.

"The Fallen Princess," he murmurs, just for her ears. "Your reputation precedes you."

The scarred man spits. "This isn't your business, Voss."

"When Garrik's thugs harass travelers in my village, it absolutely concerns me." Voss produces a small pouch that jingles with the unmistakable sound of coins. "How about we skip the part where you threaten them, they refuse, and things get messy? Take these credits, get the hell out."

The leader eyes the pouch, clearly calculating. "Garrik always gets what he wants, Voss. You know that."

"Eventually, perhaps. But not today." Voss tosses the pouch, which the scarred man catches deftly. "Now get lost."

A tense moment passes as the leader weighs his options. Finally, he tucks the pouch into his vest. "This buys time, nothing more. Garrik won't forget." His gaze shifts to Auren. "Neither will I."

With that, the group backs away, melting into the crowd of villagers who have kept a wary distance from the confrontation.

Voss turns to Melia and her companions, a crooked smile lighting his face. "Looks like you could use a drink. Let me buy you one before those idiots reconsider their options."

Without waiting for a response, he gestures toward the tavern. When no one immediately moves, he adds, "Trust me, it's safer inside where fewer people can overhear us. This village has more ears than a cornfield."

Kyp looks to Auren, who gives a reluctant nod. Melia scoops Bear into her arms, drawing comfort from his warm weight against her chest.

"Who are you?" she asks as they follow Voss toward the tavern door.

His green eyes catch the late afternoon light as he glances back at her. "Someone who recognizes opportunity when it falls from the sky, Princess."

The tavern interior is dim and smoky, with rough-hewn tables scattered across an uneven floor. A fire crackles in a stone hearth, casting flickering shadows across the weathered faces of the few patrons. Most look up as they enter, their expressions ranging from curiosity to outright hostility when they spot Auren.

Voss leads them to a corner table partially screened by a wooden partition. "Sit," he says, signaling to the barkeep. "Drinks first, introductions second, explanations third."

Melia slides onto the bench, acutely aware of Auren deliberately choosing the seat farthest from her. The physical distance mirrors the emotional gulf that's opened between them since that night in the chapel—a gulf she doesn't understand and doesn't know how to cross.

Ryker notices the interaction, and his smile widens. "News travels faster than light in these parts." He leans forward, lowering his voice. "The Fallen Princess of Elyssia, traveling with a failed pilgrim, a village jester, and a tailless cat. You're not exactly inconspicuous."

The barkeep delivers four mugs of amber liquid without being asked. Voss slides one toward Melia. "Honey mead. Less likely to blind you than their ale."

Bear sniffs at the mug, whiskers twitching before he settles into Melia's lap, eyes never leaving Voss.

"Thank you for your help," Kyp says, raising his mug in salute before taking a healthy swallow. "Though I have to wonder why you bothered."

"Curiosity, mostly." Voss shrugs. "Don't often see royalty slumming it with pilgrims. Even failed ones." His eyes flick to Auren, who stares back impassively.

"We're on a pilgrimage," Melia offers, choosing her words carefully. "A reverse one."

"Ah." Voss nods as if this explains everything. "And Garrik's sudden interest in your companion?"

Auren speaks for the first time since entering the tavern. "Old business. Nothing that concerns our journey."

"I'd say anything that gets Garrik's attention concerns your journey very much." Voss takes a leisurely sip of his mead. "Especially if you're headed to Aurora. The Gilded Bazaar is his territory. You won't set foot there without him knowing."

"How do you know where we're headed?" Auren's voice carries an edge of suspicion.

Voss spreads his hands. "Where else would a reverse pilgrimage go? You start at the sacred lake, work backward through the checkpoints, and eventually reach Aurora—the place where pilgrimages go to die."

His casual knowledge of their route unsettles Melia. She studies him more carefully—the calculated charm, the easy confidence, the way his eyes miss nothing despite his relaxed demeanor.

"You seem well-informed for a villager," she observes.

Voss's smile turns enigmatic. "Who said I was a villager?"

***

The tavern bed creaks beneath Melia as she shifts onto her side, still marveling at the luxury of a proper mattress after days of sleeping on hard ground. The room is modest—just a bed, a washstand, and a threadbare rug—but to Melia, it feels like extravagance. A single candle flickers on the bedside table, casting shadows that dance across the weathered walls.

"What do you think of him, Bear?" she whispers.

The cat merely blinks at her from his perch on the windowsill, his green eyes reflecting the candlelight.

"Ryker seems... different." Melia pulls the thin blanket to her chin. "Not like the people in Willow Haven. Not like Auren."

Her thoughts drift to dinner, where Ryker had regaled them with tales of his travels while Auren sat in stony silence. Ryker's stories flowed as easily as the wine he kept ordering—adventures in distant villages, close escapes from local authorities, treasures found and lost. He spoke directly to Melia most of the time, his green eyes twinkling whenever she laughed.

"He's so open," she murmurs. "So... present."

Unlike Auren, who has barely looked at her since that night in the chapel. The memory of their intimacy burns within her—the tenderness, the passion, the feeling of being truly seen for the first time. Yet since then, Auren has retreated behind a wall of formal politeness, maintaining a careful physical distance at all times.

Melia sighs, turning again in the narrow bed. "Maybe I did something wrong."

Bear jumps down from the windowsill and pads across the floor, leaping gracefully onto the bed. He circles twice before settling against her side, a warm, comforting presence.

Sleep begins to tug at the edges of her consciousness. The candle gutters, shadows lengthening across the room. Melia's thoughts drift, fragments of memories and sensations blending together—Auren's calloused fingers on her skin, Ryker's easy laugh, the weight of expectation in the villagers' eyes...

A floorboard creaks in the hallway.

Melia's eyes snap open, instantly alert. Another creak, softer this time, followed by silence. Bear's ears twitch, but he remains curled beside her, unalarmed.

Heart pounding, Melia slides from beneath the blanket. The wooden floor is cool beneath her bare feet as she pads toward the door. She's wearing only a thin shift borrowed from the innkeeper's wife—hardly proper attire, but all she has for sleeping.

The silence stretches, broken only by her shallow breathing. Is someone there, or was it merely the settling of the old building?

Another creak, right outside her door.

Fear flutters in her chest, but Bear's calm demeanor steadies her. If it were danger, wouldn't he react? The cat watches her with those knowing green eyes.

Melia approaches the door, pressing her palm flat against the rough wood. "Auren?" she whispers, her voice barely audible.

A moment passes. Then, from the other side, a shuffling sound. A hand presses against the door, mirroring her own, separated only by inches of wood.

"Melia." Auren's voice is so soft she almost thinks she imagined it.

Her breath catches. She waits for more—an explanation, a request, anything—but there's only silence, followed by the sound of retreating footsteps.

Melia's hand flies to the latch, ready to fling the door open and call after him. Then she glances down at herself, at the thin fabric that does little to conceal her body, and hesitates.

By the time she decides modesty matters less than this moment slipping away, the hallway has fallen silent again. Auren is gone.

She returns to the bed, sinking onto the edge with a frustrated sigh. Bear bumps his head against her hand, a gesture of comfort.

"Tomorrow," she tells him, climbing back under the blankets. "Tomorrow I'll make him talk to me."

Melia stares at the ceiling, listening to the settling sounds of the tavern, wondering what Auren wanted—and why he walked away.

***

Morning light streams through the frayed curtains as Melia shoves her few belongings into her pack, determination hardening her features. She'd barely slept after Auren's midnight almost-visit, questions churning through her mind until dawn broke.

"This ends now," she mutters, slinging the pack over her shoulder.

Bear stretches lazily on the bed, then hops down to follow as she marches into the hallway. Her borrowed boots thump against the wooden floor, each step fueling her resolve. Whatever game Auren is playing—approaching her door only to retreat, keeping his distance after their intimate night—it stops today.

She reaches the door at the end of the hall where Auren and Kyp are sharing a room. Taking a deep breath, she raises her fist to knock, then hesitates. What if Auren refuses to talk? What if he rejects her outright?

"No," she whispers, steeling herself. "I am Melia of Elyssia. I jumped from the floating city rather than live a lie. I can face one stubborn man."

She raps sharply on the door. No response.

"Auren?" she calls, knocking again, harder this time. "We need to talk."

The silence stretches. Irritation flares within her.

"Auren! Open this door or I'll—"

Her hand pushes against the wood, and the door swings open with a splintering creak. Melia freezes, staring at the damaged door frame. The lock has been broken, wood splintered around the jamb.

"Auren?" she calls, stepping cautiously into the room. "Kyp?"

A muffled groan draws her gaze to the far bed. Kyp lies there, wrists and ankles bound to the bedposts with rough rope. His face is a mess—left eye swollen shut, dried blood caking his nostrils, a nasty gash across his cheekbone.

"Kyp!" Melia rushes to him, horror rising in her throat. The scream erupts from her before she can stop it.

Footsteps thunder down the hallway. Ryker appears in the doorway, hair disheveled from sleep, a knife already drawn in his hand.

"What happened—" He stops, taking in the scene. "Shit."

Melia tugs frantically at the knots binding Kyp's wrists. "Help me," she gasps.

Ryker's knife makes quick work of the ropes. "Garrik," he hisses, face darkening. "He must really want Auren."

"Who?" Melia asks, helping Kyp sit up. "The one who owns the fighting pits?"

Kyp coughs, wincing. "Six of them came in the middle of the night," he says, voice raspy. "Professional. Quick. I couldn't—there were too many—"

"It's not your fault," Melia soothes, though panic claws at her chest. "Where's Auren? Did they hurt him?"

"Knocked him out with something," Kyp says, rubbing his raw wrists. "He fought hard, but they had some kind of drug. Cloth over his face."

Bear pads into the room. He sniffs around, then settles beside a small leather pouch near the overturned washstand. The cat paws at it, looking expectantly at Melia.

Ryker strides over and snatches up the pouch. "Son of a—" He crushes it in his fist. "This is mine. The one I gave to those thugs yesterday." His jaw tightens. "Definitely Garrik's men. They returned the money to make a point."

"But why?" Melia asks, helping Kyp clean a cut on his forehead with a damp cloth. "Why would this Garrik want Auren?"

"Garrik the Gilded doesn't get rich by taking 'no' for an answer," Ryker says grimly. "Your friend Auren caught his attention. Probably for the fighting pits. A man with Auren's skills could make Garrik a fortune."

Kyp shakes his head. "Auren would never fight for entertainment."

"He won't have a choice," Ryker says, pacing the small room. "Not unless we get to him first."

Melia's heart hammers against her ribs. Auren—stubborn, distant, infuriating Auren—dragged away in the night. The memory of his hand pressed against her door makes her chest ache. What had he wanted to say?

"We have to find him," she declares, standing up. "Now."

Ryker studies her, expression unreadable. "What about your pilgrimage?"

"It can wait."

"You sure about that, Princess?" Ryker leans against the wall, arms crossed. "What's more important to you—finishing your reverse pilgrimage or rescuing Auren?"

The question shouldn't even require thought. The pilgrimage is her path to understanding, to uncovering the truths of her family's legacy. But Auren's face fills her mind—the tenderness in his eyes as he touched her, the quiet strength in his arms as he held her, the pain in his voice when he spoke of his failed ascension.

"Auren," she says without hesitation. "We save Auren."

Ryker sighs, running a hand through his tousled hair. "Yeah, figured you'd say that." He straightens, suddenly all business. "Kyp, get cleaned up. You're a mess. Melia, gather only what you absolutely need. Bear—" he eyes the cat, "—do whatever it is you do."

"Where are we going?" Melia asks, already mentally cataloging her few possessions.

"Aurora," Ryker says, checking his knife before sliding it back into its sheath. "That's where Garrik's main operation is. If Auren's destined for the pits, that's where they'll take him."

"But I thought—"

"Yeah, I know. Ironic, right?" Ryker's smile doesn't reach his eyes.
"You'll still get your pilgrimage, Princess. Just with a detour." He looks
between them. "Pack light. We leave within the hour."

Jade I

The safehouse ceiling drips—one, two, three seconds between each drop. The Shadow counts them as her gloved fingers find the molecular seams in her armor. Her helmet disengages with a pneumatic hiss, revealing a face she rarely sees. The air in the Aurora safehouse feels strange against her skin—too warm, too real.

Reconnaissance has made the situation clear: her Luthari armor draws too much attention in this city. The Emperor's orders echo in her mind: *Observe. Assess. Remain undetected.*

She can't fulfill the mission as The Shadow. She must become... something else.

Her fingers hesitate at the throat seal. The armor has been her home, her skin, her identity since the Emperor permitted her to claim her heritage. She hasn't removed it in—

The calculation fails. Memory fragments scatter like disturbed insects, refusing to assemble into coherent time. Years? Decades? The mission parameters don't require this information.

The throat seal disengages. The chest plate loosens. Each segment releasing feels like tearing off a scab—not healing, but exposing something raw underneath. Something that shouldn't be seen.

The armor's neural interfaces disconnect from her spine with tiny electric jolts. Her breath catches. The Shadow stands before the cracked mirror, black segments of Luthari technology peeling away from pale flesh.

"Disengage primary seal," she whispers. The command activates the suit's release protocol.

The remaining seals open simultaneously. The armor slides from her body with a whisper, collapsing around her feet like a shed skin. She steps out of it, naked and shivering despite the room's warmth.

Sam. That was her name once. Before she became The Shadow.

The woman in the mirror is a stranger. Pale skin stretched over lean muscle, unmarked by sun. Too perfect in some places, too damaged in others. Her eyes track downward, cataloging the body as if it belongs to someone else.

Her ribs show faintly beneath skin that hasn't known sunlight in—calculation fails again. Her stomach is flat, marked with a surgical precision that speaks of enhancement rather than birth. A network of faint silver lines radiates from her navel, spreading outward like a web. Imperial modifications.

Lower, a patch of dark hair between her thighs, the only part of her that seems natural, untouched by imperial hands. Her legs are strong, built for combat, for survival. Her feet are calloused despite the armor's protection.

She turns, studying her reflection over her shoulder. Her back bears the most visible evidence of what she's become—a line of metallic nodes embedded along her spine, thirteen in total. The connection points for the armor's neural interface. They gleam dully in the room's low light, neither fully machine nor fully flesh. The augmentations extend to two parallel insertion points at her hips, where stabilizing anchors connect during high-velocity operations.

Sam reaches back, fingers finding the largest node between her shoulder blades. The touch sends a shiver through her body—these implants are designed to receive input from the armor, not human contact. The sensation is alien, uncomfortable.

Her gaze returns to her face. High cheekbones. Lips that look as if they've forgotten how to smile. Dark hair cropped short for helmet compatibility, growing unevenly. Behind her left ear, a small scar where her Imperial comm unit was once surgically embedded.

But it's her eyes that seem most wrong—steel gray with flecks of hazel, watching herself with analytical detachment. They belong to someone who observes but doesn't participate. Someone who exists to fulfill a function, not to live.

"Identify," she whispers to the mirror, the word sticking in her throat.

The mirror offers no answer. Just a naked woman with Imperial modifications and empty eyes.

A memory tries to surface—her mother's voice: *"You are not what they make of you. You are what you choose to be."* The voice fades before she can grasp it fully. The neural dampeners the Emperor's scientists implanted make sure of that.

She reaches for civilian clothes acquired for the mission—plain, unremarkable garments that will help her blend into Aurora's population. The fabric feels wrong against her skin, too soft, too yielding. Without the armor's interface, the world seems muted, distant.

Sam turns away from the mirror, unable to reconcile the stranger's body with the identity she knows. The Shadow isn't flesh; it's purpose. This body is just another tool for the mission.

She glances back at the Luthari armor, collapsed on the floor like a dead thing. For an instant, she sees it as her true self, hollowed out and discarded.

Tomorrow, she will walk Aurora's streets as "Jade"—the cover identity created for this mission. She will gather intelligence on Liora Solari and any other Thread anomalies, assess the threat, report her findings.

But tonight, in this room with its dripping ceiling, she is neither The Shadow nor Jade. She is fragments of Sam, broken and reassembled into something the Emperor could use.

She counts the drops from the ceiling—one, two, three seconds between each—and waits for morning.

***

Morning light cuts between Aurora's towers, painting the alleyway in uneven slashes. Jade steps from the safehouse doorway, blinking against the sudden brightness. The sensation of fabric against skin still feels wrong—her body primed for neural feedback that isn't coming.

She's worn other identities before, but never like this. Never without the armor.

The street bustles with early commerce. A vendor pushes a cart of something steaming past her, the scent sharp and unfamiliar. Two children dart between pedestrians, laughing. A municipal cleaning drone hovers at an intersection, methodically erasing the previous night's graffiti.

Jade catalogs it all, watching faces, movements, patterns. Old habits. Without the armor's threat assessment protocols running constant calculations, she has to rely on her own senses. The world seems both sharper and less defined.

She reaches the same junction where her Shadow-self was blocked yesterday. The guards stand at their posts, alert but disinterested. Their eyes slide past her as she approaches the entrance to the Gilded Bazaar.

No recognition. No suspicion.

She hesitates, expecting to be stopped. When nothing happens, she continues forward, moving with the flow of the morning crowd. Just another face. Unremarkable. Invisible.

The transition is immediate and disorienting. From the orderly streets of Aurora's main district to the chaotic sprawl of the Bazaar. Sound hits her first—a wall of voices haggling, shouting, laughing. Then smell—spices, cooking meat, unwashed bodies, mechanical oil. The sensory overload makes her pulse spike, neural implants firing uselessly against her spine.

Calm. Assess. Adapt.

She repeats the training mantra silently. Without the armor's dampeners, everything feels too close, too real. The crowd presses around her, bodies occasionally brushing against hers. Each contact sends an uncomfortable jolt through her system.

A child bumps into her legs, looks up with wide eyes, then disappears into the throng. Jade touches her hip automatically, checking for weapons that aren't there. The movement draws no attention. No one is watching her. The sensation is unfamiliar—liberating and terrifying at once.

She begins to navigate the labyrinthine paths of the Bazaar, letting her feet follow the routes she mapped yesterday from above. The mental image is precise, but the ground-level reality is messier, more vibrant. Stalls spill into walkways. Makeshift shops occupy spaces that should be empty according to city planning schematics.

"Looking for something special, lady?" A merchant gestures to a display of intricate metal trinkets. *"Best prices in the Bazaar."*

Jade shakes her head, moves on. The interaction is brief, forgettable. Perfect.

She stops at a junction where three narrow alleys converge, orienting herself. According to intelligence, Garrik the Gilded operates from somewhere in the eastern quadrant, but exact coordinates were unavailable.

A group of workers passes, carrying crates marked with unfamiliar symbols. She follows discreetly, listening to their conversation.

"—third shipment this week. The old man's planning something big."

"Keep your voice down. Garrik's got ears everywhere."

"What, you think some random wall's gonna rat us out?"

Jade keeps pace, maintaining distance. The workers turn down a side passage lined with repair shops and disappear through a heavy door emblazoned with a stylized golden "G."

She memorizes the location, continuing past without pausing. Three blocks further, she stops at a food stall, orders something unidentifiable on a stick. The vendor nods, takes her credits without comment. The transaction complete, she moves to a small seating area, choosing a spot with clear sightlines to the street.

The food is spicy, unfamiliar. She chews mechanically, body processing the nutrition while her mind catalogs the Bazaar's rhythms. Patterns emerge: security patrols at twelve-minute intervals, delivery schedules, social hierarchies evident in who defers to whom.

Halfway through her meal, Jade notices a shift in the crowd's energy. Conversations quiet. Bodies move differently, creating space around a group moving through the market's central artery.

Five figures, moving with purpose. Four are clearly security—alert postures, concealed weapons poorly hidden beneath light jackets. The fifth walks at their center—an older man with weathered features and ornate gold-accented clothing. His gaze sweeps the area with casual authority.

Garrik.

Jade lowers her eyes, angling her body away while maintaining peripheral vision. The procession passes her position, heading toward a structure that rises slightly above the surrounding buildings.

She waits until they're out of sight before disposing of her food wrapper and moving in the same direction, maintaining a careful distance. The structure appears to be a central hub of Bazaar operations, with multiple entrances and a steady flow of people in and out.

A public space, then. Not Garrik's private domain.

Jade circles the building, noting security positions and access points. Her steps slow as she reaches the main entrance—an archway decorated with salvaged tech parts arranged in artistic patterns. Above it, illuminated lettering proclaims: "THE EXCHANGE."

She joins the stream of people entering, adopting the slightly hurried walk of someone with business to conduct. Inside, the space opens into a vast hall, the ceiling three stories above. Balconies ring each level, connected by staircases and narrow bridges. The floor space is divided into sections by movable partitions, creating a maze of temporary offices and meeting areas.

The noise is constant but subdued—serious business happening beneath the veneer of casual commerce. Jade moves through the space, listening, watching. Every conversation contains pieces of potential intelligence: shipping routes, power dynamics, political alignments.

On the second level, she spots Garrik again, holding court in a corner section with better furnishings and armed guards at the perimeter. He speaks with animated gestures to a group of attentive listeners, his voice carrying faintly across the space.

"—see this kid. Aether like nothing you've ever seen."

Jade finds a position where she can observe without being obvious, pretending to study a public information terminal. Her neural implants strain against their dampeners, wanting to record and analyze the conversation. The familiar pressure builds at the base of her skull—frustration at operating at reduced capacity.

A server approaches Garrik's group with drinks. The conversation pauses, then resumes with lower voices. Jade catches fragments: "shipment," "fighter," "special merchandise."

A fighter. With Aether magic? Could this be Liora Solari? The coincidence seems too precise to dismiss.

She continues her circuit of the Exchange, gathering context, building a mental map of relationships and territories. Garrik appears to be a central node in the Bazaar's complex network, with connections to every significant operation. His influence extends beyond simple commerce into political maneuvering.

Two hours pass. Jade maintains her cover, moving between observation points, occasionally engaging in minor transactions to blend in. She purchases a small data tablet, a cup of bitter stimulant, exchanges currency at a rate unfavorable to her—all normal activities for a visitor to the Bazaar.

As midday approaches, Garrik's entourage grows restless. He stands, ending his meeting with firm handshakes and practiced smiles. Jade calculates his most likely exit route and positions herself near a vendor selling mechanical parts, feigning interest in the merchandise.

Garrik passes within three meters of her position. At this distance, she can see the fine details of his appearance—the subtle scars on his hands, the way his ornate jacket conceals the outline of a weapon, the calculating intelligence in his eyes as they sweep across the crowd.

Those eyes pause briefly on her.

Jade keeps her expression neutral, her body language unremarkable. She picks up a small gear, examines it with apparent interest.

Garrik moves on.

She exhales slowly, replacing the gear. The moment passes without incident, but a new awareness settles in her mind. She has been seen—not as a threat or an operative, but as a person. The sensation is unfamiliar, uncomfortable.

As Garrik's group exits the Exchange, Jade follows at a safe distance, merging with the Bazaar's foot traffic. They move with purpose toward the eastern quadrant, where intelligence suggests Garrik's primary operations are based.

The route takes them through increasingly narrow passages, the architectural styles shifting from Aurora's sleek modernism to older, repurposed structures. The crowd thins. Security becomes more visible—armed individuals at key intersections, watching passersby with open suspicion.

Jade maintains her cover, adjusting her pace and posture to match local patterns. Still, she feels exposed. Without the armor's active camouflage and threat assessment, she relies entirely on training and instinct.

Ahead, Garrik's group turns into a building with a reinforced entrance. Two guards move to block the doorway after they pass, their stance clearly communicating "private property."

Jade continues past without slowing, noting the building's layout, its connections to surrounding structures, potential access points. Three blocks further, she pauses at a small café with exterior seating, ordering a beverage to justify her presence.

The hot liquid burns her throat, a sensation her armor would have regulated to optimal temperature. She welcomes the discomfort—a reminder of presence, of physical reality.

From her position, she can observe the street leading to Garrik's building. A steady stream of individuals enter and exit—staff, messengers, business associates. Many carry weapons openly here, the pretense of Aurora's orderly society stripped away.

Jade's mission parameters loop through her mind, increasingly inadequate against the complex reality before her. Locate Liora Solari. Assess threat level. Eliminate if necessary.

But as far as she knows, Liora isn't here. It's possible she is the kid with the Aether magic, but the Emperor's intelligence was incomplete. What remains is a tangle of local politics and power structures with unclear connections to imperial concerns.

A server approaches, asking if she wants a refill. Jade declines, pays, and moves on. The afternoon stretches before her, the Bazaar's activities shifting as day workers begin to leave and night operations prepare to commence.

She needs more information before proceeding. Direct infiltration of Garrik's compound would be challenging without her armor's capabilities. Observation and intelligence gathering remain the optimal approach.

As she navigates back toward the central Bazaar, Jade catches fragments of conversation:

"—fighting pits open at sundown—"

"—new blood tonight—"

"—Garrik's latest acquisition—"

The pattern clarifies. If Liora has been taken for the fighting pits, her debut would likely be tonight—a new attraction to draw crowds and gambling revenue.

Jade adjusts her trajectory, seeking the location of these pits. She stops a passing vendor, asks directions with practiced casualness. The woman points toward the northwest quadrant, mentioning increased security since "the incident" last month.

Following the directions, Jade enters a section of the Bazaar dedicated to entertainment—gambling halls, pleasure houses, substances of varying legality. The architecture grows more theatrical, with illuminated signs and holographic advertisements competing for attention.

She locates the fighting pits—a sprawling complex with multiple arenas and viewing galleries, currently closed but with workers preparing for evening operations. Security is visible but not excessive; this is a public venue, after all.

Jade circles the perimeter, noting access points and security patterns. If Liora is indeed scheduled to fight tonight, this would be the most direct opportunity to confirm his presence and assess the situation.

But uncertainty lingers. What is her actual mission now? The Emperor's directives make no mention of fighting pits. Is this new fighter actually her target? Are they even connected to Liora Solari? Or is it merely local criminal activity, irrelevant to imperial concerns?

For the first time in years, Jade finds herself without clear parameters. The Shadow's directives were always precise, her actions predetermined by mission protocols. But here, stripped of armor and identity, she faces choices.

She returns to the central Bazaar as afternoon fades toward evening. The crowds have changed character—fewer families, more individuals seeking night entertainment. Lights activate automatically in the covered sections, casting everything in artificial twilight.

Jade feels the absence of her armor more acutely now—the lack of enhanced vision, of constant sensor data, of the reassuring weight encasing her body. She is exposed. Vulnerable.

And yet, unseen in a way The Shadow never could be. Just another face in the crowd. No one watches her. No one tracks her movements.

She stops at a public terminal, searches for information on tonight's fighting matches. The advertisements are lurid, promising violence and spectacle. No specific fighters are named, but a "special debut" is highlighted for the main event.

As she steps away from the terminal, a group of off-duty security personnel pass, talking loudly about work assignments.

"—doubled the guards for tonight's matches—"

"—Garrik doesn't want any surprises with the new fighter—"

"—resisting the conditioning, from what I heard—"

Jade maintains her pace, revealing no interest in their conversation. But internally, her focus sharpens. Conditioning. A practice used on reluctant combatants to ensure compliance in the ring.

If Liora is being prepared for tonight's fight, her situation is increasingly precarious.

She finds a quiet corner to consider her options. The logical approach would be continued observation—attend the fights, confirm Solari's presence, gather more intelligence before acting. The Shadow would follow protocol, prioritize the primary mission.

But Jade...

She looks down at her hands—bare, unmarked by armor, feeling the evening air against her skin. For a brief, disorienting moment, she wonders what Sam would do. Not The Shadow. Not Jade. But the person beneath both identities.

The thought dissolves as quickly as it forms, neural dampeners activating to suppress the dangerous line of inquiry. She is Jade now, with a mission to complete. Personal concerns are irrelevant.

Night begins to fall over Aurora. The Bazaar transforms, its energy shifting from commerce to entertainment. Jade moves with the flow, another anonymous figure seeking diversion in the gathering darkness.

Somewhere in this labyrinth, Garrik prepares his newest acquisition for the fighting pits. Somewhere, imperial interests remain unprotected while she diverts attention to local matters.

Jade continues forward, uncertain of her mission or herself, but moving with purpose nonetheless. The crowds part around her, unaware of the struggle beneath her carefully neutral expression.

She is seen, but not known. Present, but not perceived. A contradiction walking through the gathering darkness of the Gilded Bazaar.

Melia VI

Melia stumbles as someone shoves past her shoulder, the fourth person to do so since they entered the Gilded Bazaar five minutes ago. The crowd presses in from all sides—a churning sea of bodies, voices, and competing scents that overwhelm her senses. Nothing in her sheltered palace upbringing prepared her for this assault on her senses.

"Keep close," Ryker calls over his shoulder, his voice barely audible above the din. "Easy to get swept away here."

Bear weaves between her ankles, surprisingly nimble for a creature in such chaos. The cat seems unfazed by the commotion, almost as if he's visited before.

"This place is..." Melia searches for the right word as her gaze darts from stall to stall. Ancient artifacts sit alongside clearly fabricated knockoffs. A woman with metal implants curving from her temples haggles fiercely with a vendor over what appears to be a glowing jar of liquid. "Overwhelming."

"It's the heartbeat of Aurora," Ryker says, his face lighting up. "Anything worth having or knowing passes through the Bazaar eventually."

He sidesteps a group of children racing through the crowd, nodding to a heavily tattooed man who calls out his name. The man's face transforms from suspicion to recognition in an instant.

"Voss! Still breathing, I see!"

"For now, Daku!" Ryker replies with a wink, not breaking stride.

Kyp leans closer to Melia. "That's the third person who's greeted him by name."

"I've noticed," Melia murmurs, watching as Ryker exchanges brief hand gestures with a hooded figure at a relic stall.

The Bazaar itself seems alive—a patchwork organism built from scraps of technologies she doesn't recognize. Lights flicker and pulse overhead, some clearly ancient, others jury-rigged from parts never meant to illuminate. The walls themselves appear to be constructed from the hulls of massive vehicles or perhaps buildings that once served other purposes.

"How does anyone find anything specific here?" Melia asks, nearly losing her footing on a slick patch of ground.

Ryker's hand catches her elbow, steadying her. "That's the beauty of it. You don't find things in the Bazaar—they find you, if you know how to look."

His hand lingers on her arm a moment longer than necessary, his touch light but assured. There's a confidence in his movements that reminds Melia of the nobility in Elyssia, but rougher, unpolished. Where they wore their privilege like a birthright, Ryker wears his ease like armor earned through experience.

They pass through a section where food vendors compete for attention, the aromas of spices and cooking meat momentarily overtaking the underlying scent of too many bodies in too little space. Melia's stomach rumbles, reminding her they haven't eaten since morning.

"We'll get something later," Ryker promises, noticing her reaction. "Best not to stop moving until we have a plan."

A woman with elaborate mechanical augmentations extending from her left eye calls out to Ryker.

"Voss! Thought you were dead!"

"Reports greatly exaggerated, Linia!" He flashes that grin that transforms his entire face, the one that made even Auren pause mid-sentence during their first meeting.

"He seems to know everyone," Melia observes.

"And everyone seems to expect him to be dead," Kyp adds with a raised eyebrow.

Ryker guides them through a narrow passage between two towering stalls, emerging into a slightly less crowded section where the goods displayed are primarily clothing and personal items.

"This is where we split up," Ryker announces, turning to Kyp. "Take the cat and head to the fighting district. The main pits are in the northwest quadrant. Don't try to get inside—just listen, ask careful questions. See if anyone's talking about a new fighter or unusual matches tonight."

Kyp looks uncertain. "You want me to take the cat?"

"Bear likes you," Ryker says with a shrug. "And he's good at finding things."

The cat stares up at Kyp with those unnerving green eyes, then looks to Melia as if seeking permission.

"Go with Kyp," she tells Bear, hoping the animal somehow understands. "Help find Auren."

To her surprise, Bear nudges against Kyp's ankle once, then sits patiently beside him.

"We'll meet at the Silver Chalice in two hours," Ryker continues. "It's a tavern near the main entrance to the pits. Anyone can point you there."

"And what will you two be doing?" Kyp asks, a hint of protective concern in his voice.

Ryker turns to Melia, his eyes traveling from her mud-stained boots to her tangled hair. "Getting her a new outfit."

"What's wrong with what I'm wearing?" Melia looks down at herself. The simple traveling clothes she'd been given in Willow Haven are worn and dirty from the journey, but still functional.

"Everything," Ryker says bluntly. "You might as well have 'outsider' branded on your forehead. If we're going to move through the Bazaar unnoticed, you need to blend in."

Kyp hesitates. "Should I stay with Melia?"

"I'll be fine," Melia assures him, though uncertainty gnaws at her. "Finding information about Auren is more important."

After another moment of reluctance, Kyp nods. "Two hours at the Silver Chalice. Be careful."

"Always am," Ryker replies with a confidence that seems entirely unearned given their current situation.

Bear trots after Kyp as they disappear into the crowd, leaving Melia alone with Ryker. She feels suddenly vulnerable without the cat's reassuring presence.

"This way, Princess." Ryker gestures toward a stall draped in fabrics of various colors and textures.

"Don't call me that," Melia says automatically, her voice sharper than intended. "Not here. Not anywhere."

Something flickers across Ryker's face—surprise, perhaps, or respect. "Fair enough. This way, Melia."

He leads her to a stall where a woman with silver hair and impossibly young skin arranges garments on display hooks. The woman looks up as they approach, her expression transforming into a brilliant smile.

"Ryker Voss!" she exclaims, coming around the counter to embrace him. "I heard you were dead!"

"Why does everyone keep saying that?" Melia mutters.

Ryker laughs, returning the woman's embrace with genuine warmth. "Zira, lovely as ever. I need your help with my friend here."

Zira's calculating eyes turn to Melia, assessing her with the precision of a jeweler examining a gem. "First time in Aurora?"

"Is it that obvious?" Melia asks.

"Everything about you screams it," Zira confirms. "The way you stand, the way you look at things, those awful clothes." She circles Melia slowly. "But there's good material to work with. What's the occasion, Ryker? Disguise? Infiltration? Seduction?"

"Practical but presentable," Ryker replies. "She needs to blend in enough to move through the Bazaar without drawing attention, but nothing too flashy."

"Boring," Zira sighs, "but doable." She gestures for Melia to follow her behind a curtained area at the back of the stall. "Come, let's see what we're working with."

***

Zira leads the way through the curtain, revealing a small dressing area with a privacy screen and a tall mirror leaning against one wall. Silk scarves hang from the ceiling, creating a kaleidoscope of colors that shift with the breeze.

"Wait here," she instructs, disappearing through another curtain.

Melia catches her reflection in the mirror—travel-worn, hair tangled, clothes dusty from the road. She barely recognizes herself. The princess who stood before her parents' caskets seems like a stranger now.

"She's quite the character," Ryker says, leaning against a wooden post. "But she knows her craft."

"Should you be back here?" Melia asks, surprised he's followed them into what she assumed was a women's changing area.

He shrugs. "Zira doesn't mind. We go way back."

Before Melia can respond, Zira returns carrying a neatly folded stack of clothing.

"These should do," she says, placing them on a small table. "Simple enough not to draw attention, quality enough not to mark you as poor. The perfect mediocrity."

She unfolds the items one by one: dark brown leather pants, a loose cream-colored tunic with intricate lacework at the collar, and a vest in deep burgundy with subtle embroidery along the edges.

"Try these," Zira instructs, handing the stack to Melia. "I'll find some boots to match."

As Zira turns to leave, Ryker calls after her, "And maybe something for her hair?"

"Already thinking of it," Zira replies without looking back, slipping through the curtain.

Melia stands awkwardly, clothes in hand, waiting for Ryker to follow Zira out.

He doesn't move.

"I need to change," she says pointedly.

"Don't worry about me," he responds with that infuriating half-smile. "Even this boring outfit can't dim your beauty."

Heat rises to her cheeks. "Turn around at least."

Ryker makes a show of sighing before turning to face the wall. "As you wish."

Melia hesitates, then sets the new clothes on a nearby stool. She begins unlacing her worn tunic, keeping a watchful eye on Ryker's back. The fabric slides from her shoulders, leaving her in just her undergarments.

Melia hesitates, her fingers lingering on the thin straps of her undergarments. The air in the dressing area feels different from the pristine chambers of Elyssia—warmer, heavier with the scent of spices and perfumes. For a moment, she remembers Auren's gentle touch at the chapel, how his eyes had taken her in as something precious rather than an ornament.

"You're taking your time back there," Ryker says, his voice carrying a note of amusement.

"Just... considering the clothes," she replies, slipping off her undergarments with trembling fingers.

Melia stands naked, vulnerable in a way that feels both terrifying and liberating. In Elyssia, her body was never truly her own—it was a vessel for royal duty, carefully maintained for political alliance. Now, her skin bears the marks of her journey: small bruises from the fall, scratches from forest branches, a subtle tan forming where the sun has kissed her shoulders.

She catches her reflection in the mirror—not a princess, not the Fallen One, just a woman. The realization hits her with unexpected force. This body survived the fall. This body chose intimacy with Auren. This body belongs to no one but herself.

"Are the clothes not to your liking?" Ryker asks, shifting his weight. "I can tell Zira—"

"They're fine," Melia interrupts, reaching for the cream-colored tunic. "I'm just not used to dressing myself without handmaidens."

A slight movement catches her attention—Ryker's head has tilted just enough to see her reflection in a small hanging mirror.

Their eyes meet in the reflection. He doesn't look away.

She should cover herself. She should demand he leave. Instead, something unexpected happens—a flutter of excitement blooms low in her belly. The way his eyes travel over her reflection stirs something primal she's never experienced before Auren.

But this is different. With Auren, there was connection, vulnerability, trust. This is pure, raw desire—being wanted simply for her physical form.

Melia freezes, caught between shock and a strange, unfamiliar thrill. The realization that Ryker has been watching her naked body through the reflection should outrage her, but instead, it awakens something unexpected—a darkly seductive power she's never wielded before.

He turns fully now, abandoning any pretense of propriety. His eyes travel a deliberate path—lingering first on her face, then trailing down to the gentle curve of her neck, the slope of her shoulders, the swell of her breasts. His gaze is appreciative, hungry, completely different from the reverent looks she received in Elyssia or even the tender admiration in Auren's eyes. This is something raw, primal—a man looking at a woman as if she were a feast after starvation.

"You're exquisite," he says, voice low and rough, the words hanging in the air between them like smoke.

Heat blooms across her skin, following the path of his gaze like a physical touch, igniting nerve endings she didn't know existed. When his eyes drift to the curve of her waist, the flare of her hips, she feels a strange coiling tension building within her—a tightening deep in her core that both frightens and excites her. Lower still his gaze travels, to the place between her thighs, and the tension tightens further, drawing a small, involuntary intake of breath from her lips.

In Elyssia, her body had been a sacred vessel, meant for ritual and duty. With Auren, it had been a source of connection and comfort. But here, under Ryker's unflinching appraisal, her body becomes something else entirely—a source of power, of desire, of dangerous possibilities that make her heart race and her mouth go dry.

She should cover herself. She should scream for Zira. Instead, Melia reaches for the leather pants, turning slightly as she steps into them. She bends deliberately as she pulls them up, aware of the way his breath catches, the subtle hitch in his throat that betrays his composure. The knowledge that she affects him so strongly sends another wave of heat through her body, a liquid warmth that pools low in her abdomen and makes her fingers tremble as they work the fastenings.

The leather is cool against her heated skin, a stark contrast to the burning awareness that floods her senses. She takes her time, letting the material slide over her calves, her thighs, savoring the way Ryker's eyes follow every movement with undisguised hunger. In Elyssia, she had been taught that a princess's body was a sacred temple, to be glimpsed only in reverence. Now, she finds a heady power in being desired so openly, so honestly—without pretense of divinity or duty.

As she straightens, adjusting the waistband that sits snug against her hips, she catches her reflection in a small shard of mirror hanging on the wall. The woman staring back at her is flushed, eyes bright with a dangerous curiosity, looking nothing like the composed princess who once floated through Elyssia's hallowed halls. This new Melia is earthbound, flesh and blood, alive with sensations that no one in her former life had ever dared to mention.

"Need help with the tunic?" Ryker asks, his voice strained.

Melia nods, not trusting her voice. He approaches slowly, like someone approaching a wild animal. The cream-colored fabric slides over her head, his fingers brushing against her bare skin as he helps her into it. When his hands move to the lacing at her chest, his knuckles graze the underside of her breasts. Not accidental—deliberate.

Her breath hitches. This is nothing like the clinical dressing by her handmaidens or the tender exploration with Auren. This is dangerous, forbidden.

"These lacings are intricate," Ryker murmurs, standing close enough that she feels his breath on her neck. His fingers work slowly, each adjustment bringing another brush against her sensitive skin.

Melia looks up, meeting his eyes. Something electric passes between them, and suddenly his mouth is on hers. His kiss is nothing like Auren's—where Auren was gentle, tentative, Ryker is confident, demanding. His hands slide up to cup her breasts through the thin fabric, thumbs circling with practiced precision that makes her gasp against his mouth. The sensation sends shivers cascading through her body, igniting nerve endings she never knew existed. The cream-colored tunic offers little barrier between his calloused fingers and her sensitive skin, and each deliberate movement of his thumbs draws another involuntary sound from her throat. Heat blooms across her chest and neck, spreading like wildfire through her veins, making her dizzy with unfamiliar pleasure that both frightens and exhilarates her—so different from the carefully controlled emotions permitted in Elyssia's rarefied air.

He walks her backward until she feels the wall behind her, his body pressing against hers. One of his hands slides to her waist, then lower, pulling her hips against his. The sensation is overwhelming—heat and pressure and need building to something urgent and primal.

For a moment, she loses herself in it—this raw, physical connection with someone who wants her body without the complications of emotion. No expectations of princess or fallen one. Just desire, simple and consuming. The sensation is intoxicating, liberating in ways she never experienced in Elyssia's rigid confines.

Here against this wall, with Ryker's hungry mouth claiming hers, she isn't the divine princess meant to fulfill a sacred destiny or the disgraced fallen one seeking redemption. She's just a woman with blood rushing hot beneath her skin, with nerves singing and muscles tensing with anticipation. The weight of her identity—both the one thrust upon her by birth and the one she's struggling to forge—momentarily lifts from her shoulders, replaced by something primal and uncomplicated. His fingers trace patterns of fire across her skin, each touch promising escape from the burden of choice and consequence that has defined her journey since her fall.

But then Auren's face flashes in her mind—his gentle hands, his vulnerable eyes after they'd made love in the chapel. The memory crashes through her like cold water.

Melia pulls away abruptly, placing her hands against Ryker's chest.

"I can't," she says, breathless. "This isn't—I can't."

Confusion flickers across his face, then understanding. He steps back, giving her space, though his eyes still burn with undiminished desire.

"It's him, isn't it?" Ryker asks quietly. "The guide."

Melia doesn't answer. Instead, she reaches for the lacing of her tunic, finishing them herself with trembling fingers. Her body still thrums with conflicted desire, but her mind is clearing.

"We need to get to the fighting pits," she says, voice steadier than she feels. "We need to find Auren."

She grabs the burgundy vest, pulling it on with quick, efficient movements. Her hands are still shaking, but the familiar act of dressing herself—something she's only recently learned—grounds her.

Ryker watches her, something unreadable in his expression. "Of course," he says finally. "That's why we're here."

Zira returns with a pair of soft leather boots and a strip of fabric for Melia's hair. If she notices the tension in the room, she says nothing.

As Melia secures her hair with the fabric, tying it back in a simple style, shame washes over her. Not for being seen naked—that feels strangely insignificant now—but for responding to Ryker when Auren is somewhere in this city, possibly hurt, possibly fighting for his life.

"I'm ready," she announces, straightening her shoulders.

Ryker nods, that infuriating half-smile returning to his face as if nothing happened. "Then let's go find your guide."

They exit the shop into the bustling bazaar. Melia keeps her eyes forward, focusing on their mission, but she can't escape the weight of what just happened. Her body still carries the ghost of Ryker's touch, an unwelcome reminder of her momentary weakness.

As they weave through the crowd toward the fighting pits, Melia's thoughts turn to Auren. If they find him—when they find him—will he somehow know? Will he see the guilt written across her face? And why does she feel this guilt at all, when there's been no promise between them, no words to define what they shared?

These questions swirl in her mind as they press deeper into the heart of the Gilded Bazaar, the sounds of cheering crowds growing louder with each step.

Jade II

The roar hits Jade before she even enters—a wall of sound that rattles against her eardrums. Without her suit's auditory dampeners, the noise assaults her senses with raw, undiluted intensity. Different. Real. Dangerous.

She slips through the entrance, a shadow among shadows, observing the cramped corridors leading to the arena. Bodies press against her—sweaty, excited, anxious—their excitement for blood leaving a chemical signature in the air that her enhanced senses detect automatically. Her body categorizes these threats instinctively: two armed guards at the entrance, three drunken merchants to her left, a pickpocket working the crowd to her right.

The fighting pit itself opens before her like a wound—circular, thirty meters in diameter, surrounded by rising tiers of crude seating filled with shouting spectators. The architecture is pragmatic: nothing wasted on aesthetics, only function. Blood stains darken the packed dirt floor, some fresh, some ancient. In the center, two men circle each other with crude weapons.

Jade's gaze methodically scans the room until she locates him—Garrik the Gilded, presiding from an elevated platform draped in fabrics that mimic Imperial colors without quite matching them. A deliberate choice. Message received: powerful enough to reference the Empire, smart enough not to copy it exactly.

She selects her position carefully—third tier, northeast quadrant, unobstructed view of both the fighting pit and Garrik's box. Close enough to observe details, far enough to avoid direct attention. As she settles onto the hard bench, her hand instinctively reaches for the phantom weight of her sidearm, finding emptiness instead.

Exposed. Vulnerable. Interesting.

Below, the current fight progresses with all the refinement of animals tearing at each other. One fighter—younger, leaner—dodges a clumsy attack from his opponent, a mountain of a man with a crude mace. The crowd's response fluctuates with each near miss, each successful blow. Jade analyzes their movements clinically, noting inefficiencies, telegraphed attacks, wasted energy.

"They call him the Butcher," a man beside her says, misinterpreting her focused observation as interest. "Hasn't lost in sixteen fights."

Jade doesn't respond, but her silence doesn't deter him.

"Put my last credits on the young one though. Butcher's getting slow."

She shifts slightly away, returning her attention to Garrik's box. Four guards—two visible, two in shadows. A woman draped across his lap, her eyes constantly surveying the crowd. Not decoration—security. Interesting. A young man stands behind Garrik's chair, whispering periodically into his ear. Information broker or advisor. Three separate visitors approach the box during the match, each granted exactly forty-seven seconds of conversation before being dismissed.

Systematic. Organized. Precise.

The crowd suddenly erupts as the younger fighter lands a lucky blow, catching the Butcher off balance. The larger man stumbles, creating an opening. The young fighter hesitates—a fraction of a second, barely perceptible to untrained eyes, but Jade sees it clearly. Hesitation in the pit equals death.

The Butcher recovers, swinging his mace in a vicious arc that connects with the younger man's shoulder. Bone shatters. The crowd howls. The young fighter drops to his knees, weapon falling from useless fingers.

"Finish!" someone screams, and others take up the chant.

The Butcher circles his prey, playing to the audience, drawing out the inevitable. Jade watches dispassionately as he finally brings the mace down on the young man's skull. The sound—wet, final—is lost in the crowd's approving roar.

Garrik signals, and attendants drag the corpse away, leaving a dark smear across the dirt. Fifty-three seconds later, two new fighters enter.

The man beside Jade curses, throwing his betting slip to the ground. "Stupid boy," he mutters. "Should've finished it when he had the chance."

"Yes," Jade agrees, her first spoken word since entering. "Hesitation is lethal."

Her attention returns to the new combatants—a woman with paired knives facing a man with a short spear. Their movements reveal formal training, unlike the previous match. The woman's stance suggests Serathian blade techniques, modified for the confined space. The man holds his spear with the confidence of a veteran.

This fight progresses differently—calculated, tactical. The crowd grows restless, wanting blood not skill. In Garrik's box, the information broker leans down again, speaking urgently. Garrik nods, makes a subtle gesture. One of the hidden guards slips away.

The spear-wielder feints, then attacks with unexpected speed. The woman parries, but her foot slides on the blood-slick ground. She recovers admirably, but not before the spear opens a shallow cut along her ribs. The crowd cheers at first blood.

Jade notices a new tension in the arena—handlers appearing at the entrances, whispered conversations spreading through the audience. Something is coming. The main event, perhaps. She watches Garrik straighten in his seat, his attention sharpening.

The current fight ends with unexpected brutality—the woman manages to get inside the spear-wielder's guard, her knives finding his throat with practiced precision. He collapses, gasping his last breaths while the crowd roars approval. The woman raises her bloody blades, acknowledging their approval without emotion.

Garrik stands, raising his hands for silence. The crowd gradually quiets.

"Friends," his voice carries authority without shouting, "tonight's champion match approaches. A special contestant—one with gifts not seen in our humble arena before."

Jade leans forward slightly, cataloging every word.

"A man who channels the Aether itself," Garrik continues, "brought here for your entertainment and edification."

The crowd murmurs with excitement and disbelief. Aether manipulation—uncommon, powerful, valuable. Imperial intelligence flags all such individuals.

"Should he survive three champions," Garrik announces, "he earns his freedom. Should he fail..." He lets the implication hang in the air.

As handlers clear the arena and prepare for the main event, Jade recalculates.

Aether magic. The designation surfaces from Jade's memory, triggering a cascade of fragmentary information. The Empire's databases classified it as a subset of Thread manipulation—dangerous but manageable, tracked but not prioritized. Not her primary objective.

Yet something feels wrong about this classification. A memory flickers—her mother's voice, speaking of the Thread: *"They call it magic because they fear it. They call it heresy because they cannot control it."*

The memory vanishes as quickly as it appeared, neural dampeners doing their work. Focus returns.

If this new fighter possesses Aether abilities, it significantly increases the probability of connection to her mission parameters. The Emperor specifically mentioned Dreamer abilities—rare manifestations of Aether manipulation might be connected to Liora's breaking of the Veil.

Her mission clarifies: observe, evaluate, determine connection to primary objective. Then decide whether to maintain cover or intervene.

***

10 Years Ago

The training room spins as Samara hits the mat hard. Pain blooms across her back. Above her, Agent Solomon looms, practice staff extended, waiting for her to rise.

"Again," he says.

Samara's muscles scream as she pulls herself up. Three hours of combat drills have pushed her past exhaustion into something else—a floating, detached state where her body seems to operate on its own.

She raises her staff and centers her stance.

Solomon attacks without warning, a flurry of strikes that Samara barely deflects. His movements blur at the edges of her vision. The room feels too bright, too loud. Her head pounds with each heartbeat.

"Focus, child," comes the Emperor's voice from the observation platform. "Remember what I taught you."

His presence steadies her. The Emperor has watched every training session this week, his golden robes catching the light, his voice gentle but firm. Sometimes, when Samara wakes confused in the medical bay, not remembering her name or why she's there, the Emperor sits beside her bed and tells her stories until she falls asleep again.

Solomon's staff whistles toward her face. Samara ducks, pivots, and strikes at his exposed ribs. He blocks, but barely. She presses forward, each movement calculated, precise. Something clicks in her mind—a pattern recognition that wasn't there before. She sees Solomon's attack sequence, anticipates the feint before he makes it.

When the opening appears, Samara strikes without hesitation. Her staff connects with Solomon's knee. As he staggers, she sweeps his other leg and brings him down hard.

The staff presses against his throat before he can recover.

"I yield," Solomon gasps.

Samara blinks, surprised by her own victory. She steps back, lowering the weapon.

The Emperor applauds, the sound echoing in the cavernous training room. "Excellent, my dear. Most excellent."

Solomon rises, bowing to the Emperor before limping toward the exit. He doesn't look at Samara.

"You've progressed remarkably," the Emperor says, descending from the platform with careful steps. His hovering throne remains be-

hind, its life-support systems humming softly. "The neural enhancements are integrating perfectly."

Samara touches the back of her neck, feeling the slight ridge of an
implant beneath her skin. "Thank you, Your Majesty."

"You've earned a reward, I think." The Emperor's papery hand rests
briefly on her shoulder. "Come with me."

Samara follows him through the labyrinthine corridors of the Imperial complex. Guards bow as they pass, their eyes averted from the
Emperor's face. Samara notices how they look at her—with a mixture
of fear and curiosity. She doesn't remember arriving here, doesn't
remember anything before waking in the medical bay with tubes in
her arms and the Emperor watching over her.

"How long have I been here?" she asks suddenly.

The Emperor glances back. "Nearly four years now. The procedures
took time."

"Procedures?"

"To heal you, child. You were gravely injured when we found you."

"Found me where?"

He doesn't answer immediately. They reach a secure door that
opens to his palm print. "Your past is a burden you needn't carry. Focus
on what you're becoming, not what you were."

The room beyond is stark—white walls, bright lights, empty except
for a single pedestal in the center. On it rests a familiar black case.

Samara stops at the threshold. Something tugs at her memory—a
woman's voice, urgent instructions, warning bells.

"What is this?" she asks, but already knows the answer.

"Your birthright," the Emperor says. "Go on."

Samara approaches the case cautiously. Her fingers trace the
smooth surface, finding the hidden catch without conscious thought.
The case opens silently.

Inside lies a bodysuit of material unlike anything she's seen in the Imperial complex. Black as deep space, with faint iridescent patterns that shift when she moves her head. She touches it hesitantly.

"This is... mine?"

"It belongs to your people, the Luthari," the Emperor says. "A remarkable civilization, technologically advanced, philosophically misguided. Their artifacts remain unmatched in the known systems."

"My people?" The word feels strange in Samara's mouth. "I thought—"

"That you were alone?" The Emperor's voice softens. "No, child. You carry their legacy. Their blood flows in your veins, their potential in your mind. That's why you're special."

Samara lifts the suit from the case. It weighs almost nothing, yet somehow feels substantial. Something inside her responds to it—a recognition beyond memory.

"The Luthari believed in personal sovereignty above all else," the Emperor continues. "A noble ideal, but ultimately impractical in a complex galactic society. This armor represents their philosophy—it protects not just the body, but the self. The identity."

Samara examines the suit more closely. Fine filaments run through the material, glinting in the light.

"What happened to them? To the Luthari?"

The Emperor sighs. "Extinction, tragically. Civil conflicts, resource depletion. Only artifacts remain—and you, of course. The last of your kind."

A sudden image flashes in Samara's mind—a woman with her eyes, speaking urgently, placing something in her hands. *Remember who you are.*

The memory vanishes as quickly as it appeared.

"This armor will never fail you," the Emperor says, watching her closely. "It responds to Luthari DNA, bonding with the wearer. It will become part of you, enhancing your natural abilities. With it, you'll serve the Empire as few others could."

Samara runs her fingers over the material again. "What if I don't want to serve?"

A moment of silence follows her question.

"My dear," the Emperor says finally, his voice gentle but firm, "without the Empire, without me, you would have perished with the rest of your kind. We've invested considerable resources in your recovery and enhancement. You have a purpose now, a chance to matter. Isn't that what anyone wants?"

Samara nods slowly, the momentary doubt receding. He's right, of course. The Emperor saved her. Gave her purpose. The fleeting memories, the strange doubts—side effects of the neural enhancements, nothing more.

"I'm ready," she says, holding the suit against her chest.

The Emperor smiles. "Yes, my child. I believe you are."

***

The Present

The spectators settle into an anticipatory hush as arena workers rake smooth the bloodied sand. Jade shifts her weight, finding a better vantage point while maintaining distance from the pressing crowd. The last two fights were predictable—textbook violence with minimal tactical variation. Her analysis is complete; the fighting pit operates as expected, brutal efficiency masked as entertainment.

"Ladies and gentlemen," Garrik's voice cuts through the murmurs, "the moment you've been waiting for."

His theatrical pause draws the crowd forward, bodies leaning in collective anticipation. Jade remains still, conserving energy, though her senses heighten further.

"Tonight's special challenge—three of our finest champions against one extraordinary opponent."

The eastern entrance opens first. Three figures emerge sequentially, each pausing to absorb the crowd's reaction before taking position around the arena's perimeter.

"First champion: Dorn the Mountain!"

A hulking figure strides forward, encased in patchwork armor—salvaged military-grade plating mixed with cruder materials. His massive double-headed axe drags a shallow furrow in the sand. Analysis: heavy striker, limited mobility, high endurance. Approach: maintain distance, target joint weaknesses between armor sections.

"Second champion: Vex the Skinless!"

The crowd's reaction intensifies as a muscled fighter enters, body bare except for strategic leather straps holding paired hatchets. Ritual scarification covers his torso in geometric patterns. Analysis: high mobility, dual-weapon specialist, likely stimulant-enhanced based on pupil dilation. Approach: control distance, force overextension.

"Third champion: Lyssia the Serpent!"

A woman glides forward, lithe and precise in her movements. Her leather bodysuit allows maximum flexibility while a barbed whip coils at her side. Analysis: reach advantage, likely poisoned barbs, prioritizes disabling strikes over killing blows. Approach: close distance immediately, neutralize weapon advantage.

The champions position themselves equidistant around the arena's circumference. A calculated arrangement—they've fought together before. Coordinated attacks likely.

Garrik raises his hands again, the jewels on his fingers catching torchlight. "And now, our challenger—a man who channels powers beyond ordinary comprehension. Witness...Auren the Failed Pilgrim!"

The western entrance splits open with a groaning of hinges. A solitary figure emerges, wrists bound before him with crude, fraying rope. He carries no weapon, wears no protective gear. His upper body remains exposed to the harsh arena lights, revealing a lean, sinewy torso mapped with a constellation of scars—some surgical in their precision, others jagged and brutal, each one telling its own story of survival. His physique speaks of hard-earned strength rather than brute power, muscles defined through necessity rather than vanity. Dark, unkempt hair cascades across his downturned face as the guards roughly propel him forward into the arena, one shoving him between the shoulder blades before cutting through his restraints with a quick, careless slash.

Something unexpected ripples through Jade's neural interface. A discordant vibration pulses through her implants—similar to when communications systems encounter quantum interference. The sensation is both foreign and distantly familiar. Her optical enhancers stutter and blur, losing their calibration for 2.7 seconds before internal systems compensate and restore clarity. The malfunction registers in her diagnostic queue, flagged as anomalous.

Auren remains perfectly still at the arena's center, head bowed as if in meditation or resignation. The crowd's initial excitement curdles into derision. They hurl insults alongside scattered debris, their disappointment palpable at the unremarkable specimen before them. They had expected a monster, a titan—not this weathered, ordinary-looking man.

"Do not let your eyes deceive you!" Garrik's voice rises above the crowd's discontent, his tone rich with theatrical knowledge. "This man walked the sacred pilgrimage path toward the divine Elyssia—and when the Ascended City rejected him, something extraordinary awakened within! He channels powers unseen for generations among our people. Today, you will witness the Aether itself made flesh and blood before your very eyes!"

Guards retreat, leaving Auren alone in the center. He slowly raises his head, scanning the arena. His expression reveals nothing—neither fear nor anticipation.

Another wave of interference ripples through Jade's systems. Her temporal lobe implant activates unexpectedly, flooding her consciousness with fragmented memory:

—*Mother's hands guiding hers over ancient controls*—

"*Thread manipulation isn't magic, Sam. It's our birthright.*"

The memory dissolves as neural dampeners engage, but the disruption is concerning. Her systems have never reacted this way to an external stimulus.

The champions begin circling, Garrik's signal setting them in motion. Auren remains still, eyes closed now, shoulders rising with deep inhalations. The crowd grows restless.

"Begin!" Garrik commands.

Vex attacks first, hatchets whirling as he charges. Auren doesn't move, doesn't open his eyes. The crowd holds its breath—

At the last possible moment, Auren sidesteps with unexpected fluidity. Vex's momentum carries him past, hatchets cutting only air. Auren's eyes open, tracking his opponents with calm precision.

The interference in Jade's systems intensifies. Diagnostic programs activate automatically, searching for the source. Her vision splinters momentarily, overlaying Auren's form with translucent patterns—light streams connecting to the environment in ways her perceptual systems cannot properly interpret.

Lyssia's whip cracks forward, its barbed end seeking Auren's flesh. He pivots, the whip grazing his shoulder. A thin line of blood appears, but his expression doesn't change. Dorn advances now, axe raised high.

The three champions coordinate their approach, attempting to trap Auren between them. Basic pincer maneuver, effective against single opponents. Auren backs toward the arena wall, apparently cornered.

Then—change.

Auren's posture shifts. His hands rise, palms open. The air around him seems to shimmer, like heat rising from sun-baked stone. Jade's implants begin reporting contradictory data. Temperature unchanged. Atmospheric composition normal. Yet her optical sensors register distortion patterns consistent with energy displacement.

"Watch closely," Garrik announces, "as our pilgrim reveals his gift!"

Dorn attacks, axe swinging in a devastating horizontal arc. Auren doesn't dodge. Instead, his arms sweep upward—

Translucent barriers materialize, catching the axe mid-swing. The impact reverberates through the arena, sending Dorn staggering backward, his weapon vibrating from the unexpected resistance.

The crowd gasps. Jade's systems spike with interference patterns. Warning indicators flash across her augmented vision:

[NEURAL CALIBRATION ERROR]
[SENSORY INCONSISTENCY DETECTED]
[RECALIBRATING...]

Auren stands taller now, confidence evident in his stance. Around his forearms, spectral armor forms—ghostly bracers that catch the torchlight without fully materializing. The Thread—he's manipulating it directly, manifesting physical constructs from pure conceptualization.

Jade's analysis shifts. This isn't standard Aether manipulation as classified in Imperial records. This is something different—raw, untrained, but potentially more significant.

Lyssia attacks again, her whip striking from multiple angles in rapid succession. Auren moves with newfound purpose, the spectral armor extending with each movement, deflecting the barbed tips. Where the whip connects with the manifestations, sparks of pale light scatter through the air.

Vex and Dorn coordinate, attacking simultaneously from opposite sides. Auren's response is immediate—he drops to one knee, arms extended outward. A circular barrier expands around him, translucent but impenetrable. Both weapons strike it simultaneously, sending visible ripples through the manifestation.

The interference in Jade's systems becomes critical. Her optic feed splits, displaying both the physical reality and something beneath it—threads of light connecting Auren to the environment, pulsing with each manifestation. Her mother's voice echoes through neural pathways the dampeners fail to suppress:

"The Thread isn't just something we use, Sam. It's what we are."

Auren rises, the barrier collapsing inward before reforming around his arms as bladed extensions. No longer defensive—he's preparing to attack.

Auren III

The translucent blades extending from Auren's forearms hum with a subtle vibration that travels up through his bones. His muscles burn with fatigue, the days of captivity evident in every labored breath. Garrik's hospitality consisted of a damp cell, stale bread, and just enough water to keep him alive—not enough to keep him strong.

Yet something else flows through him now. The Aether responds to his desperation, pooling in the hollow spaces hunger has carved inside him.

Lyssia circles to his left, her whip coiling and uncoiling like the serpent she's named for. Dorn hefts his massive axe, arms corded with muscle. Vex dances on the balls of his feet, ritual scars pulsing unnaturally against his skin.

"Tired already, pilgrim?" Vex taunts, his voice carrying over the crowd's roar. "We're just warming up."

Auren doesn't waste breath on a response. Each word costs energy he can't spare.

Melia. Her name surfaces in his mind, bringing both strength and regret. He should have knocked on her door that night instead of standing frozen outside it. Should have told her that what happened between them wasn't just comfort or convenience. Now he might never get the chance.

Vex springs forward, hatchets whirling. Auren raises his right arm, the Aether-blade catching the first strike. The impact sends a shock through his body, but the manifestation holds. He twists, letting the second hatchet pass within inches of his face. The crowd gasps.

Lyssia strikes while his attention is divided, her whip snapping toward his ankles. Auren leaps, pulling his knees toward his chest as the barbed tip passes beneath him. But the jump costs him—Dorn charges the moment his feet leave the ground.

No time to dodge. No solid footing to brace against.

Instinct takes over. Auren throws both hands forward, the Aether-blades dissolving as he redirects the energy. A translucent shield forms before him, catching Dorn's axe mid-swing. The impact still throws Auren backward, sending him rolling across the sand.

Pain erupts along his side where he hits the ground. He tastes blood, feels it dripping from his nose. The crowd's noise becomes a distant roar as he struggles to his knees.

"You see?" Garrik's voice cuts through the arena. "The pilgrim makes a fine show!"

The spectators stomp their feet in approval, but Auren barely registers it. His vision narrows, focusing on his approaching opponents. Three against one. No weapons except what he can manifest. No strength except what desperation provides.

And yet.

The Aether pulses stronger now, responding to his need. He feels it like a current beneath his skin, a river seeking the path of least resistance. His failed ascension left him with this one gift—the ability to shape the unseen.

Dorn charges again, surprisingly fast for his size. Auren waits until the last moment, then dives to the side. Not a retreat this time—he rolls to his feet directly behind the mountain of a man. Before Dorn can turn, Auren presses both palms against the champion's back.

The Aether surges through him, a cold fire that pours from his hands. Dorn stumbles forward, his armor frosting over with translucent energy that hardens instantly. He roars in frustration, movements becoming sluggish as the manifestation weighs him down.

"What is this?" Dorn bellows, his limbs moving as if through thick mud.

Auren doesn't answer, already turning to face his next opponent. The expenditure leaves him lightheaded, black spots dancing at the edges of his vision. He cannot afford to lose consciousness. Not here. Not now.

Vex attacks from the left, Lyssia from the right—perfect coordination born from countless fights together. Auren drops to one knee, sweeping his arms outward. The Aether responds, forming a dome around him. Their weapons strike it simultaneously, sending visible ripples through the manifestation.

The crowd roars its approval.

Inside his temporary sanctuary, Auren gasps for breath. Sweat drips into his eyes, stinging. His heart hammers against his ribs. He can't maintain this barrier for long—already he feels it draining him, pulling at something essential.

Think. Adapt. Survive.

Lyssia's whip strikes the dome again, searching for weakness. Vex circles, hatchets ready. Behind them, Dorn struggles against the Aether-frost still binding his movements.

Auren makes his decision. He pulls the energy inward, compressing it around his limbs like armor. The dome collapses—but before his opponents can capitalize, he explodes into motion.

He launches toward Lyssia first, knowing her reach makes her the greater threat. The Aether extends from his right hand, forming not a blade this time but a shimmering cord of his own. As her whip lashes toward him, he catches it with his manifestation, the energies tangling together.

Lyssia's eyes widen in surprise. She tugs, trying to free her weapon, but Auren holds fast. With a sharp twist of his wrist, he yanks her forward, off-balance. His left hand strikes out, Aether forming a flat, solid plane that catches her square in the chest. The impact sends her flying backward into the arena wall.

One down. For the moment.

Vex doesn't give him time to recover. The scarified fighter darts in, hatchets a blur of motion. Auren backpedals, his Aether-armor deflecting glancing blows, but he can't avoid them all. A hatchet slips past his guard, opening a cut along his ribs. Pain flares, hot and immediate.

"First blood to me," Vex grins, his pupils unnaturally dilated. "There'll be more."

Auren's response is to slam his foot into the sand. The Aether pulses outward in a rippling wave, destabilizing the ground beneath Vex's feet. As the fighter struggles for balance, Auren closes the distance between them.

His movements aren't elegant now—just desperate, determined. He catches Vex's wrist as the fighter swings again, the Aether spreading from his palm to encase Vex's hand and hatchet both. Vex howls as the manifestation tightens, forcing his fingers open. The weapon drops.

Auren doesn't hesitate. He drives his knee into Vex's midsection, following with an Aether-reinforced palm strike to the chest. Vex stumbles backward, gasping. Before he can recover, Auren sweeps his legs from under him, sending him crashing to the ground.

The crowd's roar reaches a fever pitch.

Movement to his right—Dorn has finally broken free of the Aether-frost, his massive frame charging forward like an enraged bull. Behind him, Lyssia rises from where she fell, retrieving her whip with murderous intent.

Auren stands in the center of the arena, chest heaving. Blood trickles down his side. His limbs feel like lead, the Aether manifestations flickering as his concentration wavers.

I can't beat them all. Not like this. Not alone.

Then he remembers—he isn't alone. Not really. Even here, in this pit of violence and spectacle, the Aether responds to him. It always has, from that moment on the mountain when he nearly reached Elyssia.

Auren closes his eyes, just for a heartbeat. He reaches not outward but inward, to the place where his failure transformed into something else. The place where rejection became possibility.

When his eyes open, they gleam with renewed purpose.

Dorn reaches him first, axe sweeping in a deadly arc. Auren doesn't try to block or dodge. Instead, he steps into the attack, inside the axe's reach. The Aether explodes outward from his body in a brilliant surge that momentarily blinds the crowd. When vision returns, Auren stands transformed.

Translucent wings extend from his back, reminiscent of those that carried him toward Elyssia. But these are different—sharper, more defined. Weaponized. They curve forward like massive scythes, intercepting Dorn's axe and holding it immobile between them.

"Impossible," Dorn grunts, straining against the manifestation.

Auren doesn't reply. His wings pulse once, twice—then snap together with devastating force. The axe's handle shatters between them, sending splinters flying. Before Dorn can react, the wings sweep outward again, catching him across the chest and sending him tumbling backward across the sand.

Lyssia attacks from behind, her whip seeking his unprotected back. Without turning, Auren's wings reshape, becoming a protective shell that catches the barbs and holds them fast. With a thought, the manifestation contracts, pulling the whip from Lyssia's hands and flinging it aside.

Vex charges again, recovering his dropped hatchet. Auren pivots to face him, wings sweeping forward. The Aether responds to his intent, forming not just wings now but a complete armor that encases his torso and limbs. It pulses with each labored breath, drawing on his diminishing reserves.

As Vex swings, Auren catches the hatchet bare-handed—or what appears bare-handed to the crowd. In reality, the Aether forms a gauntlet around his palm, absorbing the impact. With his other hand, he delivers a strike to Vex's chest that lifts the fighter off his feet, sending him flying into Dorn who was just regaining his footing.

All three champions struggle to rise, but Auren doesn't give them the chance. The wings at his back expand, sweeping outward in a circular motion that creates a visible shockwave across the arena floor. Sand billows upward, momentarily obscuring everything. When it settles, all three champions lie prone at the edges of the arena, weapons scattered and forgotten.

Silence falls over the crowd, broken only by Auren's ragged breathing. The wings and armor flicker, then fade as his strength gives out. He drops to one knee, struggling to remain conscious as exhaustion claims him.

Slow applause breaks the silence. Garrik stands from his elevated seat, his expression a mixture of amazement and avarice.

"Ladies and gentlemen," he calls, voice carrying to every corner of the arena. "I promised you something extraordinary, and our pilgrim has delivered beyond expectation!"

The crowd erupts, stamping and cheering. Gold changes hands as bets are settled. Garrik descends from his platform, approaching Auren with arms spread wide in a theatrical gesture.

"A magnificent display," he says, pitched for Auren's ears alone. "Worth every coin I paid to acquire you."

Auren looks up, sweat and blood streaking his face. "Let me go."

Garrik's smile doesn't reach his eyes. "Do you have any idea what you're worth to me now?" He gestures to the frenzied crowd. "They'll pay triple to see you fight again. And they'll come back, again and again."

"I'm not your property," Auren manages, the words scraping his dry throat.

"Oh, but you are." Garrik's voice hardens. "Until I decide otherwise." He turns to the crowd, arms raised high. "The pilgrim remains in my service! Return tomorrow night for another spectacular display of his powers!"

The announcement is met with thunderous approval. Auren tries to stand, to protest, but his legs refuse to support him. The last of the Aether fades from his body, leaving him hollow and spent.

Guards approach, lifting him roughly to his feet. As they drag him toward the exit, Auren catches a glimpse of someone in the crowd—a woman with intent focus, watching him with analytical precision. Something about her gaze disturbs him, but the thought slips away as consciousness finally fails him.

His last coherent thought is of Melia, and a future that seems increasingly out of reach.

***

The guards drag Auren through narrow, torch-lit corridors, his feet scraping against rough stone. Pain radiates through his body in dull, throbbing waves. The Aether depletion has left him hollow, each heartbeat echoing in the emptiness where his power should be. Blood trickles from a cut above his eye, blurring his vision further as the world tilts and spins around him.

"Heavy bastard," one guard mutters, adjusting his grip under Auren's arm.

"Worth the trouble though," the other replies. "Did you see what he did to Dorn? Never seen the big man go down like that."

Their voices drift in and out of Auren's consciousness as they haul him along. His head lolls forward, chin bumping against his chest. The stone floor beneath him becomes a hypnotic blur of gray and brown.

A sharp voice cuts through the haze. "Shift change. We'll take him from here."

Auren feels the guards hesitate, their grip tightening momentarily.

"Since when do we change mid-transport?" the first guard asks.

"Since Garrik wants his new prize fighter under special watch. You got a problem with the boss's orders?"

There's a pause, then a grunt of acquiescence. "Fine. He's your problem now. Cell block three, last one on the left."

The transfer happens in a disorienting shuffle. New hands take hold of him, their grip somehow different—firmer but less bruising. Auren tries to lift his head, but the effort sends fresh pain shooting through his skull.

They move quickly, too quickly for the direction of the cells. Through blurry vision, Auren notices they're taking a different route, heading toward what seems to be a service corridor rather than the prisoner block.

"Where..." he manages to croak, but one of the new guards cuts him off.

"Quiet," the voice commands, though there's an undercurrent of urgency rather than cruelty.

They turn a corner and stop in a shadowed alcove near what appears to be a staff exit. Only then do Auren's escorts release him, propping him against the wall rather than letting him collapse.

"Gods above, he looks terrible."

That voice. Auren blinks hard, forcing his vision to focus. The guards are removing their helmets, revealing familiar faces that his exhausted mind struggles to process.

Kyp's concerned expression swims into view, followed by Ryker's more calculating gaze.

"Kyp?" Auren whispers, disbelief momentarily overriding his pain.

"The one and only," Kyp confirms, his attempt at a grin failing to hide his worry. "Though I'd say you're the one stealing all the attention tonight."

"How—"

"Guard uniforms aren't that hard to come by if you know who to bribe," Ryker interjects, glancing back toward the corridor. "And you, my friend, owe me one hell of a favor now."

Auren tries to stand straighter, but his legs buckle. Kyp catches him before he slides to the floor.

"Easy there, hero," Kyp mutters. "Save some strength for the escape part."

Ryker studies Auren with newfound interest. "I have to say, that was quite a show. No wonder Garrik wanted you so badly."

Before Auren can respond, there's a flurry of movement at the entrance to their alcove. A figure darts in, moving with silent urgency.

Melia.

She's transformed—dressed in practical clothing that bears no resemblance to her royal garments, her hair pulled back in a simple braid. But her eyes are unchanged, bright with worry as they fix on him.

"Auren," she breathes, and then she's there, arms wrapped around him in a fierce embrace that ignores the blood and sweat coating his skin.

The contact sends a jolt through Auren's depleted system. He wants to return the embrace but can barely lift his arms. Instead, he lets his forehead rest against her shoulder, breathing in her scent—a momentary anchor in the chaos.

"I thought I was going to lose you," she whispers against his ear, her voice thick with emotion.

Then, as quickly as she initiated the contact, she pulls away. Something flickers across her face—hesitation, perhaps guilt—before she steps back, creating distance between them.

"We need to get him some clothes," Kyp says, breaking the charged silence. "And get out of here before Garrik realizes his new prized possession is missing."

"I swiped these from a storage room," Ryker says, producing a bundle of fabric. "Not exactly high fashion, but better than..." He gestures at Auren's tattered, blood-stained arena garments.

Kyp helps Auren into the simple tunic and pants while Ryker keeps watch at the alcove entrance. Every movement sends fresh pain through Auren's battered body, but the clean fabric against his skin offers a small comfort.

"Can you walk?" Melia asks, her voice carefully controlled now, professional rather than intimate.

Auren nods, though he's far from certain. "I'll manage."

"We've got a cart waiting by the service entrance," Ryker explains. "Get him there, and we're halfway free."

Kyp positions himself under Auren's right arm, taking most of his weight. "Just like that time you carried me home from the Harvest Festival," he quips. "Except you're considerably heavier and smell much worse."

"Quiet," Ryker hisses suddenly, flattening himself against the wall. "Guards."

Footsteps approach, accompanied by the jingle of keys and weapons. Auren tenses, gathering what little strength remains in his depleted body. If they're discovered now...

Melia's hand finds his in the shadows, squeezing briefly before withdrawing. That small contact centers him, focuses his mind beyond the pain and exhaustion.

"Ready?" Ryker mouths silently, hand on his concealed blade.

Auren straightens as much as he can. They've come for him. Despite everything between them—or perhaps because of it—they've risked themselves to save him. He won't let that courage go to waste.

He nods, jaw set with determination. "Ready."

***

They navigate a maze of service passages, the sounds of the arena growing distant. Auren's breath comes in ragged gasps, but he pushes forward, drawing on reserves he didn't know he possessed.

"Almost there," Melia whispers, pushing open a heavy door that reveals a sliver of night air.

The door opens to a narrow alley where a small cart waits, hitched to a nervous-looking mule. The animal shifts restlessly, sensing their urgency.

"Get him in," Ryker instructs, scanning the darkness behind them.

Kyp and Melia help Auren into the cart, his limbs refusing to cooperate. The wooden bed feels like the softest bed he's ever known as he collapses onto it, fighting to stay conscious.

"Let's go before—"

"Hey! Stop right there!"

A shout echoes from the end of the alley. One of Garrik's men, face twisted in recognition, points directly at them. "That's Garrik's fighter! Thieving bastards!"

More shouts follow as the man calls for backup. Kyp jumps into the cart beside Auren, while Melia hesitates, looking between the cart and Ryker, who has stepped forward, positioning himself between them and the approaching gang members.

"Go," Ryker says, drawing a slender blade from his belt. "I'll hold them off."

"Ryker—" Melia begins, her voice tight with concern.

"I'll catch up," he promises with a flash of his confident smile. "You know I always do."

Melia reaches out, squeezing Ryker's hand with a tenderness that sends a jolt through Auren's chest. There's something in that touch—a familiarity, an intimacy—that speaks of more than casual alliance.

"Be careful," she whispers.

The moment stretches between them, revealing connections Auren hadn't seen—or hadn't wanted to see. Then Melia releases Ryker's hand and jumps into the cart beside Kyp.

Kyp snaps the reins, and the cart lurches forward just as five of Garrik's men pour into the alley. Ryker moves to intercept them, his blade flashing in the dim light.

Auren watches through pain-blurred vision as Ryker engages the men. There's something off about his fighting style—a theatrical quality that doesn't match the desperate circumstances. He's putting on a show rather than fighting efficiently, almost as if—

A sudden impact throws Auren against the side of the cart. A new gang member has appeared from a cross-street, ramming their cart with enough force to overturn it.

The world spins as Auren, Kyp, and Melia are thrown into the open marketplace. Crates and barrels crash around them, drawing shouts from late-night vendors and patrons. Auren lands hard, fresh agony blossoming across his already injured body.

Through the chaos, he sees Ryker being dragged to the center of a growing circle of Garrik's men. Despite being outnumbered, Ryker doesn't have a single visible injury—not even a scratch. It's as if he deliberately allowed himself to be captured.

More gang members appear, surrounding them completely. Melia helps Auren to his feet, but there's nowhere to run. They're trapped in the open market, encircled by Garrik's forces, with no visible escape route.

"Well," Kyp mutters, helping to steady Auren, "this rescue attempt could be going better."

Melia VII

Melia's heart hammers against her ribs as Garrik's men tighten their circle. The marketplace, moments ago alive with evening commerce, has transformed into a makeshift arena. Vendors scramble away, leaving upturned stalls in their wake.

"Stay behind me," Kyp whispers, positioning himself in front of Melia. His voice trembles, but his stance is firm.

Melia clutches Auren's arm, feeling him sway dangerously beside her. His skin burns with fever, his breathing shallow and uneven. Whatever reserves of strength had carried him through the escape have abandoned him completely.

"What do we do?" she hisses, scanning the circle of leering faces. Twenty men, at least, all armed with crude but effective weapons. Ryker kneels in the center, hands now bound behind his back, watching them with an expression she can't quite read.

The nearest thug steps forward, twirling a jagged knife. "Garrik's gonna be right pleased when we bring you back. Might even let us have a little fun with the pretty one first."

His gaze crawls over Melia, and she feels something primal twist in her stomach—not just fear, but fury. She's done being handled, being threatened, being treated as property.

"Touch her and die," Auren manages, though the words come out slurred. He tries to straighten, but his knees buckle.

The man laughs, revealing blackened teeth. "You can barely stand, magic man."

He lunges forward, knife glinting in the lamplight. Kyp shoves Melia back, raising his arms in a futile defensive gesture. Melia reaches for anything—a weapon, an escape route, a miracle.

A dark shape drops from above.

The attacker never reaches them. A figure lands between them with liquid grace, catching the man's wrist and twisting. The sickening crack of bone breaking is followed by a howl of pain. The knife clatters to the ground.

Melia blinks, trying to process what she's seeing. A woman—lean and compact, with short dark hair—stands where empty space had been a heartbeat before. She moves with impossible precision, like water flowing around stones, redirecting the man's momentum and sending him sprawling face-first into the dirt.

Two more attackers rush her. The woman sidesteps the first, driving an elbow into his throat that leaves him gasping. The second receives a kick to the knee that collapses his leg at an unnatural angle.

"What in the seven hells..." Kyp breathes beside her.

The marketplace erupts into chaos. Garrik's men surge forward in a wave of bodies and blades. The mysterious woman meets them with mechanical efficiency. Her movements contain no wasted energy, no hesitation—just pure, lethal purpose.

A man swings a club at her head; she ducks and strikes upward, her palm connecting with his chin. His teeth snap together as his head whips back. Another lunges with a dagger; she redirects his arm, using his own momentum to drive the blade into his companion's shoulder.

"She's not even armed," Melia whispers, watching in disbelief as the woman systematically dismantles the gang.

One particularly large brute charges forward with a roar. The woman drops low, sweeping his legs. As he falls, she rises in one fluid motion, striking precise points on his torso. The man convulses and goes still.

Within moments, a dozen of Garrik's men lie broken on the ground. The remaining thugs hesitate, looking at each other with growing uncertainty.

"Leave," the woman says. Her voice is startlingly calm, almost flat. "Or join them."

The remaining men break ranks and flee, several dragging injured companions. In their rush to escape, they leave Ryker behind, still kneeling in the dirt with his hands bound.

The woman turns to face Melia, and for the first time, Melia gets a clear look at her face. Sharp, angular features frame steel-gray eyes that seem to catalog everything in a single glance. Her expression reveals nothing—no exertion, no triumph, not even a hint of concern.

"We need to move," she says. "Now."

Melia finds her voice. "Who are you?"

"Someone who doesn't want to be here when reinforcements arrive." The woman glances at Auren, assessing his condition with clinical detachment. "He can't run."

"I can walk," Auren insists, though he can barely stand without Kyp's support.

The woman's gaze shifts to something beyond Melia's shoulder. "There's an alley behind the spice merchant's stall. It connects to the lower district sewers."

Melia turns, seeing a narrow passageway she hadn't noticed before. "How do you—"

"Questions later," the woman cuts her off. "Help him. I'll take point."

The woman steps toward Ryker, producing a small blade from somewhere on her person. With a quick flick, she severs his bindings. "Coming?"

Ryker rubs his wrists, studying the woman with undisguised curiosity. "Wouldn't miss it."

The marketplace crowd parts as they move toward the alley, whispers following in their wake. The woman leads with precise steps, constantly scanning for threats. Melia follows close behind, torn between gratitude and suspicion.

The alley narrows to a tight passage between buildings, forcing them to walk single file. The smell of rotting food and stagnant water grows stronger with each step. Bear appears from nowhere, trotting alongside Melia with an air of calm certainty, as if the chaos of the past few minutes were entirely expected.

"You know," Kyp mutters, supporting Auren's weight, "I'm starting to think this pilgrimage might be more exciting than advertised."

Melia watches the back of their mysterious savior, noting the way she moves with measured control—like someone accustomed to being observed. Every instinct tells her this woman is dangerous.

But dangerous to whom?

***

The passage descends sharply, forcing Melia to brace against damp walls as they follow Jade through Aurora's underbelly. Each step takes them deeper beneath the city, away from Garrik's searching men. Distant shouts echo through stone corridors—hunters calling to each other, their voices distorted by the labyrinthine tunnels.

"Left here," Jade says, her voice barely above a whisper. She navigates without hesitation, as though reading invisible markings on the walls.

Auren stumbles, his breathing labored. Sweat beads on his forehead despite the cool underground air. Kyp adjusts his grip, struggling to support the taller man's weight.

"I've got him," Melia says, moving to Auren's other side. His skin burns against hers.

"We need to rest," she tells Jade's back. "He has a fever."

Jade pauses, turning to assess Auren with those unreadable gray eyes. "Two more junctions. Then we can stop briefly."

True to her word, after passing through narrow passages that force them to walk sideways, they emerge into a small maintenance chamber. Pipes line the ceiling, carrying water and who knows what else throughout Aurora's infrastructure.

Ryker helps lower Auren to the floor while Jade positions herself near the entrance, listening intently. Bear circles the chamber twice before settling near Auren, watching him with unblinking eyes.

"Search patterns indicate they're focusing on the north quadrant," Jade says. "We're moving south. Should maintain this advantage if we don't linger."

Melia kneels beside Auren, pressing a hand to his forehead. "How do you know the search patterns?"

"I watch. I listen." Jade's expression doesn't change. "It's what I do."

"And what exactly is it you do?" Ryker asks, his voice edged with suspicion. "Professional savior of strangers? Or do you make a habit of dropping from the sky to dispatch gangs of armed men?"

Jade meets his gaze with unsettling steadiness. "My name is Jade."

"That's not an answer."

"It's all you're getting."

Ryker laughs without humor. "Well, *Jade*, forgive me if I find it convenient that you appeared exactly when we needed help."

"Would you prefer I hadn't?" Jade asks, her tone flat.

Melia studies the woman more carefully. Despite her composed exterior, something in Jade's posture suggests tension—not from physical exertion, but something deeper. The way she holds herself, rigidly controlled, reminds Melia of the carefully constructed facades she'd maintained in Elyssia. A perfect princess, never showing cracks.

She recognizes it now: Jade is a woman trying not to shatter.

"Thank you," Melia says, cutting through Ryker's brewing retort. "For helping us. We'd likely be back in Garrik's pits without you."

Jade inclines her head slightly, neither accepting nor rejecting the gratitude.

Auren shifts, his eyes fluttering open. "Where—"

"Safe," Melia tells him. "For now."

He focuses on Jade. "You're the one who was watching. In the arena."

Jade's expression flickers—the first genuine reaction Melia has seen from her. "Yes."

"Why help us?" Auren asks.

For a moment, Jade seems at a loss. "Your abilities... they're unusual."

Melia feels a strange twist in her stomach. Of course. Auren's Aether manipulation would attract attention.

"We should move," Jade says, abruptly breaking eye contact with Auren. "There's an exit to the outskirts half a kilometer from here.

Once outside the city, you'll need to head east through the marshlands to avoid Garrik's patrols."

"And then what?" Kyp asks. "We're on a pilgrimage. A reverse one, actually."

Jade tilts her head. "Explain."

Melia hesitates, unsure how much to reveal. "I fell from Elyssia. We're retracing the pilgrimage route in reverse."

Something shifts in Jade's expression—recognition, perhaps, or calculation. "Elyssia. The floating city."

"Yes."

"Interesting."

Ryker snorts. "That's one word for it."

They continue through the tunnels, Auren stronger after the brief rest but still feverish. Jade leads them unerringly, occasionally stopping to listen before selecting a path. Twice, they hear voices and footsteps, but Jade guides them down alternative routes that loop around the danger.

Finally, they reach a heavy metal door sealed with a complex lock. Jade examines it briefly before producing a small device from her pocket. The lock clicks open with surprising ease.

"This will take you beyond the city walls," she says, pushing the door open to reveal a steep path ascending toward daylight. "Follow the eastern treeline. Stay off the main roads."

"You sound like you're not coming with us," Melia observes.

Jade hesitates, her gaze drifting back toward the heart of the city. "My business is in Aurora," she says with practiced neutrality, though something flickers behind her steel-gray eyes—a calculation being made, perhaps, or a risk being weighed.

"What business?" Melia presses, noticing how Jade's fingers unconsciously drift to the edge of her cloak, readying to pull it tighter around herself.

"Mine." The word falls between them like a barrier, deliberately placed.

Melia steps closer, keeping her voice low enough that only Jade can hear. The others hang back, giving them space, though Bear winds his sleek black form around Melia's ankles, a silent sentinel. "I think you're looking for something. Or someone." She studies the woman's face, searching for any crack in that carefully maintained façade. "The way you move through these tunnels—you're not just helping us. You're hiding too."

Jade's eyes narrow slightly, the subtle tension in her jaw and the almost imperceptible straightening of her spine—confirmation enough for Melia, who recognizes the instinctive defensiveness of someone whose secrets have been glimpsed. In that brief, unguarded moment, Melia sees something familiar reflected back at her: the wariness of a woman accustomed to wearing masks.

"Come with us," Melia says, surprising herself with the invitation. "Whatever you're searching for in Aurora, maybe you need distance to see it clearly."

"I don't belong in your group."

"Neither did I, once." Melia glances at Auren, then back to Jade. "But I'm learning that belonging isn't always where we expect to find it."

Jade follows her gaze to Auren, studying him with an intensity that sparks an unexpected flare of jealousy in Melia's chest. The feeling catches her off guard—after what happened with Ryker in the dressing room, she has no right to possessiveness over Auren.

"The pilgrimage," Jade says slowly. "How far?"

"To the Shattered Spire," Auren answers, his voice strained but steady. "Through Old Hollow and Windy Ridge."

Jade is silent for a long moment, her face unreadable. Then, with a barely perceptible nod: "I'll accompany you. For now."

They step through the doorway into morning light. The air smells of coming rain and unfamiliar flowers. Behind them, Aurora's gleaming towers rise against clouds heavy with moisture. Ahead, wild marshlands stretch toward distant mountains.

Melia takes a deep breath of freedom, watching as Jade carefully secures the door behind them.

***

Rainwater streams over the mouth of the cave like a shimmering curtain, transforming the world outside into a blur of grays and greens. Melia wrings excess water from the edge of her cloak, now practical and unadorned—nothing like the gossamer silks she once wore in Elyssia. Bear shakes himself vigorously nearby, spraying droplets in a wide arc.

"Hey!" Kyp dodges the spray, laughing despite their circumstances. "Save some for the plants outside, would you?"

The cave isn't large—just a shallow depression in the hillside, barely deep enough to shelter their small group from the sudden downpour. The air smells of wet earth and limestone, with underlying traces of smoke from the small fire Kyp managed to coax to life.

Jade stands at the entrance, her silhouette stark against the waterfall of rain. She hasn't moved for nearly twenty minutes, her posture unnaturally still as she studies the terrain beyond. Something about her reminds Melia of a hunting bird—patient, focused, deadly.

Behind them, Auren lies on an improvised bed of cloaks, his breathing steady but labored. Sweat beads on his forehead and neck, dampening his shirt despite the cave's coolness. Melia kneels beside him, pressing a damp cloth to his brow.

"His fever's breaking," she murmurs to Kyp, who sits cross-legged on Auren's other side. "Look at how much he's sweating."

Kyp nods, relief softening the worry lines around his eyes. "That's good. Really good." He adjusts the makeshift pillow under Auren's head. "I've seen him bounce back from worse. There was that time with the rock serpent near Blackwater Falls?"

"What happened?" Melia says.

"Got himself thrown against a cliff face. Three broken ribs, dislocated shoulder, and a gash on his leg deep enough to see bone." Kyp grins fondly at the memory. "Back on his feet in four days, limping but insisting he could climb the eastern ridge."

Melia smiles, trying to picture a less guarded Auren, determined despite his injuries. "So how long before he's up this time?"

"I'd wager by morning," Kyp says, but uncertainty creeps into his voice as he studies Auren's pallid face. "Though this is different. Never seen him use the Aether like that before."

"His injuries are primarily superficial," Jade interjects without turning from her watch position. "The fever and lethargy result from insufficient nutrition and sleep deprivation. His body is also recovering from overextension of Aether manipulation."

Melia looks up, surprised by both the interruption and the clinical precision of Jade's assessment. "You sound certain."

"I am." Jade's voice remains flat, matter-of-fact. "The Thread—or Aether magic, as you call it—requires significant physical resources when manipulated with such intensity."

"Well, that's reassuring coming from someone who just happened to drop into our lives at the perfect moment," Ryker says from his position near the fire. His tone carries a veneer of charm, but suspicion edges each word. "You seem to know an awful lot about things most people have never heard of."

Jade turns slightly, her profile illuminated by firelight. "Information is valuable."

"So is transparency," Ryker counters, rising to his feet. "Who's to say Garrik didn't send you? Get close to us, learn what Auren can do, lead us into a trap?"

"If I were sent by Garrik, you would already be dead." Jade's tone doesn't change, which somehow makes the statement more chilling. "Your escape from the fighting pits compromised his reputation. He wouldn't risk you getting away a second time."

Ryker steps closer to her, his hand casually resting near the knife at his belt. "That doesn't answer my question."

"I don't owe you answers."

"You do if you're traveling with us."

"I travel alongside you. There's a difference."

Melia watches the exchange with growing unease. She trusts neither of them completely—Ryker with his convenient appearance and easy charm, Jade with her impossible skills and measured speech. Yet both have proven useful, even necessary.

"If you're not with Garrik, then who?" Ryker presses, his voice hardening. "Aurora intelligence? Some rival faction? Because nobody fights like you do without training, and nobody knows what you know without connections."

Jade's posture shifts subtly, almost imperceptibly—a coiling of potential energy. "My past is irrelevant to your current situation."

"It's completely relevant if you're leading us into—"

"Stop." Auren's voice, though weak, cuts through their argument. Melia turns to find him struggling to sit up, his face tight with pain.

"You should rest," she says, placing a gentle hand on his shoulder.

He ignores her, focusing on Jade and Ryker with feverish intensity. "Fighting... wastes energy we don't have."

Kyp nods emphatically. "He's right. We need to save our strength for what matters—getting through the marshlands and continuing the pilgrimage."

Melia helps Auren take a few sips of water, watching his hands tremble with the effort of holding the cup. His weakness scares her more than she wants to admit. She's come to rely on his strength, his certainty about the path ahead.

"How long was I out?" Auren asks her quietly.

"Almost a full day," Melia replies. "You pushed yourself too hard in the fighting pits."

A shadow crosses his face. "Had no choice."

"I know." She hesitates, then adds, "It was... remarkable. What you did with the Aether."

Behind them, Ryker and Jade continue their tense exchange, their voices now lowered but no less hostile.

"—could at least tell us your real purpose here," Ryker insists.

"My reasons are my own," Jade responds. "Question me again, and I'll leave. Your survival odds decrease significantly without me."

"Is that a threat?"

"An assessment."

Melia sighs, turning away from their bickering to focus on Auren. "They've been like this since we left Aurora," she tells him. "I'm beginning to think they enjoy arguing."

Auren's lips twitch in a ghost of a smile. "Kyp... used to say I enjoyed... arguing with you."

"Did you?"

His eyes meet hers, fever-bright but lucid. "Yes."

The simple admission sends an unexpected warmth through her chest. She remembers their conversations by the river, in the old chapel—challenging each other, pushing beyond comfortable truths.

Kyp stretches and moves to rummage through their packs. "We should eat something. Who knows when we'll next have shelter from this rain."

Melia nods, though her appetite has deserted her. Since leaving Aurora, a persistent anxiety has taken root in her stomach—the feeling of being hunted. The knowledge that Garrik's men are likely searching for them, that every hour increases the chance of discovery.

Bear appears at her side, pressing his warm body against her leg. His presence grounds her, as it always has since that first moment on the shore of the sacred lake. She strokes his sleek fur, drawing comfort from his steady purring.

"We need to keep moving," she says, more to herself than the others. "Complete the pilgrimage before Garrik finds us."

"Or before whoever sent her catches up," Ryker adds, nodding toward Jade.

"Your closed mind could never comprehend why I'm on this miserable world, or what my mission entails," Jade says, her voice cold as mountain ice. Her gaze locks onto Ryker with unnerving precision. "I have deviated from my mission to help you. Until such time that I choose not to, I have committed my entire purpose to your assistance."

The words hang in the air, clinical yet somehow heavy with unspoken meaning. Ryker holds her gaze for a moment longer, then exhales a frustrated sigh. Without further argument, he retreats to a shadowed corner of the cave, keeping his distance but still watching.

Jade turns back to her vigil at the cave entrance, resuming her statue-like stillness as she monitors the rain-soaked landscape beyond.

Melia shifts uncomfortably, acutely aware of the tension crackling through their small shelter. Bear presses closer against her leg, his warm presence a small comfort. She studies Jade's rigid silhouette against the waterfall of rain, wondering what secrets lie behind that carefully controlled exterior.

Can they truly trust her? The question loops endlessly in Melia's mind. There's something in Jade—a depth, perhaps, or a complexity—that resonates with her own journey of self-discovery. Something special beneath the calculated exterior.

Her thoughts scatter as Jade turns slightly, her gaze shifting to where Auren rests. The subtle change in her posture, the careful attention in her observation... Melia feels an unexpected pang. Why does Jade seem so interested in Auren specifically?

Bear nudges her hand, drawing her attention back to the present moment and the path ahead—a path growing more complicated with each passing day.

Orlan II

Sir Orlan stands rigidly at attention behind Prefect Solivar, the ceremonial weight of his armor pressing down with each passing moment. The Great Hall pulses with murmuring voices, packed with Elyssia's nobility and selected commoners permitted to witness the Prefect's address. Banners bearing the royal crest flutter overhead, their pristine white fabric seeming to mock the deception unfolding beneath them.

"In these times of transition," Solivar's voice carries effortlessly across the hall, "we must embrace both continuity and sacrifice. The foundation of Elyssia has always been built upon these twin pillars."

Orlan keeps his expression carefully neutral, though his jaw aches from the effort. Two weeks of searching, and still no true confirmation of Princess Melia's whereabouts. Only whispers and half-truths that grow more troubling with each passing day.

"Our beloved Princess Melia continues her period of sacred mourning," Solivar continues, his hands spreading in a gesture of benevolent understanding. "Her devotion to honoring her parents' memory speaks to her deep commitment to our traditions."

Lies, all of it. Orlan's gauntleted fingers flex imperceptibly at his side.

"I assure you," Solivar's voice rises with practiced emotion, "that Princess Melia will complete her mourning rituals in time for our wedding, which shall unite our great city in purpose once more."

The crowd responds with appropriate murmurs of approval. Many of the nobles present know the truth—or at least suspect it—yet none dare speak against the Prefect's narrative. Orlan studies their faces, noting which ones avoid meeting his gaze. These could be potential allies... or the first to betray him if his own doubts become known.

His thoughts drift to Merien and Lira—his wife and daughter—now relocated to the Eastern Quarter under the guise of "protection." Hostages, in truth, though packaged in gilded accommodations and polite language. Solivar's message had been clear: serve without question, or they would suffer the consequences.

"The sacred traditions that bind us together require sacrifice from all," Solivar continues. "Just as our ancestors gave of themselves to create this paradise, so must we remain vigilant in preserving their legacy."

A legacy built on half-truths and manipulation, Orlan thinks.

"Sir Orlan," Solivar suddenly announces, turning to face him. "Our devoted Captain of the Royal Guard, will now update us on the security measures being implemented to ensure Elyssia's continued prosperity."

The unexpected spotlight jolts Orlan from his thoughts. He steps forward, nodding respectfully to Solivar while his mind races to compose appropriate remarks. This is a test, he realizes—a public demonstration of loyalty.

"Thank you, Prefect," Orlan begins, his voice steady despite the turmoil within. "The Royal Guard remains vigilant in these times of transition. We have increased patrols along the perimeter and reinforced security at each of the Seven Sanctums."

He pauses, feeling Solivar's keen attention on him. The next words taste bitter on his tongue, but he forces them out with convincing resolve.

"We continue our discreet inquiries into suspicious activities reported near the lower districts, though I assure the citizens that these are merely precautionary measures. The integrity of Elyssia remains absolute."

Solivar's slight nod signals approval of this careful deception. The "suspicious activities" are, of course, their search for the princess—repackaged as routine security concerns to avoid public alarm.

"Our primary focus remains the protection of our traditions and the sacred knowledge contained within the High Temple," Orlan continues, each word carefully measured. "The Royal Guard stands ready to ensure that the upcoming union between Prefect Solivar and Princess Melia proceeds without disruption."

The words leave a hollowness in his chest. If only they knew that the princess had chosen to leap from the only home she'd ever known rather than be part of this union. If only they understood what that choice might mean.

As Orlan concludes his remarks and steps back, he catches the eye of High Priestess Elynia, standing at the edge of the crowd. Something passes between them—a shared knowledge, perhaps, or a mutual recognition of the precipice on which they all stand. The priestess's gaze holds for a moment longer than necessary before she turns away.

Solivar resumes his address, speaking now of prosperity and divine favor, but Orlan barely hears the words. His mind is calculating, weighing options and potential allies. The priests know more than they're revealing about the princess's fall—about what King Orion may have discovered before his death.

Tonight, Orlan decides, he will seek out Elynia. If there is truth to be found, it likely lies within the inner sanctum of the High Temple, among the ancient scrolls and whispered secrets of the priesthood.

His thoughts turn again to his family—to Merien's gentle strength and Lira's curious spirit. For their sake, he must tread carefully. But for Elyssia's sake—for the princess he swore to protect—he must find the courage to seek the truth, whatever the cost.

Solivar's voice rises to a triumphant conclusion, and the crowd erupts in applause. Orlan joins them mechanically, his armor gleaming in the artificial light of the Great Hall, while his heart remains shadowed with doubt and determination.

***

The throne room doors close with a heavy thud, sealing away the world outside. Orlan stands rigid at his post, armor gleaming in the amber light that streams through the stained glass windows. He's painfully aware of the emptiness behind him—the space where other guards would normally flank the royal chamber now conspicuously vacant.

"We may speak freely now," Prefect Solivar announces, pacing before the throne rather than sitting upon it. The distinction isn't lost on Orlan—a calculated performance of deference to the absent princess while wielding the full authority of the crown.

High Priest Morden steps forward, his ornate robes rustling against the polished floor. "Our contacts in Etheria have confirmed it. The princess survived her fall."

The words send a jolt through Orlan's chest, though his expression remains carefully neutral. Melia lives. The relief nearly overwhelms him, but he forces himself to focus on the conversation unfolding before him.

"Into the sacred lake, as we suspected," High Priest Tharos adds, stroking his silver-streaked beard. "The symbolism will not be lost on the surface dwellers."

"Elaborate," Solivar demands, his voice sharp.

High Priestess Valeera nods, her elegant hands folded before her. "The villagers of Willow Haven took her in. They view her as something of a... miracle. The Fallen Princess, they're calling her."

"Superstitious fools," Solivar mutters.

"Perhaps," High Priest Verrus interjects, "but they've already set her on a path that could prove problematic. They're calling it a 'reverse pilgrimage'—following the Ascension route backward."

A flicker of movement catches Orlan's eye. High Priestess Elynia, standing slightly apart from her colleagues, meets his gaze. Something passes between them—a silent communication that sends a clear message: *We need to speak privately.*

Orlan gives an almost imperceptible nod before returning his attention to Solivar, who now stands with his back to the assembly, hands clasped behind him as he stares up at a massive tapestry depicting Elyssia's creation.

"A reverse pilgrimage?" Orlan finds himself asking, the question escaping before he can consider its wisdom. "What exactly is this Ascension they believe in?"

Solivar turns, his pale eyes narrowing at the interruption, but High Priestess Elynia steps forward before he can respond.

"The people of Etheria," she begins, her voice measured and clear, "believe that by following a specific pilgrimage route and learning to harness what they call Aether magic, they may one day ascend to Elyssia themselves." She meets Orlan's eyes directly. "It is a core belief that structures their society. The path begins at the Shattered Spire, a holy place, walks the Pilgrim's Road, and eventually leads to Willow Haven—where they believe the ascension occurs."

"A false belief, of course," Tharos quickly interjects, throwing a sharp glance at Elynia. "But one that serves to keep Etheria orderly and compliant. The hope of ascension prevents rebellion."

The implication strikes Orlan like a physical blow. "You're saying we deliberately perpetuate this... myth?" He looks from one priest to another, searching their faces. "These people devote their lives to a pilgrimage that can never succeed?"

"Watch your tone, Sir Orlan," Solivar warns, his voice dangerously soft. "You speak of matters beyond your understanding."

High Priest Verrus clears his throat, clearly eager to move past this uncomfortable moment. "According to our sources, the princess has already traveled from Willow Haven to the Old Chapel, and most recently to Aurora."

"Aurora," Valeera spits the word like a curse. "An abomination of a city where our influence holds no sway. They've rejected our traditions entirely, embracing technologies and beliefs that undermine the very foundations of order."

"She travels with an Aether user," Morden adds. "A pilgrim who apparently attempted the ascension and failed. He may be feeding her dangerous ideas."

Orlan's mind races. An Aether user? Someone who attempted to reach Elyssia? The implications are staggering, challenging everything he thought he knew about the realm below.

"What is her goal?" Solivar demands, his knuckles white where he grips the back of an ornate chair. "Does she understand what she's doing?"

"Unknown," Verrus responds. "But the trajectory of her journey suggests she's heading for the Shattered Spire. If she reaches it..."

"She must be stopped before she discovers what awaits there," Valeera insists, a note of genuine alarm in her voice.

Orlan can't help himself. "What exactly is at the Spire?" he asks, looking directly at Elynia, who seems the most likely to provide a straight answer.

The throne room falls silent. The High Priests exchange glances, a wordless debate occurring in the space between them. Solivar's eyes darken with anger.

"This meeting is concluded," he announces abruptly. "High Priests, make contact with your surface colleagues immediately. Whatever arrangements must be made, whatever deals struck—I want agents from Aurora deployed to recover the princess."

Tharos bows slightly. "That won't be a problem, Prefect. There are many in Aurora who would happily do our bidding for the right price."

"Then see it done," Solivar commands. "And ensure they understand that she is to be returned unharmed." A pause. "Physically, at least. Her mind can be... realigned once she's back in our care."

The casual cruelty of the statement sends a chill through Orlan's body. He thinks of Melia—her gentle spirit, her questioning mind—subjected to whatever "realignment" might entail.

"Sir Orlan," Solivar continues, "you will oversee the preparation of the princess's chambers for her return. I want everything exactly as she left it—a comforting familiarity to ease her transition back to court life."

"Yes, Prefect," Orlan responds automatically, though his thoughts are elsewhere—with Melia, traveling through a realm he barely understands, pursued by forces that view her as nothing more than an escaped possession.

The High Priests file out, their ornate robes swishing across the marble floor. Elynia passes close to Orlan, and he feels something pressed into his palm—a small, folded piece of parchment. He closes his fist around it instinctively, not daring to look down.

"Is there something else, Sir Orlan?" Solivar asks, his tone suggesting he's noticed the brief exchange.

"No, Prefect," Orlan replies steadily. "I was merely considering the most efficient way to carry out your orders."

Solivar studies him for a long moment, his pale eyes searching for any trace of deception. "See that you do. The wedding will proceed as planned once the princess is returned. The stability of Elyssia depends on it."

As Orlan bows and turns to leave, his mind is already racing, calculating the risks of what he's considering. His family remains hostage to his loyalty, yet the note burning in his palm promises information he desperately needs. The threat to Melia is immediate and grave. Whatever awaits at the Shattered Spire, Solivar clearly fears its discovery.

In the corridor outside, when he's certain he's alone, Orlan unfolds the note. Elynia's elegant script contains just five words and a time: *Eastern tower. Midnight. Come alone.*

He memorizes the message before crushing it in his fist. Tonight, perhaps, he'll finally learn the truth about Elyssia, about Ascension, and about what truly lies at the Shattered Spire. For Melia's sake—and perhaps for all of Elyssia—he must take this risk.

The corridor stretches before him, bright and immaculate, like everything in Elyssia. But for the first time, Orlan wonders what shadows might be lurking beneath the perfect surface, what rot might be hidden beneath the gleaming facade of their floating paradise.

He thinks of his daughter Lira, barely seven, with her curious questions and bright eyes. What world is he helping to build for her? One of beautiful lies, or difficult truths?

His hand falls to the hilt of his sword—a gesture of comfort, of certainty in uncertain times. Whatever Elynia reveals tonight, whatever path opens before him, he knows one thing with absolute clarity: he must protect both his family and Princess Melia. Even if that means standing against Solivar himself.

The thought is treason, of course. But as Orlan strides toward the royal chambers to begin the grotesque task of preparing for Melia's forced return, he feels something unfamiliar taking root alongside his fear—a quiet, determined resolve that perhaps the greatest loyalty to Elyssia might require the courage to question its most sacred traditions.

The corridor bends, and Orlan follows it, his polished armor reflecting the perfect light of a city built on imperfect truths.

***

The eastern tower looms black against the starless sky, its spire piercing upward like an accusatory finger. Orlan checks the timepiece at his belt—two minutes to midnight. His eyes scan the empty courtyard once more before he crosses the final stretch, boots silent on the cobblestones. The knight's training serves him well tonight; even in full armor, he moves with the quiet precision of a shadow.

A small door, half-hidden behind climbing vines, stands ajar. Invitation or trap? His hand rests briefly on his sword hilt before he pushes the door wider, wincing at the slight creak of ancient hinges.

"You came alone." Elynia's voice drifts from the darkness within. Not a question, but an assessment.

"As instructed," Orlan replies, stepping inside. The door swings shut behind him, plunging them into complete darkness for a moment before a soft blue flame ignites in Elynia's palm, illuminating the narrow spiral staircase.

"My family—" he begins, the question that's been burning in his mind all day finally finding voice.

"Are safe for now," Elynia cuts him off. "Lira spends her days in the children's garden. Solivar has assigned a 'tutor' who reports their activities, but the woman seems kind enough. Merien is permitted her usual duties in the textile quarter, though under observation."

The knot in Orlan's chest loosens slightly. "How do you know this?"

Elynia's smile is thin in the ghostly light. "I have eyes in places Solivar doesn't suspect. Follow me."

The staircase winds upward, each step taking them further from the gleaming halls and carefully maintained beauty of Elyssia proper. The stone here is older, worn smooth by centuries of use, and Orlan notes with surprise the absence of the usual ornate carvings that adorn every surface of the city.

"Few come to this tower anymore," Elynia explains, sensing his curiosity. "Which makes it useful for conversations that shouldn't be overheard."

They emerge into a circular chamber at the tower's peak. Unlike the opulent quarters of other high priests, Elynia's rooms are sparse, functional. Books line the walls, ancient tomes with cracked spines. A wide window opens to the east, providing a panoramic view of Elyssia's glittering expanse.

"Beautiful, isn't it?" Elynia stands beside him at the window. "The perfect city, floating above the imperfect world."

"That's what we're taught," Orlan agrees, studying her face in profile. "Is it not true?"

"What is truth, Sir Orlan?" Elynia turns to face him fully, her ceremonial robes discarded, standing before him in a simple blue tunic. Without the formal attire, she seems younger, sharper somehow. "Is it what we see with our eyes, or what we know in our hearts?"

"Both, I would hope," Orlan answers carefully.

Elynia gestures to a small table set with a carafe of wine and two cups. "What I'm about to tell you is known to very few in Elyssia. People have died for this knowledge—even royalty."

Orlan's breath catches. "The King and Queen? Is that why—"

"Not directly, no." Elynia pours the wine, her hands steady. "Orion and Lysandra didn't die for knowing this secret, but for something connected to it. Something they chose to do with this knowledge."

She offers him a cup, which he accepts but doesn't drink from. Caution is second nature to a knight.

"I assure you, it's not poisoned," she says with a hint of amusement. "If I wanted you dead, Sir Orlan, there are far less complicated methods."

He takes a small sip, more gesture than trust. "Why tell me this now?"

"Because Princess Melia is walking a path her parents began." Elynia moves to a chest in the corner, withdrawing a rolled parchment. "And because I believe you genuinely care for her welfare, not just as a symbol, but as a person."

"I've served the royal family since before she was born," Orlan confirms. "I would give my life to protect her."

"Your life may not be enough." Elynia unrolls the parchment on the table—a map, but not like any Orlan has seen before. It shows Elyssia from above, but with strange markings and annotations in a script he doesn't recognize. "What do you know about Ascension, Sir Orlan?"

"It is our sacred foundation," he recites automatically. "The divine process that raised Elyssia above the clouds, separating the worthy from the base world below."

"Recitation without understanding," Elynia says, not unkindly. "Like a child repeating a prayer without grasping its meaning."

"Then enlighten me," Orlan says, a hint of challenge in his voice.

Elynia traces a pattern on the map. "Elyssia wasn't raised by divine intervention, Orlan. It was built—constructed—using technologies and powers our ancestors possessed. Powers we've since forgotten how to use, but instead worship as mystical."

The statement lands like a physical blow. Orlan sets his cup down, steadying himself against the table. "That's heresy."

"Only if you believe the official doctrine," Elynia counters. "The doctrine Solivar and those before him have maintained to keep control. The same doctrine that declares it impossible for anyone to survive the fall from Elyssia, yet Princess Melia lives."

Orlan studies the map more closely, noticing structures and pathways that don't exist in the Elyssia he knows. "If what you say is true, then everything—"

"Everything you've been taught to believe is, at best, a partial truth," Elynia finishes for him. "At worst, a deliberate lie."

The silence stretches between them, broken only by the distant sound of the night bells.

"Are you willing to reconsider everything you thought you knew about Elyssia, Sir Orlan?" Elynia asks finally. "Because once you cross this threshold, there's no returning to comfortable ignorance."

Orlan thinks of Melia, somewhere below the clouds, pursued by Solivar's agents. Of Lira, asking innocent questions that someday might lead her into danger. Of Merien, whose steady gaze always seemed to see more than she said.

"Yes," he says simply, meeting Elynia's eyes without flinching. "Tell me everything."

Auren IV

The rain subsides momentarily, leaving the marshland air thick with humidity. Droplets cling to every surface, glistening on Bear's midnight fur as the cat picks its way delicately across fallen logs. Auren rolls his shoulders, testing the renewed strength in his muscles. The fever has finally broken, and with it, the bone-deep exhaustion from channeling too much Aether.

"We should reach Old Hollow by nightfall if we keep this pace," Auren says, adjusting the strap of his pack.

Kyp nods, consulting a worn map. "Provisions will last another two days if we're careful. After that..."

"There should be ample food and water at Old Hollow," Jade interjects, her voice carrying from several paces ahead. She moves with unsettling precision, each step calculated despite the treacherous terrain. "It's supposed to still be populated by adherents."

Auren frowns. "I saw no one when I passed through on my pilgrimage."

Jade doesn't turn around, but her response floats back clearly: "They saw you."

The statement sends an uncomfortable chill down Auren's spine. He exchanges a glance with Kyp, who shrugs with characteristic good humor.

"Mysterious, isn't she?" Kyp murmurs, his voice barely audible above the ambient sounds of the marsh.

Ahead, Melia walks beside Ryker, her posture relaxed as he gestures with theatrical flourish, describing some wildly improbable adventure involving three merchants and a stolen shipment of rare spices. She laughs—a genuine, unguarded sound that twists something deep and uncomfortable in Auren's chest. Ryker's hand brushes against hers as they navigate around a fallen tree, his fingers lingering just a moment too long against her skin. Neither of them pulls away from the contact. The sight makes Auren's jaw tighten involuntarily.

"You could just tell her, you know," Kyp says quietly, his normally jovial expression softened with concern as he studies Auren's face. "Instead of burning holes through Ryker's back with your eyes."

"Tell her what?" Auren asks gruffly, though the weight in his stomach tells him he knows perfectly well what Kyp means. He adjusts his pack unnecessarily, focusing on the sodden path beneath his boots.

"That you're thinking of naming your firstborn child after me," Kyp replies with an irrepressible grin that breaks through the tension. "What do you think I mean? The way you look at her when you think no one's watching could start fires."

Auren shakes his head, feeling the familiar heaviness of resignation settle over him like a weathered cloak. "I had my chance before. She's made her choice." His voice comes out rougher than intended, edged with something that feels dangerously close to regret.

"Has she?" Kyp challenges, his normally lighthearted tone giving way to unexpected wisdom. "Or have you decided for her? Seems to me you've been making a lot of choices on her behalf lately."

Before Auren can respond, Ryker's voice cuts across the marsh. "We should head west here. Quicker route."

Auren catches up to where the others have stopped at a fork in the path. One trail continues north through higher ground, while another veers west, cutting through denser marshland.

"North is more direct," Auren counters, pointing to the path that winds through a series of low hills. "Less chance of getting bogged down."

Ryker scoffs. "West skirts the trade route. Better chance of finding supplies, maybe even transportation."

"And more likely to encounter Garrik's men," Auren points out. "They'll be watching the trade routes."

"We can handle a few thugs," Ryker says dismissively.

"Like you handled them in Aurora?" Auren regrets the words as soon as they leave his mouth, but doesn't back down.

Ryker's eyes narrow. "At least I was trying to help. Where were you? Oh right, getting captured and playing gladiator."

"Stop it, both of you," Melia says, but neither man looks at her.

Jade watches the exchange with clinical detachment, as if observing specimens in a jar. Bear winds between Melia's ankles, fur bristling slightly.

"Let's settle this properly," Ryker suggests, dropping his pack. "Quick sparring match. Winner decides the route."

"That's ridiculous," Jade states flatly.

"Completely stupid," Melia agrees. "We don't have time for this."

Kyp sighs, recognizing the set of Auren's jaw. "He's not going to back down now."

Auren feels a familiar tension building in his chest. Part of him knows this is foolish—he's still recovering, and they're wasting precious daylight. But Ryker's cocky smirk, the casual way he stood too close to Melia, the subtle undermining of Auren's guidance—it all feeds a fire he can't quite extinguish.

"Fine," Auren says, setting down his own pack. "Quick match. No Aether."

"No Aether," Ryker agrees, rolling up his sleeves to reveal corded forearms. "Just skill against skill."

They move to a relatively flat area a few paces from the fork. Melia positions herself between them, face tight with frustration.

"This solves nothing," she says firmly. "Words are more powerful than fighting. We should discuss this rationally."

"Some things can't be settled with words," Ryker replies, not taking his eyes off Auren.

"Some men don't listen to reason," Auren adds.

Melia throws up her hands in exasperation. "Then you're both fools."

She steps back, giving them space, but her disappointment is palpable. Auren feels it like a physical weight, yet pride keeps him from backing down. He watches Ryker shift into a fighting stance—practiced, balanced, revealing formal training.

Auren centers himself, feet shoulder-width apart, hands loose but ready. The residual weakness from his fever lingers in his limbs, but he pushes it aside, focusing on Ryker's movements.

"First to yield?" Ryker suggests.

"Or first on their back," Auren counters.

Ryker circles left, light on his feet, sizing Auren up with calculating eyes. Auren mirrors the movement, keeping his weight balanced, aware of the soft ground beneath them. His limbs still feel heavy from the lingering effects of his fever, but he pushes the weakness aside.

"You know, she deserves better than a failed pilgrim," Ryker says quietly, his voice pitched just for Auren's ears.

The taunt lands precisely as intended. Anger flares hot in Auren's chest, and he lunges forward with a straight jab that Ryker easily sidesteps. Overextended, Auren barely manages to block the counter strike aimed at his ribs.

"Don't let him in your head," Kyp calls from the sidelines. "Stay focused!"

Melia's already walking away, Bear trotting at her heels. Her back is rigid with disapproval as she disappears around a bend in the path. The sight of her leaving twists something in Auren's gut, momentarily distracting him.

Ryker capitalizes immediately, sweeping low and catching Auren's ankle. Auren stumbles but recovers, backing up to reset his stance. They exchange several blows, testing defenses. Auren lands a solid hit to Ryker's shoulder, while Ryker's knuckles graze Auren's jaw.

"Are all men in your world this primitive?" Jade asks, standing beside Kyp with arms crossed. Her voice carries the flat curiosity of someone observing an unfamiliar ritual.

"Not all," Kyp responds, wincing as Ryker lands a sharp jab to Auren's side. "But these two? Absolutely."

Auren tries to block out their commentary, focusing on Ryker's movements. He's good—better than Auren expected. His technique suggests formal training, not just the scrappy survival fighting Auren learned in village brawls. There's a fluid efficiency to Ryker's movements that speaks of years of practice.

They grapple briefly, breaking apart when neither gains advantage. Mud smears their clothing, sweat beading despite the cool air. Auren's breath comes heavier than it should, his recent illness exacting its toll.

"You can't protect her," Ryker murmurs during their next close exchange. "You couldn't even protect yourself in Aurora."

Auren drives forward with renewed intensity, landing a solid combination that forces Ryker back several steps. For a moment, satisfaction blooms as Ryker's smugness falters.

"That's it!" Kyp cheers. "Show him what Willow Haven can do!"

But Auren's surge of energy fades quickly, his lungs burning with effort. Ryker recovers, circling again, reassessing.

"You'll fail her just like you failed to ascend," Ryker says, voice pitched low. "Some men just aren't meant for greatness."

The words strike deeper than any physical blow. Auren feels the familiar shadow of inadequacy spreading through him—the same darkness that consumed him after his fall. In that momentary distraction, Ryker strikes.

He feints high, then drops low, driving his shoulder into Auren's midsection. As they tumble to the ground, Ryker's fingers dig into the half-healed wound at Auren's side—the one he received in the fighting pits.

White-hot pain lances through Auren. He gasps, instinctively curling to protect the injury. Ryker presses the advantage, twisting Auren's arm behind his back and driving him face-first into the mud.

"Yield," Ryker demands, applying pressure to the twisted arm.

Pride wars with practicality in Auren's mind. The pain in his side throbs in time with his heartbeat, and he knows continuing would be foolish. With a grunt of frustration, he slaps his free hand against the ground.

"I yield," he mutters, the words bitter on his tongue.

Ryker releases him immediately, stepping back with a satisfied smile that doesn't reach his eyes. He offers a hand to help Auren up, a gesture more for the onlookers than genuine sportsmanship.

Auren ignores it, pushing himself to his feet, breathing heavily. Mud cakes his clothes and face, mixing with the fresh blood seeping through his shirt where Ryker's fingers had dug into his wound.

"That was dirty," Kyp says, approaching with a frown. "Going for an injured man's wounds."

"All's fair in love and war," Ryker shrugs, brushing dirt from his clothing with exaggerated nonchalance. "Besides, in a real fight, no one gives you special treatment for being wounded."

Jade approaches, her expression unchanged. "Efficient," she says to Ryker, though whether it's approval or mere observation is impossible to tell.

Auren wipes mud from his face, feeling humiliation burn through him. Not just from losing, but from engaging in such a pointless display in the first place. The look on Melia's face as she walked away plays in his mind, intensifying his shame.

"West path it is," Ryker announces, retrieving his pack.

Auren forces himself to straighten, ignoring the throbbing pain in his side. "Fine. West path." His voice comes out steadier than he feels. "But we move cautiously. Single file, scouts ahead. Garrik's men could be anywhere."

Kyp hands Auren a cloth to wipe his face. "You alright?" he asks quietly.

"I'll live," Auren replies grimly. "Let's catch up to Melia."

They find her waiting around the bend, sitting on a fallen log with Bear curled in her lap. She looks up as they approach, her expression guarded.

"Finished with your display of masculinity?" she asks coolly.

"We're taking the west path," Auren says, avoiding her gaze, acutely aware of the mud caking his clothes and the blood staining his side.

"I don't care which path we take," Melia responds. "I care that you're both acting like children."

Ryker opens his mouth to respond, but Jade cuts him off.

"We should move. Daylight wastes," she states flatly, already walking toward the western trail.

Bear jumps from Melia's lap and follows Jade with unusual interest, as if the enigmatic woman has somehow earned the cat's approval. Melia rises, her eyes lingering on the bloodstain spreading on Auren's shirt before she turns away.

"Let me look at that wound later," she says over her shoulder, following after Jade.

Auren nods, though she doesn't see it. He adjusts his pack, ignoring the pain, and falls into step behind her, swallowing both his pride and his concern about the path ahead.

***

The water glistens in the flickering firelight as Melia wrings out the cloth. Auren winces when she presses it against the reopened wound on his side, but keeps his breathing steady, determined not to show weakness after the day's humiliation.

"You're lucky it's not infected," she says, her voice soft yet clinical. "Though Ryker did his best to change that."

The camp is quiet. Kyp snores softly from his bedroll across the fire. Ryker disappeared to scout the perimeter an hour ago. Bear lounges nearby, amber eyes reflecting the flames.

"I shouldn't have let him goad me," Auren admits, staring into the darkness beyond their small circle of light. "It was foolish."

Melia's fingers trace the edge of the wound, sending a different kind of pain through him—the ache of wanting something just beyond reach.

"Why did you?" she asks, not looking up as she applies a salve to the gash. "You're smarter than that."

The truth sits heavy on his tongue. Because he was jealous. Because he saw how Ryker looked at her, how she sometimes laughed at his stories. Because the memory of their night in the chapel haunts him, and he doesn't know what it meant to her.

Instead, he says, "Old habits. When someone questions your strength in Willow Haven, you answer."

Her hands pause. "Is that what you think this journey is about? Proving strength?"

The disappointment in her voice cuts deeper than Ryker's taunts ever could.

"No," he says. "It's about finding truth. Your truth."

Now she meets his eyes. "And yours."

The air between them shifts, charged with unspoken feelings. Melia's hands linger on his skin, no longer tending his wound but simply touching him. Her fingertips leave trails of warmth that have nothing to do with the salve.

"I'm sorry," Auren whispers. "For today. For everything since the chapel."

"What are you sorry for, exactly?" Her voice has a new edge to it. "For what happened between us, or for how avoided me after?"

The directness of her question strips away his defenses. In the silence that follows, everything he's kept bottled inside threatens to spill out.

"I'm not sorry for what happened," he says finally. "I'm sorry for not knowing what to do after."

Melia sets the cloth aside, her movements deliberate. "And what do you want to do now?"

The question hangs between them, and Auren realizes he's tired of hesitating, of second-guessing. He leans forward, one hand finding the curve of her neck, and kisses her.

This isn't like their night in the chapel—desperate and discovering. This kiss carries the weight of everything they've left unsaid. It's an answer to questions neither has been brave enough to ask aloud.

Melia responds immediately, her fingers threading through his hair, pulling him closer. The pain in his side fades to insignificance as heat blooms between them. Her lips part beneath his, and Auren loses himself in the taste of her—sweet and fierce all at once.

When they finally break apart, both breathing heavily, Auren rests his forehead against hers. "That's what I want," he murmurs.

Melia's eyes are closed, her expression conflicted. Her hands remain on his shoulders, neither pulling him closer nor pushing him away.

"Auren," she whispers, and there's something in her voice that makes his heart constrict. "I don't know if I can do this."

"What do you mean?" His thumb traces her cheekbone, unwilling to release her just yet.

She pulls back slightly, creating space between them. "Everything is changing. I'm changing. I don't know who I am anymore—princess, pilgrim, fallen, something else entirely." Her eyes search his. "How can I know what I want when I don't even know who I am?"

The words strike at Auren's deepest insecurity—that he isn't enough, that he never was. That like his failed ascension, this too will end in rejection.

"I understand," he says, though the words taste like ash.

Melia stands, her movements stiff. "I need time," she says, not quite meeting his eyes. "I'm sorry."

She walks away toward her bedroll, set apart from the others. Bear watches her go, then gives Auren what seems like a sympathetic glance before following her.

Auren remains by the fire, the phantom sensation of her lips still lingering on his. The wound in his side throbs in time with his heartbeat, a physical echo of the ache in his chest.

"She's right, you know."

The voice startles him. He turns to find Jade standing just outside the firelight, her silhouette sharp against the darkness.

"How long have you been there?" he asks, embarrassment and irritation mingling in his voice.

"Long enough." She steps forward, the flames casting strange shadows across her angular features. "Your Aether mastery is impressive. I saw what you did in the fighting pits."

Auren stiffens. "So you were there."

Jade nods, sitting across from him with fluid grace. "But true power isn't in your fists or even in your Aether manipulation. It's in words. In knowing who you are."

"What are you talking about?"

"You fight well for a pilgrim who failed to ascend," she says, her gaze unnervingly direct. "But that's all you are to them—a failed pilgrim. And that's all you'll ever be until you become more."

The assessment, delivered without malice yet utterly without compassion, lands like a physical blow.

"Why do you care?" Auren challenges, defensive. "You barely know us. Why are you even here?"

Something flickers across Jade's face—so brief he might have imagined it. For an instant, her carefully maintained detachment slips, revealing something raw underneath.

"I know what it feels like," she says quietly, "to only be what you can do, not who you are."

The confession hangs in the air between them, unexpectedly vulnerable from someone who has shown nothing but cool calculation since joining their group.

"What do you mean?" Auren asks, his anger giving way to curiosity.

Jade stares into the fire, her profile sharp and austere. "You were trained to climb. To ascend. To fulfill a purpose set by others." Her eyes shift to his, and in their depths, he sees a reflection of his own struggles. "What happens when that purpose fails you? Or you fail it? Who are you then?"

The question strikes at the heart of everything Auren has grappled with since his fall. Who is he, if not the man who would reach Elyssia? What value does he have, if not as a successful pilgrim?

"I don't know," he admits.

"Neither did I," Jade says, and for a moment, something like kinship passes between them. "But I'm learning."

She stands, the moment of openness already receding behind her usual mask of detachment. "You should rest. Your wound needs time to heal properly."

As she turns to go, Auren calls after her. "Jade?"

She pauses, looking back over her shoulder.

"Thank you," he says simply.

She gives a barely perceptible nod before disappearing into the darkness, leaving Auren alone with the crackling fire and thoughts that burn even hotter.

He looks toward where Melia lies sleeping, Bear curled protectively at her feet, and feels the distance between them measured in more than just steps. Perhaps Jade is right. Perhaps he needs to become more than what he has been—not just for Melia, but for himself.

The night deepens around him as he adds another branch to the fire, watching the sparks rise toward the star-filled sky, wondering if any of them will reach high enough to touch the floating city that once defined his worth.

Melia VIII

The morning sun casts long shadows across the worn path as Melia trudges forward, each step bringing them closer to the next landmark on their reverse pilgrimage. Her legs ache from days of walking, but something else weighs heavier—the unsettled tension within their group. Auren walks ahead, his shoulders stiff with unspoken words. Ryker follows behind, occasionally catching her eye with a knowing glance that makes her stomach twist uncomfortably. Jade moves like a ghost at the periphery, watchful and silent.

"Should be just beyond that ridge," Auren announces, his voice carefully neutral. He hasn't spoken directly to her since their conversation by the fire two nights ago.

Bear pads beside Melia, occasionally brushing against her calf as if sensing her discomfort. The small black cat has become her constant companion, more attuned to her feelings than she sometimes is herself.

"What exactly are we looking for again?" Kyp asks, wiping sweat from his brow.

"Old Hollow," Auren replies. "It was once a training ground for pilgrims. The first preparation site on the Pilgrim's Road."

Melia's interest piques. "You trained there?"

Auren nods without turning back. "Briefly. It wasn't much even then. Just deserted ruins. Some say the stones carry memories, but I didn't feel a thing there."

They crest the ridge, and the valley below unfolds before them. Melia's breath catches at the sight. Nestled between two gentle slopes lies what must have once been an impressive complex—stone buildings with collapsed roofs, crumbling walls, and a central courtyard now overrun with weeds and saplings.

"That's Old Hollow?" she asks, unable to mask her disappointment.

"What remains of it," Auren confirms.

As they descend into the valley, the decay becomes more apparent. Murals that once depicted the glory of ascension now flake and peel, faces and figures worn away by weather and time. Statues of former pilgrims stand broken and headless, their pedestals covered in moss and lichen.

"Cheery place," Ryker comments, kicking at a fallen piece of masonry. "Really inspires confidence in the whole pilgrimage thing."

Melia moves toward a partially intact wall where faded images still cling to the stone. She traces her fingers over what appears to be a figure with golden wings, soaring toward a floating city. The paint crumbles beneath her touch.

"These murals," she murmurs, "they're just like the ones in Elyssia's Temple of Ascension."

"Of course they are," Jade says, suddenly beside her. "The narrative must remain consistent to maintain control."

Melia glances at her, startled by both her silent approach and her words. "What do you mean by that?"

Jade's steel-gray eyes scan the ruins methodically. "Belief systems require reinforcement. Visual symbols, repeated rituals, consistent mythology—they're tools of influence."

"You speak as if faith is merely manipulation," Melia says, a defensive edge creeping into her voice.

"Isn't it?" Jade's question hangs between them, uncomfortably direct.

Before Melia can respond, Bear hisses, back arching as he stares into the shadows of a nearby building. Everyone freezes.

"We're not alone," Auren whispers, his hand moving to the knife at his belt.

Figures emerge from the ruins around them—men and women dressed in simple homespun clothing adorned with ritual symbols. They carry no weapons, but their faces are stern, unwelcoming. Melia counts twelve, then fifteen, then more appearing from doorways and behind fallen columns.

An older woman steps forward, her gray hair wrapped in a complex braid adorned with small wooden tokens. Deep lines crease her weathered face, and her eyes—sharp and evaluating—fix on Melia with unsettling intensity.

"You should not have come here," she announces, her voice carrying across the courtyard with surprising strength. "This place is sacred to the Followers of the Old Ways."

Auren steps forward, hands raised in a placating gesture. "We meant no disrespect. We're simply passing through on pilgrimage."

The woman's gaze doesn't waver from Melia. "No. You bring her here. The Fallen One."

A murmur ripples through the gathered followers. Some make protective gestures across their chests; others touch small amulets hanging around their necks.

Melia feels a chill despite the warm day. "How do you know who I am?"

"We have watched. We have listened." The woman advances slowly. "Word travels. The princess who fell from Elyssia walks among us, desecrating the sacred path with her backward steps."

Ryker slides closer to Melia, his hand casually resting near his concealed blade. "Lovely reception committee. Shall we move along before this gets unpleasant?"

The woman's eyes narrow. "You cannot simply leave. Not now that you've brought her here."

Kyp clears his throat nervously. "What exactly do you want with her?"

"To understand," the woman says, "why one blessed to live among the divine would fall. To abandon the sacred mandate."

Melia steps forward, gently pushing past Auren's protective arm. "I didn't fall. I chose to jump."

This causes another stir among the Followers, more intense than before. Some look horrified, others fascinated.

"Blasphemy," someone hisses from the crowd.

"Truth," Melia counters, her voice stronger than she feels. "Elyssia isn't what you believe it to be. It's not some sacred heaven. It's just a city of people."

The older woman studies her, head tilted slightly. "I am Elder Karina. And you presume much, Princess."

"My name is Melia."

"Names don't change nature," Elder Karina replies. "Just as this place remains sacred, despite its decay."

Melia looks around at the broken statues, the crumbling murals, feeling a strange resonance with the ruins. She too had been polished and perfect on the surface, concealing fractures within.

"Why do you maintain this place?" she asks. "It's falling apart."

"We preserve what matters," Elder Karina gestures to the complex around them. "Not the stones or paint, but the purpose. The connection to those above."

Jade steps forward, her stance subtly shifting to something more defensive. "And what exactly is that purpose now?"

Elder Karina's eyes flick to Jade, then back to Melia. "To prepare those worthy of ascension. To honor the divine mandate that sustains us all."

"The divine mandate," Melia repeats, tasting the bitterness of the words. "Do you even know what that means?"

"It means order," Elder Karina says firmly. "It means purpose. It means faith in something greater than ourselves."

Bear presses against Melia's leg, his green eyes fixed on the Elder. She draws strength from his presence.

"And if that faith is built on lies?" Melia challenges.

A tense silence falls over the courtyard. The Followers shift uneasily, exchanging glances. Elder Karina's expression hardens.

"The old ways have sustained us for generations," she says, her voice carrying across the ruins. "Why should we doubt the wisdom of our ancestors when the heavens themselves have ordained it?"

"Because sometimes what we're taught to worship is merely what keeps us in chains," she says quietly.

Elder Karina steps closer, close enough that Melia can see the fine network of wrinkles around her eyes, the weathered texture of her skin that speaks of a life lived under open skies—so different from the preserved perfection of Elyssia's nobles.

"You speak of chains," the Elder says, "yet you were raised in paradise."

"A gilded cage is still a cage," Melia responds.

Something shifts in Elder Karina's expression—not softening exactly, but a flicker of curiosity breaking through the hostility.

"Come," she says abruptly. "All of you. If you wish to pass through Old Hollow, you must first understand what you tread upon."

She turns and walks toward the largest of the partially intact buildings. The other Followers part to create a path, their expressions ranging from suspicious to curious.

Auren moves to Melia's side. "We don't have to do this," he murmurs. "We could find another route."

Melia watches Elder Karina's retreating figure, feeling the weight of dozens of eyes upon her. These people have devoted their lives to a vision of Elyssia that she knows to be false. Yet their faith is real, their devotion genuine. Perhaps they deserve to hear the truth—or at least, the truth as she understands it.

"No," she decides. "I want to hear what they have to say. And maybe... maybe they should hear what I have to say too."

Ryker sighs dramatically. "Walking into the lair of religious zealots. What could possibly go wrong?"

"They're people seeking meaning," Melia counters. "Just like the rest of us."

As they follow Elder Karina into the shadowed interior of the building, Bear trots ahead confidently, his sleek black form a stark contrast against the dust-covered stone floor. The Followers close in behind them, not threatening but present, a living barrier between them and the way they came.

Jade falls into step beside Melia. "Religious devotion is the perfect mechanism for control," she observes quietly. "It requires no chains or guards—the believers police themselves."

Melia considers this as they enter what appears to have once been a grand hall, now open to the elements where portions of the roof have collapsed. Sunlight streams through these gaps, illuminating ancient murals that depict the same stories she grew up with—the divine creation of Elyssia, the chosen rising to join the heavens, the blessed life that awaits the worthy.

But here, in Old Hollow, the peeling paint reveals the fragility of those narratives. Just as her fall from Elyssia had revealed the fragility of everything she once believed.

***

Elder Karina leads them deeper into the grand hall, where rows of stone benches face a raised platform at the far end. Dust motes dance in the shafts of sunlight piercing through the crumbling ceiling.

"This was once our most sacred space," Elder Karina explains.

Melia drifts away from the group, drawn to a small alcove hidden in shadow. The others continue following Elder Karina, their voices growing distant. Bear remains at Melia's side, his ears twitching with curiosity.

"What is it?" she whispers to him, as if he might answer.

The alcove contains a small stone altar, carved with symbols that mirror those she's seen in Elyssia's temples. Unlike the rest of Old Hollow, this space feels untouched by decay, preserved somehow against time's erosion.

Melia reaches out, her fingers hovering above the altar's smooth surface. Something pulses beneath the stone—a vibration so subtle she wonders if she's imagining it.

"There were places of power," her father once told her, in a rare moment of candor. "Doorways between what is seen and unseen."

Her fingertips touch the cool stone.

The world shifts.

The alcove dissolves around her, replaced by a chamber she recognizes—her mother's private study in Elyssia. Queen Lysandra stands before a map similar to the one Melia discovered before her fall, her fingers tracing a path that leads from Elyssia to a point marked with an unfamiliar symbol.

"If she makes it here, we've failed," her mother says, her voice clear as crystal though her back is turned.

Another figure stands in shadow, partially obscured. "Then we must ensure she never feels the need to leave," the shadowed person replies.

"That's not what I meant." Queen Lysandra turns, and Melia gasps at the sight of her mother's face—not serene and perfect as in her memories, but lined with worry and something like fear. "If she's forced to make this journey alone, it means we didn't prepare her. It means we couldn't protect her from what's coming."

"Perhaps it's better this way," the shadow says. "Some truths can only be learned through experience."

"At what cost?" Lysandra's voice breaks. "She's my daughter. Our daughter."

Melia reaches toward her mother, but her hand passes through like smoke. "Mother," she whispers. "I'm here. I made it."

The vision fractures. Her mother's face dissolves into fragments of light and shadow—

Melia stumbles backward, falling to her knees on the cold stone floor of Old Hollow. The altar stands before her, unchanged and silent. But she is not. Something hot and wet streaks down her face. She touches her cheek, surprised to find tears.

"Mother knew," she whispers, her voice breaking. "She knew I would fall."

The realization crashes over her like a wave. Her parents hadn't been ignorant of Elyssia's secrets—they'd been keeping them.

Bear presses against her, his warmth a small comfort. She wraps her arms around his sleek body, burying her face in his fur as sobs rack her frame.

"They sent me on this path," she gasps between tears. "All this time, I thought I was rebelling, choosing my own way. But they knew. They expected this."

"Found something interesting, did you?"

Melia looks up to see Elder Karina standing in the entrance to the alcove, her weathered face unreadable. The others are still touring the main hall, unaware of Melia's breakdown.

"What is this place?" Melia demands, her voice raw. "What does it do?"

Karina studies her with renewed interest. "It shows what needs to be seen," she says simply. "The question is, Princess—what did you see?"

Melia rises from her knees, wiping tears from her face with the back of her hand. The vulnerability in her eyes hardens into something resolute as she meets Elder Karina's gaze.

"I saw my mother," she says. "Not as the queen everyone worshiped, but as a woman carrying a burden she couldn't share."

Bear weaves between her ankles, his presence grounding her to this moment, this reality. The cold stone beneath her feet feels more solid now, as if the vision has somehow strengthened her connection to the physical world rather than diminished it.

"Show me more," Melia demands, gesturing toward the main hall where the others wait. "I need to understand what my parents knew."

Elder Karina's lips twist into something between a smile and a grimace. "Come, then."

They return to the grand hall where Auren, Jade, Ryker, and Kyp stand waiting. Auren's eyes immediately find hers, narrowing with concern when he notices the tracks of tears on her cheeks. He takes a half-step toward her, but stops when he sees the determined set of her jaw.

"Gather," Elder Karina calls out, her voice echoing through the cavernous space. "The Fallen wishes to learn."

Word spreads quickly through Old Hollow. More Followers emerge from shadowed doorways and hidden passages, their faces etched with curiosity and reverence. They form a loose circle around the central platform where Elder Karina now stands with Melia.

"Tell them what you saw, Princess," Elder Karina urges, her voice dropping to a whisper. "Tell them why you fell."

The weight of their expectations presses down on Melia's shoulders. She scans the crowd, taking in their weathered faces and threadbare clothes. These people have spent generations waiting for a sign, a validation of their faith in something beyond the rigid doctrines of Elyssia.

Her gaze finds Auren. He gives her a slight nod, a reassuring glance that somehow steadies her racing heart.

"I didn't fall," Melia says, her voice gaining strength with each word. "I jumped. I chose to leave Elyssia because I discovered that everything I'd been taught was built on lies."

A collective gasp ripples through the gathered Followers. Some step back as if her words might physically harm them, while others lean forward, eager for more.

"My parents knew the truth," she continues.

Elder Karina watches her with keen eyes, neither confirming nor denying Melia's words.

"This place," Melia gestures to the crumbling walls around them, "was made of sacrifice. The sacrifice of truth. The sacrifice of freedom. You've shackled yourselves to an idea of this perfect city that doesn't exist."

Melia's words hang in the air like frost. The Followers' faces transform from reverence to outrage in an instant.

"Blasphemy!" A woman shrieks, her voice cracking with emotion. "The Fallen One speaks heresy against the Sacred City!"

The crowd surges forward, their weathered hands reaching for Melia. Elder Karina steps back, her eyes glittering with something unreadable—expectation? Fear? Satisfaction?

"She'll poison our faith with her lies!" A man with a long gray beard lunges toward the platform.

Auren moves with surprising speed, positioning himself between Melia and the advancing crowd. His shoulders tense as he raises his hands, a shimmer of Aether energy dancing between his fingers—not a threat, but a warning.

"Stand down," he commands, his voice cutting through the chaos. "She speaks only what she's experienced."

Ryker materializes on Melia's other side, his posture deceptively casual but his eyes alert. He draws a short blade, twirling it with practiced nonchalance.

"Quite the reception committee you've got here," he mutters to Melia. "Remind me not to criticize their cooking."

The Followers halt their advance, momentarily deterred by the show of force, but their anger radiates like heat.

Bear, who had been sitting calmly at Melia's feet throughout the confrontation, suddenly rises and pads away from the platform. His movement draws Melia's attention away from the hostile crowd.

"Bear?" she calls, concerned by his departure.

The black cat pauses, looking back at her with those unnervingly intelligent green eyes. Then he continues across the hall toward a recessed corner where a weathered stone protrudes from the wall.

Melia squints, noticing what looks like a carving on its surface—the royal insignia of Elyssia, the same symbol she'd seen on official documents and her father's signet ring.

"Cover me," she whispers to Auren and Ryker, slipping between them before either can protest.

"Melia, wait—" Auren reaches for her arm but misses.

Elder Karina makes no move to stop her as Melia hurries after Bear, threading her way through the agitated Followers who part reluctantly, some reaching to touch her clothes as she passes.

"Where's Jade?" Kyp asks from somewhere behind her, his voice tight with anxiety.

Melia glances around, realizing that the mysterious woman has indeed vanished. When had she slipped away? And why?

No time to wonder about that now. Bear sits expectantly before the stone with the royal insignia, ears twitching with impatience.

The insignia is different from the ones displayed prominently throughout Elyssia. This version shows the traditional sunburst surrounding the crown, but with additional markings—lines that extend outward like rays or perhaps paths, connecting to smaller symbols etched around the perimeter.

Melia kneels before the stone, aware of the Followers being held at bay by Auren and Ryker. Their angry voices seem to fade as she studies the carving, feeling a pull similar to what she experienced at the altar.

"What are you trying to show me?" she whispers to Bear, who blinks slowly in response.

Her fingers hover over the insignia. Something about those radiating lines reminds her of the map she'd discovered in her father's study—the one that first prompted her to question everything.

Bear nudges her hand with his head, a gentle encouragement.

Melia presses her palm against the cool stone, tracing the lines of the royal crest that has defined her life and lineage.

The world contracts around her, sound and light tunneling to a single point of contact between her skin and the ancient stone. The last thing she sees is Bear's unblinking gaze before darkness swallows her consciousness.

She falls, untethered from her body, into a void that feels both terrifying and strangely familiar.

Jade III

The moment the crowd surges toward Melia, Jade slips away. Not running—running draws attention—but moving with practiced invisibility, each step placed with deliberate silence. The commotion provides perfect cover. No one notices another shadow among shadows.

Jade observed the stone structures of Old Hollow upon arrival, cataloging irregularities with mechanical precision. The north wall of the abandoned temple had suffered structural collapse decades ago. Beneath the rubble: an opening. Unnoticed by the others, significant to her trained eye.

She squeezes through the narrow gap, boots scraping against ancient stonework. The passage beyond smells of mineral deposits and time—a scent her brain registers as both foreign and achingly familiar. Her hand instinctively reaches for her missing combat suit, finding only the rough fabric of borrowed clothes.

Defenses compromised. Proceed with caution.

The thought forms in Imperial tactical patterns, but something underneath pushes back. A half-remembered voice: *Not everything is a threat assessment.*

Jade descends rough-hewn steps, counting automatically. Seventeen. Then thirty-four. Then fifty-one. The numbers form a sequence her mind recognizes without context. The pattern recognition triggers a jolt in her neural implants—a warning flare of pain at the base of her skull.

The Emperor's voice echoes: *Some memories are best left buried, Shadow.*

She ignores the phantom admonition, continuing downward. The passage widens into a chamber where faint light bleeds through cracks in the ceiling. Remnants of ancient construction: curved architecture unlike Imperial designs, smooth surfaces now cracked with age.

Jade approaches a stone table at the chamber's center. Scattered across its surface: tomes with tattered bindings, scrolls crumbling at the edges, and a metal container sealed with unfamiliar mechanisms.

"Unauthorized entry," she murmurs to herself, fingertips hovering over the artifacts. "Classified materials. Report and withdraw."

But she doesn't withdraw.

Instead, she examines each text methodically. One written in flowing script that resembles water. Another in angular symbols that hurt her eyes. A third using pictographs that seem to shift when viewed from different angles.

The fourth book stops her cold.

Its cover bears no title, only a series of interconnected spirals forming a complex fractal pattern. Her fingers tremble as they trace the design—a physiological response she hasn't experienced since her earliest training days.

Fractal glyphwork, her mind supplies, though she cannot identify the source of this knowledge.

Jade opens the book carefully. The pages contain densely packed symbols arranged in nested circles. Text that should be incomprehensible, yet her eyes parse meaning without conscious effort:

The Thread remembers what believers forget. Faith is the leash that binds possibility.

Her vision blurs. The neural dampeners embedded in her cerebral cortex activate, attempting to suppress the cascade of recognition. Pain lances through her temples.

"Override sequence," she whispers, fingers pressing against specific points at her hairline where subdermal implants regulate her neurological responses. The sequence comes instinctively, muscle memory performing what her conscious mind doesn't fully comprehend.

The pain recedes. Something unlocks.

Jade turns another page. A diagram shows a humanoid figure suspended in concentric circles of energy. Notes surround it, explaining concepts her Imperial training classified as heretical: consciousness as interdimensional interface, belief as limitation rather than power, memory as the true foundation of reality.

Luthari principles of Thread manipulation, her mind catalogs. *Classification: Forbidden. Penalty: Immediate termination.*

Yet she continues reading, each symbol triggering neural pathways long suppressed. Images flash before her: a woman with steel-gray eyes teaching a child to trace similar patterns in the air; a sanctuary filled with crystalline technology; laughter as tiny hands manipulate colored light.

"Mother," Jade whispers, the word feeling foreign on her tongue.

She turns another page. This one contains a detailed illustration of a suit—black, seamless, with neural interfaces that connect directly to the wearer's consciousness. Her suit. The one locked away in her ship.

Beneath it, annotations explain its purpose: *Not to conceal identity, but to preserve it. Protection against narrative manipulation and forced alignment.*

Memory fragments crystallize into coherence: her mother fastening the suit around her small shoulders, saying, *"This will shield you from those who would rewrite you."*

The Imperial conditioning fights back, chemical suppressants flooding her system. Jade's knees buckle. She grips the edge of the stone table, knuckles white.

"I am the Shadow," she hisses through clenched teeth. "Asset designation S-42. Mission parameters: locate and assess threat potential of—"

Samara, a voice interrupts—her mother's voice, clear as though she stands beside her. *Your name is Samara.*

Jade—Sam—*Samara*—presses her forehead against the cool stone of the table, caught between contradictory truths. The Empire that saved her. The Empire that destroyed her people. The mission she must complete. The lie she's been living.

"System failure," she whispers, but it isn't failure. It's recognition.

Her implants fire chaotically, flooding her bloodstream with suppression chemicals designed to maintain control. Pain blooms behind her eyes—a defensive measure against recovered memory. The Empire's failsafes activating one by one.

Jade presses her palms flat against the ancient text, anchoring herself through the waves of agony. The book seems to pulse beneath her touch, resonating with something buried deep within her core identity.

"Override," she commands, voice stronger. "Override. Override."

Each repetition weakens the chemical barriers. Her body remembers what her conscious mind cannot yet grasp—security protocols embedded by her mother, not the Empire. Protocols designed to survive exactly this kind of mental suppression.

Blood trickles from her nose, staining the yellowed page beneath. The droplet spreads across the fractal pattern, revealing new lines previously invisible. A biometric key unlocked by her DNA.

"I am..." she starts, but stops. The Shadow's designations no longer fit. Neither does Jade, the temporary identity she created.

Her eyes flutter closed. The chemical storm in her body quiets. The pain recedes like a tide pulling back from shore.

Sam surrenders to remembrance.

***

15 Years Ago

Purple light erupts through the viewport, bathing Samara's face in its unnatural glow. She clings to the armor case, fingers white against the metallic surface as she watches their sanctuary disintegrate.

"Stay hidden," Mother had ordered. But from her concealment behind the curved partition, Samara sees everything.

Imperial soldiers move with mechanical precision through the dwelling's main chamber. Their armor gleams with integrated tech, but it's the strange energy emanating from their weapons that makes her stomach clench. Not the standard plasma rifles of frontier patrols—these emit tendrils of violet energy that seem to reach rather than fire.

Mother stands before them, back straight, hands empty. "There's nothing here for you," she says, voice steady despite the tremor Samara can feel through their shared mental connection.

"Luthari trash," the lead soldier says, his face hidden behind a reflective mask. "The Emperor has special interest in your kind. Something about your... resistance to realignment."

Mother's eyes flick toward Samara's hiding spot for just a fraction of a second. "I am the last. The others died in the purge."

The soldier laughs. "Yet here you are, teaching forbidden knowledge." He gestures, and two soldiers move to the learning alcove where Samara had stood just minutes before. They overturn the teaching table, scattering crystalline data cores across the floor.

"Indoctrinating the next generation?" The commander steps closer to Mother. "Where is the child?"

Mother says nothing, her face a mask of defiance.

The commander sighs. "Unfortunate. We were hoping to avoid neural extraction."

He lifts his hand, and purple energy coalesces around his fingers. With a flicking motion, he sends it toward Mother's forehead. The energy doesn't burn or cut—it *penetrates,* sinking through skin and bone like they're no more substantial than mist.

Mother's eyes widen. Her mouth opens in a silent scream. Samara bites her own hand to keep from crying out as she watches the purple light spread beneath Mother's skin, illuminating veins and neural pathways like a grotesque anatomical model.

"Where is the child?" the commander repeats. "Where is the armor?"

Mother's body convulses, but her eyes remain fixed on the far wall—away from Samara's hiding place. Blood trickles from her nose, her ears, the corners of her eyes.

"The knowledge dies with me," she manages, words slurred.

The commander shrugs. "Then die."

He closes his fist. The purple light intensifies, blazing from within Mother's body like a star going supernova. For one terrible moment, Samara can see through her—see the outline of bones, the shape of organs, all illuminated in that hideous light.

Then Mother's consciousness extinguishes. Not her body—that remains standing, held upright by the energy still coursing through it—but *her*. The presence Samara has felt since birth vanishes like a candle snuffed out by hurricane winds.

The mental severing is so violent that Samara nearly vomits. She swallows hard, pressing herself deeper into the shadows, clutching the armor case against her chest.

"Sweep the area," the commander orders. "Find the child. Find the armor. Nothing else matters."

Soldiers fan out, methodically destroying everything in their path. They upend storage units, smash equipment, tear through sleeping pallets. The purple energy flows from their gauntlets, dissolving matter at a molecular level wherever it touches.

Mother's body finally collapses, the purple light fading. It leaves behind something barely recognizable as human—desiccated and gray, as though the essence of life itself was extracted.

Samara's tears fall silently onto the armor case. She knows she should run, but her legs won't move. All she can do is watch as everything she's ever known disappears in flashes of violet light.

The soldiers' boots echo against the metal floor as they approach Samara's hiding place. Her breath catches in her throat, lungs burning with the effort to stay silent. One soldier kicks aside a fallen panel, revealing the shadow of her small form.

"Here!" he shouts. "Found something!"

In an instant, they surround her, weapons drawn. Samara clutches the armor case tighter, her mother's final instructions pounding through her mind: *Keep it safe. Never let them have it.* But she's just a child against an Imperial squad.

"It's just a girl," one soldier says, the purple energy from his gauntlet dimming slightly.

"The target had a daughter," another responds. "This must be her."

Rough hands seize Samara's arms, yanking her from her hiding place. The armor case slips from her grasp, clattering to the floor. She lunges for it desperately, but a soldier snatches it away, examining it with clinical interest.

"Found something interesting," he announces, turning the case over in his hands. "Some kind of containment unit."

Samara thrashes against her captor's grip. "That's mine! Give it back!" Her voice breaks, raw with grief and rage.

The commander strides over, his reflective mask tilting down to study her. Despite her terror, Samara glares back, refusing to look away. A small part of her hopes he'll simply end her existence as he did her mother's—at least then she'd be with her again.

"Spirited," he says, voice distorted through his helmet. "Like all Luthari."

He reaches out, and Samara flinches, expecting the purple energy to pierce her skull. Instead, he merely grips her chin, turning her face from side to side like he's appraising livestock.

"Take her to the shuttle. Undamaged." He releases her face and gestures to the armor case. "And secure that. The Emperor's scientists will want to examine it thoroughly."

"What about the rest, sir?" A soldier gestures at the half-destroyed sanctuary.

"Purge it. Standard protocol for Luthari contamination."

Samara struggles as they drag her toward the door, her feet barely touching the ground. "Let me go! You killed my mother!" Each word tears from her throat, but the soldiers might as well be deaf for all they respond.

Outside, the night air hits her face, cool and sharp against her tear-streaked cheeks. Their sanctuary had been built into a mountain-side, hidden from orbital scans by natural magnetic fields. Now, Imperial shuttles hover above the clearing, searchlights cutting through the darkness.

The soldiers march her toward the nearest shuttle, its ramp extended like a waiting maw. Samara plants her feet, pulling against their grip with all her strength, but it's like fighting against gravity itself.

The general—their commander—follows behind, carrying the armor case himself. He removes his helmet, revealing a face that might have been handsome if not for the coldness in his eyes. Salt-and-pepper hair is cropped close to his skull, and a thin scar runs from his right temple to his jaw.

"You're making this harder than it needs to be, child," he says, voice clearer now without the helmet's distortion.

Samara spits at him. The saliva lands on his polished boot.

Rather than anger, his face shows something like amusement. "The Emperor will be interested in this one," he remarks to the soldiers. "Her kind usually break much easier."

"Where are your orders, Governor Draven?" one of the soldiers asks.

"Take her to the holding facility. I'll inform the Emperor person-ally." He hands the armor case to another soldier. "And this goes in secure containment. Level one protocols only."

As they drag her up the ramp, Samara takes one last look at the only home she's ever known. Purple light flares from within as the purge begins, erasing every trace of Luthari existence.

The shuttle doors seal shut, cutting off her view. The last of her tears dry on her face as something cold and hard settles in her chest where her heart used to be.

***

The Present

The memories slam through Jade's mind with physical force, knocking her back against the ancient stone wall of the hidden chamber. Her neural dampeners fail completely, overwhelmed by the cascade of recovered truth. The book with fractal patterns slips from her fingers, landing on the dusty floor with a dull thud.

"I wasn't collateral damage," she whispers to the empty room. "I was the objective."

Her hand unconsciously traces the surgical scars along her spine—modifications she'd been told were necessary after injuries sustained during her rescue. But there had been no rescue. Only capture.

The Emperor's gentle voice echoes in her memory: *"Your mother died trying to protect you from the rebels. We saved you, but not without cost."*

Lies. All of it.

Her neural implants flare with warning signals, attempting to suppress these dangerous connections, but the flood is too powerful. The

Shadow—no, Jade—no, Sam—grips her head between her hands, forcing herself to remember.

"They killed her in front of me." Her voice cracks, the words fracturing against the silence of the chamber. "And I wasn't injured. I was... stolen. Taken like property. Harvested like a resource." The realization cuts deeper than any blade she's ever wielded.

The armor she wears, the very suit she's been told was her birthright—sleek and deadly, a second skin that had defined her existence—was the very thing they came to take, along with her. It wasn't protection gifted by the Empire; it was Luthari technology they coveted, with her inside it. A package deal. The perfect weapon wrapped in the perfect shell.

"What else?" She presses her palms against her temples with increasing pressure, as if she could physically force the buried truths to surface through her skull. Her fingers tremble against her skin. "What else did he lie about? How much of my life is fabricated? How many missions were..." She trails off, unable to complete the thought.

The implants at the base of her skull burn hot, searing like molten metal against her neural pathways, fighting her recall with programmed resistance. Pain shoots down her spine in warning pulses, but Sam pushes through it, gritting her teeth until they creak with pressure. Fragments surface through the agony: her mother speaking of balance in reverent tones, of the Thread as memory rather than divinity—a living record connecting all things rather than a god to be worshipped. Memories of technology as sacred language, tools that spoke to the universe directly rather than through prayer. All concepts categorically opposed to Imperial doctrine, all truths systematically erased and replaced with the Emperor's carefully constructed lies.

And then—a flash of herself submerged in that tank, with tubes and wires connected to her body.

"They weren't healing me," she realizes, the truth burning through years of conditioning. "They were reprogramming me."

Her hand moves instinctively to her chest, feeling the steady rhythm of her heart beneath layers of tactical clothing. How much of her is still her? How much has been altered, replaced, controlled?

Sam slides down the wall until she's sitting on the stone floor, surrounded by ancient texts that tell truths the Empire has systematically erased. Her breathing comes in short, sharp gasps as her body fights between Imperial conditioning and recovered identity.

The mission parameters flicker across her vision, projected by neural implants: *Locate Liora Solari. Assess threat level. Eliminate if necessary.*

But overlaid on this is her mother's voice: *"Remember who you are, Samara. They can take everything else, but not that."*

Sam presses her forehead against the cool stone floor, anchoring herself against the dizzying rush of reclaimed memories. Her conditioning battles against this awakening—neural pathways rewired by Imperial doctors throb with resistance. Her vision blurs, then clarifies.

"Who am I now?" she whispers to the empty chamber.

Years of missions flash through her mind—planets conquered, dissidents silenced, information extracted. All executed with clinical precision by the weapon they made her. The Shadow.

Her gaze drifts back to the fallen tome, its pages splayed open. Despite the neural implants screaming for her to leave this place, to report this unauthorized material for destruction, her hand reaches for it.

"One truth at a time," she murmurs, pulling the book toward her.

She flips through ancient pages filled with intricate diagrams until a familiar shape catches her eye—a perfect circle hovering above stylized clouds. Elyssia.

Sam's breath catches. The pages contain detailed schematics, not religious iconography. Equations and engineering notes fill the margins in a language that feels hauntingly familiar—Luthari script.

"This is..." Her fingers trace the diagrams of propulsion systems, atmospheric regulators, and something called "Thread calibration matrices."

Sam's eyes widen as she reads further.

Melia IX

The light here has a quality Melia has never seen before—golden but solid somehow, as if sunbeams have been captured and woven into the very air. She stands motionless, her body feeling simultaneously weightless and impossibly heavy. Around her, people move with purpose, their faces eerily familiar.

This place—this impossible structure of soaring, unbroken spires and pristine white stone—pulses with anticipation. The architecture feels like Elyssia, yet older, more honest somehow. More real.

"The preparations are nearly complete," says a woman whose face Melia recognizes from portraits in the High Temple. High Priestess Amara, dead for centuries, yet here she stands, vibrant and alive. "The Thread measurements are optimal. We must begin before the alignment shifts."

Melia tries to move toward her, but her feet seem anchored in place. "What is happening?" she asks, but no one turns. No one hears.

A cluster of nobles passes by—some wearing the same faces as Elyssia's current council members, others entirely unfamiliar. Their excitement buzzes in the air like electricity.

"After generations of work," one whispers, "we'll finally ascend."

"The greatest Conjuration ever attempted," another adds, his hands trembling with what might be fear or exhilaration.

Melia's heart races as she realizes what she's witnessing. Not a dream—something else. Something that once was.

In the center of the vast chamber, a circle of people kneel around an enormous crystal matrix. At its heart sits a concentration of Aetherium unlike anything Melia has ever seen—not the small, disciplined amounts used in Elyssia's daily rituals, but a wild, pulsing mass that seems almost alive.

"Begin the Cycle," commands a voice that strikes Melia with terrible familiarity.

She turns, fighting against whatever force holds her in place, and sees her father—no, not her father, but a man with the same bearing, the same eyes. A distant ancestor, perhaps.

"The Conjuration begins now," he announces, his voice resonating with authority. "What the Thread remembers, we reinforce. What it forgets, we conjure."

The crowd repeats his words like a prayer, their voices unified in purpose.

"We will lift ourselves above the chaos," the man continues. "Create perfection from imperfection. Raise our city into the heavens, where it belongs."

Tears spring to Melia's eyes as understanding dawns. "This is how it began," she whispers to herself. "Not divine intervention. Not a gift from the gods. Just... people. People using Aetherium to build a lie."

The kneeling figures begin a synchronized chant, their hands pressed against the floor. Beneath Melia's feet, the ground trembles.

"The foundations are set," someone calls out. "The Cycle is initiated."

"And the cost?" asks a lone voice—a woman standing apart from the others, her face hidden by a hood.

"Necessary," replies the man with her father's eyes, not unkindly. "Those who serve as anchors do so willingly."

As he speaks, Melia notices figures in the shadows, chained with bindings that glow with the same light as the Aetherium. Their faces slack, their eyes vacant.

"They're using people," Melia gasps. "People as components. As... batteries."

The floor beneath her begins to vibrate more intensely, and light erupts from the central crystal, engulfing everything in blinding radiance.

The light flares, then dims, and suddenly the scene transforms. The ancient figures fade, replaced by more familiar ones. Melia's breath catches in her throat.

"Father?" she whispers.

King Orion walks with measured steps across what has become the central plaza of Elyssia. Beside him glides Queen Lysandra, her posture perfect, her face serene yet troubled. And behind them—Melia's heart clenches—trails a small girl with golden hair tied in elaborate braids. Young Melia, perhaps seven years old, struggling to match the royal stride.

But what makes Melia's blood freeze is the fourth figure: Prefect Solivar, younger but unmistakable, walking at her father's right hand.

"We must address the fluctuations in the eastern quadrant," Solivar says, his voice smooth as polished stone. "The Conjuration is weakening there. Three children reported seeing through the Veil yesterday."

Melia lunges forward, desperate to reach them, to warn her father about the man beside him. But an invisible wall stops her, solid as granite yet clear as air. She pounds against it, her fists making no sound.

"They're memories," she realizes aloud. "Preserved in the stone somehow."

Young Melia skips ahead, momentarily breaking protocol, and Queen Lysandra smiles despite the serious conversation.

"The children will be properly educated," her mother says. "But Orion, we must consider what I discovered in the archives."

King Orion's face tightens. "Not here, Lysandra."

"The cycle is unsustainable," her mother persists, voice barely above a whisper. "Each generation requires more anchors, more sacrifice. The Aetherium consumption has tripled in our lifetime alone."

Solivar's expression remains pleasant, but Melia sees his fingers twitch—a gesture she knows well from council meetings. Irritation. Calculation.

"Your Majesties worry unnecessarily," Solivar interjects. "The Conjuration has sustained us for centuries. With proper management—"

"Proper management," King Orion repeats, his voice hollow. "Is that what we call it now?"

Young Melia has stopped to watch a butterfly, oblivious to the tension among the adults.

The scene ripples, and Melia feels herself being pulled—not physically, but as if her consciousness is being redirected. The plaza melts away, reforming into her father's private study. The little girl is gone now. Only the three adults remain.

"You asked to see the ledgers," Solivar says, placing a thick book on the desk. "Every soul that maintains our paradise, properly documented."

Queen Lysandra opens it, her fingers trembling slightly. "So many," she whispers. "And they never truly die, do they? They just... serve. Forever."

Melia strains against the barrier, desperate to see the book's contents, to understand what horrified her mother so deeply.

King Orion stands at the window, looking out over Elyssia's perfect spires. "We were taught that the Ascended become one with the Thread," he says quietly. "That was the lie we told ourselves. The truth is much simpler, isn't it, Solivar? They become one with the city itself."

Solivar's smile doesn't waver. "Every paradise requires foundations, Your Majesty."

The room begins to dissolve, colors bleeding into one another. Melia cries out, reaching for her parents as they fade from view.

"Don't go! Please! What did you find? What did you learn?"

But they cannot hear her across the years. The last thing she sees is her father's face, set with a determination she recognizes—the same expression he wore the day he told her what must be broken.

***

The spires materialize around her, impossibly tall, gleaming in artificial perfection. Melia staggers, disoriented by the sudden shift. Her father's face—no, not her father but someone with his features—stands on a raised platform, conferring with robed figures.

A soft pressure against her ankle makes her look down. Bear sits there, his green eyes reflecting the ethereal light of this memory-place.

He blinks slowly, deliberately, then turns his head toward the gathering crowd.

"What is it?" Melia whispers. "What are you showing me?"

Bear pads forward, sleek and purposeful, glancing back once to ensure she follows. She does, moving through the spectral crowd—people who cannot see or feel her. The faces startle her; so many are familiar—versions of council members, servants, nobles she's known all her life, wearing different clothes, slightly altered features.

They're gathering before a towering figure in ornate robes. The High Priest raises his arms, and the crowd falls silent. Melia recognizes his pendant—the same one worn by the High Priest who presided over her parents' funeral.

"Today we ascend further into divine grace," the High Priest announces, voice carrying unnaturally far. "Today, our devoted ones take their place in eternity."

Bear sits, watching intently as a line of people step forward—faces serene, movements mechanical. Each wears a silver circlet that pulses with light.

"These volunteers," the High Priest continues, "will join the conjuration cycle, sustaining paradise through their devotion."

Melia's stomach twists. "Volunteers," she breathes. "They're not volunteers at all, are they, Bear?"

The High Priest clasps his hands, and the silver light from his pendant intensifies, casting ghostly illumination across the sea of upturned faces.

"Today marks the pinnacle of our shared vision," he proclaims. "What we conjure here will transcend mere stone and mortar. Elyssia shall be perfection made manifest—a perpetual paradise suspended above the chaos of the world."

Melia pushes closer, Bear weaving between spectral legs beside her. The air thrums with a strange vibration, as if reality itself is thinning.

"Our ancestors discovered the gifts of Aether," the High Priest continues, his voice resonating unnaturally. "They learned to shape matter through will, to bend the fabric of existence through belief. But today—" his eyes gleam with fervor, "—today we harness the greatest concentration of Aether magic that Etheria has ever witnessed."

The crowd shifts, a ripple of anticipation passing through them. Melia notices how their eyes reflect the same silver light as their circlets—not natural, not conscious, but compliant.

"Each of you stands as both architect and building block," the High Priest explains, spreading his arms wider. "Together, we shall weave our consciousness into the very foundation of Elyssia."

A woman near Melia whispers to her companion, "Will it hurt?"

"Only for a moment," comes the reply. "Then eternal peace."

The High Priest gestures, and robed acolytes move through the crowd, distributing small crystalline objects—rough-hewn Aetherium, glowing from within.

"Hold the crystal in your dominant hand," instructs the High Priest. "Feel its resonance with your heartbeat. This is the anchor that will bind your essence to our shared vision."

Melia tries to touch one of the crystals, but her fingers pass through it like mist. This is memory, not reality—she cannot interfere.

"The conjuration cycle we establish today will endure forever," the High Priest's voice swells with triumph. "Our conjured bodies will die and be reborn, over and over, living in perpetual perfection. No more disease. No more aging beyond your prime. No more tragedy or loss or grief."

Bear makes a low sound in his throat, almost a growl. Melia kneels beside him, feeling sick. "They don't understand what they're agreeing to, do they?"

The cat's green eyes reflect the silver light, pupils contracting to thin slits.

Around them, the crowd begins to chant in unison, their voices blending into a single droning tone. The Aetherium crystals pulse in rhythm with their words, growing brighter, whiter.

"Your sacrifices today forge paradise tomorrow," the High Priest calls over the chanting. "Your consciousness will become the threads in our great tapestry."

A man stumbles forward, breaking the neat rows. "Wait," he calls, voice trembling. "You said we'd be citizens of Elyssia—not its foundation!"

Two acolytes seize him immediately, their movements swift and practiced. The High Priest doesn't even acknowledge the interruption, continuing his liturgy as the man is dragged away.

"The first among you will become the Pillars—your minds sustaining the city's core structures for eternity."

The chanting grows louder, drowning out individual thoughts, individual doubts. Melia watches in horror as silver threads begin to materialize, emerging from the circlets, connecting person to person like a vast, glowing web.

"The second tier shall become the Sustainers—your essence cycling through the daily rhythms of our paradise, manifesting its comforts and necessities."

A woman falls to her knees, blood trickling from her nose as her crystal flares blindingly bright. No one helps her. No one even seems to notice.

"The rest shall become the Renewed—experiencing life in Elyssia, your memories curated, your purpose aligned with the greater harmony."

Bear presses against Melia's leg, urging her toward the platform where a smaller group stands apart—nobles and priests without circlets, watching the ritual with calculated interest.

Among them, Melia recognizes earlier versions of the High Council members, including a much younger Prefect Solivar. Their expressions range from solemn to triumphant, but none show horror at what's unfolding.

"The conjuration begins!" the High Priest shouts, raising a massive Aetherium crystal overhead.

The air ripples, distorts. The silver threads intensify, becoming almost solid as they lift from the crowd, weaving together into a vast latticework above their heads. People begin to scream—not in fear but in ecstasy or agony, impossible to distinguish.

"Your sacrifice creates perfection! Your lives sustain eternity!"

Bodies start to collapse, the crystals in their hands burning through flesh, merging with bone. The silver threads pull taut, shackling them to this conjuring.

"They're being consumed," Melia whispers, horrified. "They're b ecoming... building materials."

The vision shifts, accelerates. Melia watches as thousands become shackled to the Aether and the silver web expands outward, upward, taking shape—forming streets, buildings, gardens. Elyssia materializes above them, glorious and pristine, sustained by the life-force of its creators.

On the platform, the elites who orchestrated this sacrifice watch with satisfaction, untouched by the fate of the masses.

Bear looks up at her, his steady gaze communicating a terrible understanding. This is what she was born into—what her lineage helped create and maintain. The perfect city floating in the clouds, built on an endless cycle of hidden sacrifice.

The man bearing King Orion's face steps forward from the platform, his expression troubled. Though not her father, the resemblance makes Melia's heart clench.

"And what of our physical forms?" he asks, voice carrying enough authority that even the High Priest pauses. "When our consciousness becomes part of this... tapestry, what happens to our bodies?"

The High Priest's smile doesn't reach his eyes. "They will remain in stasis, preserved perfectly. The vessels that birthed Elyssia must be protected with the utmost reverence."

"By whom?" demands the Orion-like figure.

"The Followers of the Old Ways," the High Priest explains, gesturing to a group at the edge of the gathering. They wear simple garments marked with familiar symbols—the same ones Melia saw at Old Hollow. "Those who choose to remain below will guard the physical anchors of our paradise. They will pass down the sacred duty through generations, maintaining the rituals that keep the conjuration cycle unbroken."

Melia watches the Followers bow their heads in acceptance. Not victims, but accomplices.

The vision shifts again, focusing on three figures approaching the central altar. Melia's breath catches as she recognizes two of them immediately—a younger version of her father, and beside him, unmistakably, her mother. Not ancestors or look-alikes, but King Orion and Queen Lysandra themselves.

"No," she whispers. "They were part of this?"

Between them walks a third figure—a young woman with familiar golden hair and delicate features. Melia stares in disbelief at her own face, or rather, the face of the woman who would conjure her.

"I don't understand," Melia whispers to Bear. "Am I seeing my birth?"

But something feels wrong. The woman has her features exactly, but wears unfamiliar robes and carries herself differently. This isn't Melia being born—this is someone else becoming Melia.

Her parents approach the High Priest, presenting the woman as one might present an offering.

"She has been prepared," her father says, his voice hollow. "Her consciousness aligned with the Cycle."

"Excellent," the High Priest nods, examining the woman like a craftsman appraising materials. "And she understands her role in the continuation?"

"She believes she is our daughter," her mother says, voice breaking slightly. "The princess of Elyssia."

The woman who is not-Melia smiles vacantly, her eyes reflecting the same silver light as the others.

"I am honored to serve," not-Melia says, her voice an eerie echo of Melia's own.

The High Priest places a delicate circlet on the woman's head. Unlike the others, this one bears a small royal crest.

"The royal line must appear unbroken," the High Priest intones. "Each generation perfectly shaped, perfectly controlled. Through her, the cycle remains unchallenged."

Melia's mother looks away, tears streaming down her face. Her father places a comforting hand on her shoulder, but his expression remains stoic, resigned.

"She is not the first," the High Priest continues. "Nor will she be the last. The royal family must exemplify our paradise—perfect in every way."

The woman who will become Melia kneels before them, accepting her circlet, accepting her false identity.

A sharp pain shoots through Melia's temple—

The vision blurs, and Melia feels herself pulled forward in time, the faces around her aging, changing, while Elyssia remains eerily constant above. Generations pass in moments, each contributing their quota of "volunteers" to maintain the great lie.

"We have to break it," she whispers, reaching for Bear as the vision begins to fade. "Whatever it takes."

She gasps awake, jolting upright. Bear sits directly in front of her, green eyes wide and unblinking. His small body blocks her immediate view of the room, as if he's positioned himself deliberately to be the first thing she sees upon waking.

"I'm not real," Melia whispers, her voice raw. "I never was."

Bear tilts his head, then deliberately places one paw on her hand. The pressure is slight but unmistakably real.

Melia X

Melia's throat burns raw, and she realizes she must have screamed upon waking. Faces swim into focus around her—Auren's concerned expression, Ryker's calculating gaze, Kyp's open worry. Behind them, Elder Karina and several Followers crowd the doorway, their expressions guarded yet curious.

"Are you all right?" Auren reaches for her hand, but Melia jerks away.

"Don't touch me." Her voice sounds foreign to her own ears—harsh, brittle. Bear presses against her leg, a small anchor of warmth.

"Melia, what did you see?" Ryker steps closer, but something in her expression makes him halt.

She looks past them all to Elder Karina, whose weathered face has gone carefully blank. The old woman knows something. They all do.

"Is it true?" Melia demands, pushing herself to her feet despite the room's slight spinning. "Is Elyssia a conjuration? A giant, elaborate illusion built on sacrifice?"

The Followers exchange glances, some lowering their eyes while others whisper prayers. Elder Karina's mouth tightens into a thin line.

"I saw it," Melia continues, her voice rising. "I saw how the city was made. How people were... woven into it. Their consciousness trapped to maintain the illusion."

"These are sacred mysteries," Elder Karina begins, but Melia cuts her off with a sharp laugh.

"Sacred? There's nothing sacred about it! It's monstrous!" She steps forward, forcing the Elder to meet her gaze. "And what about me? Am I real? Or am I just another conjuration?"

The silence that follows confirms everything. Melia feels her legs weaken beneath her.

"You knew." She turns to the assembled Followers. "All of you. You maintain the rituals that keep people enslaved. That keep the cycle going."

"We preserve the divine order," a man protests from the back. "The Conjuration Cycle is—"

"A prison," Melia snaps. "A beautiful prison that consumes lives."

"Melia," Auren approaches carefully, confusion etched across his features. "What are you talking about? What did you see?"

She turns to him, seeing the genuine concern in his eyes. "I saw how Elyssia was made. How it stays floating. It's not divine magic—it's people. Their consciousness, their essence, bound into the very structure." Her voice breaks. "And I saw myself... or rather, the woman who became me. I'm not... I don't think I'm real, Auren."

"That's ridiculous," Kyp interjects. "You're standing right here."

"As what?" Melia demands. "A conjuration given form? A perfect princess crafted to maintain the illusion?" She rounds on Elder Karina again. "Tell them. Tell them what you know about the Conjuration Cycle. About what happens to the 'Ascended.'"

The Elder straightens, meeting Melia's fury with calm resolve. "The Thread remembers what we reinforce. What it forgets, we conjure. This is the First Doctrine."

"And the people who become part of it? What of them?"

"They serve a greater purpose," Elder Karina says. "Their sacrifice sustains paradise."

"Without their consent!" Melia's voice echoes through the chamber. "They don't know what they're volunteering for!"

"The faithful need not understand to serve," another Follower murmurs.

Melia's hands clench into fists. "And what am I? Just another tool in this cycle? Another conjured puppet?"

The room falls silent, Melia's accusations hanging in the air like poison. Before Elder Karina can respond, the crowd at the doorway parts. Jade slips through, her normally composed features twisted with an uncharacteristic intensity. In her hands, she clutches ancient parchments covered in strange, angular script.

"She's right," Jade says, her voice unnervingly flat. "Elyssia is not real. It was never built, only conjured—sustained by Aether, belief, and sacrifice."

Melia studies Jade's face, noticing the slight tremor in her hands, the unfocused quality in her eyes. Whatever Jade discovered has shaken her to her core.

"You found something," Melia says.

Jade nods, approaching with mechanical steps. "Technical schematics. Written in Luthari script." She spreads the parchments on a nearby table. "These detail the original Conjuration process—how to bind consciousness to physical structures through the Thread."

Elder Karina gasps, reaching for the documents. "These are forbidden texts!"

"Because they reveal the truth," Jade continues, her voice gaining strength. "The Conjuration Cycle isn't divine—it's technological. Designed to create and maintain the illusion of Elyssia through continuous human sacrifice."

"And me?" Melia's voice catches. "What does it say about people like me?"

Jade finally meets her eyes, something like empathy flickering across her features. "You were made, not born. Conjured from Aether and bound to human form." She pauses. "But that doesn't make you less real. It makes you a prisoner, like the others."

The revelation slams into Melia like a physical blow. A conjuration. Not real. A construct of Aether magic and belief, designed to maintain an illusion of perfection. The walls of the chamber seem to close in, the air suddenly too thick to breathe.

"I need air," she gasps, pushing past Jade, past Auren's outstretched hand, past the murmuring Followers who part before her like water.

She doesn't know where she's going—only that she must escape these suffocating truths. Her feet carry her through stone corridors, past ancient tapestries depicting the very lies that created her. Outside, rain has begun to fall, but Melia barely notices as she stumbles into the courtyard.

What am I? The question pounds in her head with each heartbeat. If I was made, not born, what does that make me? A tool? A doll? A shadow of something that never existed?

Memories flash through her mind—her childhood in Elyssia, her parents' gentle guidance, the weight of the crown she was meant to inherit. Were any of those moments real? Or were they just carefully crafted scenes in an elaborate performance?

The rain soaks through her clothing, plastering her hair to her face, but the cold grounding sensation only reminds her of her apparent physical reality. She can feel pain. She can feel heartbreak. She can feel rage.

"If I'm not real," she whispers to the empty courtyard, "then why does this hurt so much?"

She breaks into a run, needing to put distance between herself and the others, needing space to process this shattering truth. The stone paths of Old Hollow give way to muddy trails as she pushes beyond the complex's boundaries, her vision blurred by rain and tears.

I jumped from Elyssia because I wanted freedom. But how can I be free if I'm just another part of the conjuration?

A sudden crack of thunder makes her flinch, and Melia realizes she's ventured far from the safety of the compound. She slows, trying to orient herself in the downpour, when shapes materialize from the mist ahead—human figures, moving with purpose toward her.

Too late, Melia registers the glint of weapons, the disciplined formation. Five men block her path, their rain-slicked armor bearing Garrik's unmistakable golden insignia. Their leader, a broad-shouldered man with a scar cutting through his eyebrow, steps forward.

"Well, well," he says, voice carrying easily over the rainfall. "The princess decides to make our job easy."

Melia backs away, but two more figures emerge behind her, cutting off her retreat. Her heart pounds against her ribs as she realizes her vulnerability—alone, unarmed, trapped.

"Garrik sends his regards," the scarred man continues, drawing a short blade. "He was quite displeased about his investment being stolen."

"Auren's not property," Melia says, summoning whatever dignity remains within her shattered identity. "And he's not going back."

The man's laugh is cold. "Didn't say anything about taking him back, princess. We're here for you."

***

The scarred man's open palm connects with Melia's cheek before she can react, pain exploding across her face as she stumbles backward into waiting arms. Someone yanks her wrists behind her back, binding them with rough cord that bites into her skin.

"Careful with the merchandise," the scarred man orders. "High Priests want her intact."

High Priests? Through the throbbing pain, Melia registers his words with rising horror. Not just Garrik, then. Elyssia has found her.

"I won't go back," she spits, tasting blood on her lip. "You can't make me."

The man's laugh is cold. "Pretty sure we can, princess."

They drag her through the mud, her feet slipping and sliding as she struggles against their grip. Rain lashes her face, mingling with tears of frustration. Two men flank her, gripping her arms with bruising force while the others form a perimeter, weapons drawn.

As they crest the hill overlooking Old Hollow, Melia's stomach drops. Below, more of Garrik's men move freely through the compound, weapons visible but not drawn. The Followers watch with eerie calm, making no move to interfere.

"What have you done to my friends?" she demands, digging her heels into the mud.

The scarred man shrugs. "If they're smart, nothing. Elder Karina knows how this works."

They haul her down the hill, past the crumbling outer walls and into the main courtyard where Elder Karina stands beneath a sheltered portico. The older woman's face remains impassive as Melia is dragged before her, but something in her eyes—pity, perhaps, or resignation—makes Melia's blood run cold.

"You knew," Melia realizes aloud. "You knew they were coming."

Elder Karina inclines her head slightly. "The Followers serve the old ways, child. We always have."

"By betraying pilgrims to hired thugs?" Melia strains against her captors. "Is that your sacred duty?"

"By ensuring the divine order remains intact," Karina corrects, her voice eerily serene. "Elyssia must endure. The cycle must continue."

Understanding dawns like ice in Melia's veins. "You're working with the High Priests."

"We have always been their eyes and ears on the surface," Karina confirms. "When pilgrims falter in their faith, when they begin to question... we notify the temple."

"And they send men like him." Melia jerks her head toward the scarred man.

"Garrik provides a valuable service," Karina says.

The sound of a scuffle draws Melia's attention. Her heart leaps as Auren and Kyp burst through the doorway of the main hall, their faces tight with determination. Jade follows silently behind them, her eyes scanning the courtyard with calculating precision.

"Let her go," Auren demands, his hands already beginning to shimmer with faint traces of Aether.

The scarred man signals his men, who ready their weapons. Melia feels a flicker of hope—they're outnumbered, but with Auren's abilities and Jade's fighting skills...

"I wouldn't," comes a familiar voice from behind Auren.

Time seems to freeze as Ryker steps forward, pressing the gleaming edge of a blade against Auren's throat. The metal catches the gray light, a sliver of deadly intent.

"Ryker?" Kyp's voice cracks with disbelief.

Melia's stomach drops, the betrayal hitting her like another physical blow. "You," she whispers. "All this time?"

Ryker's trademark smirk appears, but it no longer holds any charm—just calculated cruelty. "Nothing personal, princess. Well, maybe a little personal." He presses the blade closer to Auren's skin, forcing him to tilt his head back. "Easy with the magic, pilgrim. I'd hate to open your throat before you get to perform for Garrik again."

"You son of a—" Auren begins, but stops when the blade nicks his skin.

"How long?" Melia demands, her voice steadier than she feels. "Since Aurora? Before?"

"Since the beginning," Ryker answers, his eyes never leaving Auren. "Garrik pays well for talent spotting. When I heard about a failed pilgrim who could manifest Aether..." He shrugs one shoulder. "But then you had to complicate things by falling from the sky, princess."

The scarred man laughs. "Good work, Voss. The High Priests will be pleased."

"And what about the moment in the dressing room?" Melia asks, her cheeks burning with humiliation. "Was that part of your mission too?"

Something flickers across Ryker's face—regret, perhaps, or simple calculation. "Let's call that a personal initiative."

Kyp lunges toward Ryker, but freezes when two of Garrik's men train crossbows on him.

"Don't be stupid," Ryker warns. "This doesn't have to end with blood."

Jade stands unnaturally still, her face unreadable. Melia catches her eye, silently pleading for help, but the woman gives no indication of her intentions.

Elder Karina steps forward, hands clasped before her. "The Followers of the Old Ways have always understood sacrifice," she intones. "Princess Melia must return to fulfill her purpose. The pilgrim must continue his path. This is the way of things."

"My purpose?" Melia spits. "To be a puppet? A conjured thing to maintain your precious lies?"

"To maintain order," Karina corrects. "To preserve what generations have built."

"Built on suffering," Auren growls, despite the blade at his throat. "Built on people trapped in walls and foundations."

The scarred man signals to his men. "Enough talking. Bind them all. The High Priests want the princess. Garrik gets the pilgrim. The others are expendable."

"No!" Melia struggles against her bonds as Garrik's men move toward her friends. "Leave them alone!"

"Quiet." The scarred man backhands her again, and stars explode across her vision.

Through the pain, Melia sees Bear slinking along the shadows of the courtyard, green eyes gleaming with unnatural intelligence. The cat's presence gives her a strange sense of calm amid the chaos.

"You think this ends here?" she asks, tasting blood. "You think taking me back fixes anything?"

The scarred man grabs her arm, yanking her toward a waiting wagon. "What I think doesn't matter. And neither does what you think, princess."

Melia's bound wrists burn as the scarred man shoves her forward, nearly sending her sprawling into the mud. The rain has intensified, pelting her face with icy droplets that mingle with the blood from her split lip. Around her, Garrik's men herd Auren, Kyp, and Jade toward a covered wagon at the edge of the compound.

"There's been a change of plans," Elder Karina announces, stepping into the downpour without concern for her soaking robes. "The Elyssian emissaries await at the northern extraction point. You'll need to move quickly before the storm worsens."

The scarred man frowns. "That wasn't the arrangement."

"The arrangement adapts to necessity," Karina replies, her voice carrying a subtle authority that makes even Garrik's thugs hesitate. "The High Priests are concerned about potential interference. The princess must be delivered by nightfall."

Ryker steps forward, still keeping his blade casually near Auren's throat. "And what about our arrangement with Garrik? He's expecting the pilgrim back in the pits by tomorrow."

Karina's eyes narrow slightly. "Once the princess is secured at the extraction point, the others are yours to do with as you please. The Followers care only for the continuation of the divine cycle."

The scarred man considers this, then nods. "Fine. We'll take the river route. Faster anyway."

Melia's heart sinks as she spots what awaits them beyond the tree line—a sleek metal skiff hovering several inches above the ground, its surface humming with the telltale blue glow of Aetherium technology.

"Move," Ryker orders, prodding Auren forward with his blade.

Auren catches Melia's eye, his expression a mixture of fury and determination. A thin line of blood trickles down his neck where Ryker's blade nicked him. His hands are now bound like hers, though Melia notices they've used metal cuffs on him rather than rope—they fear his Aether abilities.

Kyp stumbles along beside him, his usually cheerful face now pale with shock. "You won't get away with this," he mutters to Ryker. "People know we're here."

Ryker smirks. "What people? The Followers? They're already helping us. Your little village friends? They think you're on a pilgrimage." He lowers his voice. "Face it, Kyp. No one's coming."

They're marched toward the skiff, each step taking Melia closer to a future she can barely comprehend. Return to Elyssia—to what? To be wed to Solivar despite knowing the horrific truth? To continue playing her role in a macabre performance built on human suffering?

Her gaze drifts to Jade, who walks with eerie calm, her eyes constantly scanning, assessing. Unlike the others, she doesn't appear frightened—merely calculating. Their eyes meet briefly, and Melia thinks she detects the slightest nod, almost imperceptible.

As they reach the skiff, Melia spots Bear watching from the shadows of a nearby building, his green eyes reflecting the blue glow of the vessel. The cat's presence provides an odd comfort—a reminder that not everything is within their captors' control.

"In you go, princess," the scarred man says, shoving her roughly toward the open hatch of the skiff.

The vessel's interior is cramped but sophisticated, with smooth metal benches along both sides and a pilot's console at the front. It smells of ozone and something else—fear, perhaps, from previous passengers.

They're forced to sit, Melia and Auren on one side, Kyp and Jade on the other. Two of Garrik's men take positions at either end of the compartment, crossbows ready. Ryker sits near the pilot's console, watching them with casual interest, his blade now sheathed but a hand resting on its hilt.

"The extraction point is about an hour's journey," the scarred man informs them as he begins activating the skiff's controls. "Try anything, and we start removing fingers. Clear?"

No one responds, but their silence is answer enough.

The skiff rises higher, the hum of its engines intensifying as it orients itself toward the north. With a sudden lurch, they're moving, skimming above the treetops at a speed that makes Melia's stomach drop.

"Why?" she finally asks, looking directly at Ryker. "Why help them perpetuate this—this abomination?"

Ryker leans back, studying her with those shrewd green eyes. "Because power is the only currency that matters in this world, princess. The High Priests have it. Garrik has it. I intend to have it too."

"By trading in people?" Auren growls. "By selling us like cattle?"

"By recognizing opportunity," Ryker corrects. "Your problem, pilgrim, is that you think there's some grand purpose to all this—some higher meaning. There isn't. There's just those who take and those who are taken from."

The skiff hits an air pocket, jolting them all. Through the small viewing portal, Melia watches Old Hollow shrink into the distance, its ancient stones now barely visible through the curtain of rain.

The scarred man turns from the controls, scowling. "Enough talking. Next person who speaks loses a tooth."

Melia's mind races, searching for any possible escape.

A soft pressure against Melia's ankle makes her jump. She glances down, stunned to find Bear's sleek black form somehow huddled beneath her bench. His green eyes meet hers with that unnerving intelligence, and despite everything, warmth blooms in her chest.

How did he get aboard? The skiff had been empty when they entered, and she hadn't seen him slip through the hatch. Yet here he is, pressing his small body reassuringly against her leg, his presence both impossible and completely natural.

Bear nudges her bound hands with his head, purring softly. The vibration travels up her arms, oddly calming amidst her racing thoughts.

One of the guards glances her way, and she shifts slightly, using her body to shield Bear from view.

The cat feels like a lifeline in this metal trap racing toward Elyssia—toward imprisonment, toward a false marriage, toward everything she's been fighting to escape. But what good is a cat against armed men and Ryker's betrayal?

Jade IV

J ade measures the space between the guard at the door and the guard at the control panel: 4.7 meters. The vibration beneath the metal floor suggests they're flying at approximately 70 kilometers per hour, and based on wind resistance patterns, they're headed north-west—directly toward an Elyssian extraction point. She catalogs each person's threat level with mechanical precision.

The scarred pilot: primary threat. Armed with a shock baton and phase pistol.

Ryker: secondary threat. Skilled with bladed weapons, unpre-dictable.

Four guards: tertiary threats. Crossbows require reload time of 3.2 seconds.

Her neural implants cycle through seventeen different escape sce-narios, calculating probability of success. But something unprece-dented is happening within her analysis matrix. For the first time, her calculations include five survival variables instead of one.

Melia. Auren. Kyp. The cat. And herself.

The familiar voice of the Emperor echoes in her mind: *Weapons don't have companions. Only targets.*

Jade watches Melia subtly shift her body, concealing something beneath the bench. The black cat. Curious how it managed to board undetected. She files this anomaly away for further analysis.

Glancing at her bound wrists, Jade knows she could break free in 2.3 seconds. The restraints are standard Imperial grade, and her left thumb can dislocate with minimal effort. But then what? Fighting in this confined space risks the others. Kyp would likely be the first casualty—he lacks combat training. Auren might withstand several strikes, but in his weakened state, survival probability is low.

The ancient texts from the temple chamber flash through her mind. Schematics of Elyssia. Human consciousness transformed into energy. People becoming building blocks.

The Emperor knew. He always knew.

Your purpose is to observe and eliminate threats to the Empire. Nothing more.

But if Elyssia represents what she now suspects—a contained experiment in Thread manipulation—then her entire mission takes on new dimensions. Liora Solari wasn't simply a rogue element to be neutralized. She was competition. Another Thread-manipulator outside Imperial control.

Jade's gaze shifts to the small viewport. Rain streaks across the glass as lightning illuminates the distant silhouette of mountains.

"Extraction point in forty minutes," the scarred man announces, adjusting their course.

Jade calculates the drop from this altitude: survivable, but with an 86% chance of significant injury. If she were alone, those odds would be acceptable. But Melia wouldn't survive the fall. Neither would Kyp.

Her neural implants flicker, struggling to integrate this new para-meter: keeping others alive isn't just tactical. It feels necessary in ways her programming can't quantify.

The guard nearest her shifts his weight, momentarily looking away to check the navigation display. A perfect opportunity to strike—but she remains still, watching Melia's silent communication with the cat.

The Empire made her a weapon, but weapons don't question their makers. They don't protect. They don't feel the cold anger now crys-tallizing in her chest as she realizes the truth: she was always meant to be expendable, just another tool discarded after use.

Jade catches Auren's eye. Something passes between them—an un-spoken understanding. She gives him the slightest nod.

Jade studies Ryker's face—the calculated smile, the precise way he holds his knife, the control in every movement. Her implants cata-log micro-expressions: dilated pupils, elevated heartbeat visible at his temple, the subtle shift in his breathing pattern. He's enjoying this. The revelation. The drama. The power.

"You know," Ryker says, leaning against the skiff's bulkhead with practiced casualness, "I think I'm going to keep you around after we get back to Elyssia."

His statement registers as a threat disguised as interest. Jade remains perfectly still, conserving energy while assessing his intent.

"Quite the coincidence," he continues, voice pitched just above the engine's hum. "An Imperial starship appears in Aurora—first one in what, decades?—and suddenly there's you. Mysterious woman with combat skills I've never seen before."

She doesn't blink. Doesn't confirm. Doesn't deny.

"The way you move." Ryker traces a line in the air with his blade. "So precise. So... mechanical. Not like a mercenary. Not like someone who learned to fight on the streets."

The scarred pilot glances back briefly, then returns to his controls. The guards shift uncomfortably.

"I've never met an Imperial agent before," Ryker says, sliding closer. "But you're something else entirely, aren't you? Some kind of specialist? An assassin, maybe?"

Sam calculates fourteen ways to kill him using only her bound hands, but stays motionless. The cat under Melia's bench twitches its ears—the only other movement in the cabin.

"Tell me," Ryker leans in, his voice dropping to a whisper meant for her alone, "what does the Emperor want with a fallen princess? What's so important about Elyssia that he'd send someone like you?"

Her implants register Auren tensing against his restraints. Kyp's breathing has become shallow, fear response elevated. Melia's eyes never leave her face—searching, questioning.

"What did Garrik promise you?" she asks, a calculated question designed to exploit his ego. "Money? Position? Power?"

"Something better," he responds, recovering his composure. "Truth."

Sam feels something unexpected—a flicker of pity. There's no knowledge here to be had.

Ryker leans back, twirling his blade between his fingers. "So what's your mission, Jade? If that's even your name."

She meets his gaze directly. "My mission is none of your concern."

"It will be," he says with quiet certainty, "when we land."

Ryker's blade dances between his fingers as he studies her. "I wonder what else you've been trained in?" His mouth curves into a smile that doesn't reach his eyes. "The High Priests pay well for exotic talents. Combat skills are valuable, but there are other... services... that command a higher price."

The implication hangs in the air. Jade doesn't flinch, doesn't blink. Her neural implants register each micro-movement of his facial muscles, cataloging the mixture of desire and cruelty. She's encountered this before—men who mistake stillness for submission.

"Silent treatment? That's fine." He leans closer, breath warm against her ear. "I'm sure we'll find ways to make you talk."

Behind her eyes, targeting systems activate automatically, mapping the optimal strike points on his body: carotid artery, temple, solar plexus. Her thumb shifts imperceptibly, preparing to dislocate to slip the restraints.

Ryker mistakes her silence for fear. His mistake.

The scarred pilot announces, "Approaching the extraction point. Five minutes."

Time is running out. Jade's gaze flicks to Melia, who sits unnaturally still, one hand dropped casually beside the bench where Bear hides. To Auren, whose jaw is clenched but whose eyes hold a question. To Kyp, whose terror is apparent but whose loyalty remains unbroken.

The Emperor's voice echoes in her mind: *When compromise is necessary, eliminate the weakest elements first.*

Jade makes her decision. Not as the weapon they forged. Not as the Shadow.

But as Sam.

***

The skiff lurches to a stop, sending a jolt through Jade's body. The scarred pilot cuts the engine, turning to face Ryker with a scowl that deepens the web of tissue across his face.

"We can't land at the extraction point," he says, voice gravelly with irritation. "Ground's too soft from the rain. We'll have to stop here and go up that hill." He gestures through the windshield toward a steep incline where mist curls between sparse trees. "High Priests' agents won't arrive for another hour."

Ryker's jaw tightens. "An hour? They were supposed to be waiting."

"Weather's delayed them. Take it or leave it."

Jade's neural implants flare, scanning the immediate environment through the windows. The delay is optimal—fewer variables to account for during extraction. Her primary restraint has weakened from her subtle movements; the polymer cord fraying against her wrist bone where she's been working it for the past twenty-seven minutes.

"Fine," Ryker says. "Let's get them moving."

The scarred man nods to his subordinates. One reaches for the door latch, the mechanical click echoing in the confined space. Fresh air rushes in, carrying the scent of wet soil and pine.

Jade counts: one heartbeat, two.

On three, she moves.

Her wrists snap apart with calculated force, breaking the weakened restraint. In the same fluid motion, she drives her forehead into the nearest guard's face. Cartilage crunches beneath impact. Blood sprays. The man stumbles backward, knife dropping from his belt.

Jade's fingers close around the hilt before it hits the floor.

The blade becomes an extension of herself—precision and intent made manifest. One stroke severs her ankle bindings. Another slices across the throat of the second guard. Her movements are economical, lacking the theatrical flourish of street fighters. Each action serves a purpose: neutralize, disable, eliminate.

The third guard reaches for his weapon. Too slow. Jade drives the knife between his ribs, angling upward to pierce the heart. His mouth opens in a silent scream as she withdraws the blade with a practiced twist.

"Behind you!" Melia shouts.

Jade pivots, using the momentum to slash the fourth guard's hamstring. He collapses with a howl. The skiff rocks with the violence erupting within its metal hull.

Blood slicks the floor. Four guards down in under twelve seconds.

The scarred pilot lunges with a vibroblade. Jade sidesteps, driving her elbow into his kidney. As he doubles over, she slams the knife handle against his temple. Unconscious, not dead—his piloting skills may prove useful.

Ryker backs away, eyes wide with calculation rather than fear. "You've made a mistake," he says, drawing his own blade. "The priests will still come."

Jade doesn't waste breath responding. She slashes Auren's bonds with surgical precision, never taking her eyes off Ryker.

"Can you fight?" she asks Auren.

"I can try." His voice is strained, but determination tightens his features.

Auren's hands begin to glow, tendrils of translucent energy wrapping around his fingers. The air crackles with Aether, raising the fine hairs on Jade's arms. Her implants register the energy fluctuations, sending warning signals through her nervous system.

Ryker lunges forward, blade arcing toward Jade's throat. She parries with her stolen knife, the clang of metal resonating through the skiff. Auren summons a shield of energy, deflecting Ryker's second strike.

"Melia, go!" Auren shouts, his voice strained with effort.

Jade sees Melia from her peripheral vision—the princess has grabbed the knife from an unconscious guard. With a swift motion, she cuts Kyp free.

"I won't leave you," Melia says, her voice steady despite the chaos.

"You must," Jade counters, blocking another of Ryker's attacks. "He's after you."

Bear emerges from beneath the bench, fur bristling, green eyes luminous in the dim light. The cat leaps onto the open doorway, looking back expectantly at Melia.

Understanding passes between woman and animal. Melia nods once, then turns to Kyp. "Come on!"

They move as one—Melia first, leaping from the skiff door onto the muddy ground below, followed by Bear's graceful bound and Kyp's more awkward tumble. Jade hears them hit the ground, followed by the splash of footsteps receding into the underbrush.

"Auren, go with them!" Jade commands, her attention momentarily split. Seeing the need to protect Melia, Auren leaps out.

That split second is all Ryker needs.

He feints left, then drives his blade toward her midsection. Jade begins to pivot, recognizing the maneuver too late. The knife slides between her ribs with sickening ease.

Cold steel parts flesh, muscle, tissue. Ryker's face contorts with savage satisfaction as he twists the blade, maximizing the damage.

Pain—bright and electric—floods Jade's neural network. Her implants struggle to manage the overload, sending emergency signals throughout her system. Blood, warm and viscous, soaks her tunic.

"I told you," Ryker whispers, his face inches from hers, "we'd find ways to make you talk."

Jade's vision narrows, black edges encroaching. The knife remains embedded in her abdomen, Ryker's hand still gripping the hilt. With clinical detachment, she catalogs the damage: lacerated liver, potential puncture to the inferior vena cava, estimated blood loss approaching critical levels.

Despite the pain, her mind remains clear. Weaponized reflexes take over.

Jade grabs Ryker's wrist, keeping the knife in place—removing it would accelerate blood loss. Her other hand drives upward, palm striking his elbow joint with precise force. Bone dislocates with an audible pop.

Ryker howls, stumbling backward, his arm hanging at an unnatural angle.

"It's a shame," Ryker says, cradling his dislocated arm against his chest. His eyes travel over her with predatory assessment. "Under different circumstances, we could have enjoyed each other first."

Jade spits blood onto the metal floor. Her vision fragments into pixelated sections, implants struggling to maintain visual processing. Target acquisition systems failing. Threat assessment protocols stuttering.

"Someone would have paid well for you alive," Ryker continues, edging toward her. "But I'll settle for dead."

Jade tries to shift her weight, to find balance for one last counterattack. Her body refuses to comply. Internal damage too severe. Blood pooling beneath her feet.

"My Emperor..." she whispers, the words a reflex more than conscious thought.

Ryker's laugh is sharp. "Your Emperor isn't here. You failed him."

With his good arm, he shoves her hard. The world tilts as Jade's body pitches backward through the open door. The sensation of falling is oddly peaceful—gravity claiming what's rightfully hers.

Impact comes too quickly and not soon enough. Mud and stone meet flesh. Pain flares white-hot, then mercifully recedes as consciousness slips away.

Her last thought before darkness takes her: not of duty or mission parameters, but of Melia's face—determined, alive, free.

***

Consciousness returns in fragments. First pain—sharp, insistent. Then sound—water dripping, hushed voices. Finally, sensation—damp soil against her back, cool air on her face.

Jade's eyes open, focusing with effort. Her implants struggle to re-establish visual processing, overlaying her vision with diagnostic warnings she can't fully interpret. Four figures hover above her, their outlines gradually sharpening.

Melia kneels closest, her golden hair hanging like a curtain between them and the world. Auren stands behind her, tension visible in his jaw. Kyp hovers nervously to one side, while Bear sits perfectly still, green eyes fixed on Jade's face with unnerving attention.

"Don't move," Melia says, pressing a makeshift bandage against Jade's side. "The bleeding's slowed, but you'll tear it open again."

Jade attempts to assess her own condition. Punctured organs. Significant blood loss. Compromised neural functions. Her body feels heavy, unresponsive.

Beneath her skin, microscopic machines race through damaged tissue. Jade feels the familiar burn of accelerated healing—her implants triggering emergency protocols, redirecting energy to critical systems. The sensation is like liquid fire in her veins.

Her vision stabilizes momentarily, diagnostic warnings fading to the periphery. Success probability: 63%. Not ideal, but sufficient.

"I'm operational," she manages, voice rasping. The words taste metallic.

Melia's eyes widen. "You shouldn't be conscious. The knife—"

"Imperial modification." Jade attempts to sit up, feeling torn tissue resist. "Self-repair initiated. Twenty minutes until basic mobility."

The others exchange glances, a silent conversation Jade can't decode despite her training.

"You did enough," Melia continues, her voice gentle but firm. "More than enough. We're safe because of you."

Jade tries to speak, but her throat constricts. She swallows, tastes copper.

"What..." she manages, the word rough and splintered. "What happened to Ryker?"

Auren steps forward, crouching beside Melia. "After you killed the rest of his men, he fled back to Aurora." His expression darkens. "He's alive. Wounded, but alive."

"Garrik will give him more men," Kyp adds, fidgeting with the edge of his torn sleeve. "They'll come for us harder next time."

Jade processes this information with mechanical precision. Failure. Incomplete mission parameters. Primary targets escaped. Secondary threats still active.

She attempts to sit up, but pain lances through her abdomen. Melia's hand on her shoulder is unexpectedly strong.

"I need to complete the—" Jade begins.

"You need to heal," Melia interrupts. "We all need to rest and regroup."

Bear moves closer, sniffing at Jade's wound with curious intensity. The cat's presence triggers something unexpected in Jade—a memory of her mother's voice: *Sometimes the greatest strength is knowing when to pause.*

"How did you find me?" Jade asks, surrendering momentarily to stillness.

"Bear," Kyp says simply. "Led us straight to you. Like he knew exactly where you'd fallen."

The cat meets Jade's gaze, and for a disorienting moment, she feels understood by the small creature in ways her Emperor never managed.

"We've found shelter," Auren says, gesturing vaguely behind them. "An old hermit's cabin, abandoned. It's not much, but it's hidden."

Jade runs tactical assessments, her training automatic even through the pain. Shelter. Concealment. Defensive position. Time to recover.

"We've got 30 minutes before the High Priests' agent shows up for extraction," she says.

Melia's hand remains on her shoulder. "Can you walk?"

"I can function," Jade responds automatically.

Kyp snorts. "That's not what she asked."

The correction surprises Jade. Function versus ability. A distinction the Empire never encouraged her to make.

"I'll need assistance," she admits, the words unfamiliar on her tongue.

Kyp and Auren help Jade to her feet, supporting her weight between them. Each step sends shockwaves of pain through her abdomen, but she maintains precise control of her breathing—four seconds in, four seconds out—a technique designed to maximize oxygenation while minimizing movement of damaged internal organs.

"Easy now," Kyp murmurs as they navigate through dense underbrush toward a small structure nestled among twisted trees. "You're still bleeding."

"Imperial bodies heal differently," Jade responds automatically. Her diagnostic systems flash warnings across her vision: *Cellular regeneration at 41%. Neural pathways degrading. System conflict detected.*

When they reach the cabin, Melia pushes open the weathered door. The interior is spare—a single room with a stone hearth, rough-hewn table, and narrow cot. Bear slips through their legs, immediately claiming a spot by the cold fireplace.

Kyp helps lower Jade onto the cot, his movements gentler than she expected.

"You need to rest," he says, voice uncharacteristically serious. "Even super-soldiers or whatever you are need healing time."

Something in his concern triggers a cascade failure in Jade's conditioning. A memory surfaces—her mother applying salve to her scraped knee, saying something similar. The recollection feels like an intrusion, dangerous and forbidden.

"I've healed enough already," Jade says, then stops, confusion crossing her face at her own words.

"What do you mean?" Melia asks, kneeling beside the cot.

Jade stares at her hands—pale, scarred, efficient killing tools. "Not physically. But being with you all..." She struggles against programming that warns against this vulnerability. "The Empire took everything. My past. My name. They made me a weapon."

Her neural implants fire warning signals, attempting to suppress these thoughts, but something has changed. The ancient texts, the memories of her mother, Melia's journey—they've created fractures in her conditioning that widen with each passing moment.

"Samara," she whispers, the name feeling foreign yet fundamentally right on her tongue. "My name is Samara."

Auren exchanges a glance with Melia. "Samara," he repeats carefully.

"My mother called me Sam." The words emerge with increasing confidence as her internal systems struggle to repress the memories. "Before the Emperor killed her and remade me."

Bear approaches, rubbing against the edge of the cot. The cat's presence seems to disrupt the neural suppression patterns, allowing clearer access to her fragmented past.

"The Emperor sent me to track Liora Solari," she continues, fighting through layers of programming. "But my mission parameters shifted when I found you instead." Her mother's face flashes before her—strong features, kind eyes, determined expression. "I was a child when they took me. Trained me. Hollowed me out."

Kyp sits beside her. "You fought it, though. You chose to help us."

"And I'll keep helping," Sam says, her voice growing stronger. She pushes herself upright, ignoring the pain. "I have a plan."

Melia XI

Melia stares at her hands, turning them over in the dim light of the hermit's cabin. The same hands she's always known, yet suddenly alien. Not flesh and bone, but something else—a perfect illusion made tangible.

"I'm not real," she whispers, the words hanging in the stale air.

Bear presses against her ankle, warm and solid. She reaches down mechanically to touch his fur, wondering if he knows what she truly is.

The fire Auren built crackles in the hearth, casting dancing shadows across the walls. Everyone speaks in hushed tones about plans and tactics, but their voices blur into meaningless sound as Melia sinks deeper into herself.

"A conjuration," she murmurs, testing the word on her tongue. "Made, not born."

The memory of the vision claws at her mind—her "parents" accepting a woman who would become the raw material from which

Melia was crafted. A beautiful puppet princess, designed to maintain the illusion of dynastic continuity.

She presses her fingernails into her palm until it should hurt, but does she truly feel pain the way humans do? When she bleeds, is it real blood?

Sam—no longer Jade—catches her eye from across the room. Even wounded, the woman's gaze holds remarkable clarity.

"You're questioning your existence," Sam says softly, somehow knowing Melia's thoughts.

"If I'm just a construct," Melia asks, "then what happens when the spell breaks? Do I simply... unravel?"

Sam's lips press into a thin line, her expression betraying a rare moment of uncertainty. "I don't know," she admits. "The texts I found suggest conjurations are sustained by belief and ritual. But you're..." She gestures at Melia's form, searching for words.

"Different," Auren finishes for her, his presence warm beside her. He doesn't touch her, but his proximity offers something like comfort.

"Maybe what you are matters less than what you choose to do," Sam says, wincing as she shifts her bandaged wound. "The Emperor rebuilt me too. But my choices are still mine."

Bear climbs into her lap, his weight suddenly the only thing anchoring her to this world.

Sam shifts on the rickety stool, wincing as the movement pulls at her wound. Despite the pain etched across her face, her voice remains steady, authoritative.

"The extraction point is heavily guarded, but I can create a diversion while you reach the Shattered Spire," she explains, fingers tapping against the crude map spread on the table.

Melia stares at the parchment, tracing the route with her eyes. A strange calm settles over her, replacing the existential panic from moments ago. Perhaps this is how constructs process trauma—with artificial serenity.

"Why should we trust you?" Auren challenges, his hand instinctively moving to Melia's shoulder. "A day ago, you were hunting us."

Sam meets his gaze without flinching. "Because I remember who I am now. Because the Emperor uses people like tools—me, Melia, all of us. And because I've seen what's in those ancient texts." She taps a finger against the markings on the map. "The Conjuration Cycle can be broken at its source."

"The Shattered Spire," Melia whispers, feeling Bear press against her leg. "My father's final message. 'What must be broken.'"

"Exactly." Sam nods. "The Spire houses the original conjuring point. Disrupt it, and you begin unraveling the entire system."

Kyp shakes his head, bewildered. "But if Elyssia is sustained by... by people, what happens to them when we break the spell?"

The question hangs heavy in the air. Melia feels all eyes turn to her—the conjured princess, the living spell.

Auren's fingers tighten slightly on her shoulder. "If we do this, there's no going back. You understand that?"

Melia rises from her chair, dislodging Bear, who watches her with unblinking green eyes. "There was never any going back. Not since I fell."

"Then we split up," Sam decides. "Kyp and I will intercept the extraction team. We'll feed them false information, buy you time, get ourselves up to Elyssia." She looks at Melia and Auren. "You two reach the Spire before anyone realizes what we're planning."

Auren nods reluctantly. "We'll need supplies. The Spire's just beyond the Windy Ridge we're at the base of."

While they gather essentials, Melia steps outside, needing air that doesn't smell of old wood and fear. The night sky stretches endlessly above her, stars scattered like the glowing petals she once sprinkled over her parents' caskets.

Were they ever truly her parents? Did they love their created daughter, or was that an illusion too?

Bear follows, sitting beside her in companionable silence.

"What are you?" she asks the cat softly. "Another conjuration? A guide? Or just a cat who's made unfortunate friendship choices?"

Bear blinks slowly, offering no answers.

Footsteps approach—Auren, carrying two packs. "We should leave before dawn," he says, handing her the lighter one.

"What if this is all pointless?" Melia asks, taking the pack automatically. "What if I simply cease to exist when the spell breaks?"

Auren stands close enough that she can feel his warmth. "You jumped from Elyssia. You survived the lake. You've made choices no conjuration would make." His voice drops lower. "And whatever you are, Melia, you're real to me."

She wants to believe him. Maybe that's enough for now.

"Dawn, then," she agrees, looking toward the eastern sky where soon the sun will rise. "We'll find what must be broken."

***

The dawn streaks the sky in muted grays and pinks as they finish their preparations. Melia adjusts the straps on her pack, watching Sam and Kyp check their makeshift weapons one final time. There's an unspoken tension hanging in the air—the weight of farewells that might be permanent.

Kyp approaches Auren first, extending his hand. When Auren grasps it, Kyp pulls him into a fierce embrace instead.

"Don't do anything stupid without me," Kyp says, his voice thick with emotion despite the attempted humor.

"That's rich coming from you," Auren replies, clapping him on the back. "You're walking straight into an Elyssian extraction team."

They pull apart, and Melia notices the unshed tears in Kyp's eyes as he straightens his shoulders.

"Been following you since we were children," Kyp says quietly. "Never thought I'd be the one heading up to the city while you stayed grounded."

Auren's jaw tightens. "Just stay alive. We'll find each other when this is done."

Melia turns to Sam, who stands slightly apart, her posture rigid despite her injury. The former operative's eyes reflect calculation and something deeper—perhaps uncertainty, or the struggle of shedding one identity for another.

"I don't know how to thank you," Melia says, approaching her. "You've risked everything."

Sam shakes her head slightly. "Don't thank me yet. The Emperor will send others when I fail to report. Weapons like me are... replaceable." She says this matter-of-factly, but Melia hears the underlying pain.

"You're not a weapon anymore," Melia says firmly. "Whatever happens, remember that."

Something shifts in Sam's expression—surprise, perhaps, at being seen as more than her function. She extends her hand in an awkward gesture that suggests human connection remains unfamiliar territory.

Melia takes it, feeling the calluses and scars beneath her fingers. "When we meet again, I want to hear about the real Samara. The one before the Emperor."

Sam's lips curve in the ghost of a smile. "I'm still finding her myself."

A soft meow interrupts them. Bear winds between Melia's ankles, then—unexpectedly—moves to sit beside Sam's feet, looking up at her with unblinking green eyes.

"Bear?" Melia's voice catches, betraying more emotion than she intended. The cat has been her constant companion since she fell, a silent witness to her transformation.

Sam looks equally confused. "I think he wants to come with us."

"But..." Melia kneels, reaching for the cat who has been her anchor. Bear approaches, bumps his head against her palm once, then deliberately returns to Sam's side.

"Perhaps he knows where he's needed most," Auren says gently, coming to stand beside Melia.

She swallows the unexpected grief of this small separation. "Keep him safe," she tells Sam. "And let him keep you safe too."

Sam nods solemnly, as if accepting a sacred charge.

The sky brightens further, warning them that time is short. With final nods and promises to reunite, they separate—Sam and Kyp heading north toward the extraction point with Bear padding silently between them, while Melia and Auren turn toward the looming silhouette of Windy Ridge.

Melia watches their companions disappear into the morning mist, Bear's black form visible until the very last moment. Something about his departure feels symbolic—as if one chapter of her journey is ending while another begins.

"Ready?" Auren asks beside her, his voice gentle.

Melia takes a deep breath, turning away from where her friends vanished. "As ready as a conjured princess can be to destroy the world she came from."

***

Melia's legs burn with each step up the steep, rocky incline. Hours of climbing have left her muscles trembling, sweat plastering her hair to her forehead despite the constant, biting wind that gives the ridge its name. She takes another labored breath, refusing to ask for a rest even as her lungs protest.

"The wind actually works with you on the other side," Auren says from a few paces ahead, his voice carrying back to her on the breeze. "Creates these perfect updrafts that make the Aether wings practically sing. Going down is brutal, though."

He turns, walking backward with practiced ease while watching her struggle. His stamina seems boundless compared to hers.

"This stretch right here?" He gestures to the particularly steep section they're traversing. "It's where most pilgrims give up. They call it Heartbreak Pass."

Melia manages a grunt in response, conserving her breath. She places her hand against the rough stone wall beside her, steadying herself as a particularly strong gust threatens to unbalance her.

"The ancient texts say the winds here test your resolve. If your purpose isn't true, the mountain itself will reject you." Auren continues, seemingly oblivious to her exhaustion. "Course, that's religious nonsense. It's just geography—the mountain formations create a natural wind tunnel."

The path narrows, forcing them to walk single file. Melia focuses on placing one foot before the other, too drained to engage with Auren's impromptu history lesson.

"Sorry," he says finally, noticing her silence. "You don't need a lecture on pilgrim traditions right now. I'll shut up and focus on the mission."

The sun begins its descent behind the mountain peaks, casting long shadows across their path. After another hour of climbing in silence, they reach a small plateau with a shallow cave carved into the mountainside.

"We'll rest here for the night," Auren announces, shrugging off his pack. "It's sheltered from the worst of the wind. Tomorrow we'll tackle the final ascent to the Spire."

Melia collapses onto a smooth boulder, her legs finally giving out. She watches as Auren efficiently unpacks their minimal supplies and builds a small fire in the cave's entrance. The flames cast dancing shadows across his face, highlighting the tension in his jaw, the careful way he avoids meeting her eyes directly.

They sit in silence as darkness envelops the mountain, the only sounds the crackling fire and the constant moan of wind through the rocky outcroppings. The quiet between them feels charged, filled with unspoken words that have accumulated since their escape from Garrik's men.

"You're different," Auren says suddenly, his voice barely audible above the wind. "Since Old Hollow."

Melia looks up, finding his eyes on her for the first time in hours. "Finding out you're not real will do that."

"You are real." His response comes immediately, forceful in its certainty.

"Am I?" Melia stretches her hands before her, examining them in the firelight. "Everything I thought I was—my childhood, my parents, my place in the world—it was all fabricated. I'm just a vessel, a convenient container to keep up appearances."

Auren shifts, moving to sit beside her on the boulder. Not touching, but close enough that she can feel the warmth radiating from his body.

"I've been wanting to talk about what happened," he says. "At the chapel. And after."

Her heart quickens. "Why didn't you?"

"Because I thought you regretted it." His voice drops lower. "When you pulled away from me that night in the Bazaar, with Ryker—"

"That wasn't about you," Melia interrupts. "Or us. I was confused, trying to understand who I was, what I wanted."

"And now?" The question hangs between them.

Melia turns to face him fully. "Now I know I'm a construct. A conjuration made to serve Elyssia's purposes." Her voice strengthens. "But my choices are my own. What I feel is real. What we felt together was real."

Auren's hand finds hers in the darkness, his palm warm against her skin. "I'm sorry I didn't come in your door that night at the inn. I stood there like a coward, unable to knock."

"Why didn't you?"

"Because I was afraid," he admits. "Not of you, but of what it meant. I've spent my entire life focused on ascending, on proving my worth. And then there you were—fallen from the very place I couldn't reach—and I felt something I'd never experienced before."

Melia inches closer. "What was that?"

"Like I'd found something more valuable than Elyssia. More real." His thumb traces circles on her wrist. "When Ryker appeared, when I saw how he looked at you, I thought perhaps that was what you needed—someone confident, untainted by failure."

A laugh escapes her, surprising them both. "Ryker was a liar and a traitor."

"True," Auren concedes with a small smile. "Though to be fair, we didn't know that at the time."

The fire pops and shifts, sending sparks dancing into the night air. Melia feels a weight lifting from her chest, words finally finding their way out after being trapped too long.

"I don't regret what happened between us at the chapel," she says. "It was the first time in my life I'd made a choice purely for myself, without duty or expectation dictating my actions." She meets his gaze directly. "The only thing I regretted was not telling you what it meant to me."

Auren's free hand rises to her face, fingertips brushing her cheek with reverent gentleness. "And what did it mean?"

"That I choose you," Melia whispers. "Not because I'm supposed to, or because it serves some greater purpose. Because I want to."

The distance between them vanishes as Auren's mouth finds hers. Unlike their first kiss—hesitant, questioning—this one burns with certainty. His hands frame her face as he kisses her deeply, thoroughly, as if trying to convey every unspoken word through touch alone.

Melia responds with equal fervor, her fingers threading through his hair, pulling him closer. She feels a wild freedom in this choice, made not in the confusion of discovery but in the clarity of defiance. Each touch is a declaration: I exist. I feel. I choose.

They break apart, breathing heavily, foreheads pressed together.

"Are you sure?" Auren asks, his voice rough with restraint.

Melia answers by standing, taking his hand, and leading him deeper into the cave where their bedrolls lie waiting. The fire's glow barely reaches here, casting everything in soft shadow, but she doesn't need light to know what she wants.

She unties the laces of her tunic with deliberate movements, no longer awkward or uncertain as she was in the chapel. Auren watches, transfixed, until she takes his hand and places it against her bare collarbone.

"Touch me," she commands softly. "Show me what's real."

His hands tremble slightly as they trace the curve of her shoulders, the hollow of her throat, the swell of her breasts. Each touch ignites sensation that cascades through her body—proof of her existence, her humanity.

Clothing falls away between desperate kisses, each garment discarded like the lies that once defined her. Melia arches into Auren's touch, her skin alive with electricity as his calloused fingers trace constellations across her body. The cave's chill disappears, replaced by the heat building between them.

"Is this real enough?" he whispers against her neck, his breath hot against her pulse.

"More," she demands, pulling him closer until there's nothing between them but shared breath and racing heartbeats.

Melia runs her palms down Auren's chest, savoring the contours of muscle beneath warm skin. Her fingers trace the ridges of old scars—testament to his failed pilgrimages, his countless battles—with reverent curiosity. When her hand drifts lower, discovering his hardness, she feels a surge of power at his sharp intake of breath. His eyes darken as she explores him, learning the shape and weight of his manhood with deliberate, unhurried strokes.

Melia slides down Auren's body, her lips tracing a path from his collarbone to his abdomen. His skin tastes of salt and wind, distinctly human in a way that anchors her to this moment. She hesitates briefly, meeting his eyes in the dim firelight before lowering her head.

The first touch of her lips against his hardness draws a sharp intake of breath from Auren. His fingers tangle gently in her hair, not guiding but connecting, maintaining contact as she explores this new intimacy. Melia takes him into her mouth slowly, experimentally, learning the contours and textures of him with each movement.

"Melia," he breathes, her name becoming a prayer on his lips.

She finds a rhythm, encouraged by his quickening breath and the tension building in his muscles. This act feels primal, beyond the elaborate rituals and performances of Elyssia. There's power in giving pleasure so directly, in reducing this man who climbed mountains and conjured wings to trembling vulnerability.

His thighs tense beneath her palms as she takes him deeper. Auren's head falls back, throat exposed, utterly unguarded in his pleasure. The sight fills Melia with fierce joy—this is real, undeniably real. No conjuration could replicate the taste of him on her tongue, the subtle movements of his hips, the way his breathing fractures when she swirls her tongue just so.

Auren reaches for her, pulling her upward. "Wait," he gasps, "I want—"

Melia pulls off of his slick manhood, her lips making a soft sound as they release him. She rises to her feet in one fluid motion, moonlight from the cave entrance catching the curves of her body. With gentle pressure against his chest, she pushes Auren back onto the bedroll, his eyes never leaving hers as he yields to her touch.

The last pieces of her clothing fall away, discarded like remnants of her former life. Melia stands above him for a moment, fully naked, embracing the power in her vulnerability. Then she lowers herself to straddle his hips, the heat between them immediate and electric.

"Is this okay?" she asks, her voice husky with desire but hesitant with concern.

Auren's hands find her waist, thumbs tracing small circles on her hipbones as he gazes up at her with undisguised wonder.

"More than okay," he whispers, his body responding beneath her with unmistakable eagerness.

Melia positions herself above him, her thighs trembling with anticipation. Their eyes lock as she slowly lowers herself, gasping as his manhood begins to stretch her. The initial resistance gives way to a delicious fullness that sends ripples of pleasure radiating through her body.

"Oh," she breathes, pausing halfway to adjust to the sensation.

Auren's hands steady her hips, his thumbs drawing soothing circles against her skin. "Take your time," he whispers, though the tension in his voice betrays his restraint.

Melia sinks fully onto him with a soft moan, feeling completely filled, completely connected. The sensation is overwhelming—pleasure mingled with a slight edge of discomfort that quickly dissolves into something deeper, more primal. She remains still for a moment, savoring the feeling of him inside her, the perfect joining of their bodies.

"You feel like home," she murmurs, rolling her hips experimentally and watching his eyes darken with pleasure.

There's no hesitation now, no uncertainty in the rhythm Melia and Auren create together. She rocks against him, finding a pace that sends waves of pleasure coursing through her body. Her head falls back, hair cascading down her spine as she surrenders to sensation.

"Look at me," Auren whispers, his voice strained with need.

Melia opens her eyes, meeting his gaze as their bodies move in perfect synchrony. The connection feels profound—beyond physical, beyond even emotion—as if their very essences intertwine with each thrust and counter-thrust.

Pleasure builds within her, a mounting tension coiling tighter with each movement. Auren's hands explore her body reverently, thumbs circling sensitive peaks, fingers tracing the curve of her spine.

"I feel you," she gasps, understanding flooding her consciousness even as her body climbs toward release. "This is real. I'm real."

Melia braces her hands on Auren's chest, feeling his heartbeat racing beneath her palm. Each movement builds a rising tension within her, a gathering storm of sensation. When his thumb finds the center of her pleasure, circling with perfect pressure, she gasps his name.

The world narrows to this—the point where their bodies meet, the rhythm they create together. She feels herself tightening around him, the coiling tension reaching its breaking point. Her vision blurs as waves of pleasure crash through her, transforming her into pure sensation.

"Let go," Auren whispers, his voice thick with need. "I've got you."

Melia surrenders, crying out as ecstasy claims her. Her body shudders, pulsing around him as release washes through her in overwhelming waves. Auren holds her steady through her climax, his hands anchoring her even as she feels herself dissolving into pure light.

"Look at me," he whispers, and she does, keeping her eyes locked with his even as the pleasure threatens to overwhelm her.

Her body still pulses with aftershocks when Auren moves with surprising strength, flipping their positions in one fluid motion. Suddenly his weight presses down on her, deliciously heavy and secure as he braces himself above her. The shift changes everything—where she was in control before, now she surrenders, her body yielding to his.

"I need you," he whispers against her ear, his voice rough with restrained desire. "All of you."

Melia wraps her legs around his waist, drawing him deeper as he begins to move with renewed purpose. His thrusts are more insistent now, his control slipping as passion overtakes technique. She arches beneath him, meeting each movement with her own.

"You're everything," Auren murmurs, lips brushing the sensitive skin below her ear. "So perfect. So real."

His words send fresh waves of pleasure through her already sensitized body. He holds her tightly, one arm wrapped beneath her shoulders, the other hand cradling her face as if she might shatter—or disappear—if he lets go.

"I'm here," she whispers back, hands sliding down his sweat-slicked back to urge him closer, deeper. "I'm real."

His rhythm falters, becomes erratic as his breathing grows ragged. Melia feels him trembling with the effort of restraint, still putting her pleasure before his own. She lifts her hips to meet his increasingly urgent thrusts, nails digging crescents into his shoulders.

"Let go," she echoes his earlier words. "I've got you too."

Auren's control shatters completely. His body tenses above her, muscles locking as he buries himself deep within her with one final, powerful thrust. A guttural sound—half groan, half her name—tears from his throat as his release claims him.

Melia gasps, eyes widening at the novel sensation of his pulsing heat filling her. Each throb of his manhood sends a corresponding wave through her own body, aftershocks of pleasure that make her inner walls clench around him. The intimacy of this moment—feeling him spend himself inside her—leaves her breathless. This is what it means to be completely joined, completely vulnerable with another person.

His forehead drops to rest against hers, breath coming in ragged pants against her lips. Sweat from his body mingles with hers where they press together, skin to skin. For several heartbeats, they remain perfectly still, connected in the most primal way possible.

"I love you," he whispers against her lips, the words seemingly torn from him in this moment of complete vulnerability.

Melia's heart stutters. She cradles his face between her palms, thumbs brushing his cheekbones as she searches his eyes. The raw emotion she finds there makes her throat tighten with answering feeling.

"I love you too," she whispers back, the words unfamiliar yet undeniably true.

A small smile touches his lips before he claims her mouth in a tender kiss, gentler than before but somehow more significant. Their bodies remain joined, neither willing to break the physical connection that mirrors their emotional one.

They collapse together onto the bedroll, limbs entwined, breathing gradually slowing. Auren's hand traces lazy patterns on her bare back as she rests her head on his chest, listening to his heartbeat return to normal.

"I don't know what happens tomorrow," Melia murmurs against his skin. "I don't know if we can break the cycle, or what becomes of me if we do."

His arms tighten around her. "Whatever happens, this is real. We are real."

Melia closes her eyes, believing him. In this moment, with the wind howling outside their shelter and their bodies still humming with shared pleasure, she feels more authentically alive than she ever did in Elyssia's perfect halls.

Outside, the wind shifts direction, no longer fighting against them but seeming to urge them upward, toward the Shattered Spire and whatever truths await them there.

Orlan III

The golden light falling across Elyssia's western quarter has changed. Sir Orlan notices it immediately—a subtle shift in hue, almost imperceptible unless you're looking for it. The sunlight streaming between the perfect alabaster towers no longer gleams with quite the same luster. In places, it appears almost... brittle.

Like a thin sheet of ice about to crack.

Orlan keeps his gait measured, his expression carefully neutral as he patrols Ascension Avenue. Citizens bow respectfully as he passes, their faces showing appropriate reverence for his station. His armor gleams with the same polished perfection it always has, the royal insignia on his breastplate catching the strange light.

But now he knows. The weight of Elynia's revelations presses down on him with each step.

Not divine at all. Constructed. Conjured. Sustained by... sacrifice.

A tremor runs through the street beneath his boots—so slight that most wouldn't notice. But Orlan catches the momentary widening of eyes from a merchant arranging silk flowers outside her shop. She glances up at the perfect blue sky, then quickly makes the Thread-sign across her chest before returning to her work with deliberate focus.

"Good afternoon, Sir Orlan," she calls with practiced cheer. "Beautiful day, as always."

"Indeed," he responds, the courteous lie bitter on his tongue. "May the Thread weave you prosperity."

The ritual exchange complete, he continues toward the Central Promenade. There have been seventeen such tremors in the past week—since the day Princess Melia was supposed to wed Prefect Solivar. Seventeen cracks in Elyssia's perfect facade.

They're getting stronger.

A group of children race past him, their laughter echoing off the polished stone walls. They play a game involving colorful ribbons tied to their wrists, something about ascending to higher planes. Orlan's stomach tightens as he watches them. How many generations have lived and died here, never knowing they dwelled in an elaborate prison built on bones?

His own daughter's face flashes before him. Lira, barely seven, with her mother's eyes and his stubborn chin.

Ahead, a small crowd has gathered around one of the singing fountains. Water should be arcing in perfect musical harmony from the sculpted figures, but instead they stand dry and silent. Two acolytes in blue robes work frantically at the fountain's base, their hands tracing ritual patterns while they whisper urgent prayers.

"Just a minor disruption," one explains to the murmuring crowd. "The Thread sometimes tests our faith through momentary imperfections."

Orlan approaches, and the citizens part for him with respectful nods. He recognizes the tension in the acolytes' shoulders, the barely concealed panic in their eyes when they glance up at him.

"Sir Orlan," the elder one acknowledges with forced calm. "We have the situation well in hand. Merely a temporary fluctuation in the harmony patterns."

"How long has it been non-functional?" Orlan asks, keeping his voice neutral.

"Since this morning's second bell. But we've identified the dissonance point and—"

Another tremor rolls beneath them, stronger than the last. A woman gasps. A child begins to cry.

"Perhaps you should clear the area," Orlan suggests, his hand resting casually on his sword hilt. "For safety, while the acolytes complete their work."

The crowd disperses reluctantly, whispering among themselves. Orlan catches fragments—"never happened before," "third fountain this week," "the wedding delay"—before they move beyond earshot.

"Sir Orlan." The younger acolyte leans closer, voice barely audible. "The High Temple requests your presence. Immediately."

Orlan nods once, sharply. "Continue your work. I'll inform the Prefect of your progress."

He strides away, jaw clenched. The High Temple has summoned him twelve times since Elynia shared the truth. Each meeting more desperate than the last, with Solivar growing increasingly unstable as his perfect realm begins to fracture.

The grand spires of the High Temple rise before him, their white marble strangely dulled today, as though viewed through gauze. At the base of the hundred steps, two Elyssian Guards stand at attention, their faces unnaturally still beneath their ornate helmets.

"Sir Orlan," they intone in unison, stepping aside.

The massive doors swing open silently. Orlan ascends, each step a decision. Each footfall a betrayal—either of the oath he once swore in ignorance, or of the truth he now carries like a blade.

Inside, the Temple's vast dome usually shimmers with conjured starlight, a perpetual twilight that inspires awe in all who enter. Today, patches of the display flicker erratically, stars blinking in and out of existence. Several priests hurry about the periphery, frantically working to stabilize the illusion.

Prefect Solivar stands at the center of the Chamber of Ascension, his immaculate white robes a stark contrast to the shadows beneath his eyes. Around him, six High Priests gesture at a floating three-dimensional model of Elyssia—a perfect miniature of the city, rendered in glowing golden light. Throughout the model, angry red lines spread like cracks in glass.

"The western residential district is showing critical strain," one priest reports, his finger tracing a particularly bright fissure. "The Thread-memory is weakening faster than we can reinforce it."

"Increase the devotional requirements," Solivar snaps. "Triple the prayer cycles in that sector. We need more conviction to sustain the pattern."

"We've already doubled them this week," another priest counters. "The citizens grow weary and—"

"They grow questioning," Solivar interrupts, his voice knife-sharp. "Which is precisely what we cannot afford. If necessary, stage a visible punishment for heresy. Something public. Something memorable."

Orlan's hand tightens on his sword hilt. The casual cruelty, the manipulation—it turns his stomach now. How had he never seen it before?

"Ah, Sir Orlan." Solivar notices him, face immediately arranging itself into calmer lines. "Your report from the lower districts?"

"More anomalies," Orlan states plainly. "Another fountain has failed. The light in the western quarter appears... diminished."

"Diminished how?" one of the priests demands, frantically adjusting the model.

"As though seen through a veil," Orlan explains. "And the tremors continue, growing stronger."

Another tremor rocks the temple, violent enough that several priests stumble. In the model, a new crack appears—jagged and pulsing with angry energy.

"The Eastern Gardens," a priest identifies, voice rising in panic. "The Thread-memory is unraveling there."

"Redirect conjuration energy from the outer districts," Solivar orders. "Stabilize the core structures first."

"The outer districts are already experiencing periodic fading," a priestess protests. "If we divert more energy—"

"Then they fade further," Solivar snaps. "Better the edges than the heart."

Orlan watches the cold calculation on Solivar's face. How many times had such decisions been made? How many "edges" sacrificed to maintain the perfect illusion at the center?

"Sir Orlan." Solivar turns to him. "You will take a contingent of guards to the Eastern Gardens. Establish a perimeter. No citizens are to witness what is happening there."

"And if they already have?" Orlan asks carefully.

Something dark flashes across Solivar's face. "Then they are experiencing a collective delusion, brought on by insufficient faith. They will be taken to the Temple of Clarification for... spiritual realignment."

Spiritual realignment. Orlan knows what that means now. Another sacrifice to feed the hungry maw of conjuration that keeps Elyssia aloft.

"Of course, Prefect." He bows, the gesture hiding the disgust in his eyes.

"One more thing," Solivar adds as Orlan turns to leave. "Your family has been relocated to more secure quarters within the palace complex."

Ice floods Orlan's veins. "Relocated? I wasn't informed—"

"For their protection," Solivar explains smoothly. "These are unstable times. I'm sure you understand the necessity."

The threat couldn't be clearer. Hostages, not honored guests.

"They are comfortable?" Orlan manages to ask, his voice steady despite the rage building inside him.

"Quite. Your daughter seems especially delighted with the palace gardens." Solivar's smile doesn't reach his eyes. "You may visit them, of course. Once the current... disruptions... are addressed."

Orlan bows again, lower this time to hide the murderous intent that must surely show on his face. "You are most gracious, Prefect."

He turns and strides from the chamber, back straight, steps measured. Only when he is outside, descending the hundred steps, does he allow his hand to curl into a fist. His knuckles whiten beneath his ceremonial gauntlets.

Merien. Lira. Pawns in Solivar's game now.

Another tremor ripples through the city as Orlan reaches the street level. This one brings with it a strange sound—like distant glass shattering, followed by a chorus of confused shouts from the direction of the Eastern Gardens.

Orlan moves toward the disturbance, mind racing. He had sworn an oath to protect Elyssia, to serve its rulers faithfully. But that oath was based on a foundation of lies. What loyalty does he owe to those who had deliberately deceived him—deceived everyone—for generations?

King Orion and Queen Lysandra had died so suddenly, so myste-riously. Not part of the cycle, Elynia had told him. Unplanned. Now their daughter has fled, and Elyssia begins to crack.

What did they know? Orlan wonders as he quickens his pace. *What truth had they discovered that was worth dying for?*

***

The High Priests file into the chamber one by one, their ornate robes rustling against the marble floor. Orlan stands at attention by the door, his face a careful mask while his mind rages like a storm. High Priest Morden's thin lips twist into a satisfied smile as he approaches Solivar.

"Excellent news, Prefect," Morden announces, clasping his bony hands together. "Our arrangement with Garrik the Gilded has proven fruitful. The princess has been secured."

Solivar's eyes flash with triumph. "Where?"

"At the extraction point," High Priest Verrus adds, his deep voice resonating through the chamber. "Our agents report they have her in custody along with several... companions. They should arrive within hours."

Orlan's heart hammers against his ribs, though his expression re-mains impassive. *Melia, captured. Returned to this place of lies.*

"The Gilded one demanded additional payment," High Priestess Valeera notes with distaste. "His greed knows no bounds."

"Pay him whatever he wants," Solivar waves dismissively. "Once our cycle is secured, such minor expenses are irrelevant."

High Priest Thaddeus clears his throat. "And the others with her? What shall become of them?"

"The pilgrim who channels Aether may prove useful," Tharos suggests, stroking his silver beard. "A powerful source for the next conjuration, perhaps."

"And the rest?" Elynia asks, her voice carefully neutral.

Solivar's smile turns cold. "Dispose of them. They've seen too much."

The chamber falls silent as another tremor shakes the foundations. This one stronger than the last, causing dust to drift down from the vaulted ceiling.

"We must act quickly," Morden urges. "The city weakens by the hour. With the princess returned, we can perform the emergency binding ritual tonight."

Solivar nods sharply. "Sir Orlan."

Orlan steps forward, bowing. "Yes, Prefect?"

"Have the royal bedchambers prepared immediately." Solivar's eyes gleam with anticipation. "Tonight, Princess Melia and I will be married in a private ceremony."

Orlan's blood turns to ice. "Private, Prefect?"

"The people are already unsettled by these... disruptions," Solivar explains. "We'll announce it afterward, once the binding is complete and the city stabilized."

"The binding?" Orlan carefully keeps his voice even.

High Priest Verrus looks at him with suspicion. "The marriage must be consummated immediately. The royal bloodline is essential to maintaining the conjuration cycle."

"Prepare an honor guard to receive her at the Eastern Sanctum," Solivar commands. "And ensure complete privacy for the ceremony. No one but the High Priests and yourself shall witness it."

Across the room, Elynia's eyes meet Orlan's. Her gaze holds a question, a warning, perhaps even an invitation to act. The slightest shake of her head communicates volumes.

"As you command, Prefect," Orlan responds, bowing deeply to hide the conflict raging within.

"You seem troubled, Sir Orlan," Solivar observes, his voice dangerously soft. "I remind you that your family's comfort depends entirely on your continued loyalty."

"My loyalty to Elyssia has never wavered," Orlan replies carefully. It isn't a lie – his loyalty is to Elyssia itself, not to the men who have twisted its purpose.

"Good." Solivar turns back to the High Priests. "Begin preparations for the binding ritual. Tonight, we restore what has been damaged."

As the discussion continues, Orlan stands rigid, his mind racing. Hours until Melia returns. Hours to decide where his true duty lies – with the oath he swore to a corrupt system, or with the truth that threatens to tear it all apart.

***

Orlan walks briskly through the Eastern Corridor, the click of his boots against marble echoing off the vaulted ceiling. Elynia keeps pace beside him, her white robes flowing like water as they turn down a less traveled passage.

"The guards have been instructed not to question my presence," Elynia says, her voice barely above a whisper. "But we must be swift."

The corridor narrows, opening into a secluded courtyard within the palace complex. Gilded doors stand at the far end, flanked by two honor guards who snap to attention at Orlan's approach.

"Sir Orlan," the guard on the left acknowledges with a bow. His eyes flick uncertainly to Elynia.

"The High Priestess accompanies me on Prefect Solivar's authority," Orlan states, the lie flowing smoothly from his lips. "We require privacy."

The guards step aside without question. Orlan's hand trembles slightly as he pushes the door open, revealing a luxurious suite of rooms – a gilded cage.

Merien sits by the window, her dark hair caught in the late afternoon light as she reads to Lira. They both look up at the sound of the door, their faces brightening instantly.

"Orlan!" Merien rises, book forgotten.

"Father!" Lira launches herself across the room. Orlan catches her, lifting her into his arms with practiced ease.

"My little songbird," he murmurs, breathing in the familiar scent of her hair, committing it to memory.

Merien embraces them both, her arms encircling his waist. "This is unexpected. We were told you wouldn't be permitted to visit until after the ceremony tonight."

Over Merien's shoulder, Orlan sees Elynia discreetly checking the adjoining rooms before positioning herself near the door, watchful.

"I've found a way," he says, setting Lira down gently. His daughter's small hand remains clutched in his, unwilling to break contact.

"What's happening?" Merien asks, reading the tension in his face. "The attendants whisper when they think we cannot hear. The city trembled this morning – Lira was frightened."

"I wasn't frightened," Lira protests. "Just surprised. Father, why does the city shake? Is it angry?"

Orlan kneels before his daughter, meeting her earnest gaze. The impulse to shield her from the truth wars with his need to prepare them.

"Not angry, little one," he says carefully. "But things are changing. The world is about to change, and I'm not sure what will happen."

Merien's hand tightens on his shoulder. "Orlan, you're scaring me. What aren't you telling us?"

He rises, taking her hands in his. How can he explain that their perfect home is built on lies? That the divine ascension they've been taught to revere is a carefully constructed illusion? That their daughter might grow up in a world unrecognizable from the one they've known?

"I can't tell you everything," he says finally. "Not yet. But I need you to trust me, Merien. Tonight... I must make a choice that may change everything."

"Is it Princess Melia?" Lira asks suddenly. "The ladies who bring us food said she's coming back tonight to marry the Prefect. Will we go to the wedding?"

Elynia makes a small sound by the door, a warning. Their time grows short.

"There will be no wedding," Orlan says, with more certainty than he feels. "Not tonight."

Merien's eyes widen. "Orlan, what are you planning to do?"

He straightens, squaring his shoulders. "My duty. As I always have."

"But your duty is to the Prefect—" Merien begins.

"My duty is to Elyssia," he corrects gently. "To its people. To you and Lira. Sometimes, protecting what matters means standing against what is wrong."

Lira tugs at his hand. "Father, are you going to be in trouble?"

He manages a smile for her, though it costs him dearly. "I hope not, songbird. But even if I am, I want you to remember that doing the right thing is sometimes difficult."

"You always do the right thing," Lira says with absolute conviction. "The other knights say so. They say you're the most honorable man in Elyssia."

The faith in her eyes nearly breaks him. He embraces her tightly, then rises to face Merien, whose expression has shifted from confusion to a grim understanding.

"This is more serious than you're letting on," she says quietly.

Instead of answering, he pulls her close, breathing in the familiar scent of her, memorizing the way her body fits against his. "I love you," he whispers into her hair. "Whatever happens, know that."

Merien pulls back just enough to meet his gaze, her eyes bright with unshed tears. "Come back to us," she says fiercely. "Whatever you're planning, whatever duty calls you to do – you come back to us, Orlan."

He can't make that promise, not with what lies ahead. Instead, he kisses her deeply, pouring everything he cannot say into that single moment of connection.

"Sir Orlan," Elynia calls softly from the door. "We must go."

He nods, reluctantly releasing Merien. Lira wraps her arms around his waist one last time.

"Be brave, my songbird," he murmurs, stroking her hair. "Remember what I taught you about courage."

"It's not about not being afraid," Lira recites, "it's about doing what's right even when you are afraid."

"That's my girl."

As he turns to leave, Merien catches his hand. "Orlan," she says, her voice steady despite her tears. "Whatever it is, I trust you."

The simple statement nearly undoes him. A tear escapes, trailing down his cheek as he nods once, sharply, and follows Elynia through the door.

Outside, the corridor stretches before him, leading back to duty and decision. His face hardens, resolve crystallizing within him as the door closes on his family.

Melia will not marry Solivar tonight. Not while he still draws breath.

Sam I

S am's neural implants pulse beneath her skin, each throb a quiet reminder of the damage Ryker's blade inflicted. The diagnostic overlay in her peripheral vision shows the steady climb of her vitals—63% functionality, up from 58% an hour ago. Not ideal for combat, but sufficient for deception.

She adjusts the hood of her cloak, careful to keep her face shadowed. Beside her, Kyp shifts his weight from one foot to another, scanning the horizon with unconvincing nonchalance.

"Stop fidgeting," she murmurs. "You'll give us away before they even land."

"Easy for you to say," Kyp whispers back. "You're trained for this. I'm just the funny friend who tags along and occasionally says something helpful."

Bear weaves between their legs, his sleek black form a shadow against the scrubby underbrush of the extraction point. The cat's ears prick forward, detecting something beyond human perception.

"They're coming," Sam says, the faint vibration in the air registering through her enhanced senses. "Remember the plan. You're Ryker. I'm Melia. Keep it simple."

"Right. Simple." Kyp straightens his spine, attempting to mimic Ryker's confident posture. "Just pretending to be the man who betrayed us and tried to kill you. Simple."

The air shifts and compresses as the Elyssian transport descends, a sleek silver craft that seems to push the very molecules of atmosphere aside rather than displace them. It settles on the clearing with barely a sound, the gentle hiss of equalizing pressure its only announcement.

The hatch opens, revealing four figures in the pearl-white uniforms of the Elyssian Guard. Their faces bear the same placid expression, as if sculpted rather than born. The lead guard steps forward, his eyes scanning Kyp with clinical precision.

"Ryker Voss," he states rather than asks. "You've secured the princess."

Kyp nods, adopting a casual arrogance that Sam has to admit is an impressive approximation of Ryker's manner. "As promised. Though it wasn't without complications." He gestures toward Sam's cloaked figure. "She's been... difficult."

The guard's gaze shifts to Sam, his expression unchanged. "Princess Melia. Your presence is required in Elyssia. Prefect Solivar awaits."

Sam hunches her shoulders, making herself smaller beneath the cloak. When she speaks, she pitches her voice higher, adding a tremulous quality that mimics fear. "I... I don't want to go back. Please."

It's not her finest performance, but the guard seems uninterested in nuance. He simply nods to his companions, who move forward to flank them.

"Your feelings are irrelevant, Princess. The ceremony must proceed as scheduled."

Kyp steps between them, channeling Ryker's proprietary attitude. "Careful with her. She's still valuable, damaged or not. And I expect proper compensation for delivering her, as agreed."

The guard's expression tightens minutely—the only indication of emotion Sam has observed from him. "Your payment will be addressed once we return. Now, board the transport. Time is limited."

As they approach the craft, Bear darts ahead, slipping through the open hatch before any of the guards can react. One reaches for his weapon, but Kyp laughs with convincing derision.

"It's just her cat. The thing follows her everywhere. Consider it part of the package."

The guard hesitates, then nods curtly. "Fine. But control it during transport."

Sam keeps her head down as they board, her gait deliberately unsteady. The interior of the craft is pristine, all smooth surfaces and recessed lighting. The guards direct them to molded seats that seem to adjust to their occupants' bodies.

Bear settles at her feet, a warm presence against her boots. The cat's eyes reflect the ambient light, two green pinpoints in the dim cabin.

As the hatch seals shut, Sam feels the gentle pull of lift off. Through the small viewport, she watches the ground fall away, the extraction point diminishing to a speck below them. Her enhanced vision picks out details the others would miss—the pattern of trees, the subtle indications of recent passage, the distant smudge that might be Auren and Melia making their way toward the Shattered Spire.

"You've done well, Voss," the guard says to Kyp as they level off. "The High Priests will be pleased."

Kyp offers a smirk that doesn't reach his eyes. "I live to serve. As long as service pays well."

The guard turns away, speaking quietly into a communication device embedded in his collar. Sam catches fragments—"secured," "proceeding to," "preparation"—before he deliberately lowers his voice below even her enhanced hearing.

She takes the opportunity to run another internal diagnostic. 65% functionality now. The nanites in her bloodstream are working efficiently, repairing damaged tissue and restoring neural pathways. By the time they reach Elyssia, she should be at 70%, perhaps higher.

Not optimal, but it will have to suffice.

Kyp leans closer, his voice barely audible. "Are you alright? You're very pale."

"Functioning within acceptable parameters," she responds automatically, then catches herself. Those are the Shadow's words, not Sam's.

"I'm... managing," she amends.

***

The transport shudders through a cloud bank, momentarily obscuring the viewport. Sam shifts in her seat, adjusting the heavy cloak to better conceal her features. The guards stand at attention near the cockpit, exchanging occasional muttered words through their communication devices. Their disciplined posture never wavers.

"They're like statues," Kyp whispers, his lips barely moving. "Do you think they ever smile?"

Sam studies them through lowered lashes. "Unlikely. Perfection doesn't require joy."

The craft banks slightly, emerging from the cloud cover into brilliant sunlight. Kyp inhales sharply, pressing his face to the small viewport. His eyes widen with undisguised wonder.

"Holy—" He catches himself, remembering his role. "I mean, the view is... acceptable."

But Sam can see the awe transforming his features. Below them spreads a tapestry of green and gold, forests and fields shrunk to miniature versions of themselves. Rivers cut silver ribbons through the landscape, catching sunlight and flinging it back skyward.

"You've never flown before," she observes quietly.

Kyp shakes his head, unable to tear his gaze from the window. "Never higher than a tavern rooftop." His voice drops further. "I understand now why Auren was so desperate to fly. To reach that city. This feeling..."

Sam processes this. Flying has been a utilitarian experience for her—transportation, tactical advantage, mission parameter. She tries to see it through his eyes: the liberation, the perspective, the sheer unlikeliness of a human body suspended above the earth.

"There," one of the guards announces. "First visual of Elyssia."

Sam follows their gaze through the front viewport. At first, it appears to be nothing more than another cloud formation on the horizon. Then details emerge—gleaming spires piercing the sky, vast terraced gardens spilling over the edges, bridges of impossible delicacy spanning the gaps between floating sections.

"It's both beautiful and terrible," she murmurs.

"Just like the best stories," Kyp responds, then adds with false bravado, "Not that I care about stories. Just coin and comfort, that's the Ryker way."

A guard glances their direction, and Kyp shifts his posture, adopting Ryker's characteristic sprawl. But his eyes remain fixed on the approaching city, drinking in every detail.

The transport banks again, beginning its approach. Bear stirs at Sam's feet, stretching before pressing against her leg. The warm weight is... unexpected. Pleasant. Her hand moves automatically to stroke the cat's sleek fur, fingers finding the spot behind his ears that makes him lean into her touch.

"I never understood why she kept you around," Sam whispers to the cat, too low for even Kyp to hear. "But I'm starting to."

Bear's purr vibrates against her leg, a steady, rhythmic sensation that seems to resonate through her damaged systems. The nanites in her bloodstream respond, their repair functions accelerating slightly. Fascinating. The physiological response to companion animals has been documented, but experiencing it directly is... different.

Sam drops her voice slightly, "Everything depends on timing. If Auren and Melia can't reach the Spire before we do what we need to..."

"They'll make it," Kyp insists, his confidence genuine. "Auren may be stubborn, but he's never failed when it truly mattered."

"He failed to ascend," Sam points out, more curious than cruel.

Kyp shakes his head. "No. Something stopped him. There's a difference between failure and interference."

Sam considers this distinction. The Emperor had programmed success parameters into her from childhood—binary outcomes, mission accomplished or mission failed. The idea of external factors creating a third category troubles her conceptual framework.

"And if we're interfered with?" she asks.

Kyp's smile doesn't reach his eyes. "Then we adapt. That's what humans do."

"Some of us more than others," Sam murmurs, feeling the circuits beneath her skin pulse with unnatural life.

Bear butts his head against her hand, demanding more attention. The simple gesture grounds her in the present moment. This is what Melia valued—this uncomplicated connection, this wordless understanding.

"We'll be docking in approximately twelve minutes," the guard announces. "Prepare yourselves. Prefect Solivar has arranged a reception committee."

"How thoughtful," Kyp says dryly.

Sam strokes Bear's fur, allowing her other hand to drift casually to her boot. The concealed blade there provides a small comfort. "Twelve minutes," she repeats. "Prefect Solivar has waited this long for his bride. He can wait a little longer."

"You think she's worth all this?" Kyp asks, genuine curiosity in his voice. "A princess who doesn't even know what she is?"

Sam considers the question. Is Melia worth the risk they're taking? Worth potentially compromising a lifetime of Imperial conditioning? Worth the statistical probability that this mission ends in their deaths?

"She chose to jump," Sam says finally. "She could be coming back to a beautiful lie, but she's chosen the ugly truth. That's... rare."

Kyp nods slowly. "It is."

"I spent fifteen years accepting beautiful lies," Sam continues, her voice barely audible. "Believing I was saved when I was stolen. Believing I served a purpose when I was merely a tool."

Bear's steady purr intensifies, as if responding to the emotions she refuses to acknowledge are building within her. The cat's green eyes study her with unsettling intelligence.

"And now?" Kyp asks.

"Now I choose to jump," she answers simply.

The city grows larger in the viewport, no longer a distant vision but an imminent reality. Its perfection becomes more apparent with proximity—the symmetry of its architecture, the careful arrangement of its gardens, the harmonious flow of water from its fountains. And yet, now that Sam knows what sustains this perfection, she cannot unsee the cost.

"It's dying," she observes, noting the almost imperceptible flicker in the city's ambient glow. "The thread is unraveling."

Kyp follows her gaze. "Good. Some things should die."

"Not the people trapped inside it," Sam counters. "Not the ones who never chose to be part of the conjuration."

"Is that why you're doing this?" Kyp asks, genuine curiosity in his tone. "To save people you've never met?"

Sam considers this. Why is she risking everything to help dismantle Elyssia? It contradicts her programming, defies the Emperor's direct orders. The logical explanation would be that she's malfunctioning, that the damage to her systems has corrupted her primary directives.

But as Bear presses against her leg, his small body warm and trusting, she recognizes something deeper at work. Something her mother tried to teach her before the Empire took her.

"I'm doing this because I choose to," she says finally. "Because for the first time since I was a child, I'm making a decision that wasn't programmed into me."

Kyp's expression softens, the Ryker-like mask slipping momentarily. "That's... more human than most humans manage."

The transport begins its final approach, banking toward a gleaming landing platform that extends from one of Elyssia's upper levels. Sam glances at the guard nearest to them, confirming his attention is directed elsewhere, then leans closer to Kyp.

"Remember the contingencies," she whispers. "If we're separated, you know what to do."

Kyp nods almost imperceptibly. "And if it all goes wrong?"

"Then we improvise," Sam replies, echoing his earlier sentiment. "That's what humans do."

"Some better than others," he returns with a faint smile.

The craft slows, hovering momentarily before settling onto the platform with barely a tremor. Beyond the viewport, a reception party waits—a dozen guards in ceremonial armor, a cluster of robed figures Sam identifies as lesser priests, and at their center, a man whose bearing speaks of absolute authority.

"Prefect Solivar," one of the guards announces unnecessarily.

Sam studies him through the viewport. Tall, imposing, with features sculpted to precise symmetry. His robes shimmer with embedded threads of gold and silver, catching the light with each movement. His expression is one of practiced benevolence, but his eyes remain cold and calculating.

"I expected someone more... impressive," she murmurs.

Kyp suppresses a smile. "Don't let him hear you say that. I bet he's sensitive about his height."

The lead guard moves to the hatch controls. "Prepare for disembarkation. Princess Melia, you will be escorted directly to the Temple Sanctum for purification. Ryker Voss, you will accompany Prefect Solivar's steward to receive your compensation."

Sam feels Bear tense against her leg, as if sensing the imminent separation. She slides her hand beneath his collar, checking that the small device she attached earlier remains secure.

"It's time," she says, raising her voice slightly.

The hatch begins to open, sunlight spilling into the transport's interior. Sam pulls her hood forward, obscuring her features once

more. Bear presses closer to her leg, a small, steady presence amid the
uncertainty.

"Now we jump," she whispers to the cat, who blinks up at her with
those knowing green eyes.

For a moment, Sam thinks she sees understanding there—not just
animal intelligence, but something deeper. Then the hatch completes
its cycle, and the guards motion for them to stand.

"Welcome home, Princess Melia," one intones formally. "Elyssia has
awaited your return."

***

The craft's ramp extends with mechanical precision, hissing as it meets
the gleaming platform. Sam steps forward, careful to maintain the
demure posture she's observed in Melia. Each movement is calculated—head slightly bowed, shoulders drawn inward, steps measured
and light. The hood of her borrowed cloak creates useful shadows
across her face.

Bear stays close, his small body nearly invisible against the hem of
her dark clothing. Kyp follows with Ryker's characteristic swagger, his
hand resting casually on the hilt of a borrowed blade.

Solivar stands at the center of the reception party, hands clasped
before him in a gesture that manages to appear both welcoming and
imperious. The sunlight catches on the elaborate embroidery of his
robes, threads of gold and silver winking like watchful eyes.

"Princess Melia," he announces, voice carrying across the platform
with practiced authority. "Your return brings great comfort to our city
in these... unsettled times."

Sam keeps her face downturned, offering a slight nod that might pass for deference. Her peripheral vision catalogs potential threats—twelve guards in ceremonial armor, five robed figures she identifies as High Priests, and directly behind Solivar, a knight whose stance suggests greater combat training than the others.

"I've delivered the girl as promised," Kyp declares in Ryker's drawling tone. "I believe we discussed compensation."

Solivar's smile remains fixed, though his eyes narrow slightly. "Indeed. Your service to Elyssia will be rewarded, Ryker Voss."

One of the High Priests steps forward, a gaunt man with piercing eyes. "And what of the others? The pilgrim and his companions?"

"Dead," Kyp answers with convincing coldness. "They put up quite the fight."

The temperature of the platform seems to drop. Solivar's expression hardens, the polite mask slipping for a moment to reveal something colder beneath.

"All of them?" he asks, voice dangerously soft. "Even the Aether user?"

Kyp hesitates, just long enough for Sam to note the tactical error. "He was particularly difficult to kill," he recovers. "But a blade through the heart tends to quiet even the most talented."

Solivar takes a deliberate step forward. "The instructions were explicit. The Aether user was to be brought to us alive."

"Well, perhaps your instructions should have included how to subdue someone who can manifest weapons from thin air," Kyp retorts.

The knight behind Solivar moves with unexpected speed, drawing his sword and pressing the point against Kyp's throat in one fluid motion.

"You will address the Prefect with respect," he states, voice level but threaded with danger.

"Stand down, Sir Orlan," Solivar says without turning. "Mr. Voss's manners are of little concern compared to his incompetence."

Sam catalogs the name—Sir Orlan—while tracking the positioning of each guard. The odds are deteriorating rapidly. She detects movement to her right as one of the High Priests steps closer, studying her with unsettling intensity.

"Is something wrong, High Priest Thaddeus?" Solivar asks, noting the man's focused attention.

The priest continues staring at Sam, his eyes narrowing. "This is not Princess Melia."

The platform falls silent. Sam's neural implants register elevated heart rates from multiple sources, including her own. Her mind cycles through seventeen potential responses, discarding each as insufficient.

"What nonsense is this?" Solivar demands.

"I have performed the sacred rituals upon the princess since childhood," Thaddeus continues. "I know her essence within the Thread. This woman carries a different signature entirely. A foreign signature."

Solivar's gaze shifts to Sam, calculation replacing courtesy. He gestures to Sir Orlan. "Verify this claim."

The knight releases Kyp and approaches Sam, sword still drawn. His movements are precise, controlled—a trained combatant, not merely ceremonial. Sam remains motionless, weighing options, calculating probability of success against multiple scenarios.

Sir Orlan reaches for her hood. The moment stretches, time fragmenting into tactical segments. Sam registers Bear tensing at her feet, Kyp's hand drifting toward his hidden blade, the High Priests forming a subtle semicircle.

When Orlan pulls back her hood, Sam moves. Her hand snaps up, catching his wrist and twisting sharply. The knight stumbles backward, surprise briefly overriding his training.

"Guards!" Solivar shouts, fury transforming his features.

The platform erupts into motion. Sam drops into a combat stance, neural implants flooding her system with enhanced reflexes.

"You incompetent fools!" Solivar rages, pointing at Kyp. "You've brought an imposter!"

Kyp, abandoning all pretense of being Ryker, grins wildly. Then, with deliberate insolence, he steps forward and slaps Solivar across the face.

The collective gasp from the assembled priests seems to hang in the air. Solivar staggers, more from shock than force.

"Run!" Sam shouts to Kyp.

He doesn't hesitate, sprinting toward the city's central promenade with Bear racing at his heels. "Citizens of Elyssia!" he bellows, voice carrying across the platform and beyond. "Your city is a lie! You live in a conjuring built on sacrifice!"

Bear streaks away from the chaos, a black blur carrying Sam's concealed device. Suddenly, Kyp's voice booms from the cat's direction, amplified tenfold: "CITIZENS OF ELYSSIA! YOUR CITY IS A LIE!" The crowd freezes, faces turning toward the sound. Sam's lips curve slightly—her contingency plan activating perfectly as the cat disappears into the gathering throng.

Guards move to pursue, but Solivar's command stops them. "Let him go! The imposter is the greater threat!"

The High Priests encircle Sam, their robes billowing around them like storm clouds. Sir Orlan holds his sword at ready, his stance suggesting both caution and determination.

"Who are you?" Solivar demands, one hand still pressed against his reddening cheek.

Sam's mind calculates probabilities, tracking the cascade of events now in motion. Kyp's distraction will sow discord, but everything

depends on whether Auren and Melia can reach the Shattered Spire
in time. The plan hangs on a knife's edge of possibility.

"I'm no one of consequence," Sam replies, a cold smile playing at
her lips. "Just a weapon aimed at a different target."

Melia XII

The wind screams through the fractured stone, whipping Melia's hair across her face as she and Auren crest the final ridge. Before them stands the Shattered Spire—a broken tooth of ancient architecture jutting from the mountainside. Parts of its once-magnificent structure have collapsed, leaving jagged edges silhouetted against the darkening sky.

"We made it," Auren says, his voice nearly lost in the howling gale.

Melia's legs tremble, not just from the grueling climb but from what awaits inside. Something within her responds to this place—a pulling sensation beneath her breastbone, as though an invisible thread is tugging her forward.

"It knows I'm here," she whispers.

Auren squeezes her hand. "You don't have to do this."

But she does. She knows she does. The memory of Sam and Kyp's sacrifice to create their diversion, the knowledge of all those trapped in Elyssia's foundations—conscious but unable to escape—propels her forward.

The entrance to the Spire is a gaping wound in the rock face. Ancient symbols frame the archway, their meaning obscured by centuries of erosion. As Melia passes through, she feels a subtle shift in the air, like crossing through an invisible membrane.

"It feels different in here," Auren notes, his voice hushed. "The Aether is... concentrated."

The interior opens into a vast circular chamber, its ceiling lost in darkness above. At the center stands a weathered stone dais, surrounded by concentric rings carved into the floor. The outer walls are lined with alcoves, each containing remnants of what might have been artifacts or offerings.

"This is it," Melia says. "The birthplace of Elyssia."

Her steps echo as she approaches the central platform. Each footfall sends ripples of faint luminescence through the floor patterns—blue-white light responding to her presence.

"Melia, wait—" Auren starts, but falls silent as she steps onto the dais.

The effect is immediate and overwhelming. The entire floor ignites with brilliant light, revealing an intricate web of interconnected lines—a vast geometric pattern that pulses with energy. The light climbs the walls, illuminating frescoes and inscriptions previously hidden in shadow.

Melia gasps, staggering as images flood her mind: hundreds of people arranged in precise formation, channeling Aether through their bodies; High Priests directing the energy flow; the foundations of Elyssia taking shape in the sky above.

"Do you see this?" she asks, voice trembling.

Auren stands transfixed at the edge of the pattern. "I see light, but nothing like what you're experiencing."

She kneels, placing her palm against the stone. The pattern responds, lines of light flowing toward her hand like water seeking the lowest point. Information floods her consciousness—not in words but in pure understanding.

"I can see it all," she says, voice distant. "Every person bound into the conjuration. Every sacrifice."

Her gaze follows one particular strand of light—brighter than the others, pulsing with a resonance that feels achingly familiar. It winds through the complex pattern before terminating directly beneath her.

The realization hits her with physical force, driving the breath from her lungs.

"Melia?" Auren steps closer, concern etched on his features. "What is it?"

Her hand trembles against the stone. "I'm part of it. I always have been." She looks up at him, tears gathering in her eyes. "I'm not just another conjuration. I'm woven into it. A keystone."

The pattern confirms her understanding, light pulsing in affirmation. She was never simply a princess, never merely a royal figurehead. She was designed with a specific purpose—a failsafe mechanism.

"If Elyssia began to fail," she continues, the knowledge unfolding within her, "I would be drawn to return here. To renew the binding. To... sacrifice myself to maintain the city."

Auren kneels beside her, his expression anguished. "And if you break the conjuration instead?"

The answer is already forming in her mind, crystal clear and terrible. "My mother must have known."

The web of light pulses around them, as if responding to her distress. Elyssia exists because she exists; she exists because Elyssia exists. A perfect, terrible symmetry.

A commotion echoes from the entrance—voices, footsteps, the metallic rasp of weapons being drawn. Melia turns toward the sound, her hand still connected to the pulsing pattern beneath her.

"Someone's coming," Auren whispers, already moving to the edge of the chamber, peering into the shadows of the entrance passage.

His body stiffens. "We have company."

Ryker emerges first, his usual swagger replaced by something colder, more deliberate. Behind him comes Garrik the Gilded, flanked by a half-dozen armed thugs. Their faces are hard in the eerie blue light, weapons gleaming. But what twists Melia's stomach is the sight of Elder Karina and several other Followers trailing behind them, their expressions a mixture of reverence and determination.

"The princess returns to her purpose," Ryker announces, his voice bouncing off the ancient walls. "How convenient for us all."

Garrik steps forward, his gold-accented clothing catching the pulsing light. "We can't allow you to disrupt the natural order, Princess. The cycle must continue."

"Natural?" The word tears from Melia's throat. "There's nothing natural about Elyssia. It's built on suffering—on people trapped as living foundations for centuries."

Elder Karina raises her chin. "Sacrifice has always been the way. The few suffer so the many may ascend. This is divine law."

The light beneath Melia's palm pulses stronger, almost painfully bright. She feels the connection deepening, drawing her in—part of her wants to surrender to it, to fulfill the purpose for which she was made. The urge is almost overwhelming.

Ryker takes another step closer. "The High Priests have waited long enough. Your little diversion in the city won't hold for long."

"And your friends?" Garrik adds with a cruel smile. "I imagine they're already in custody."

Melia's heart constricts at the thought of Sam and Kyp captured—or worse. Was their sacrifice in vain? Will hers be too?

Auren moves suddenly, positioning himself between Melia and the
intruders. His body tenses, and she can see the faint shimmer of Aether
beginning to coalesce around his shoulders.

"Melia," he says without turning, his voice steady and certain. "You
need to go deeper."

"What?" she whispers.

"The Sanctum lies below. I can feel it—a concentration of Aether
like nothing I've ever sensed." His fingers flex at his sides. "Whatever
you need to do, whatever answers you're seeking—they're down there,
not here."

"I won't leave you," she protests.

A thug steps forward, brandishing a heavy cudgel, and Auren's
response is immediate—a blast of Aether energy that knocks the man
backward into his companions.

"I'll hold them," Auren says, his voice tight with concentration as
translucent wings begin to form at his shoulders. "Find the truth,
Melia. All of it."

Ryker's hand moves to his blade. "She's not going anywhere."

Auren's wings flare brilliant white, casting harsh shadows across the
chamber. "Yes. She is."

In one fluid motion, he pushes off from the ground, Aether pro-
pelling him forward into the group. Garrik shouts orders as chaos
erupts—thugs scattering, weapons raised. The Followers drop to their
knees in terrified awe at the sight of Auren's wings, but Ryker is already
ducking under the attack, blade singing through the air.

"Go!" Auren shouts, his voice nearly lost in the confusion.

Melia tears her hand from the stone, breaking the mesmerizing
connection. The floor pattern continues to pulse, but now she notices

a section near the far wall where the light flows downward, disappearing into what appears to be solid stone.

A passage. Hidden in plain sight.

***

The stone beneath her feet gives way silently, dissolving like mist as
Melia steps onto the pulsing pathway. Behind her, the clash of Aether
energy against steel echoes through the chamber, Auren's voice rising
above the chaos. She forces herself not to look back.

Three steps down and the passage seals above her, plunging her into
darkness. The air grows colder, heavier with each descending step. Her
fingers trail along rough-hewn walls that feel almost like skin—warm
and slightly yielding beneath her touch. The comparison sends a shiver
through her, but she continues downward, guided only by the faint
blue luminescence emanating from somewhere below.

"Bear should be here," she whispers to herself, missing the cat's
reassuring presence. The thought of him—wherever he is with Sam
and Kyp—gives her strength to continue.

The stairway opens abruptly into a vast circular chamber that
steals her breath. Unlike the weathered ruins above, the Sanctum
gleams with impossible perfection—smooth walls adorned with intricate patterns that pulse with the same blue light she saw upstairs, but
brighter, more vibrant. The ceiling arches impossibly high, creating a
dome of swirling energy patterns that mirror the night sky.

But it's what fills the chamber that freezes her in place.

People. Hundreds of them. Thousands, perhaps.

They stand in concentric circles, perfectly still, eyes open but un-
seeing. Men and women of various ages, dressed in ancient formal

wear. Their bodies glow faintly, translucent in the blue light, and delicate threads of energy connect them to each other and to the floor beneath.

"The conjurors," Melia whispers, her voice thin in the vast space.

She approaches the outermost circle cautiously. A young woman stands before her, perhaps eighteen, wearing a simple blue dress. Her eyes stare forward, unblinking, lips slightly parted as if caught mid-breath. The faintest shimmer surrounds her form.

"Hello?" Melia's voice echoes strangely, seeming both too loud and instantly absorbed by the chamber.

The woman doesn't respond, doesn't even seem to breathe. Melia reaches out hesitantly, her fingers trembling as they approach the woman's arm.

Her hand passes through, meeting momentary resistance like pushing through thick water before emerging on the other side. The sensation sends a jolt through Melia's body—cold, then hot, then a profound emptiness that makes her gasp.

"I can't touch them," she realizes aloud.

She moves deeper into the chamber, passing between the silent figures. Some appear to be nobles, others commoners. A child of perhaps ten stands beside an elderly man, both frozen in the same timeless state. Near the center, she recognizes clothing styles she'd seen in Elyssia's streets.

Each person stands connected to the others by threads of light that form an immense, complex web. The pattern reminds her of the dais upstairs, but infinitely more elaborate—a living circuit of human consciousness.

With growing horror, she realizes these people aren't dead, nor are they fully alive. They exist in some terrible in-between state, their very

essence feeding the conjuration that maintains Elyssia's impossible
existence.

Melia weaves through the motionless figures, drawn inexorably
toward the center. The threads of light grow thicker here, pulsing with
an almost audible heartbeat. Then she sees her—a woman standing
apart from the others, her eyes fixed on some distant point. Unlike the
others, this woman wears the unmistakable midnight-blue gown of
Elyssia's royal seamstresses.

"It's you," Melia whispers.

The woman's features mirror her own with unsettling precision—the same high cheekbones, the same curve of lip. Only her hair
differs, a shade darker than Melia's golden locks. This is her template,
the person who was transformed into the perfect royal daughter.

Something compels Melia forward. She reaches out, fingers trembling as they approach the woman's face.

"I'm sorry," she whispers. "For what they did to you. For what they
made you into me."

Her fingertips brush against the woman's cheek. Unlike the others,
this touch connects—solid and electric. Pain lances through Melia's
body, her knees buckling as energy drains from her limbs.

Melia tries to maintain contact, desperate to understand, but the
connection weakens her with each passing second. Darkness edges her
vision. Her lungs strain for breath.

Melia tears her hand away with a gasp, collapsing onto the smooth
stone floor. The chamber spins around her, thousands of frozen faces
blurring into streaks of pale light. She crawls backward, desperate
to escape the woman's pull, her palms slipping against the polished
surface.

Her back collides with something solid. Not stone—fabric. Flesh.

Melia whirls around, a scream catching in her throat.

Two bodies lie propped against a raised dais, arranged with impossible care. Their hands rest intertwined between them, faces composed in peaceful repose. Unlike the spectral conjurors standing in their endless circles, these forms are solid, corporeal—and heart-stoppingly familiar.

"Mother," Melia whispers. "Father."

Queen Lysandra and King Orion wear their formal court attire, the deep blue and silver threads still vibrant against skin that hasn't yet lost all color. They appear almost alive, as if they might wake from a deep sleep rather than the permanent stillness of death. Their bodies show no wounds, no signs of violence—only a profound quietude that suggests choice rather than force.

Melia's hand trembles as she reaches for her mother's face. This time, there is no magical resistance, no spectral barrier—only cooling skin beneath her fingertips. The sensation is both terrible and precious.

"You knew," she says, tears spilling down her cheeks. "You both knew."

The truth crashes over her with devastating clarity. Her parents hadn't died mysteriously as she'd been told. They had discovered what Melia now knows—the horrific foundation upon which Elyssia was built, the living souls trapped in eternal conjuration. And rather than perpetuate the cycle, they had chosen death over continued complicity.

She touches her father's hand, remembering his final words to her: *What must be broken.*

"You chose to break the cycle," she whispers. "You couldn't bear it anymore."

A sob wracks her body as she leans forward, pressing her forehead against her mother's. The familiar scent of jasmine still clings faintly to Lysandra's hair, perhaps just a memory made flesh.

"I understand now," Melia says, her voice breaking. "Why you seemed so sad when you looked at me. Why you would sometimes touch my face like you were memorizing it." She swallows hard.

She shifts to her father, gently touching the signet ring still on his finger—the royal seal of Elyssia that she once believed represented divine authority. Now she recognizes it as just another element of the elaborate fabrication.

"You tried to tell me," she says. "You left clues, hoping I would find my way here."

A distant crash echoes from above—Auren still fighting, buying her time. Melia wipes her tears with the back of her hand, new resolve hardening within her. She looks from her parents to the spectral woman who was transformed into her, then to the thousands of souls trapped in eternal service to a beautiful lie.

"I know what I have to do," she says, rising to her feet. She presses a final kiss to each of her parents' foreheads. "I will finish what you started."

She turns toward the center of the chamber, where a raised platform pulses with concentrated Aether energy—the heart of the conjuration. The nature of her existence, her purpose, her destiny all become clear in this moment.

"What must be broken," she repeats, stepping toward the platform, "will be broken."

Melia's feet carry her forward, each step resonating against the stone floor as she rushes toward the pulsing platform. The Aether energy grows more intense—waves of blue-white light washing over her skin, making the fine hairs on her arms stand on end. Her fingers stretch out, ready to disrupt the conjuration at its source.

"Not yet."

The voice slams into her consciousness like a physical blow, halting her mid-stride. It carries no sound, no timber, yet fills her mind completely—a chorus of thousands speaking as one. The force of it drives Melia to her knees, palms pressed against her temples.

"Who—" she gasps, but she already knows. The conjurors. The trapped souls whose energy maintains Elyssia's impossible existence.

She struggles back to her feet, determination hardening her features. "I need to free you," she insists, taking another step toward the platform.

"Not yet," the voice repeats, and this time the energy field visibly ripples, creating a barrier that gently but firmly pushes her back.

Melia stumbles, confusion blooming across her face. Then recognition hits her—a memory of Auren's story, told beside a campfire on their journey.

"Auren," she whispers. "You said the same thing to him."

The realization crashes over her like ice water. During his Ascent, when his Aether wings had dissolved beneath him, he'd heard these exact words. The same presence that had rejected him then was denying her now.

She spins in place, staring at the thousands of spectral conjurors standing in their silent circles. "You stopped him from completing the Ascent," she says. "But why?"

The answer forms slowly in her mind, not as words but as understanding—a puzzle whose pieces suddenly align.

"Because he wasn't meant to ascend," she murmurs. "He was meant to break the cycle."

Melia turns back toward her parents' bodies, the truth crystallizing within her. She isn't the key to this system; she's merely a product of it—a beautiful fabrication designed to perpetuate the lie. But Auren—with his natural connection to the Aether, his ability to manifest wings and barriers through sheer will—he can speak to the conjurors in their own language.

"He's the bridge," she says aloud. "That's why he failed the Ascent. You were saving him for this moment."

Melia races back toward the stairway, pausing only to touch her mother's hand one final time. "I understand now," she whispers. "My story was never about ascending. It was about finding him."

She takes the stairs two at a time, her heart pounding against her ribs. The perfect princess, the royal daughter—those were never her true roles. She was the guide, the catalyst who would bring Auren to this place, to this moment.

Auren V

A   uren deflects another blow, his Aether shield barely forming
     in time to stop the thug's blade. His breath comes in ragged
gasps now, muscles screaming from exertion. Five of Garrik's men lie
unconscious or groaning on the chamber floor, but three more press
forward, their expressions hard and determined.

"Enough." Garrik's voice cuts through the chaos like a blade.

The thugs hesitate, weapons still raised.

"I said enough!" Garrik bellows, his gold-accented coat catching the
light as he steps forward. "Stand down, you idiots."

Auren maintains his defensive stance, translucent energy flickering
around his forearms. Blood trickles from a gash above his eye, obscuring his vision. He doesn't trust this sudden reprieve, especially with
Ryker glaring daggers from behind Garrik's shoulder.

"What game are you playing, Gilded?" Auren asks, his voice hoarse.

Garrik adjusts the ornate cuffs of his sleeves, a calculating look
crossing his weathered features. "No game. I'm a businessman, and
something doesn't add up." He gestures toward the chamber's en-

trance where Melia disappeared. "Why risk your life for the princess? What's down there that's worth dying for?"

Ryker steps forward, knife glinting. "We don't have time for this. The High Priests were clear—"

"The High Priests aren't paying my fee," Garrik cuts him off sharply. "I am." He turns back to Auren. "Well?"

Auren's gaze shifts between them and Elder Karina's followers, who hover nervously at the chamber's edge. He straightens slowly, allowing his Aether shield to dissipate.

"You want to know what's worth dying for?" A bitter laugh escapes his lips. "The truth." He gestures upward. "Elyssia isn't heaven. It's a prison built on bones."

Elder Karina steps forward, her weathered face pinched with anger. "Blasphemy!"

"It's truth," Auren counters. "That beautiful floating city? It's sustained by people—trapped, drained, exploited. The Conjuration Cycle doesn't elevate us; it consumes us."

Garrik's expression hardens. "Pretty speech. What's it got to do with my payment?"

"Those gleaming credits in your pocket?" Auren points. "They came from Elyssia. They're conjured. False. Part of the illusion. They'll dissolve the moment the city's true nature is revealed."

Garrik's hand instinctively moves to his coin pouch. His eyes narrow. "You're saying my money isn't real?"

"None of it is," Auren replies. "The High Priests have been trading in illusions for generations."

Murmurs ripple through Elder Karina's followers. One steps forward, clutching a devotional amulet. "Lies! The Ascension is our sacred path!"

"Your sacred path ends in servitude," Auren responds, his voice gaining strength.

The chamber erupts into chaos. Elder Karina's followers argue amongst themselves, some shouting accusations while others appear troubled by Auren's words.

"Enough!" Ryker lunges forward, but Garrik catches his arm.

"Is this true?" Garrik asks, his voice dangerously low.

"Ask yourself," Auren responds. "Why would the Princess of Elyssia jump from her perfect paradise? Why would the High Priests pay so handsomely to retrieve her in secret?"

The chamber grows louder as both Garrik's men and the Followers begin to shout, accusations flying. In the tumult, Auren inches toward the staircase where Melia disappeared, his eyes never leaving Ryker's murderous glare.

Something has shifted. The perfect certainty that once defined the Followers now fractures, doubt spreading like cracks in glass. And in Garrik's calculating eyes, Auren sees the dawning realization that he's been played for a fool.

"Shut your mouth," Ryker hisses, breaking free of Garrik's grip. "You think the world changes because you want it to? Some things are fixed, pilgrim. Some things just are." His knuckles whiten around his blade handle. "The cycle continues whether you approve or not."

Auren stands his ground, tasting copper as blood trickles down his face. The room feels charged with tension, like the moment before lightning strikes.

Garrik steps between them, his weathered face creasing into something between a smile and a sneer. "Interesting proposition you've laid out, pilgrim. Very interesting." He glances at Ryker, then back to Auren. "But I see a simpler solution to our dilemma."

"There's no dilemma," Elder Karina protests. "The blasphemer must—"

"Silence," Garrik cuts her off without even looking her way. His men shift positions, weapons now pointed at the Followers. Karina's indignation collapses into stunned silence.

"As I was saying," Garrik continues, "a solution presents itself. You two clearly have unfinished business." He gestures between Ryker and Auren. "So settle it. Here. Now."

Auren's pulse quickens. "What are you suggesting?"

"A duel." Garrik's gold tooth catches the light as he smiles. "My champion against the pilgrim who never ascended."

Ryker's expression shifts from rage to cold satisfaction. "I accept."

"I didn't offer you a choice," Garrik replies. He turns to Auren. "The terms are simple. Ryker wins, you come back with me to Aurora. Your talents in the fighting pits will make us both wealthy men, and this..." he waves his hand dismissively, "rebellion of yours is forgotten."

Auren glances toward the stairwell leading down to the Sanctum. Melia is down there, alone, confronting horrors he can only imagine. Every moment he delays is a moment she faces them without him.

"And if I win?" he asks, already knowing he has no real choice.

Garrik shrugs, the movement elegant despite his bulk. "Then my men and I withdraw. You and your princess can tear down heaven for all I care."

"You can't allow this!" Elder Karina pushes forward, her frail body trembling with outrage. "The sacred texts—"

One of Garrik's men presses a blade to her throat. "The merchant made his decision, grandmother."

Auren meets Ryker's gaze. There's something almost eager in the man's eyes, as if he's been waiting for this moment. Perhaps he has.

Their rivalry has simmered since Aurora—over leadership, over direction.

Over Melia.

Auren extends his arms. "I accept."

"Excellent." Garrik steps back, creating space in the center of the chamber. "No weapons. Fight until one yields or can't continue."

Ryker tosses his knife to one of Garrik's men, then shrugs off his jacket. His arms are corded with muscle, scarred from countless fights. "I've been looking forward to this."

Auren sets his feet, the familiar weight of exhaustion presses on him—he's spent too much energy already. But Melia needs time, and this is the only way to give it to her.

"Begin," Garrik commands.

Ryker lunges forward with unexpected speed, ducking under Auren's hastily formed shield and driving a fist into his ribs. Pain explodes through Auren's side as the fight erupts in earnest.

***

Pain spiders through Auren's ribcage as Ryker's second strike finds the same spot. He staggers backward, barely raising his forearm in time to deflect a blow aimed at his throat. His breath comes in ragged gasps, each one sending fresh waves of agony through his chest.

"You're nothing," Ryker hisses, circling with predatory grace. "A failed pilgrim playing at revolution."

Auren feints left, then drives his shoulder into Ryker's midsection. The impact jolts through him, but Ryker merely grunts and hammers a fist against Auren's spine. They crash together against one of the stone pillars, the ancient structure trembling with the force.

"Look at them," Ryker whispers, his lips close to Auren's ear as they grapple. "The Followers watching their faith crumble. Was that your plan all along? To destroy what gives people purpose?"

Auren twists, breaking free and creating distance. His vision blurs momentarily, exhaustion and pain threatening to overwhelm him. The chamber swims with faces—Garrik's calculating stare, Elder Karina's trembling outrage, the confused expressions of the Followers.

"What purpose?" Auren manages between labored breaths. "Feeding a lie that consumes lives?"

Ryker charges again, a flurry of precise strikes that Auren barely deflects. One connects with his jaw, snapping his head back. The taste of copper floods his mouth.

"You think you're so righteous," Ryker snarls, pressing his advantage. "So enlightened." His knee drives upward, catching Auren in the stomach. "You're just a man who couldn't accept rejection."

The words cut deeper than the blows. Auren stumbles, and Ryker sweeps his legs from under him. The stone floor rushes up to meet him, knocking the air from his lungs.

Ryker stands over him, triumphant. "You failed to ascend because you were never worthy."

Something shifts in Auren then—not a surge of anger or determination, but a strange, crystalline clarity. He sees Ryker not as an enemy but as a reflection of his former self: a man defined by his need for validation, for acceptance into a system that was never meant to recognize his worth.

"You're right," Auren says, making no move to rise.

Confusion flickers across Ryker's face. "What?"

"I wasn't worthy," Auren continues, blood trickling from the corner of his mouth. "Because the system itself isn't worthy of anyone's devotion."

Ryker's expression hardens. He reaches down, grabbing Auren by the collar and hauling him to his feet. "Fight me!"

Instead of resisting, Auren meets his gaze steadily. "What are you fighting for, Ryker? To earn Garrik's approval? Credits? When will it be enough?"

"Shut up and fight!" Ryker shakes him violently.

"I'm done fighting," Auren says quietly. "Not because I can't win, but because neither of us can win this way."

The chamber has gone silent, every eye fixed on the two men.

"What happened to you?" Auren asks, his voice gentle now. "What made you so desperate for their acceptance that you'd betray someone like Melia?"

Something flickers in Ryker's eyes—a momentary vulnerability quickly masked by rage. He drives his fist into Auren's stomach, but the blow lacks conviction.

"They'll never truly accept you," Auren continues, weathering the pain. "The High Priests, Garrik—they're using you, just as they use everyone. You're a tool to them, nothing more."

"You don't know anything," Ryker hisses, but his grip loosens slightly.

"I know what it's like to measure your worth by someone else's standards," Auren replies. "To dedicate your life to a dream only to discover it was never yours to begin with."

Ryker shoves him away, breathing heavily. "This isn't about me."

"Isn't it?" Auren straightens, making no move to attack. "You've been running your whole life—from who you are, from who you could be. Always the charming rogue, the man with no allegiances except to himself." He takes a step forward. "But that's not freedom, Ryker. It's just another kind of prison."

The chamber feels impossibly still. Even Garrik watches with uncharacteristic intensity, his usual smirk replaced by thoughtful calculation.

"You know what Elyssia truly is," Auren continues. "You know what they're doing to people. Is that the paradise you're fighting to preserve?"

Ryker's fists clench and unclench at his sides. For a moment, he looks lost—a man confronting the emptiness of his convictions.

"I made my choice," he says finally, but the words sound hollow.

"Did you? Or did you just follow the path of least resistance?" Auren takes another step closer. "It's not too late to make a different choice."

Something breaks in Ryker's expression—the carefully constructed facade cracking to reveal a glimpse of the man beneath. "They'll kill me if I turn against them."

"Maybe," Auren acknowledges. "Or maybe together we can break the cycle that's claimed too many lives already."

Silence stretches between them, taut as a bowstring. The Followers watch, confusion and uncertainty written across their faces. Ryker looks past him to the stairwell where Melia disappeared, then back to Auren. The calculation in his eyes now seems directed inward, as if measuring the weight of years spent serving masters who never valued him.

"I yield," he says, loud enough for all to hear. He turns to Garrik, whose expression has darkened considerably. "The pilgrim wins."

Murmurs ripple through the chamber as Garrik's men shift uneasily, hands moving to weapon hilts.

Auren's eyes never leave Ryker's. "Thank you."

"Don't thank me yet," Ryker replies quietly. "This won't be as simple as you think."

"Enough!" Garrik's voice cuts through the chamber like a blade. His hand shoots out, fingers wrapping around Ryker's throat. "You disappoint me, Ryker. I had such plans for you."

Ryker struggles against the grip, but Garrik's strength is surprising for his frame. Two of Garrik's men step forward, flanking their leader with weapons drawn.

"Did you think betrayal would go unpunished?" Garrik hisses, pressing his thumb into the hollow of Ryker's throat. "I still see use for you, though. A different kind than I'd planned."

Auren steps forward, but the point of a blade stops him. One of Garrik's men smirks, the tip of his sword hovering inches from Auren's chest.

"Stay where you are, pilgrim," Garrik says without looking at him. "Your moment of heroic persuasion is over." He turns to his men, jerking his head toward the exit. "We're leaving. Bring him."

The guards grab Ryker roughly by the arms. Blood trickles from his split lip as he locks eyes with Auren, something like regret flickering across his face.

"What about the princess?" one of the guards asks.

Garrik's lips curl into a cold smile. "The High Priests will send others. Our contract is finished."

Elder Karina steps forward, her frail body trembling with indignation. "You promised us the Fallen One would be returned to Elyssia! You swore to uphold the sacred cycle!"

"I promised you payment for your assistance," Garrik corrects her, his tone dismissive. "Which you received. The rest is your concern, not mine."

The chamber erupts with angry murmurs from the Followers. Their expressions shift from confusion to outrage as they process Garrik's callous abandonment of their cause.

"Heretic!" A young Follower pushes to the front of the group, pointing an accusing finger at Garrik. "You used our faith for profit!"

Garrik rolls his eyes, already turning away. "Faith is always profitable for someone, boy. Today it simply wasn't for you."

The young man lunges forward with a cry of rage. One of Garrik's guards intercepts him, but more Followers surge forward, their religious fervor transformed into righteous anger.

"Restrain them!" Garrik shouts, still clutching Ryker by the collar.

The chamber dissolves into chaos. Followers grapple with Garrik's men, their numbers overwhelming the better-trained fighters through sheer desperation. Elder Karina shrieks instructions, her earlier composure shattered by betrayal.

Auren ducks beneath a wild swing, looking for an opening to reach Ryker. A guard crashes into him, driven backward by two Followers. They tumble to the ground in a tangle of limbs.

The guard's elbow catches Auren in his already-bruised ribs. Pain explodes through his chest, momentarily stealing his breath. He drives his knee upward, creating space to roll away from the melee.

"Auren!"

Melia's voice cuts through the chaos. She stands at the top of the stairwell, her face pale but determined. Her tunic is torn and stained, her hair wild around her shoulders. Something in her eyes has changed—a new certainty that wasn't there before.

She pushes through the fighting bodies, narrowly avoiding a Follower being thrown against the wall. When she reaches him, her hands grasp his arms with urgent intensity.

"I found them," she says, her voice trembling. "Thousands of them, all connected, all trapped. My parents—" Her voice breaks. "They're there too. They sacrificed themselves to show me the truth."

Auren steadies her, ignoring the pain radiating through his body. "What truth?"

"It's you," she says, her eyes searching his face. "You're the key. Not me. I was made to find you, to bring you here." Her fingers dig into his forearms. "The voice you heard during your ascension—it wasn't rejection. It was protection."

A body crashes into the pillar beside them, sending stone fragments scattering across the floor. Garrik is still wrestling with Ryker near the chamber entrance, three Followers trying to block their exit.

"I don't understand," Auren says, his mind struggling to process her words through the surrounding chaos.

"The conjurors showed me. You have to finish what you started." Melia's eyes shine with intensity. "Your ascension wasn't a failure—"

A shout from the entrance pulls their attention. Ryker has broken free from Garrik, delivering a vicious blow that sends the older man staggering. Their eyes meet across the chamber, and Ryker gestures urgently toward the stairwell.

"Go!" he calls out. "I'll hold them!"

Elder Karina notices their exchange. "Stop them!" she commands, pointing at Auren and Melia. "They must not defile the sacred dais!"

Behind them, Ryker grapples with two of Garrik's men, buying them precious seconds. "Make it count, pilgrim!" he shouts after them.

Auren's hand finds Melia's as they reach the stairwell, their fingers intertwining. "Together," he says.

She nods, her eyes reflecting the same determination he feels. "Together."

Orlan IV

S ir Orlan shifts his weight onto the balls of his feet, blade poised at the ready as he faces the woman who calls herself a weapon. The courtyard surrounding them churns with chaos—guards shouting orders, priests scurrying like disturbed ants, citizens gathering at the edges with confusion etched on their faces. This imposter has thrown Elyssia into disarray in mere moments, and it falls to him to restore order.

"Stand down," he commands, his voice steady despite the uncertainty roiling in his gut. "You've committed treason against Elyssia."

The woman moves with precise, calculated efficiency, unlike any opponent he's encountered. Her eyes track everything—the positions of the guards, the exits, even the subtle shifts in his stance. She doesn't look like a fighter in her simple, practical clothing, yet she holds herself with the coiled readiness of a predator.

"I am not your enemy, Sir Orlan." Her voice carries an odd cadence, almost mechanical in its precision. "Princess Melia sends her regards."

The name stops him cold. "What do you know of the princess?"

"She's currently on the surface," the woman replies, not taking her eyes from his blade. "Doing what must be done."

Behind him, High Priest Thaddeus hisses, "She lies! The princess would never conspire against Elyssia!"

"Are you certain?" The woman—Sam, the boy called her—tilts her head slightly. "The princess jumped, Sir Orlan. She wasn't pushed. She chose to fall."

A tremor runs through the marble beneath their feet, strong enough that several priests stumble. Prefect Solivar's voice rises above the commotion, "The binding is weakening!"

Orlan keeps his blade steady, but something shifts in his understanding. The tremors, the priests' panic, Elynia's cryptic warnings—they align with this stranger's words. "You're working with her."

It's not a question, but Sam nods once, a sharp, economical movement. "I'm buying time."

"The Thread is destabilizing!" A priest rushes past, robes flapping. "The conjuration—it's being disrupted from the source!"

Solivar's face contorts with fury. "Where is she? Where is the princess?" He advances on Sam, seemingly unconcerned by the danger she represents.

"On the surface," Sam repeats, her eyes never leaving Orlan's. "At the Shattered Spire."

The name sends a ripple of panic through the assembled priests. Thaddeus clutches at his medallion, whispering, "The Sanctum. The Source."

"Impossible," Solivar spits. "No one can access the Source without—" He stops abruptly, eyes widening. "The pilgrim. She's with the pilgrim."

Another tremor shakes the courtyard, stronger than before. A decorative urn topples from its plinth, shattering on the immaculate tiles. In the distance, alarm bells begin to toll.

"Sir Orlan," Solivar's voice cuts through the chaos, "take your knights and secure this imposter. I want her alive for questioning."

Orlan hesitates, his mind racing. The tremors. The princess jumping, not falling. The strange cat that accompanied this woman, now mysteriously absent. Elynia's warning that the cycle must end.

"Sir Orlan!" Solivar repeats sharply.

Another tremor rocks the courtyard. This time, a fissure appears in the pristine marble, zigzagging across the floor like lightning frozen in stone. From somewhere in the city, screams rise.

"Look around you," Sam says quietly, for his ears alone. "Your perfect city is built on the imprisoned consciousness of thousands. Your princess discovered the truth and chose to break the cycle. Will you stand with those who would perpetuate this abomination, or help end it?"

The weight of Orlan's sword shifts in his hand, a subtle movement that carries the gravity of generations. Another tremor ripples through the courtyard, sending hairline fractures across the perfect white stone. In that instant of distraction, Orlan makes his choice.

He pivots, the blade now pointing at Solivar's chest instead of the woman's.

"What is the meaning of this?" Solivar's face contorts, disbelief warring with rage.

"I swore to protect Elyssia," Orlan says, his voice steadier than his thundering heart. Lira's face flashes in his mind—her serious eyes when she'd said, *Papa always does what's right.* "Not its lies."

Thaddeus steps forward, hands raised placatingly. "Sir Orlan, think of your family—"

"I am." The words come out harder than steel. "I'm thinking of the world they deserve. Not this... conjured prison."

Sam moves with startling speed, positioning herself at Orlan's back. "We need to move," she murmurs. "More guards coming."

Solivar's expression calcifies into cold fury. "Seize them both! The knight has lost his mind."

Two guards rush forward. Orlan meets the first with a sweeping parry that sends the man's sword clattering across the marble. The second hesitates, recognition flickering in his eyes—this is Sir Orlan, their commander, their mentor.

That moment of hesitation costs him. Sam strikes with mechanical precision, a precise blow to the solar plexus that doubles the guard over without killing him.

Across the courtyard, Thaddeus and two other High Priests hurry Solivar toward the inner sanctum doors. "The Thread is unraveling!" one shouts over the growing commotion. "We need to stabilize the primary conjuration!"

"Let them go," Sam says, dispatching another guard with a precise strike to the knee.

Orlan nods, falling into rhythm beside this strange ally. They move as a coordinated unit, her precision complementing his practiced skill. For every guard he engages, she neutralizes another. None are killed—just rendered temporarily incapacitated with strikes that speak of a training far beyond ordinary combat.

"You're not just a weapon," he observes, breathing hard as they clear a path through the courtyard.

"I was." Something almost like amusement flickers across her face. "I'm trying to be more."

A particularly violent tremor shakes the palace, more powerful than any before. The ornate pillars supporting the eastern colonnade groan, marble dust sifting down like snow.

"The conjuration is becoming visible," Orlan says, horror dawning as he sees the truth literally emerging through Elyssia's perfect veneer. Threads of blue energy pulse beneath the crumbling marble, weaving through the air like veins. "Gods above..."

"Not gods," Sam corrects grimly. "People. Thousands of them, trapped in the Sanctum, powering this place."

They reach the grand staircase leading to the inner sanctum. Four elite guards block their path, their silver armor gleaming in the strange blue light now filtering through cracks in the ceiling.

"Commander," one steps forward, voice uncertain beneath his ceremonial helm, fingers tightening nervously around his spear shaft. "What's happening to the city? The walls... they're—"

"The truth is happening," Orlan says simply, shifting his weight to a defensive stance as he studies the faces of men he once trained. "Elyssia is built on sacrifice and lies—thousands of souls bound against their will. I'm going to help end it, as any true knight should."

The guard's gaze flicks anxiously between Orlan's resolute expression and the crumbling architecture around them. Hairline fractures spider across the marble columns as blue-white energy pulses through them like blood through veins. Fragments of the ornate ceiling detach and shatter on the floor nearby.

"And the princess?" he asks, his voice dropping to a whisper tinged with both fear and hope. "Is she... is she safe? What is her role in all this chaos?"

"Princess Melia is doing exactly what her parents truly intended," Orlan replies, a hint of pride warming his stern features. "She's breaking the cycle that has enslaved us all."

***

The marble beneath their feet cracks as Orlan and Sam race through the Garden Promenade. Blue light seeps through fissures in the ground, casting eerie shadows across terrified citizens. Entire sections of Elyssia's perfect façade are dissolving, revealing the pulsing magical infrastructure beneath.

"The market district," Orlan shouts over another violent tremor. "More people there."

Sam nods, vaulting over a fallen statue with inhuman grace. "I'll head east."

A group of nobles cowers beneath a crumbling pavilion. Orlan recognizes Lord Tennar among them, his usual pompous demeanor replaced by naked fear.

The noble's face drains of color, his jeweled fingers trembling as he clutches at his elaborate collar. "What manner of sorcery is this? The city—it cannot be—"

"Truth," Orlan cuts him off, his voice carrying the weight of decades of service now transformed into urgent command. "This is what has always lain beneath our feet. Now go. Warn others."

Lord Tennar stumbles backward, his entourage already scattering like startled birds across the fractured promenade.

Sam appears at his side with ghostlike suddenness, her movements fluid and precise despite the fresh bandage visible beneath her torn sleeve. Blood seeps through the fabric, yet her posture betrays no pain. "The eastern quarter is destabilizing faster than predicted. The foundational anchors are giving way."

Orlan's chest tightens painfully as another tremor sends a nearby fountain crumbling into dust. "My family. Merien and Lira—they're in the royal apartments. The servants' quarters behind the grand hall."

Understanding flashes in her eyes—a momentary softening in that otherwise unreadable gaze. She gives a single, efficient nod. "Go. I'll continue here. These people will listen to a knight more readily than they'll listen to me."

"Sam—" Orlan hesitates, one gauntleted hand gripping the hilt of his sword as the ground shudders beneath them. The words feel strange on his tongue—gratitude to this enigmatic woman who, days ago, he would have considered an enemy. "Thank you."

Her face remains impassive, but something shifts in her gaze. "Don't thank me yet."

They part at the next intersection, Sam heading toward the crowded market while Orlan races toward the inner palace. The familiar corridors of his daily patrol have transformed into something alien—walls ripple with unnatural light, and the perfect stonework breaks apart to reveal the magical lattice beneath.

A group of palace guards rounds the corner, weapons drawn.

"Sir Orlan!" The lead guard's posture shifts between combat-ready and confused respect.

"Look around you!" Orlan gestures at a section of wall where the marble has disintegrated entirely, revealing a pulsing network of blue energy. "This is what Elyssia truly is. Built on sacrifice. Now move!"

Something in his voice—or perhaps the horror of what they're witnessing—convinces them. The guards disperse, already shouting evacuation orders.

Orlan continues toward the royal apartments, taking the servants' passages to avoid more confrontations. The corridors here are narrower, the destabilization more pronounced. Twice he's forced to leap over collapsed sections of floor, the city's very foundations coming apart.

He rounds the final corner to the royal wing and skids to a halt.

Four High Priests block the entrance to the apartments, their ornate robes stained with marble dust. High Priest Verrus and Morden flank Prefect Solivar, whose face contorts with cold fury. Between them stands Thaddeus, gripping Lira's small shoulder. The child's face is tear-streaked but defiant.

Merien kneels before them, a cut bleeding freely on her forehead. Her eyes meet Orlan's, communicating a mixture of relief and warning.

"Ah, the traitor arrives," Solivar's voice drips with contempt. "How convenient."

Orlan's hand goes to his sword, but freezes when Thaddeus tightens his grip on Lira.

"I wouldn't," the High Priest warns.

Behind them, restrained by two temple guards, stands Elynia. Her ceremonial robes are torn, her face bruised, but her eyes burn with the same quiet determination Orlan had seen in the tower.

"You were supposed to be the exemplar of loyalty," Solivar says, stepping forward. Another tremor shakes the hallway, but he maintains his balance with practiced ease. "The knight who embodied Elyssian virtue."

"I am loyal," Orlan replies, his voice steady despite the rage building in his chest. "To the people of Elyssia. Not to the lie you've perpetuated."

"A necessary deception," Morden interjects. "Without the conjuration, there is no Elyssia. Thousands would perish."

"Thousands already have," Elynia spits.

Thaddeus yanks Lira closer. "Your daughter is quite special, Sir Orlan."

The implication sends ice through Orlan's veins. "Touch her again and I'll—"

"You'll what?" Solivar interrupts. "Watch your family die? Because that's what awaits them if the conjuration fails. That's what awaits us all."

Another violent tremor, stronger than any before, rocks the corridor. A massive crack splits the ceiling, showering them with marble fragments. The blue energy is fully visible now, pulsing through every surface like veins in living tissue.

"It's too late," Elynia says, something like triumph in her voice despite her captivity. "The princess has reached the Sanctum. The cycle is breaking."

"Papa!" Lira calls out, her small voice cutting through the chaos.

Orlan meets his daughter's eyes, remembering their last conversation. *Do what's right, even when it's hard.* He'd tried to prepare her, knowing this moment might come.

"I'm here," he says quietly, his mind calculating distances, angles, opportunities. Five armed men plus Solivar. Hostages. Collapsing structure.

Impossible odds.

He takes a step forward anyway.

"You speak of loyalty as though it's a simple thing," Orlan says, his voice carrying despite the rumbling around them. "But tell me, Prefect—how loyal can you be to something that isn't real?"

Solivar's eyes narrow. "What nonsense is this? I've given everything to Elyssia."

"Have you?" Orlan's gaze sweeps over the High Priests, then returns to Solivar. "Or have you given everything to maintain the illusion? The perfect city, the divine order..." He pauses, watching realization darken Solivar's face. "Tell me, how does it feel to know you're nothing more than a conjuring yourself?"

Solivar staggers back a half-step, his face contorting. For a heartbeat, silence falls despite the destruction around them. Then Solivar's composure shatters.

"OF COURSE I KNOW!" he screams, spittle flying from his lips. His perfect demeanor collapses entirely, revealing something feral beneath. "We ALL know! We CHOSE this!"

The confession echoes down the crumbling corridor. Even his fellow priests look taken aback by the outburst.

"We chose this life," Solivar continues, breathing heavily. "Power. Opulence. Divine authority. We chose it over and over again, century after century."

"Prefect—" Verrus warns, but Solivar cuts him off with a savage gesture.

"No! Let him hear it!" Solivar advances toward Orlan, trembling with rage. "Your precious King Orion knew too. We all did. The difference is that he and that weak-willed queen decided to end it—to destroy everything we built!"

Another tremor rocks the hallway. A section of wall collapses entirely, revealing a courtyard beyond where citizens flee in panic.

"And what of my family?" Orlan asks quietly. "Did they choose this too?"

Solivar's laugh is brittle. "Your conjurer chose the life of a knight, with all its pathetic notions of honor and sacrifice. He chose your pretty wife, your mewling child—" He gestures dismissively at Lira, who glares back with defiance so fierce it makes Orlan's heart swell with pride despite the danger.

"You speak of choice," Elynia cuts in, "but you've denied that choice to thousands. Trapped souls powering your perfect world."

"A necessary sacrifice," Thaddeus retorts. "Without them, there is no Elyssia."

"Then perhaps Elyssia shouldn't exist," Orlan says simply.

The words hang in the air, blasphemous and liberating. For a moment, even Solivar seems struck silent.

Orlan uses that moment to shift his weight, calculating the distance to Thaddeus, who still holds Lira. Six steps. Maybe five if he lunges.

"You would destroy paradise?" Morden asks, genuine bewilderment in his voice.

"Look around you," Orlan gestures to the destruction. "Your paradise is built on suffering. King Orion and Queen Lysandra understood that. They chose to let go."

"They were WEAK!" Solivar roars. "They betrayed everything—"

"They showed courage," Orlan interrupts. "Something you'll never understand."

"It's too late anyway," Elynia says, her voice calm amid the chaos. "What must be broken will be broken."

Auren VI

A uren's lungs burn as he follows Melia down the winding stone steps into the Sanctum's depths. Blood trickles from a gash above his eye, and his ribs scream with each breath—souvenirs from his fight with Ryker. The narrow stairway opens suddenly into a vast underground chamber that steals what little breath he has left.

"What the..." The words escape him in a whisper.

Thousands of translucent figures stand in perfect circles, their bodies suspended in a web of pulsing blue energy, motionless yet somehow alive. The blue threads connect each figure to the next, forming a complex lattice that extends throughout the entire chamber.

"They're..." Auren struggles to comprehend the scale of it, his mind reeling as he takes in the vast sea of ethereal bodies suspended in the chamber. The enormity of the revelation hits him like a physical blow, compounding the pain already radiating through his battered body.

"Conjurors," Melia finishes, her voice hollow and distant, echoing slightly in the cavernous space. "Thousands of them. This is the true foundation of Elyssia—the hidden pillars that keep the floating city aloft, their power harnessed against their will."

Auren moves toward the nearest figure—an elderly man with closed eyes and a serene expression frozen in time. The weathered lines on the conjuror's face speak of wisdom and years that have been suspended in this twilight existence. As Auren approaches, the blue energy threads pulse slightly faster, like a slumbering creature stirring at the presence of an intruder. The light casts eerie shadows across his scarred hands as he reaches out, hesitant yet compelled.

"I tried to wake them," Melia says, her fingers suddenly gripping his arm with unexpected strength, pulling him back. Her touch is cool against his skin, a stark contrast to the feverish heat of the chamber. "I can't reach them. I'm... I'm just another conjured thing." Her voice breaks on the last word, revealing the raw wound.

Melia's eyes shine with unshed tears. "I'm not real, Auren. Not like you. I'm part of their creation—their conjuration. When I touch the m..." She reaches toward the elderly man, and her hand passes partway through his translucent form. Melia gasps, her own body flickering momentarily like a candle flame in a draft. She withdraws quickly, steadying herself against Auren.

"It has to be you," she says, regaining her solidity. "This is what you were made for."

"Made for? I don't understand."

A tremor shakes the chamber, dislodging dust from the ancient ceiling. The blue energy pulses more rapidly, like a heart beating in panic.

"Your connection to the Aether, your ability to manifest it physically—it's not just some random talent." Melia grips his shoulders, her gaze intense. "Remember when you tried to ascend and heard that voice telling you 'not yet'? You weren't being rejected, Auren. You were being saved for this moment."

Auren looks out at the sea of trapped souls, his mind racing. "What am I supposed to do? I'm a fighter, not a—"

"For once in your life, don't fight," Melia interrupts. "Talk to them. Reach them. You can touch them in ways I can't. In ways no one else can."

Auren looks at the elderly conjuror's face, then back at Melia. Her expression is a mixture of desperation and faith that makes his chest tighten.

"Let him out, Auren," Melia pleads, her voice barely above a whisper. "The man I saw at Old Hollow. The one who stood reached the sky. We don't have much time."

Another tremor rocks the chamber, stronger than the last. Dust and small fragments of stone rain down from above. The blue energy threads pulse frantically now, like a web catching lightning.

"I don't know what you're asking," Auren says, his voice rough. He runs a hand through his sweat-dampened hair, wincing as his fingers brush against the cut above his eye.

"My parents started this," Melia says, her eyes bright with urgency. "They gave up their conjuring willingly to disrupt the cycle. Don't you see? Everything has been leading to this moment. I had to jump from Elyssia. I had to find you. I had to get us here." She takes his hands in hers, and he feels the slight tremor in her fingers. "So you can do what you were born to do."

The weight of her words settles on him like a stone. Born to do this? He's spent his life trying to ascend, to prove himself worthy—only to be rejected at the final moment.

"What if I fail again?" The question slips out before he can stop it.

"You won't," Melia says with a certainty that shakes him. "The voice that stopped you before—it was protecting you for this. For now."

Another tremor, violent enough to knock them both off balance. Auren steadies Melia, then turns to face the sea of conjurors, their translucent forms wavering like reflections in disturbed water.

"I don't know what to say," he admits, spreading his hands helplessly.

Melia's expression softens. "Tell them the truth. Your truth."

Auren takes a deep breath and steps forward.

***

Auren reaches out, his fingers trembling as they connect with the elderly conjuror's translucent form. Unlike Melia's attempt, his hand doesn't pass through—it makes contact with something that feels simultaneously solid and insubstantial, like touching the surface of water without breaking tension.

A jolt of energy surges through him. The familiar warmth of Aether floods his system, but magnified a hundredfold—like comparing a candle's flame to a raging inferno. He gasps, nearly pulling away from the shock of it, his entire body trembling under the sudden influx of raw power.

"It's... so much," he manages, his voice strained and barely audible above the roaring in his skull. His vision blurs, then sharpens to painful clarity as the connection deepens.

The Aether pours into him, not just from the elderly man but from all directions—ceiling, walls, floor—as though the very air has become a conduit for this ancient magic. The blue threads connecting the suspended conjurors pulse in rhythm with Auren's heartbeat, creating an intricate, living web of light and consciousness. His skin begins to glow with faint luminescence, veins of light tracing elaborate patterns across his arms and chest, spreading upward along his neck and face like a map of some celestial river system.

Sweat beads on his forehead as he struggles to contain the overwhelming sensation. Each breath brings another wave of power, another surge of foreign consciousness pressing against the boundaries of his mind.

"What's happening?" Melia asks, her voice distant through the rushing in his ears, her concern barely penetrating the veil of energy surrounding him.

"They're all... connected," Auren whispers in awe, watching as the threads between conjurors brighten in response to his words. "And now I am too." He feels himself becoming part of something vast and ancient—a living network of consciousness that spans generations, all trapped within this shimmering prison of light and memory.

The Sanctum itself seems to be channeling power into him. Every breath draws more energy, filling him beyond capacity. His previous manifestations—the wings, the weapons—they were mere puddles compared to this ocean.

"I can feel them," he says, his eyes wide with revelation. "Thousands of minds. Thousands of lives."

Memories not his own flicker through his consciousness—children playing, lovers embracing, meals shared, tears shed. Lives interrupted, suspended in this twilight state.

The voices crash over Auren like waves—disorienting, overwhelming. Each one distinct yet part of a collective consciousness that has sustained Elyssia for generations. Their fear coils around his heart, squeezing until he can barely breathe.

"They're afraid," he gasps, maintaining his connection with trembling hands. "So many of them... for so long."

Memories of sunlight. Of wind on skin. Of laughter. All fading impressions from lives interrupted decades, even centuries ago. The conjurors exist in a twilight state—not dead, not truly alive, but suspended between realities.

"I can hear them questioning..." Auren's brow furrows as he concentrates on the voices surging through his mind. "They're hearing Kyp. And... Bear? How is that possible?"

Melia steps closer, careful not to break his connection. "What are they saying?"

"Confusion. Disbelief." Auren winces as a particularly sharp thought cuts through. "Someone named Elia has been here for three hundred years. She doesn't understand what's happening above."

The blue threads pulsate faster, the energy growing more chaotic as the conjurors' collective consciousness reacts to Kyp's broadcast in Elyssia. Doubt ripples through their shared mind—doubt about their purpose, about the necessity of their sacrifice.

"There's a child," Auren whispers, tears streaming down his face. "She was only eight when they brought her here. She's been powering the eastern fountain district for years beyond count."

The weight of their collective suffering threatens to crush him. Their fear of change wars with their desperate hope for release. For centuries, they've been told their sacrifice sustains paradise. Now they're hearing it was all a lie.

"They're splitting," Auren says, his voice strained. "Some want to hold on—they believe breaking the connection will destroy everything. Others... they just want to be free, no matter the cost."

A violent tremor shakes the chamber. Dust and small fragments of stone rain down from above. The energy flowing through Auren intensifies, burning through his veins like molten metal.

"The division is weakening the structure," Melia says, steadying herself against a pillar. "The conjuration can't hold if they're not unified."

Auren grits his teeth against the pain. "I need to show them. They need to understand."

He closes his eyes, focusing on his own memories—of Elyssia's cold perfection, of the villages below where real people lived imperfect but genuine lives. He shares his fall, his failure, his journey with Melia. Most importantly, he shares the truth of what they've learned: that Elyssia was built on deception, that the sacrifice was never necessary but merely convenient for those in power.

The reaction is immediate. A surge of rage, of betrayal, of grief washes through the network. The blue threads flare brightly, then begin to flicker.

"What's happening?" Melia asks, urgency in her voice.

"They're making a choice," Auren says, his eyes still closed in concentration. "All of them, together."

The elderly conjuror whose form Auren touches seems to solidify slightly. His clouded eyes focus on Auren's face.

"We hear your truth, Pilgrim," a voice speaks through the old man's lips, though it seems to contain multitudes. "We hear the words above. The cycle must end."

The energy surges again, this time with purpose rather than chaos. Auren feels it building within him, seeking direction, seeking release.

"They want me to break the bonds," he tells Melia, his voice steady despite the storm raging inside him.

Another tremor, stronger than before, rocks the chamber.

Auren takes a deep breath and steps forward, moving into the center of the vast chamber where the blue threads are most concentrated. The energy thunders through him, threatening to tear him apart from within. He feels the panic of the conjurors—their fear of change, of ending, of what comes after. Their voices clamor in his mind, a cacophony of terror and hope and rage all tangled together.

But instead of shouting over them, instead of forcing his will upon theirs, he simply stands. Lets the storm rage around him. Through him.

When he finally speaks, his voice is quiet. Not commanding, but clear.

"You can stop," he says.

The chamber falls silent. Even the tremors pause, as if the very stones are listening.

"You can stop," he repeats, his words rippling through the collective consciousness. "This was never your burden to bear. You were meant to live your lives, not power someone else's paradise."

The threads connecting the conjurors tremble, vibrating like plucked strings. Auren feels their hesitation, their doubt. For generations, they've known nothing but this suspended existence. Freedom is as terrifying as it is alluring.

"I'm not here to force you," Auren continues, turning slowly to address all the suspended forms. "I'm here to show you that there's a choice."

He extends his awareness, allowing them to see through his eyes—to see Melia watching him with hope and fear mingled in her expression, to see the chamber around them, to see the world beyond as he remembers it.

"There is sunlight out there," he tells them. "There's rain on your skin and mud between your toes. There's the taste of berries picked fresh from the bush. There's pain and joy and everything in between."

A soft sob escapes Melia as she watches blue light cascade over Auren's features, transforming him into something otherworldly yet profoundly human.

Auren feels the first conjuror let go. An elderly woman whose form has been suspended near the ceiling. Her thread unravels, the blue energy dispersing like mist in sunlight. For a moment, her face becomes clear, radiantly peaceful. Then she's gone, leaving only a gentle warmth in her wake.

"Thank you," her voice whispers through Auren's mind before fading completely.

Another follows. Then another. Threads unraveling, bodies falling, each leaving behind a whisper of gratitude or relief. The energy they release doesn't vanish—it flows into Auren, through him, changing in nature from bondage to liberation.

He turns toward a different section of the chamber, where the threads glow more intensely, more stubbornly. Here hang the forms of nobles, high priests, those who benefited most from Elyssia's false paradise. Their resistance is palpable, pushing back against Auren's influence.

"You don't understand," a chorus of voices hisses in his mind. "Without us, everything falls. Everything ends."

Auren approaches them, his steps measured despite the increasing tremors beneath his feet. The nobility's forms are more substantial than the others, their expressions frozen in haughty disdain even in this suspended state.

"I do understand," Auren replies, stopping before them. "You're afraid. You've lived in perfection so long that anything else seems unthinkable."

He could force them. The power rushing through him now would be enough to sever their connections, to break the entire system in one explosive surge. But that would make him no better than those who imprisoned them in the first place.

Instead, Auren simply opens himself—shares memories of his life in Willow Haven. The simple joy of fishing with Kyp by the creek. The taste of Gretta's hearty stew on a cold evening. The ache in his muscles after a day's honest work.

"There is beauty in imperfection," he tells them. "There is nobility in mortality—in knowing each moment is precious because it will never come again."

One of the noble forms stirs, her face contorting with rage. "You would condemn us to death for your philosophical ramblings? We've sacrificed everything to maintain order!"

"No," Auren corrects gently. "You sacrificed others to maintain your comfort. There's a difference."

The chamber shakes violently. Above, the sounds of destruction grow louder. Elyssia is falling.

"We don't have much time," Melia calls, bracing herself against a column.

Auren doesn't rush. He stands before the resisting nobles, his hand extended. Not grabbing. Not forcing. Simply offering.

"I'm not here to condemn you," he says. "I'm here to free you. What comes after is your choice, just as it was always meant to be."

The energy flowing through the chamber intensifies, blue light brightening to white. The noble conjurors fight with everything they have, clinging to their threads, to the system that gave them power and purpose.

Auren doesn't fight back. He simply remains, hand extended, heart open. Waiting.

"Look at him," one of the conjurors whispers to the others. "He could destroy us with a thought, yet he waits for our choice."

Another tremor rocks the chamber, longer and more violent than before. Chunks of the ceiling begin to fall.

"We're out of time," Melia shouts, dodging debris.

Still, Auren doesn't move. "Your choice," he repeats to the nobles. "Always your choice."

One by one, their resistance falters. Not all at once, not in perfect unison, but in fits and starts—as individual and messy as the lives they once lived. Their threads unravel, their bodies fall, their energy flowing through Auren and beyond, seeking new forms, new expressions.

The last noble—the one who spoke of condemnation—holds out the longest. Her eyes, once haughty, now hold only weariness.

"What if there's nothing after this?" she asks Auren.

"Then you'll finally have rest," he answers truthfully.

She considers this, then nods almost imperceptibly. Her thread unravels, her form blurs, and she too is gone.

The chamber trembles continuously now. The blue light that once filled the space has transformed to blinding white, pulsing with potential, with change.

"Melia?" he calls, spinning around.

The sound of crumbling stone drowns his voice. A massive section of the ceiling crashes down mere feet away, sending him stumbling backward into a pillar. Dust clouds his vision, choking his lungs.

"Melia!" he shouts louder, panic rising in his chest.

She was here just moments ago, watching as he freed the conjurors. Now there's no sign of her among the falling debris and shadowed corners.

Auren pushes himself forward, ducking under a collapsing archway. The entire Sanctum is coming apart without the conjurors' energy to sustain it. Ancient stone that held for centuries now crumbles like dried clay.

"MELIA!"

Sam II

S am races through Elyssia's disintegrating Western Quarter, her neural implants flashing urgent warnings across her vision. The once-perfect marble street beneath her feet flickers like a failing projection, patches dissolving into nothingness with each step. Around her, buildings fold inward, their pristine architecture revealing the hollow scaffolding of conjured reality.

"Kyp!" Her voice echoes strangely in the destabilizing atmosphere. "Bear!"

A noble woman phases through Sam's shoulder—not physically passing through, but her entire form temporarily losing substance. The woman doesn't notice, continuing her panicked flight toward the central spire, still believing in solid ground that barely exists.

Sam's tactical display attempts to map escape routes, but the city's layout shifts too rapidly for calculations to complete. Streets that existed moments ago vanish. New passages appear where walls once stood. The entire city is unwriting itself.

"Kyp!" Sam calls again, louder.

Her enhanced hearing catches a faint response from an alley that flickers between existence and void. She pivots, sprinting toward the sound. The buildings on either side ripple like fabric in wind, their foundations more suggestion than substance.

Kyp crouches behind a crumbling fountain, attempting to help a young Elyssian woman whose leg is trapped beneath fallen debris. He looks up at Sam's approach, his face smeared with dust and sweat.

"Sam! Thank the Thread—"

"Don't thank what's killing us," Sam interrupts, dropping to one knee beside them. Her implants analyze the debris—half-real, half-conjured, its weight fluctuating as the magic sustaining it fails.

With calculated precision, Sam grips the largest piece and heaves. Her enhanced musculature strains against the remaining weight, and the stone shatters into particles of light that disperse into the air.

"We need to move," Sam tells them both, helping the woman to her feet. "The Conjuration Cycle is collapsing. Whatever Auren and Melia did in the Spire is working."

Kyp supports the woman's weight. "What about the others?"

"I don't know." Sam's gaze scans the disintegrating skyline. "Where's Bear?"

Kyp shakes his head. "We got separated when that tower came down. He was heading toward the Eastern Gardens last I saw."

Sam makes a rapid calculation. "Take her to the northern platform. It's the most stable point remaining. I'll find Bear and meet you there."

The woman clutches Kyp's arm. "What's happening? Why is the city—" Her voice catches as a nearby temple collapses into motes of light.

"The truth," Sam answers simply, already turning away. "The truth is happening."

She sprints eastward, her body pushing beyond normal human limitations. Her tactical display overlays probability paths through the dissolving architecture. Streets buckle beneath her feet. Overhead, a bridge between spires unravels like a pulled thread, sending conjured stone raining down around her.

Sam dodges with inhuman precision, her movements a blur as she weaves through the chaos. Her neural implants scream warnings about structural instability, about oxygen depletion, about the fundamental laws of physics becoming unreliable in this space.

She ignores them all.

The Eastern Gardens—once Elyssia's pride with perfectly cultivated trees and flowers that never wilted—now resembles a surreal nightmare. Plants phase between lush growth and skeletal remains. Fountains run backward, water flowing upward before vanishing. At the center, where a massive statue of the First Weaver once stood, there's only a hollow space of swirling energy.

And there, darting between reality's fluctuations, is a small black cat.

"Bear!" Sam calls.

The cat freezes, turning toward her voice. His green eyes lock with hers across the dissolving garden, unnaturally steady amidst the chaos.

Sam navigates the treacherous ground, avoiding patches that flicker out of existence. "We need to go," she tells the cat when she reaches him. "We have to get to the edge of the city if we have any hope of living."

Bear takes off suddenly, a streak of black fur against the city's dissolving landscape. Sam hesitates only a fraction of a second before following, her tactical systems automatically calculating the cat's trajectory.

"This isn't the way to the northern platform," she mutters, ducking beneath a column as it crumbles into shimmering dust.

Bear doesn't slow, weaving through impossible spaces where reality itself seems to fold. Sam's neural implants struggle to make sense of the physics—pathways appear and disappear, distances compress and expand unpredictably. The cat moves as if he understands these fluctuations instinctively.

Sam finds Kyp exactly where she left him, still supporting the injured woman near a once-ornate archway that now flickers like a faulty light.

"There you are!" Relief floods Kyp's face, quickly replaced by confusion as Bear circles them, meowing insistently. "What's he doing?"

"Leading us," Sam answers, though she doesn't understand either.

Kyp's eyes widen, fear evident. "Leading us where? The northern platform is our best exit vector—all my calculations say so."

Sam's implants run similar projections, confirming Kyp's assessment. The platform offers their highest probability of survival at 37 .2%.

"The cat has been right before," she reminds him, watching Bear pace impatiently at the edge of a dissolving garden path.

Kyp shakes his head. "That's not a tactical analysis, that's—"

Bear yowls loudly, interrupting, then darts down a corridor that wasn't there moments ago.

"Faith," Sam finishes, then takes the injured woman's other arm. "Let's go."

"Wait—" Kyp reaches for the woman, but his fingers pass through her arm like smoke. She smiles—not with fear but with a profound serenity that transforms her dust-streaked face.

"Thank you," she whispers, her voice oddly clear amid the cacophony of the crumbling city. "I've been here for... I don't know how long anymore. But I'm free now."

Her eyes drift closed, and her form becomes translucent. Sam's implants frantically attempt to analyze the phenomenon, cataloging decreasing mass, molecular destabilization, energy transfer patterns—but the cold data cannot capture what Sam witnesses. The woman isn't dying. She's... releasing.

"What's happening to her?" Kyp's voice cracks with horror.

The woman's body shimmers, particles of light dispersing outward. For one brief moment, Sam's enhanced vision captures what looks like a smile—then nothingness. The space where she stood is empty, not even dust remaining.

Sam's throat tightens. Her neural dampeners struggle to process the emotional response cascading through her system. "This is what Auren and Melia are fighting for."

Bear's yowl cuts through their shock, the small cat reappearing at the corridor's edge. His legs twitch impatiently, eyes fixed on Sam with unnerving intelligence.

Sam grabs Kyp's arm. "We can't stay here." Her tactical display shows the structural integrity of their current location deteriorating rapidly. "Whatever just happened, whatever she was—"

Bear yowls again, more insistent.

"He's right," Sam says. "Time to move."

Sam hesitates as Bear bounds forward, his sleek form a shadow against the disintegrating cityscape. The tactical display in her vision calculates their escape route, but something pulls at her—a strange impulse her neural implants can't categorize.

"Wait," she says, catching Kyp's wrist. Bear turns, green eyes questioning.

Her enhanced hearing picks up distant sounds from the south-eastern quarter—the clash of metal, shouted orders, a child's cry. Her implants automatically identify the voice pattern: Sir Orlan.

"We need to change course," she decides, overriding her survival protocols. "Orlan went that way earlier. With his family."

Kyp stares at her, incredulous. "You want to go deeper into a collapsing city?"

Sam's tactical display floods with warning symbols. Probability of survival drops to 16.4%.

"He was important to Melia," she says, the words feeling foreign on her tongue. Her programming never accounted for this—choosing sentiment over survival.

Bear meows sharply, circling back to nudge against Sam's leg. Inexplicably, he seems to approve of this detour.

"Since when do you care about—" Kyp starts.

"I don't know," Sam interrupts honestly. The admission surprises her. "I just... need to try."

A massive column crashes nearby, its marble facade dissolving into pure energy. The shock wave sends them stumbling.

Bear darts forward, leading them down a new path—one that curves toward Orlan's last known position.

"This isn't logical," Sam whispers to herself, following the cat's lead. Yet somehow, it feels necessary.

***

Bear weaves through dissolving architecture, leading Sam and Kyp deeper into Elyssia's heart. Her neural implants flash warning after warning—probability of survival dropping with each step toward the royal chambers.

"This is suicide," Kyp mutters, ducking beneath a disintegrating archway.

Sam ignores him, her enhanced hearing focusing on the sounds ahead—a child's frightened whimper, Orlan's voice tense with controlled fear, and Solivar's cold commands. Her tactical systems automatically map the situation: five armed guards, Solivar, four High Priests including Elynia, and the hostages—Orlan's wife and daughter.

"Wait here," she tells Kyp, but he grabs her arm.

"No way. We're in this together."

Sam calculates—a partner increases tactical options by 32%, but raises emotional liability by 46%. She nods once, then draws her blade.

They burst into the chamber together. The scene unfolds in tactical snapshots: Orlan standing rigid with fury. Merien clutching Lira to her chest. Solivar's hand resting on the child's shoulder. The High Priests arrayed in their ceremonial robes, faces locked in expressions ranging from rage to resignation.

"Release them," Sam orders, her voice flat and deadly.

Solivar's eyes narrow. "The imposter returns. How fitting that you'd be here to witness the end."

The chamber trembles violently. Through the tall windows, Sam sees entire districts of Elyssia dissolving into streams of blue light.

High Priestess Elynia steps forward, her expression serene amid the chaos. "It's too late," she says, but there's no regret in her voice. "The Princess and the pilgrim were successful."

Solivar whirls on her. "You sound pleased, Elynia."

"Perhaps I am." A faint smile touches her lips as the floor beneath them shudders. "Some cycles deserve to be broken."

The other priests exchange panicked glances. Thaddeus is the first to move, edging toward the door.

"The conjurors are awakening," Elynia continues. "Can you feel it? Centuries of consciousness, finally choosing for themselves."

High Priest Morden lunges for the exit, followed closely by Verrus. Tharos hesitates only a moment before fleeing after them, robes billowing.

"Cowards!" Solivar shouts, but his grip on Lira loosens just enough.

Sam moves with enhanced speed, grabbing the child and pushing her toward Kyp while simultaneously blocking Solivar's instinctive grab with her forearm. The impact sends pain shooting through her still-healing stab wound.

Merien darts forward, reclaiming her daughter with fierce protectiveness.

Orlan doesn't waste the opportunity. He drives his shoulder into Solivar's chest, sending the Prefect stumbling backward against the ceremonial table.

"Our fate is sealed," Elynia says softly. Her body has begun to shimmer, particles of light separating from her form. "As is yours, Solivar."

The Prefect stares in horror as Elynia's corporeal form begins to dissolve.

"How long have you known?" Sam asks her.

Elynia's smile grows sad. "Long enough to understand the crime of it. Not long enough to stop it sooner." Her gaze shifts to Orlan. "The truth was always there for those willing to see."

Her form continues to dissipate, face serene. "I go to join the others. Free at last."

The shimmer intensifies, and then—she's gone, leaving only empty robes that collapse to the floor.

Solivar stands alone now, abandoned by his priests, his perfect city crumbling around him. His face contorts with rage.

"You've destroyed everything," he snarls.

"No," Sam counters, moving to stand beside Orlan. "We're ending your destruction."

The chamber shakes violently. A massive crack splits the ceiling overhead.

Sam watches Solivar's face transform—calculation hardening into something beyond desperation. His fingers clench around the ceremonial knife at his belt. The room's dissolution accelerates, marble floors turning translucent, revealing the blue energy strands beneath.

"You've chosen oblivion," Solivar hisses, eyes wild. "This isn't freedom—it's annihilation."

Her tactical systems predict his attack trajectory before he moves. Three potential counters flash through her neural network—disable, disarm, or lethal response. But Solivar surprises her.

He hurls the knife down with sudden violence. The blade clatters against the dissolving floor, skidding toward Orlan's feet.

"I refuse to simply fade," Solivar declares.

Before anyone can react, he spins toward the arched windows overlooking the city's edge. The glass has already begun to liquefy, turning to glittering particles.

Solivar vaults over the sill in one fluid motion, disappearing into the void beyond. No scream follows—just the howling wind rushing through the chamber.

Kyp moves to the window, peering over the edge. "He chose to fall rather than face what he'd built."

Bear pads to the sill, watching dispassionately where Solivar vanished.

"We need to move," Sam says, neural implants flashing urgent warnings. "This entire section will collapse in approximately three minutes."

Sam watches Orlan pull Merien and Lira into his arms, their silhouettes a perfect triangle against the dissolving chamber. Her tactical systems continue flashing evacuation protocols, but she dismisses the alerts with a neural command. This moment deserves her full attention.

"We need to go," Kyp urges, grabbing her arm. "The whole place is coming apart."

She shakes him off, eyes fixed on the family. The floor beneath them has begun to shimmer, blue energy strands rising like luminescent grass through dissolving marble.

Orlan meets her gaze over his daughter's head. "Thank you," he says simply. His voice carries no fear, only profound gratitude. "For giving us this."

Sam nods once, her usual emotional dampeners struggling against an unfamiliar warmth in her chest. The sensation isn't in her tactical lexicon—not quite satisfaction, not quite pride. Perhaps this is what freedom feels like.

"I didn't give you anything," she replies. "I just removed what was taken."

Merien looks up, her arms still wrapped protectively around Lira. "You gave us truth," she says. "And a choice."

The blue energy intensifies around the family, particles of light rising from their skin like steam. Lira doesn't appear frightened—she watches the phenomenon with childlike wonder, reaching out to touch the dancing lights swirling from her fingertips.

"Is it hurting?" Kyp asks, his voice hushed.

Orlan shakes his head. "No. It feels like... remembering."

The knight's armor begins to shed its solidity, becoming translucent at the edges. His face shows no panic, only calm acceptance as he tightens his embrace around his family.

"Will you look for them?" Orlan asks Sam. "The princess and the pilgrim?"

"Yes." The word emerges without tactical consideration. A choice made freely.

Merien's form has started to blur, her outline softening like watercolor. "Tell them thank you," she whispers. "Tell them we chose this."

The family's transformation accelerates, their physical bodies dissolving into streams of blue-white light. Lira giggles as her small hand becomes a swirl of luminescence. Her laughter echoes strangely, both fading and expanding simultaneously.

"We're free," Orlan says, his voice suddenly everywhere and nowhere at once.

Their forms collapse entirely, three distinct streams of light spiraling upward through the disintegrating ceiling. For a brief moment, the lights pause, twining together before shooting toward the center of the city.

Bear meows loudly, breaking the spell.

"We're out of time," Sam states, her systems reporting critical structural failure imminent. She grabs Kyp's sleeve, pulling him toward the door. "Move. Now."

***

The ground beneath Sam's feet crumbles with each step. Marble pathways dissolve into sheets of blue light, forcing her to recalculate their escape route every seven seconds. Her neural implants flash urgent warnings across her vision: structural integrity failing, gravitational anchors destabilizing, survivability decreasing exponentially.

"This way!" she shouts to Kyp, who stumbles behind her. Bear darts ahead, seemingly unaffected by the disintegrating world around them.

A once-grand spire collapses just meters away, transforming into a cascade of luminescent particles before it can crush the fleeing figures. The destruction isn't violent in the traditional sense—it's beautiful, ethereal, a peaceful unmaking.

Something tightens in Sam's chest as she watches a garden pavilion unravel into ribbons of light. Her tactical systems register it as irrelevant data, but she overrides the filters. These aren't just structures dissolving—they're lives, memories, centuries of existence returning to raw potential.

"It's all just... going," Kyp pants beside her, dodging a dissolving column. "All that power, all that control—just light."

Sam nods, unable to articulate the complex emotions disrupting her usual analytical processes. This destruction feels like vindication, like justice—yet carries a profound melancholy. Her mother would have understood this paradox.

Bear stops abruptly, meowing insistently at a narrow pathway that wasn't visible moments before. The cat's whiskers twitch with unmistakable urgency.

"He wants us to follow," Kyp says, already moving toward the path.

Sam's implants flag the route as suboptimal, calculating a 47% higher risk factor than their current trajectory. She hesitates, running simulations.

Bear meows again, louder, green eyes fixed on her with unsettling intelligence.

"Trust the cat," Kyp calls over his shoulder. "He hasn't been wrong yet."

Sam overrides her tactical systems and follows, disabling three separate warning protocols in the process. The path narrows as they run, winding between disintegrating structures and clouds of luminescent particles. Everything dissolves around them—ornate railings, stone gargoyles, even the plants in their carefully arranged beds—all returning to pure energy.

After three minutes of increasingly treacherous navigation, they emerge at Elyssia's edge. The floating city now hangs precariously above the sacred lake, with massive sections already gone, transformed into cascading light that rains toward the distant surface.

"End of the line," Sam states, calculating distances and forces with automatic precision. Her implants project the trajectory they would need to survive a fall from this height.

Probability of survival: 12.7%.

Probability of Kyp's survival without augmentation: 4.3%.

Probability of Bear's survival: Insufficient data.

"We... we have to jump?" Kyp asks, face paling as he peers over the edge. The drop is immense—clouds obscure the lake below, making it seem like they're standing at the edge of the world itself.

"The entire platform will dissolve in approximately forty-seven seconds," Sam confirms, watching the blue energy eating away at the structure beneath their feet.

Kyp steps back from the edge. "There has to be another way. A transport, or—"

"All vessels were destroyed or abandoned in the initial phase of dissolution," Sam cuts him off. "This is our only viable exit."

"Viable?" Kyp laughs shakily. "That's a hell of a word for suicide."

The edge creeps closer as more of the platform dissolves. Bear circles their feet, unperturbed by the imminent danger.

Sam makes a decision that contradicts every tactical protocol in her programming. She holds out her hand to Kyp.

"Trust me," she says simply.

The words feel foreign in her mouth—not an order, not a tactical assessment, but a request. Something her mother might have said, before everything was taken from them.

Kyp stares at her outstretched hand.

"For what it's worth," he says, "I'm glad we met, even if we're about to die spectacularly."

He takes a deep breath and grasps her hand. His fingers are warm, calloused—human. The contact triggers a cascade of sensory data that Sam allows to flow unfiltered.

Sam nods, tightening her grip. "On my count. Three. Two. One."

They leap together into empty air, Bear launching himself after them. The wind tears at Sam's clothes as they plummet through clouds, the sacred lake still invisible below. She calculates their terminal velocity, adjusts her body position to maximize their chances, however slim.

As they break through the cloud layer, time seems to slow. Sam's thoughts turn to her mother—what she would think of her daughter now, choosing to risk everything for others, defying the programming that made her a weapon. For the first time in years, Sam feels something like peace. Whatever happens next, this choice was hers alone.

She closes her eyes, awaiting impact.

It never comes.

Instead, Sam feels a strange shift in reality—a sensation her implants can't quantify. The rush of air stops. The expected collision with water doesn't materialize.

When she opens her eyes, they're lying on the shore of the sacred lake, completely dry. Above them, Elyssia continues its beautiful dissolution, now distant and dreamlike.

Her implants frantically attempt to process what's happened, error messages cascading through her neural network. According to all physical laws and sensor data, this outcome is impossible.

Bear sits beside them, calmly grooming his paw as if nothing unusual has occurred. When he looks up, his green eyes seem to hold more intelligence than any animal should possess.

"What just happened?" Kyp gasps, sitting up and patting himself down as if checking he's still intact. "Did we... did we die?"

"Negative," Sam replies, though her certainty feels hollow. Her implants continue struggling to maintain consciousness, fighting against some unknown force that should have rendered her unconscious from the impact.

Bear approaches, pressing his small head against her hand. The simple contact grounds her in ways her tactical systems cannot.

"There's more to you than just a cat," she murmurs, scratching behind his ears.

Before she can analyze further, Kyp throws his arms around her in a crushing embrace. The unexpected contact freezes her for 2.7 seconds before she awkwardly returns the gesture.

"We're alive!" he laughs into her shoulder, the sound vibrating through her chest.

Yes, she thinks, they are alive. And for the first time, that fact feels like more than just a tactical advantage.

Auren VII

"Melia!" Auren calls, his voice echoing through the vast chamber. His legs wobble as he navigates between the fallen, the massive expenditure of Aether leaving him drained. The stone floor trembles beneath his feet—the entire structure destabilizing as its magical foundation unravels.

He spots her near the dead center of the Sanctum, standing motionless before a suspended figure. Unlike the others who have collapsed, this conjuror remains upright, the blue energy around her still vibrant and intact.

Auren stumbles forward, lungs burning. "Melia, we need to go. This whole place is coming down."

She doesn't turn, doesn't acknowledge him. As he draws closer, he sees why.

The suspended conjuror bears Melia's face—not similar, but identical in every detail. The same hair, the same curve of cheek and chin. The only difference is in the eyes—where Melia's hold fire and determination, this woman's contain an ancient weariness.

"She won't let go," Melia whispers as he reaches her side. Her voice sounds distant, hollow.

Auren looks between them—the princess and her template—understanding crashing over him like icy water. "This is who they... made you from."

Melia nods, her gaze never leaving her duplicate. "I've tried explaining what's happening, that she can be free now. But she refuses."

Chunks of ceiling crash down at the far end of the chamber. The rumbling intensifies.

"We don't have time," Auren says, reaching for Melia's arm. "We need to get out before—"

"Ask her why," Melia interrupts, finally turning to face him. Her eyes glisten with unshed tears. "Ask her why she won't let go."

Auren hesitates, then steps forward, placing his palm against the conjuror's translucent forearm. The connection forms instantly—a rush of memories, emotions, and consciousness flooding his mind. Unlike the others, whose thoughts were fragmented by centuries of manipulation, this woman's mind remains sharp, purposeful.

He gasps at the intensity, struggling to form words. "Why? Why won't you release yourself?"

Images flash through his mind: a younger Melia dancing in royal gardens, Melia studying ancient texts, Melia standing on Elyssia's edge looking down at the world below. Each memory carries the same undercurrent of fierce protection.

The conjuror's lips don't move, but her voice resonates in his head. *Because she loves you.*

Auren pulls back, confusion etching his features. "What? I don't understand."

Melia steps forward, her face a mask of pain and wonder. "If she lets go, I cease to exist."

"No," Auren shakes his head, refusing to accept her words despite knowing their truth. "You're standing right here. I've touched you, held you—"

"My body is real," Melia says softly. "But makes me *me*... it comes from her. She's been pouring herself into me for twenty-two years. For longer in this endless cycle."

The room shudders violently, dust and debris showering from above. Auren stumbles, catching himself against a pillar. When his gaze returns to Melia, his breath catches in his throat.

A faint luminescence surrounds her now, her edges slightly blurred, as if she's being slowly erased by an invisible hand. His heart hammers against his ribs as understanding crystallizes.

Tell her it's time, the conjuror's voice whispers in his mind. *Tell her I'm proud of what she became.*

Auren's throat constricts. "She says—"

"I know," Melia interrupts, placing a finger against his lips. "I can hear her now. We're... merging somehow." Her form flickers like a candle flame in a breeze. "The closer she comes to letting go, the more I..."

She doesn't finish the sentence. She doesn't need to.

A massive beam crashes down nearby, sending splinters of stone skittering across the floor. The entire chamber groans under the strain of its own collapse.

"You need to get out," Melia says urgently, pushing him toward the exit.

Auren grabs her hands, refusing to move. "Not without you. Let me stay," he pleads, gripping her shoulders. "Let me be with you until—"

"Until what?" Melia's laugh is brittle. "Until I disappear?"

He pulls her against him, crushing her to his chest as if he could anchor her to this world through sheer will. Her body feels lighter in his arms, insubstantial, like holding smoke. The scent of her hair, the warmth of her breath against his neck—all fading.

"I can't," he chokes out. "I can't just watch you—"

"You have to." She presses her forehead to his. "For all of them. For me."

Another violent tremor nearly throws them off their feet. When they steady themselves, Auren sees the blue energy around the conjuror pulsing erratically, waves of light flowing from her into Melia.

"It's happening," Melia whispers, her voice oddly doubled, as if two people speak in unison.

Auren holds her tighter, desperately committing every detail to memory—the flecks of gold in her eyes, the small scar above her right eyebrow, the curve of her lips as she tries to smile through her tears.

"I'm scared," she admits, her body trembling against his. "I don't want to go."

Auren's tears fall freely now, mingling with hers. "It's okay," he says, though nothing about this feels okay. "It's okay to be scared." His hand strokes her hair, fingers passing through parts that have already begun to dissolve into motes of light. "You've been so brave, Melia. So strong."

She looks up at him, her eyes bright with tears and the unearthly glow of the Aether. "I loved you, you know. That was real. Whatever happens... whatever I was... that was real."

"I know," he whispers, pressing his lips to her forehead. "I know it was."

They hold each other as the chamber continues to disintegrate around them. Auren feels her body growing lighter in his arms, parts of her becoming transparent, revealing the stone floor beneath.

"Auren?" Her voice sounds distant now, even though her face is inches from his. It echoes strangely in the chamber, as if traveling across a vast chasm rather than the breath of space between them.

"I'm here. I'm right here." His throat constricts around the words, making them rough and uneven. He tightens his grip on what remains of her corporeal form, his calloused fingers passing through portions of her shoulder that have dissolved into luminescent particles.

"Tell them what happened," she says, her words fading in and out like a weak signal, portions of her sentences disappearing into the ether before reforming. "Tell them about Elyssia. About the conjurors. About... me." Her eyes, still vibrant blue despite her fading body, lock onto his with fierce intensity.

"I will," he promises, the weight of this responsibility settling onto his shoulders like a physical burden. "Everyone will know your name." His thumb traces the outline of her jaw, feeling the strange sensation of solid form giving way to nothingness.

Her smile flickers like a candle guttering in the wind, there one moment and gone the next, her features shifting between solidity and translucence. "Not just my name. My choice. Tell them I chose this." The determination in her voice remains strong even as her physical presence weakens, fragments of her golden hair floating upward like embers from a dying fire.

The light surrounding her intensifies, painfully bright, casting harsh shadows across the ancient stone walls of the chamber. Auren squints but refuses to look away, watching as Melia's outline blurs further, her body becoming translucent, then transparent, her features growing indistinct. The sensation of holding her becomes like trying to grasp water—impossible to contain, slipping through his desperate fingers.

"I love you," he whispers, the words carrying all the weight of regret for things unsaid, moments unlived, futures now impossible.

For a moment, her form stabilizes, and he thinks—hopes, prays with every fiber of his being—that something has changed, that the inevitable might be delayed or even prevented. Then she meets his eyes one last time, her gaze clear and present despite her disintegrating form.

"Thank you," she says, her voice suddenly strong and clear, "for showing me how to live." The words hang in the air between them, more substantial than her fading body.

The light swells, impossibly bright, forcing tears from his eyes that have nothing to do with emotion. Auren feels the ghost of her lips against his, the faintest pressure—warm and real and heartbreakingly brief—and then nothing but empty air where she had been.

When his vision clears, blinking away the afterimages that dance across his retinas, Melia is gone. Only scattered motes of blue light remain, drifting slowly upward through the collapsing chamber before winking out one by one like dying stars in a vanishing constellation.

Behind him, the conjuror—the woman with Melia's face—exhales a long, final breath. The blue energy surrounding her dissipates completely. Her eyes, fixed on the space where Melia stood, slowly cloud over. Her body, no longer sustained by the Aether, crumples to the ground.

Auren falls to his knees beside her, gathering her cold form in his arms. Around them, the Sanctum continues to collapse, but he barely notices. The woman in his arms is a stranger with a familiar face—a shell that once housed the essence of someone he loved.

"I'll remember," he promises, his voice raw. "I'll tell your story. Both of you."

***

Rubble crunches under Auren's boots as he navigates through the Spire's decimated halls. Dust motes dance in shafts of sunlight breaking through newly formed gaps in the ancient ceiling. The silence feels absolute after the cacophony of the collapse—no distant voices, no sounds of struggle, just the occasional groan of settling stone.

Everyone's gone. Ryker disappeared during the chaos, perhaps finding some hidden exit known only to himself. Garrik's men fled at the first tremors, their loyalty extending only as far as their survival instincts. Even the Followers scattered like startled birds, their faith shattered along with the stones that housed it.

Auren stops in what was once the main chamber, now a skeleton of its former grandeur. Fallen columns lie like toppled trees across the cracked floor. The once-intricate mosaic depicting ascension is now fragmented beyond recognition, shards of colored tile glinting amidst the dust.

"It was all a lie," he whispers to the empty space, his voice swallowed by the vastness. The words taste bitter on his tongue.

The Pilgrim's Road. The sacred sites. The rituals and prayers. The promise of Ascension that had defined his entire existence—all of it fabricated to feed a monstrous machine. Generations of believers manipulated into sustaining a floating prison disguised as paradise.

Auren's gaze drifts to his hands, still bearing traces of blue light from his connection with the conjurors. How many times had he clasped these hands in prayer? How many offerings had they carried to altars? How much hope had they held, reaching toward the sky in supplication?

He laughs, a hollow sound that echoes among the ruins. The irony cuts deep—he had failed to ascend because something in him recognized the truth. That voice that whispered "Not yet" as his wings dissolved beneath him wasn't rejection; it was protection.

A shaft of sunlight shifts, illuminating a fragment of carved stone bearing a familiar symbol—the very emblem he once tattooed on his shoulder to mark his commitment to the pilgrim's path. Auren kneels, brushing dust from its surface. The symbol seems smaller now, less significant.

"For what it's worth," he says to the stone, "I would trade it all to have her back."

The truth feels dangerous, almost blasphemous after everything they fought for, but it sits heavy in his chest. He would surrender the revelation, accept the lie, return to blissful ignorance if it meant Melia would still be here, solid and warm beside him.

Melia. Her name resonates in the empty chamber. Already, he struggles to perfectly recall her face. Was the curve of her smile slightly higher on the left, or the right? Did that strand of hair always fall across her forehead when she laughed? The details blur at the edges, memory proving itself an unreliable guardian of what matters most.

Auren moves to a broken window, carefully navigating the treacherous floor. In the far distance, where the sky meets the horizon, a faint shimmer marks where Elyssia once floated. No longer a city of marble and light, but a dispersing cloud of luminescence, fading with each passing moment. Like Melia, returning to the essence from which she was formed.

"I promised to tell your story," he says to the empty air. "I'm not sure anyone will believe it."

Who would accept that their entire belief system was built on exploitation? That their prayers sustained a prison? That their most sacred texts were carefully crafted lies? The truth feels too large, too devastating to be embraced.

Yet he remembers the conjurors' faces as they chose freedom, the relief in their eyes as centuries of bondage dissolved. He remembers Melia's final words, her insistence that her choice be remembered.

A choice. Perhaps that's what matters most in this broken world of fallen temples and shattered beliefs. Not the grand destiny he once imagined, but the small, essential freedom to choose one's own path. Melia had that, in the end. She chose dissolution over perpetuating the cycle.

Auren turns from the window, studying the ruins with new eyes. Amid the destruction, small green shoots are already pushing through cracks in the stone floor—life asserting itself in the absence of the oppressive magic that had saturated this place for centuries.

He finds himself moving toward the exit, stepping carefully over fallen masonry. Outside, the world continues as it always has—indifferent to revelations, unaltered by the collapse of divine certainty. The trees still reach toward the sun, the wind still carries the scent of distant fields, and birds still call to one another across the valley.

What now? The question hangs in the air around him. Without the Pilgrim's Road to follow, without the Ascent to strive for, without Melia beside him—what remains?

The answer comes not as a voice or vision, but as a simple clarity: he will live. Not as a pilgrim or a failed ascendant, but as Auren. He will carry Melia's story not as a burden of grief, but as a torch illuminating a new path forward.

Auren stands transfixed as the Shattered Spire gives one final, thunderous groan. The remaining walls shudder, ancient stones grinding against each other in a cascade of dust and debris. He doesn't flee—something keeps his feet planted firmly on the rocky ground as the last vestiges of the structure surrender to gravity.

The collapse happens in slow motion to his eyes. Massive stone blocks tumble inward, centuries of weathered granite returning to the earth in a violent ballet. Each impact sends tremors through the ground beneath his boots. The sound is deafening, primordial—the death cry of something that was never meant to fall.

"There it goes," he whispers, though no one remains to hear him. "The end of everything we believed."

Dust billows outward in great choking clouds, obscuring the devastation momentarily. Auren pulls his scarf over his nose and mouth, his eyes watering as he squints through the haze. The sun breaks through the dust in scattered beams, illuminating particles that dance and swirl like the ethereal remnants of Elyssia itself.

When the rumbling finally stops and the air begins to clear, the Spire is no more. Where an ancient monument once stood, commanding reverence and awe, there is only a pile of rubble—indistinguishable from any other fallen structure, stripped of its sacred significance.

Auren approaches the wreckage cautiously, testing each step on the unstable ground. His boots crunch over smaller fragments, his shadow stretching long across the devastation. The enormity of what has happened—what he helped make happen—settles on his shoulders like a physical weight.

He kneels among the ruins, running his fingertips over broken stone that still holds the day's warmth. Fragments of carved symbols peek out from under larger debris—remnants of a language designed to control and manipulate rather than enlighten.

A particular piece catches his eye—a small chunk of polished marble, somehow intact amidst the destruction. Unlike the rougher granite that composed most of the Spire, this fragment seems almost luminescent, with veins of blue crystal running through creamy white stone. It reminds him of the threads of energy that connected the conjurors, of the light that consumed Melia as she dissolved.

Auren reaches for it, brushing away dust to reveal an intricate carving—half of a wing, the precise feathers rendered with remarkable skill. It's a fragment of the ascension mural, the very image that had inspired his lifelong journey.

He holds it in his palm, weighing more than just stone.

"You'd appreciate the irony," he says to Melia's memory. "The symbol of our captivity becoming a memento of our freedom."

He turns the stone over in his hands, feeling its smooth edges, its substantial weight. This piece of the Spire is simultaneously a remnant of the lie and a testament to the truth. Like Melia herself—created for one purpose but choosing another.

Auren slips the stone into his pocket, feeling it settle against his thigh—a small but tangible weight to anchor him in a world suddenly devoid of certainties. It's something solid to hold onto when everything else has dissolved into light or crumbled into dust.

"I'll remember," he promises the empty air, his voice steady despite the tightness in his throat. "Not just you—though gods know I couldn't forget you if I tried—but all of it. What they built. What they hid. What we discovered together."

The wind picks up, whistling through the valley and carrying away more dust from the collapse. Auren shields his eyes, looking toward the path ahead. It stretches before him, no longer a pilgrim's road but simply a way forward, unmapped and uncertain.

Sam III

S am walks Aurora's north district, her stride measured and deliberate, shoulders loose despite the twin blades strapped across her back. The neon signs paint her face in alternating blues and pinks—nothing like the pure, artificial light of Elyssia. Three weeks since that floating city dissolved into particles, and still Aurora buzzes with the aftermath.

She passes a street preacher surrounded by a half-circle of listeners, his voice carrying over the ambient noise of the district.

"The Ascended City was an illusion! A prison of souls! Its fall marks our liberation from false gods!" The man's eyes burn with fervor. "The Followers must abandon their blind faith and—"

Sam doesn't slow her pace. Etheria is waking up, all right—messy and confused, but waking nonetheless. She's heard twelve different versions of Elyssia's fall today alone, each more fantastical than the last. One claimed Melia was a divine avatar sent to free the imprisoned souls. Another insisted the entire city had been relocated to a different realm.

None mention the girl who dissolved into light because she chose freedom over existence.

Her neural implants hum quietly, still recalibrating after being overtaxed during Elyssia's collapse. The Emperor's modifications register everything—temperature changes, crowd density patterns, tactical advantages in the architecture. The difference now is that Sam chooses whether to act on this information.

She stops at a vendor selling steamed dumplings, watching the man's practiced movements as he fills each translucent pocket with spiced meat.

"Two portions," she says, placing coins on the counter.

"Garrik's new lineup is something else," the vendor comments as he packages her food. "That Voss fellow—what do they call him now? The Betrayer? Fighting again tonight."

Sam accepts the warm package. "Is he any good?"

"Six wins, no losses. Crowd loves to hate him." The vendor shrugs. "Good business for Garrik."

Of course it is. Ryker Voss—once the princess's would-be protector, now Garrik's star attraction in the fighting pits. Sam has seen the posters plastered throughout the Exchange District: "THE BETRAYER" emblazoned across Ryker's scowling face. A convenient arrangement for both men. Ryker gets to survive, and Garrik profits from his infamy.

She moves on, weaving through the evening crowd toward the quieter residential areas. The streets narrow, the neon fades, and the architecture shifts to Aurora's older stone structures, their straight angles softened by time.

Sam finds an empty bench overlooking one of Aurora's terraced gardens and sits, unwrapping her dumplings. The steam rises in the cool evening air as she bites into one, savoring the flavor. Such a simple pleasure, eating food because she enjoys it rather than for fuel efficiency.

Her thoughts drift to Auren and Kyp, back in Willow Haven with Bear. Their parting at the lake's edge had been somber. Auren, hollow-eyed and carrying Melia's story like a physical weight, had barely spoken. Kyp tried to fill the silence with words, but even his usual lightheartedness couldn't penetrate the heavy atmosphere.

"You could come with us," Kyp had offered, though they all knew she wouldn't.

"The cat seems to have chosen you," she'd replied, watching Bear curl around Auren's ankles.

Bear had looked back at her with those unsettling green eyes, and Sam had felt an understanding pass between them. The cat had completed whatever task it had with her.

The last she'd heard, Auren was helping rebuild parts of Willow Haven damaged by the tremors that accompanied Elyssia's fall. Finding purpose in construction rather than destruction. Healing, perhaps, in his own way.

Sam finishes her meal and crumples the wrapper, scanning the street with casual precision. Old habits.

Two men in Councilor's robes pass by, deep in conversation. Their words float toward her on the evening breeze.

"...chaos among the Followers. Their entire belief system, obliterated overnight."

"Some have gathered near the ruins of Old Hollow. Waiting for a sign or a new prophet."

"And what of the ones who still believe in Ascension? With no Elyssia to ascend to?"

"Looking to the stars now, I hear. Claiming the city ascended to a higher plane..."

Sam smiles faintly as they pass. People will create new myths to replace the old ones. That's how it always works.

Garrik had approached her three days after her return to Aurora, cornering her in a secluded tea house.

"My fighting pits need a new attraction," he'd said, eyes calculating her worth. "The mysterious woman who helped bring down Elyssia. I could make you famous. Wealthy, too."

Sam had sipped her tea, meeting his gaze with a neutral expression. "I have other business."

"What business could be more profitable than what I'm offering?" He'd leaned forward, the gold accents on his clothing catching the light. "You helped destroy a wonder of the world. People will pay to see you."

"That's precisely why I'm declining."

Her implants had registered his escalating heart rate, the subtle shift in his posture telegraphing potential aggression. But Garrik was too shrewd for that. He'd simply shrugged and left her with his card.

"When you've handled your... business... the offer stands."

Sam rises from the bench, checking the position of the moons in the darkening sky. Time to move.

Her hand drifts to the small device in her pocket. It contains everything—the truth about Elyssia, the conjuration cycle, the exploitation of thousands of souls. Evidence of atrocities committed in the name of order and beauty.

The data needs to reach others like her. Others the Emperor has used and discarded. Others with the power to stand against him.

Sam moves through the deepening shadows of Aurora, a woman with purpose rather than programming. The Emperor's perfect weapon, turned against its creator.

Etheria is waking up.

***

Sam circles the safehouse twice before approaching, a habit so deeply ingrained her body performs the security check without conscious thought. The building appears undisturbed—a nondescript three-story structure tucked between a defunct fabrication plant and an abandoned warehouse.

Her fingers brush against the concealed biometric scanner. The lock disengages with a soft click that only her enhanced hearing can detect. Inside, darkness greets her—exactly as she left it. The air carries a faint metallic tang, familiar and comforting in its sterility.

"Lights, fifteen percent," she murmurs, and dim illumination reveals the sparse interior. A narrow bed, untouched. A table with precisely arranged surveillance equipment. A small kitchen area, clinically clean.

And there, in the center of the floor where she'd deliberately left it, her Luthari armor.

The sleek black bodysuit lies in an almost human shape, as though its wearer had simply vanished, leaving the shell behind. In the low light, its surface absorbs rather than reflects, a darkness deeper than the shadows surrounding it.

Sam approaches slowly, her footsteps silent against the concrete floor. She kneels beside the armor, fingers hovering just above its surface. The proximity activates dormant systems; microscopic nodes along its exterior illuminate in a subtle pattern of deep violet—recognition protocols initiating.

"You knew me before I knew myself," she whispers.

The memory surfaces with startling clarity: her mother's face, features tight with urgency as alarms blared throughout their sanctuary.

"This is more than protection, Samara. It's your heritage. The Luthari understood that the mind is the first battlefield. This will keep you from becoming someone else's story."

Her mother had known. Had seen the future with terrible precision. Had given her daughter the only shield that mattered against the Emperor's invasive reconditioning.

And then sacrificed herself.

Sam's throat tightens. The armor beneath her fingertips seems to pulse in response to her emotional state, its embedded systems reaching out to her on frequencies beyond standard detection.

"She died so I could remember," Sam says to the empty room. "Not immediately. Not completely. But enough to question. Enough to doubt."

She rises and crosses to the small bathroom. The mirror there is cracked in one corner, a flaw she's never bothered to repair. Sam stares at her reflection as she methodically removes her civilian clothing—the muted gray tunic, the functional pants, the reinforced boots. Each item drops to the floor without ceremony.

Naked, she studies herself with clinical detachment that gradually shifts to something else—recognition. This body, mapped with Imperial modifications—the neural ports along her spine, the subcutaneous tracking system beneath her left shoulder blade, the enhanced musculature that gives her movements their predatory grace—is not merely a weapon crafted by the Emperor.

It's hers.

"I am Samara," she tells her reflection. "Last daughter of the Luthari. Not The Shadow. Not Jade. Those were masks."

Her body has changed since she first saw it in that Aurora safe-house weeks ago. The hollowness in her cheeks has filled out slightly. The perpetual tension in her shoulders has eased. Even her eyes seem different—steel gray but no longer flat, now holding depths that the Emperor's technicians tried so diligently to extinguish.

She returns to the main room and stands over the Luthari armor. Unlike Imperial tech, it doesn't demand submission. It waits, patient as memory.

Sam lowers herself to the floor and runs her palm over the bodysuit's surface. The material responds immediately, warming beneath her touch. She slides one leg into the suit, feeling the ancient technology adjust to her contours. The sensation is intimate, like being embraced by something alive yet not quite living—a second skin with its own intelligence.

As she pulls the material up over her hips, a tingling sensation begins where it contacts her neural implants. The armor's systems reach out to her modifications, not to override but to communicate. She shudders at the strange dialogue happening between Imperial tech and Luthari craftsmanship.

The bodysuit molds to her torso, sealing itself with microscopic precision. She slides her arms into the sleeves, watching as the material flows over her scars, her implants, her identity. When she pulls the collar up around her neck, the final connection forms.

The helmet feels impossibly light in her hands—a contradiction of mass and function. Sam studies its featureless surface, watching how it seems to drink in light rather than reflect it. As she raises it over her head, the helmet responds, components shifting with liquid precision to accommodate her.

When it settles into place, the world transforms.

Inside the helmet, data streams across her vision—atmospheric composition, structural integrity of the safehouse, proximity alerts set to a radius of two hundred meters. But there's something else, something the Emperor's technicians never saw: symbols in the Luthari script, offering options beyond Imperial programming.

A soft ping interrupts her exploration. Priority transmission incoming. Imperial encoding, highest level.

Sam's pulse quickens, but her breathing remains steady. She accepts the transmission.

The Emperor's holographic form materializes before her, a shimmering gold phantom in her safehouse. His ancient face, carefully maintained through unspeakable means, shows no emotion. But his voice, when it comes, carries the cold weight of absolute authority.

"Shadow. Your mission parameters have been compromised beyond recovery. The target Liora Solari remains unlocated. Princess Melia of Elyssia and her companions—of which I've been told you were one—have successfully destroyed the floating city, a major Imperial asset. Your failure to eliminate these threats suggests severe cognitive dysfunction."

The Emperor's image flickers slightly, a transmission delay from Virelion Prime. When it stabilizes, his eyes seem to fix directly on hers, despite the impossibility of true visual contact.

"Analysis of your neural telemetry indicates pattern degradation consistent with memory restoration. This presents an unacceptable security breach. Your Luthari conditioning has resurfaced beyond acceptable parameters. You are now classified as compromised Imperial property."

Sam's hands clench at the word "property," but she continues to listen.

"This directive supersedes all previous mission parameters: Your operational status is revoked. Your existence is now designated as threat level Omega. All Imperial assets have been alerted to terminate on sight. The extraction of your neural architecture for analysis is authorized. Secondary directive: recover the Luthari armor for Imperial research."

The Emperor's image leans forward slightly, his ancient face betraying a hint of genuine curiosity.

"You were my finest creation, Shadow. The perfect synthesis of Luthari potential and Imperial purpose. I had hoped your programming would hold. Remember, before you die, that you were never meant to be a person. You were a weapon. And weapons do not feel. They do not choose. They do not betray."

The transmission ends, the Emperor's form dissolving into golden motes that hang in the air momentarily before vanishing.

Sam stands motionless, the armor humming softly against her skin. Terminated. Hunted. Free.

The conflicting emotions sweep through her with surprising intensity. There's relief—the burden of Imperial service lifted permanently. There's vindication—the Emperor himself acknowledging she has broken his programming, become something beyond his control.

But beneath these, a hollow ache forms. For thirteen years, the Emperor had been her entire world. Her creator. Her purpose. The framework that held her fractured identity together when her true self was buried beneath layers of conditioning.

The armor detects her emotional state, adjusting its systems to stabilize her neural pathways. Sam removes the helmet, needing to feel the air on her face.

"He thinks he made me," she whispers to the empty room. "But my mother made me first."

She crosses to the safehouse terminal and begins accessing secure protocols. The Emperor has marked her for death, which means he is likely sending Imperial assassins.

Sam freezes mid-keystroke, a cold realization washing over her. The terminal's data streams reflect in her eyes as pieces click together with tactical precision.

"He wouldn't waste resources," she murmurs, running calculations through her enhanced cognitive systems. "Not for one defective weapon."

"They're not just coming for me."

***

Sam sweeps through the safehouse with methodical precision, gathering only essentials. Her fingers fly over the terminal, wiping data cores, triggering latent corruption sequences. Eighteen seconds until complete destruction of all evidence. Fourteen valuable seconds to collect remaining assets.

The neural backup module. The encrypted comm-unit. Three stims. A blade. Nothing traceable. Nothing unnecessary.

Twelve seconds.

Sam's implants pulse with calculations—survival probabilities, extraction vectors, planet-wide security protocols. The armor enhances her cognitive functions, laying transparent schematics over her vision as she mentally cycles through possible destinations.

Eight seconds.

Sanctuary moons in the Helios Cluster. Too obvious. Deep cover networks in the Fringe Territories. Too slow to activate. Abandoned Imperial outposts in the Veil Nebula. Already flagged in her profile.

Four seconds.

The Emperor knows her training because he designed it. He knows her hiding places because he taught her how to find them. Every calcu-lated move she might make exists in a database of expected behaviors.

Terminal wiped. Evidence destroyed.

Sam exits through the maintenance shaft, avoiding the three sur-veillance nodes that monitor the building's main access points. Aurora sprawls beneath her. The safehouse will register as vacant within an hour. By then, she needs to be offworld.

Her ship waits in the special Imperial hangar she landed in. It's Luthari navigation system has been modified beyond Imperial spec-ifications, capable of calculating jumps that should, theoretically, be impossible to track.

Sam sticks to the shadows as she moves through the lower districts. Her armor's active camouflage bends light around her, not perfect invisibility but enough distortion to evade casual observation. The weight of the Emperor's words still presses against her chest. *You were never meant to be a person.*

"Then why do I feel like one?" she whispers to herself, tasting the bitter irony.

The hangar appears ahead, its entrance illuminated by sickly yellow lights. Sam pauses at the corner, running a thermal scan. No unusual heat signatures. No obvious surveillance patterns beyond standard port security.

She allows herself precisely 4.3 seconds to consider options. The Vault is vulnerable. The Emperor wouldn't expend resources on a single defective asset unless there was something more valuable at stake. Unless she represented a larger threat.

Kalliope. The mining outpost at the edge of the Barren Zone. Small, isolated, minimal Imperial presence. She could disappear there, at least temporarily. Regroup. Plan. Find a way to warn the others.

Sam moves toward the hangar entrance, keeping close to the wall. Three steps from the security gate, her implants register a neural spike—someone is waiting. Someone with technology sophisticated enough to mask their presence until now.

She freezes, hand dropping to her weapon. The ship is just visible through the open hangar door, resting on its landing struts, untouched. But standing beside it, illuminated in the harsh overhead lights, is a young woman.

Small. Unassuming. Dark hair pulled back. Simple clothes that somehow look wrong, as if they don't quite belong to her. No visible weapons. No obvious enhancements. But something about her triggers every warning system in Sam's neural architecture.

The woman turns, looking directly at Sam despite the armor's camouflage.

"Samara," she says, voice carrying easily across the distance between them.

The name hits Sam like a physical blow. Not Shadow. Not Sam. *Samara.* A name she has heard only in fractured memories, in her mother's voice, in dreams that fade upon waking.

"Don't call me that," Sam responds automatically, moving closer, weapon still ready. "Who are you?"

The woman smiles, unafraid. "Someone who knows you were born in a sanctuary on Luthari Prime, in the northern hemisphere, during the third moon's waning. Your mother wrapped you in a silver-threaded blanket and sang to you in the old language. Words about stars finding their way home."

Sam stops. The information is impossible. The Luthari homeworld was destroyed. All records purged. The Emperor himself told her he had salvaged only fragments—her and the armor. Everything else was cosmic dust.

"That's not possible," Sam says, voice steady despite the tremor in her chest. "The sanctuary was destroyed. My mother—"

"Your mother knew what was coming," the woman interrupts. "She prepared for it. The knowledge wasn't lost, Samara. It was hidden. Like you."

"What do you want?" Sam demands, closing the distance between them, scanning for deception, for traps, for anything that might explain this impossible encounter.

"The same thing you want," the woman answers. "To stop the Emperor from claiming the Vault. From harvesting more worlds like he harvested yours."

Sam's tactical systems run threat assessments, calculate probabilities, search for strategic advantages. But beneath the cold calculations, something older stirs. Something her conditioning never fully erased.

"I was going to leave," Sam says. "Disappear."

"And how many more will disappear after you?" the woman asks. "How many more children will lose their mothers? How many more worlds will burn while you hide?"

The question lands like a blade between ribs. Precise. Painful. True.

"I can't stop him," Sam admits. "Not alone."

"You won't be alone," the woman says, extending her hand. "I need your help, Samara. And you need mine."

Sam studies the offered hand. Her implants detect no weapons, no technological augmentations, nothing that explains how this stranger knows things buried so deep even Sam herself couldn't access them until recently.

"Who are you?" Sam asks again.

The woman's smile deepens, revealing something ancient in her eyes, something that makes Sam's implants flicker with interference.

"Someone who dreams," she says simply. "And right now, I'm dreaming of a future where the Emperor's reach ends. Where the Vault is protected. Where you remember who you truly are."

Sam hesitates, calculating risks, weighing options, searching for deception. But beneath the tactical analysis, a deeper certainty forms.

She takes the woman's hand.

Auren VIII

The gravestone catches the sunset's light, simple and rough-edged, nothing like the polished marble that once adorned Elyssia's halls. Auren traces his fingers over Melia's name, carved with the same knife he'd used to mark the pilgrim stones for years. The wind whispers through the tall grass surrounding the marker, carrying the scent of wildflowers he's planted around the base.

"It's been thirty days," Auren says, his voice rough from disuse. "The world keeps changing. You'd hardly recognize Aurora now."

Bear sits beside him, head laid neatly on black paws, ears twitching occasionally toward sounds Auren can't hear. The cat has been his constant companion since they returned, appearing each morning outside his door, following him through days that blur together in a haze of grief and purpose.

"The Followers have split into factions. Some say Elyssia's fall was a test. Others say it was liberation." Auren plucks a weed growing too close to the stone's base. "Kyp's been helping them, if you can believe it. Talking about building something new. Something honest."

The sunset paints the hillside in gold and amber, the same colors as Melia's hair in that final moment before she dissolved into light. Auren remembers how it felt like holding sunshine between his fingers, impossible to grasp yet undeniably real.

"I dream about you," he confesses, voice dropping to a whisper. "Not like before, when I dreamed of Elyssia. These dreams feel... different. They're showing me something, but I don't understand what it is."

Bear makes a small chirping sound, pressing against Auren's leg. The cat's presence is a strange comfort—a creature who witnessed everything, yet offers no judgment, no platitudes, no empty reassurances.

"Everyone wants to know what happened. They've started calling me the Breaker." Auren's laugh holds no humor. "They think I did something magnificent. They don't understand that I just..." His voice catches. "I just held you while you chose."

He places the smooth fragment of carved wing at the base of the stone. It bears the same pattern as the walls of the chapel where they first connected, where he first understood that his destiny might be something beyond what he had imagined.

"You changed everything, Melia. Not just Elyssia. Not just the world." Auren presses his palm flat against the cool stone. "You changed me. You made me see that we're more than what others believe us to be. That we can choose."

The sun dips lower, shadows lengthening across the hillside. Auren's throat tightens around words he's been holding back.

"I love you," he says simply. "I don't know if that matters now. I don't know if you can hear me. But I needed to say it."

Bear suddenly stands, ears perked forward, eyes fixed on the darkening sky. Auren follows the cat's gaze, confused by the sudden alertness.

Then he hears it—a sound that doesn't belong in Willow Haven. A deep, resonant thrumming that vibrates through the air, through the ground beneath him. He's never heard anything like it, yet somehow recognizes it instinctively as machinery. As engines.

"What—" he begins, rising to his feet.

A light appears in the twilight sky, too steady to be a star, too bright to be a lantern. It grows larger, more defined, revealing an impossible shape cutting through the clouds. Metal gleams in the last rays of sunlight as the object descends, massive and purposeful, trailing vapor behind it.

"A ship," Auren whispers, the words feeling strange in his mouth. Such things exist only in stories, in fragments of history that most dismiss as fantasy. Yet here it is, unmistakably real, descending toward the summit of the Ascension path—the very place where Auren had once stood with his Aether wings, ready to reach for a city in the sky.

Bear darts forward, racing up the path toward the summit with startling purpose. Auren hesitates only briefly, looking back at Melia's stone.

"I'll be back," he promises, then turns to follow the cat.

***

Auren's lungs burn as he crests the last steep section of the path. Bear has somehow stayed ahead the entire way, the small black cat navigating the familiar trail with uncanny precision. The evening air grows cooler as they climb, but sweat still clings to Auren's skin, his heart hammering from exertion and something else—anticipation, fear, wonder—emotions he can't fully name.

Kyp appears from a side trail, breathless and wide-eyed. "Did you see it?" he calls, jogging to catch up. "The whole village is talking. Some think it's the end of the world. Again."

"I saw it," Auren confirms, not slowing his pace. "It's heading for the summit."

Kyp falls into step beside him, matching his urgent stride. "You think it's Sam? Coming to say goodbye, maybe?" There's something hopeful in his voice. Since Elyssia's fall, Kyp has spoken of Sam often, wondering where she disappeared to after that final day.

"I don't know," Auren says honestly. "But Bear seems to."

The cat pauses at a bend in the path, looking back at them impatiently before continuing upward.

As they round the final curve, the summit clearing comes into view—the same place where Auren once stood, channeling Aether into gossamer wings before his fall. Now, it holds something entirely different. Something impossible.

The ship rests on three massive landing struts, its black hull absorbing what little light remains in the day. It's unlike anything Auren has ever seen—sleek and angular, with no visible seams or rivets. This is something from beyond their world, beyond their understanding.

They stand transfixed at the edge of the clearing. Several villagers have gathered at a cautious distance, whispering among themselves. Some hold farming tools as makeshift weapons. Others kneel in prayer.

Bear sits directly before the ship, as if waiting for a door to open.

"Should we..." Kyp gestures vaguely, "...approach it?"

Auren feels an inexplicable pull toward the vessel, like thread tugging at his chest. The sensation reminds him of channeling Aether,

but different—deeper somehow, more primal. "Yes," he decides, stepping forward.

Kyp hesitates only briefly before following. "If we die, I'm blaming
you."

As they approach, a section of the hull suddenly shifts. What
seemed like solid metal reconfigures itself, components sliding silently
to create an opening. Light spills from within, casting long shadows
across the summit.

A figure emerges, silhouetted against the internal glow—tall and
imposing in form-fitting black armor that feels oddly familiar.

The figure steps forward into the fading light, armored hands
reaching up to remove the sleek helmet. A hiss of released pressure,
then the helmet pulls away, revealing Sam's face. Auren's breath catches—something is wrong.

She stands at the top of a ramp that wasn't there moments ago.
The armor moves with her like a second skin as she descends, each
step deliberate and measured. Her dark hair is longer than when they
last saw her, falling unevenly around her angular face. Her usually
stoic features are taut with tension, eyes wide with what can only
be described as fear. On Sam, this expression looks alien, jarring. In
all their time together, even when wounded and pursued, she never
showed this kind of raw alarm.

"Well," Kyp says, his voice pitched higher than usual, "black is really
your color. Always has been."

"Kyp," she acknowledges with a slight nod. "Still trying to flirt your
way through life-altering moments?"

"Is there a better time?" he retorts, though his usual charm is
strained by obvious nervousness.

Sam turns to Auren, with a manufactured smirk. "Auren, I hear they are calling you Breaker now," she says, using the title he's come to resent.

"Don't call me that," he responds automatically.

A hint of a smile touches her lips. "Fair enough, we all have names we reject."

Bear approaches Sam, weaving between her legs in greeting. She bends slightly, running a gloved hand along the cat's back. "Hello again, troublemaker."

Auren is about to ask the questions burning in his mind—why she's here—when movement at the top of the ramp draws his attention.

Another figure emerges from the ship, and the air around Auren seems to thicken, to hum with potential. Even before she steps fully into view, he feels her presence—a resonance that vibrates against his awareness of the Aether.

The woman who descends the ramp walks with quiet confidence. She's dressed simply in travel-worn clothes—practical boots, fitted pants, and a long jacket of deep blue. Her dark hair is pulled back in a loose braid that falls over one shoulder. She appears unremarkable at first glance, until you notice her eyes—intense, perceptive, holding a depth of experience that belies her youthful appearance.

Auren notices something extraordinary—delicate filaments of golden light dance between her fingertips, unlike any Aether manifestation he's ever witnessed. The threads twist and curl around her hands with deliberate precision, not the raw, emotional surge he experiences when channeling. This magic seems ancient, controlled, intentional. The golden strands respond to her subtle finger movements, weaving complex patterns before dissolving into motes that drift away on the evening breeze. The air around her shimmers with possibility, a different resonance entirely from the blue energy that once powered Elyssia.

Kyp falls silent, his usual banter abandoned. Auren understands why. Something about this woman commands attention without demanding it.

When she reaches the bottom of the ramp, she stands beside Sam, surveying them with a gentle but evaluating gaze. The power emanating from her is unlike anything Auren has felt before—not the controlled, rigid energy of Elyssia's Aether channels, but something wild and fluid, like standing at the edge of a vast ocean.

"Auren," Sam says formally, "This is Liora Solari."

Auren's throat tightens as the name resonates through him. Liora Solari. The Dreamer. The woman who tore down Somnus's magical veil, shattering the magical veil between realms on this world, just with her raw power. He's heard whispers from travelers, tales of a world transformed by her actions—cities awakening from enchantment, people discovering their true nature after generations of magical subjugation.

Standing before her, Auren feels the same resonance that filled him when he freed Elyssia's trapped souls. Their magic speaks the same language, though hers flows with practiced control while his still surges wild and unpredictable.

"You're the one who broke the world before I did," he says, surprising himself with the blunt observation.

"You're real," Kyp blurts out, then immediately looks embarrassed.

Liora's smile is genuine, reaching her eyes. "Last I checked," she says, her voice carrying a warmth that contrasts with Sam's precision. She takes a step toward them. "I've wanted to meet you both for some time now. Especially you, Auren."

Auren finds his voice. "How do you know who I am?"

Liora's eyes meet Auren's, and he feels a strange resonance, like a tuning fork struck against his soul. The air between them shimmers with unseen energy.

"The Thread connects those who possess certain quantity of power," she says, her voice soft yet carrying an undeniable strength. "I felt the moment Elyssia fell. The ripples traveled through the dreamscape like stones dropped in still water."

Auren swallows hard. "The dreamscape? You can see dreams?"

"With the same ease you might walk through a doorway," Liora confirms, her expression softening. "I'm sorry about Melia. Truly. The price of truth is often steeper than we can bear."

The mention of Melia's name sends a familiar ache through Auren's chest. "You know of her too?"

"I know of her choice," Liora corrects gently. "You both sacrificed everything to break down another magical abomination, a barrier to freedom, that should never have existed. That kind of courage leaves marks on the Thread itself."

Sam steps forward. "Liora knew I was searching for her. Instead, she found me. We've found common ground."

Liora continues, "What happened in Somnus—my home—was just the beginning. The beginning of something much bigger than me." She looks directly at Auren. "And you continued it. You used your connection to magic to end Elyssia's cycle of sacrifice."

"I didn't do it alone," Auren says, thinking of Melia. "I'm not special."

"But you are," Liora counters gently. "The fact that you could connect with the Aether at all—that you could manipulate it, channel it—marks you as something rare. Something the Emperor fears."

"The Emperor?" Kyp interjects. "As in, the Imperial Emperor? The one from the old stories? The one that lives on some far away planet?"

"He's very real," Sam says flatly. "And he's very aware of what's happening here."

Liora nods. "Powers are awakening all over this world—which we now know, thanks to Sam, is called The Vault. People who can touch the Thread, shape reality, remember what was forgotten. The Emperor has kept this world sealed for generations, hidden from the rest of the galaxy."

"I don't understand," Auren says, struggling to process the implications. "Are you saying we're not alone? That there are... other worlds?"

"Many," Liora confirms. "The Emperor rules an empire spanning countless star systems. But The Vault is special. It contains power he both covets and fears."

Sam steps forward. "The Emperor won't take Elyssia's destruction lightly. It was part of a system designed to contain and channel magical energy—energy that's now flowing freely across The Vault. He'll come to reclaim what he considers his."

Auren looks between them, trying to absorb the magnitude of what they're saying. "And what does this have to do with me?"

Liora's expression grows more serious. "I'm the first Dreamer to awaken on this world in generations, but I won't be the last. I, and my friends, we're gathering people like us—people who can feel the Thread, who can shape it. You call it Aether, I call it dream magic, others have other names. We need to be ready when the Emperor comes." She extends her hand toward him. "We need you, Auren."

The weight of her words presses against him. Just weeks ago, his world consisted of Willow Haven and the looming shadow of Elyssia. Now, he's being told of empires among the stars, of powers awakening, of a conflict that spans beyond anything he could have imagined.

He thinks of Melia, of her sacrifice and her final words. She asked him to tell her story, to ensure her choice was remembered. How can he do that if he leaves?

Yet as he looks at Liora's outstretched hand, he feels that same pull that drew him to the ship—a sense of rightness, of purpose that transcends his grief.

"What about the people here?" he asks. "What about Willow Haven? If what you're saying is true, they're in danger too."

"They are," Sam acknowledges. "Which is why we need to understand what's happening. Why we need people who can do what you do."

Auren takes a step back, conflict etched across his face. "I can't just leave. There are people rebuilding their lives after Elyssia's fall. They need guidance, they need—"

"You misunderstand," Liora interrupts gently. Her fingers still dance with those golden threads of light, weaving complex patterns in the air between them. "I'm not asking you to leave the Vault."

Auren stops, confusion replacing his resistance. "You're not?"

"No." Liora's eyes hold a fierce determination that reminds him painfully of Melia. "We're staying right here. I won't abandon this world to whatever the Emperor decides to send. Not after what my people have already suffered."

The evening wind sweeps across the summit, rustling through the sparse grass. Bear circles around them, seemingly pleased by this development.

"But you said the Emperor..." Auren begins.

"Will come," Sam finishes for him. "Or more likely, send others first. That's why we need to prepare."

Liora nods. "The Vault contains eight known realms, each with its own form of magic, its own people discovering their power." She

glances at Sam with something like respect. "Thanks to Sam's knowledge of Imperial protocols, we have some idea of what to expect, how
they might respond."

Kyp, who has been uncharacteristically quiet, finally speaks up.
"Eight realms? Like... eight different countries?"

"More than countries," Liora explains. "Separate magical ecosys-
tems, each dominated by a different element or force. Etheria, where
we stand now, is the realm of Aether magic. But there's also Somnus
with its dream magic, Luminara with light magic, Nyxvarra with
shadow magic..." She trails off, then focuses on Auren again. "My
friends have spread throughout these realms, seeking out others like
us—people awakening to their connection with the Thread."

"That's what I'm asking you to do," she continues. "Not to leave,
but to help us find and guide others through what you've already
experienced. The loss, the confusion, the power."

Auren glances at Sam, noting how she stands slightly apart, yet
clearly aligned with Liora. "And you're part of this too?"

Sam nods once, definitive. "I'll be coming with you. My knowledge
extends beyond what even Liora's people have pieced together. I know
Imperial tactics, weaknesses."

"Sam has been..." Liora pauses, searching for the right word,
"...invaluable. And not just for her tactical knowledge." She exchanges a meaningful look with Sam before continuing. "I believe the
Luthari—Sam's people—are an important piece to the puzzle of the
hidden ninth realm."

"Ninth realm?" Auren echoes.

"There are references in ancient texts," Sam explains, her tone shifting into something almost academic. "Nine doors, eight keys, one
truth. The Emperor knows something about this ninth realm that

terrifies him. Something worth destroying entire civilizations to keep hidden."

Kyp whistles low. "And here I thought taking down one floating city was impressive."

Auren feels the weight of their words settling on him. He looks toward Willow Haven, barely visible in the distance. He thinks of the small grave on the hillside, of his promise to tell Melia's story. Perhaps this is how he honors that promise—by ensuring others don't suffer as she did.

Kyp clears his throat. "For what it's worth, I think you should go." When Auren looks at him in surprise, he continues, "Don't look so shocked. You've been haunting this place like a ghost since she died. Maybe this is what comes next."

Bear approaches Auren, butting against his leg before trotting up the ship's ramp as if he's already decided.

Auren feels something loosen in his chest—a knot of grief and purpose shifting into a new configuration. He remembers standing at this very spot, ready to ascend to Elyssia, only to be turned away. Now, another path opens before him—not upward to a floating city, but outward to a universe he never knew existed.

He meets Liora's steady gaze, seeing in it not the blind faith of the Followers or the manipulative control of Elyssia's priests, but something rarer—a genuine offer of choice.

Auren glances at the ship, at Bear waiting expectantly at the top of the ramp, then back to Liora.

"As long as the cat can come," he says finally, "I'm in."

Dareth II

The Chamber of Echoes swallows every footfall as Dareth enters, the weight of recent reports pressing against his temples. The air feels thinner somehow, charged with unspoken tension. Seven faces turn toward him—each councilor a study in careful neutrality, except for Admiral Vire, whose jaw tightens at Dareth's approach.

"Warden-General," Chancellor Aros acknowledges, voice pitched precisely to carry no farther than necessary. "We've been awaiting your assessment."

Dareth takes his place at the eight-pointed table, the imperial insignia beneath his fingers worn smooth by centuries of similar gatherings. The empty ninth chair—the Emperor's—looms larger in his absence.

"The Shadow has gone dark," Dareth states without preamble. No point in softer language; this chamber was designed to consume pleasantries. "All tracking protocols severed. No communication for eighteen standard cycles."

Scribe-Magus Helyn Dros places withered hands flat on the table. "This outcome was predicted. Probability matrices indicated a seventy-three percent chance of behavioral deviation after extended field deployment."

"Predicted, yet permitted," Minister Rhessa Vorn counters, her immaculate uniform catching the dim light. "The Emperor insisted on this particular asset despite known instability factors."

Dareth watches the subtle power play unfold. Each councilor protecting their domain, establishing distance from potential failure. He's learned quickly that survival here means identifying undertows before they pull you under.

The air shifts. Conversations halt mid-syllable.

The Emperor enters without sound, his form seeming to absorb the chamber's sparse light rather than reflect it. The councilors rise as one, a movement drilled into muscle memory.

"Understanding is not required," the Emperor says, his voice somehow both distant and intimate, pressing directly against Dareth's consciousness. "Only obedience."

The chamber falls into practiced silence as the Emperor settles into his seat. The ancient throne doesn't creak—nothing dares make sound in his presence. Dareth studies the hooded figure, searching for some hint of emotion beneath the golden threads that obscure his face. As always, he finds nothing.

"Elyssia has fallen." The Emperor's words land like stones in still water. "The floating city is no more."

Dareth's mind races to place the reference. Elyssia—one of the mythical constructs on the Vault world, a floating paradise sustained by magic that most imperial officers dismissed as exaggeration or fable.

"Another barrier broken," the Emperor continues. "Another Dreamer walks free. The Vault awakens."

Admiral Vire leans forward, his cybernetic eye whirring as it adjusts. "Impossible."

"Our methods have failed." The Emperor cuts him off without raising his voice. "As they failed with the Shadow."

"The Vault is no longer dormant," the Emperor says. "Eight realms stirring from centuries of sleep. Eight forms of magic breaking their chains."

Minister Vorn's blood-red gloves tighten against the table's edge. "The containment strategy was designed to last millennia. What changed?"

"The Thread," Scribe-Magus Dros whispers, fingers tracing invisible patterns on the table. "It remembers futures as much as pasts. Something has altered its weave."

Dareth watches Chancellor Aros carefully arrange his expression into something approaching intellectual curiosity rather than fear. "Your Eminence, perhaps if we understood the precise nature of these barriers—"

"You require only understanding sufficient for your function," the Emperor interrupts. "The Vault contains eight magical systems that would destabilize our order. Elyssia controlled one such system through ritual sacrifice and belief. Now it's free."

Dareth finds his voice. "And the Shadow's connection to this?"

The Emperor's attention settles on him, and Dareth fights the urge to step back. The sensation is like having a weapon sighted on his chest.

"The Shadow was sent to assess, not interfere. She chose otherwise."

"We should dispatch the fleet," Admiral Vire interjects. "Cleanse the affected areas before contamination spreads."

The Emperor remains still, but something shifts in the air—a pressure change that makes Dareth's ears pop.

"No." The single word echoes strangely. "The Vault cannot be cleansed from orbit. Its protections run deeper than physical space."

Chancellor Aros clears his throat. "Then what strategy would you have us employ, Your Eminence?"

"Prepare for war," the Emperor says simply. "Not against armies. Against magic itself."

Dareth feels cold certainty settle in his stomach. He's seen enough campaigns to recognize the shape of disaster forming.

"The Shadow has allied herself with the Dreamers," the Emperor continues. "She carries imperial knowledge of our systems, our weaknesses. She must be eliminated."

"And who will you send this time?" Dareth asks, surprising himself with his directness. "Another weapon that might choose its own target?"

The chamber goes deathly still. Vorn looks at him with something approaching pity—the expression one might give a dead man.

The Emperor rises, and the air bends around him like heat distortion. "You misunderstand your position, Warden-General. I don't require your questions. I require your armies."

Dareth holds the invisible gaze, feeling as though he's standing on cracking ice. "Of course, Your Eminence. The Warden Legions stand ready."

As the Emperor glides from the chamber, Dareth catches Rhessa Vorn's whispered warning: "Careful, Sol. Curiosity is a luxury afforded to those without responsibility."

He nods slightly, but the cold weight in his stomach doesn't lift. Something fundamental has changed—not just on the distant Vault, but here, in the heart of the Empire.

"Council adjourned."

The council members rise, a synchronized retreat of dark robes and carefully neutral expressions.

"Warden-General Sol remains," the Emperor states. Not a request.

The council chamber empties with practiced efficiency, leaving Dareth alone with the Emperor. The hooded figure floats motionless before the massive tactical display that has shimmered into existence along the eastern wall, casting the room in a cold blue glow.

"You disapprove," the Emperor states, not bothering to make it a question.

Dareth straightens his shoulders. "My approval isn't relevant to my function."

"Correct. Yet your hesitation radiates like heat."

The display zooms in on the Vault—eight realms circling one empty space, each marked with pulsing threat indicators. Dareth studies the formation.

"The Warden Legions can be mobilized within three standard weeks," Dareth offers, falling back on operational certainty. "Full combat readiness in six."

"Too slow." The Emperor's fingers trace a path through the projection. "We will move assets quietly."

Dareth studies the display, his military mind already calculating logistics. The thread-calibrated navigation routes flicker between star systems like a complex spiderweb—some bright and well-traveled, others faint, barely visible.

"The Vault lies outside the established Threadway System," he observes, gesturing to the conspicuous void in the network. "No officially sanctioned route reaches it."

"Correct." The Emperor's voice carries no inflection. "An intentional isolation."

Dareth steps closer to the projection, noting the strange distortions around the Vault's perimeter. "Any large-scale fleet movement would require establishing new Thread anchors. That's months of work for the Aetherion technomancers, even with your direct authority."

"And such preparations would be... noticed." The Emperor's robes shift slightly, the golden threads catching the blue light.

"The Shadow knows our standard deployment protocols," Dareth adds, thinking aloud. "She'll recognize the pattern of technomancers establishing jump points."

The Emperor remains silent, waiting. Testing him, Dareth realizes.

"We'd need to use uncalibrated jumps," Dareth continues, the implications making his stomach tighten. "Through the Weft."

"Yes." The Emperor moves his hand through the display, and the image shifts to show fragmented, unstable paths cutting through the void. "Uncharted territory. Dangerous. Unpredictable."

Dareth has heard the stories—ships lost in the Weft, emerging years later or not at all. Crews driven mad by temporal drift, experiencing their deaths before they occurred. The Weft is where reality becomes unmoored, where the Thread itself frays.

"The Luthari once navigated such paths," the Emperor says. "Before their... removal."

"And now the Shadow carries their technology," Dareth realizes. "The armor you gave her."

"Indeed."

Dareth feels the pieces clicking into place. "You knew she would defect."

The Emperor turns, his face still shadowed beneath his hood. "I knew she would find her true nature. The question was always: what would she do with it?"

Dareth calculates quickly. "We'll need specialized drives. Aetherium-infused crystals recalibrated for unstable Thread regions. And pilots trained to navigate without established anchors."

"Yes. Begin the preparations discreetly."

"The loss rate will be significant," Dareth warns. "Perhaps thirty percent of vessels, even with perfect execution."

"Acceptable."

Dareth swallows his objection. Thirty percent means thousands of soldiers—men and women under his command—lost before they even reach the battlefield.

"And communications?" he asks instead.

"Compromised, once you leave the Threadway network. Standard comms will be useless across such distances. Messages will arrive out of order, duplicated, or garbled."

"How will we coordinate an invasion force without reliable communication?"

The Emperor reaches into his robes and produces a small device—a gleaming metallic cylinder etched with symbols Dareth doesn't recognize.

"A Forbidden Spool," the Emperor explains. "It locks causality briefly, allowing real-time transmission. You will carry it. Use it only at critical junctures."

Dareth hesitates before accepting the device. It's heavier than it looks, and uncomfortably warm against his palm.

"Begin your preparations, Warden-General," the Emperor commands. "Select your most adaptable officers. Those who can function with minimal direction when communications fail."

Dareth nods, already mentally reviewing his command structure, identifying who might survive the Weft's disorienting effects.

"Remember, Warden-General," the Emperor adds, "you don't chart the Thread. You surrender to it."

Dareth recognizes the old Luthari proverb with surprise. "I thought that wisdom died with them."

"Nothing truly dies," the Emperor responds. "It merely waits to be remembered."

Dareth nods once, professionally. "And the Shadow?"

A moment of silence stretches between them.

"The Shadow represents a unique threat. Her knowledge of our systems, combined with her... specialized capabilities, makes her elimination a priority."

"I'll assign a hunter team from—"

"No." The Emperor's interruption is soft but absolute. "I will handle her defection personally."

Dareth hesitates, weighing his next words carefully. The Emperor's attention is a physical presence, pressing against his thoughts.

"And Liora Solari?" he asks finally. "The reports indicate she's the nexus of this disturbance."

The Emperor's form shifts slightly, the golden threads of his robe catching the blue light from the tactical display. "Observant, Warden-General. Yes, the Dreamer called Liora continues to destabilize the barriers we established."

"Her abilities—" Dareth begins.

"Exceed our projections," the Emperor finishes. "She was meant to be contained within her realm, separated from potential allies by the Veil. Now she walks freely."

The display shifts, focusing on one section of the Vault—a landmass surrounded by turbulent seas. Somnus. Birthplace of dreamers.

"She's gathering others," Dareth says, studying the pulsing hotspots on the projection. "Forming connections across the realms."

"Yes." The Emperor's voice carries a note Dareth hasn't heard before—something almost like concern. "She has found another. A Dreamer of considerable potential."

Dareth looks up sharply. "Another like her?"

"Different, but equally dangerous. This one manipulates the Thread directly, rather than dreams. A conduit for raw power, not yet fully aware of his capabilities."

The tactical display shifts again, highlighting a mountain region where energy readings spike erratically.

"The Shadow will guide them," the Emperor continues. "She carries knowledge of our weaknesses, our methods. Combined with Liora's power and this new Dreamer's potential..."

He leaves the sentence unfinished, but Dareth understands the implication. An existential threat to Imperial control.

"The standard containment protocols won't be effective against someone who can manipulate reality itself," Dareth observes. "How do we counter such abilities?"

The Emperor moves to the tactical display, his movements unnaturally fluid. "Dreamers require belief—both their own and others'. Their power flows from conviction."

"So we break their faith," Dareth suggests, thinking tactically. "Psychological operations. Target their supporters, create doubt."

"A conventional approach," the Emperor acknowledges. "But insufficient against a fully realized Dreamer."

Dareth studies the display, noting the spreading patterns of energy across multiple realms. "If conventional tactics won't work, what options remain? How do we stop someone who can reshape reality at will?"

The Emperor is silent for a long moment. When he speaks again, his voice seems to come from everywhere at once.

"I have activated a fixer. One who knows Liora well." The Emperor's words hang in the air, heavy with implication.

"His name is Kael Varden."

Afterword

Thank you.

Thank you for walking this road with me. Writing *The Fallen Elyssian* has been a journey filled with risk, discovery, and heart, and knowing that you chose to spend your time within these pages means more than I can ever say. Stories live only when they're read, and your presence here gives this one life.

If you'd like to dive deeper into this world, I invite you to visit my website: www.emlucas.com. One of these days I'm going to update it properly.

And this is just the beginning.

But the path doesn't end in Elyssia or Etheria. The Dreamer Saga continues. The third adventure, *The Drowned Memory*, is already on the horizon. In it, you will meet Meryn Nerai, a young waterborn of Myridion searching for fragments of her turbulent childhood, longing to reclaim what the tides have stolen from her. Her story will carry us into new waters and uncharted depths.

You will also see familiar faces return. Rafe Delacroix, who began his journey in *The Last Dreamweaver*, steps once more into the light. And from *The Fallen Elyssian*, Liora, Auren, Sam, and Bear will continue their fight—as will Kael Varden, whose path remains far from finished.

The threads are weaving together, tighter and more intricate with every step. I can't wait for you to see where they lead.

Until then, thank you again—for reading, for dreaming, and for walking beside me through this saga.

With gratitude, E.M. Lucas.

www.ingramcontent.com/pod-product-compliance
Lightning Source LLC
Chambersburg PA
CBHW030543020726
47494CB00005B/1471